Black Reign Saga

D1028126

JUN 2012

Black Reign Saga

Edd McNair

www.urbanbooks.net

Urban Books, LLC
78 East Industry Court
Deer Park, NY 11729

ISBN 13: 978-1-60162-513-7
ISBN 10: 1-60162-513-8

First Printing July 2012
Printed in the United States of America

10 9 8 7 6 5 4 3 2 1

Distributed by Kensington Publishing Corp.
Submit Wholesale Orders to:
Kensington Publishing Corp.
C/O Penguin Group (USA) Inc.
Attention: Order Processing
405 Murray Hill Parkway
East Rutherford, NJ 07073-2316
Phone: 1-800-526-0275
Fax: 1-800-227-9604

Chapter One

"Hurry up, Angah," Angela's little brother yelled, unable to pronounce her name. "Mommy said, 'Hurry up now.'" He tried to annoy her.

"Shut up, boy. I'm glad I'm graduating today, so I can get the hell out of here."

"You're not out of here yet, so I would watch my mouth if I were you," her mother replied from down the stairs, surprising Angela, who thought she was outside by the car.

Angela had been the only child up to five years ago. Her parents had divorced when she was ten. Her father, a licensed electrician, had provided a comfortable life for her and her mother. Her mother got pregnant with her in high school, which made things difficult, but with the help of grandparents, she was still able to attend Old Dominion University and receive her nursing degree.

Together they worked hard to move themselves into Virginia Beach's only upper-class, all-black neighborhood, L & J Gardens, where they purchased their first two-story, three-bedroom, contemporary-style home. They felt at the time that being around other black folks who had what they had was going to classify them as "better" black folks.

As her mother left for Leigh Memorial every morning and her father for whatever he did, Angela thought to herself, *They have the perfect marriage.* Until one day she came home and all her father's things were gone. He realized that family life wasn't for him—five years after the fact—but kept on paying the mortgage, so her mother never asked for anything else.

Angela resented him for a long time, but now she was older and had learned to look at the situation from another angle. Her mother and father argued all the time, and many times she could see why her father left, but didn't dare say that to her moms. Her father always kept in touch, and she spent summers with him in Beltsville, Maryland.

After two years of being alone and trying the dating scene, Angela's mother met Dr. Statton, or Ken, which he told her to call him. Ken didn't look as good as Angela's father, but he treated her mother well. Angela remembers the trips and the long weekends Ken and her moms would take. (She would be left at her grandparent's house.)

It wasn't long before Angela's mother was pregnant with her little brother. They never married, but Ken was always in the picture. Angela admired the way Ken treated her mother and promised that any man she would even consider marrying would have to do the same.

As they traveled to her graduation, Angela was so excited about starting college in the fall, and that her parents had agreed to give her a hand if she got her own place closer to campus. If they didn't, she was going to stay on campus—no way in hell was she going to stay home and have her moms all up in her business. Most of her friends would be going to school out of state, but she and her best friend, Monica, had decided to go to Hampton University.

When they arrived at graduation, Monica was waiting for her at the door. The girls took off so they could get with their classmates. Angela was talking to Monica when someone grabbed her from behind. She turned around to see her boyfriend Ray standing there.

"You still goin' to Allen pool party after graduation? His parents suppose to be out of town, so it got to be the hype shit." Ray shook his head to confirm that what he was saying was the truth.

Angela looked at Monica. "Monica, are we going to Allen party?"

"Yeah, but we goin' to get there later on because we got to stop at Ski shit first—he havin' his party out Lake Edward at the clubhouse. And you know how them LE niggas roll." Monica gave Angela a high five, knowing it would irk Ray. "Heah, Ray," Monica said, "you comin' to Ski party?"

"I don't know—I ain't for the bullshit tonight. I'll probably just see y'all at Allen house later. That Lake Edward shit probably end early anyway . . . guaranteed."

Ray grew up in Wesleyan Chase, not too far from L & J Gardens, but just down the street from Lake Edward apartments, which was known for drugs, violence, and other illegal activities. Ray hadn't planned on going to college. Actually he never cared too much for school; he knew he was going to work for his dad and one day take over the business, Decker and Sons Plumbing.

Ray stood about five foot ten and weighed about 210 pounds solid, which kept him destroying kids on the wrestling mat. He ultimately became captain of the wrestling team and two-time state champion contender. Ray had been with Angela since the summer before their junior year. He was popular among his peers and somebody the young ladies would kill to be with, but he knew Angela was no one to give any space to. Any man would gladly scoop her up with the quickness. Her dazzling light-brown eyes, smooth golden-brown skin, full and beautifully shaped lips, perfectly shaped ass that stunned men, no matter what she wore, all packed in a size eight frame with well-proportioned breasts. When the bra fell, the breasts didn't; they stood up and begged for attention. She was set off with a short Halle Berry cut, which made her an extraordinary package.

To top it off, she carried a 4.0 GPA. Even though there were equally attractive girls at Bayside H.S., Angela was the only girl for him. He loved her more than anything, and if it went his way, right after she finished school, they would be married.

As Angela sat in the stands listening to her principal speak, she realized the day she never thought would come was here. She had everything planned; this summer she would work full-time as a receptionist. She had been there since the beginning of her senior year and really enjoyed it. Her and Monica were going to sign their lease at their new condo on the first of July, and then she'd be considered grown. The graduation class standing brought her back to reality as she heard the words, "Congratulations, class of 1996."

As they strolled out the stands, she made her way over to her father. She knew he would come. He never had anymore kids, and he always let her know that even though he was in Maryland and she in Virginia, she was the most important thing in his life. And he did a great job showing it, even if he wasn't local.

"Congratulations, baby girl," her father said as they embraced.

"Heah, Daddy." Angela smiled a wide smile, one that you could only get when in daddy's arms.

"Just because you out of school, don't mean shit—you ain't grown, goddamn!"

"Shut up, James," Lenore said. "I'm happy for you, love. Don't pay your dad any attention."

Lenore was from Washington, DC. Angela's father had met her about five years ago, and they had been living together about four years. In the beginning Angela didn't care too much for Lenore, but her father begged her to give her a chance—Angela's problem was that her father was almost forty and Lenore was twenty-eight. By the end of the summer, they were the best of friends.

Lenore was stern like her mother . . . except, hanging out with Lenore was fun. She was beautiful and, at the same time, fly as hell. She was a cosmetologist and had been doing hair since the tender age of twelve. By the time she was twenty, she had landed a job at one of the top salons in the Northern Virginia/DC area. Her appearance was always together—hair perfect, eyebrows arched, makeup applied as if it was professionally done, and a body to kill for. Over the years, Angela started to admire Lenore's style and wanted to be more like her than her mother.

Angela's mother never noticed that she was turning into a woman. She didn't want her to wear makeup, she wouldn't let her arch her eyebrows, and the thought of getting nails was totally out of the question. Angela always wore her hair long since she was a young girl, something her mother took great pride in. But last summer when she was in Maryland, Lenore was wearing a short cut that made her jealous. Angela cut hers in the same style without thinking twice. When she got back home, her mother was pissed, and she remembered her mom and dad on the phone arguing for what seemed like hours. Her mom promised her father that Angela would never spend another summer in Maryland again. Her father laughed, knowing this was the last summer before Angela graduated, and her mother wouldn't have shit else to say about that situation.

"So what you doin' tonight?" Lenore handed Angela a card.

"Me and Monica goin' to a couple parties, that's it." Angela responded as if it was nothing.

"Be safe, and no drinking and driving out here," Lenore said.

"Here come your grandparents, baby. We'll be here until Sunday at the Sheraton Downtown Waterside. The room is under my name. Call me." James leaned over and kissed his daughter again.

"Hello, James," her grandparents said.

"Hello." James turned to Angela. "Call me," he said as he strolled off.

Angela's mother came up and hugged her. She held her face, looked into her eyes, and told her how proud she was and from here on nothing could hold her back. Her eyes began to water. "Don't cry, Ma," Angela said, trying not to get emotional.

"Baby, we're all just so proud of you," her grandmother said.

Just then, Dr. Statton walked up, holding her little brother. "Congratulations, love," he said, hugging her.

Angela reached up and hugged him real tight. Even though he had never married her mother, he had been there through some tough times. Through her teenage years, many times she felt her mother didn't understand what she was going through, but Dr. Statton did, and he would come to her rescue. Many nights when her mother worked, Dr. Statton would be at the house to cook, clean, and take care of her and her brother. She referred to him as her step-dad to her friends, and even though he never told her, he was like putty in her hands. He couldn't love her anymore if she was his own.

"Thank you, Ken."

"I forgot your gift, but you'll get it tomorrow. And just because you out of school, don't forget your curfew."

"Ken," Angela said in a whining voice.

"Okay"—he smiled—"you have an extra hour."

Angela smiled and her mother just stared. They all began walking to the car when Monica and Ray came up, "Hello, Ms. Wood, Dr. Statton," Ray said.

"Hello, Raymond," her mother replied.

"Girl, what you gonna do?" Monica asked.

"Ain't nothin' change. I'll be at the house waiting on you. Don't you have to change?"

"Yeah, I was just asking. I'll see you in a few." Monica said, and she and Ray walked off.

Angela was trying to figure out what to wear. She didn't know if she was going to swim or what. She called Monica to see what was up. "Heah, what you puttin' on?"

"Shorts and a T-shirt," Monica said. "Bitches might be tryin' to act up tonight, and I ain't for it."

"I'll throw my suit on under my other shit."

"Just hurry the fuck up, girl. I'll see you in five." Angela pulled her white, two-piece body glove swimsuit out her drawer along with her sleeveless button-down that tied in the front. It was a little wrinkled, but she knew it would come off as soon as she got up the street. She twisted into her new Levi shorts, stepped back and looked into the mirror at how the jeans fit real snug on her phat ass, and let out a satisfying smile.

Just then the door to her room flew open. "Hurry up, bitch, we got some stops to make."

"Where?" Angela reached into her closet for her new white Reebok Classics.

"You'll see, come on."

Angela loved her buddy, but she knew at times she had to calm her down. She and Monica had been friends since grade school. (Monica's parents were killed in an accident when she was seven, leaving her and her brother of nine to be raised by her grandparents, who lived in L & J Gardens. Soon after, she met Angela, and they've been hanging ever since.)

"Girl, you know them shorts screamin'," Monica said.

"They'll make the niggas scream more. And look at your shit."

"Shut your mouth—I'm grown now."

They both began to laugh.

Angela was fine and she knew it, but Monica was no slouch. Monica was light skinned and stood a little taller than Angela at about five foot five". Her ass wasn't as phat as Angela's, but it stuck out farther. Her breasts were bigger, with large nipples that usually poked through her blouse. When she was younger, it bothered her; now it was an attention-getter, and she knew how to handle it. She would always catch guys staring right at them. Her hair, lightened almost to a gold to complement her complexion, hung down on her shoulders, with little spiral curls all over. She wasn't conceited but she knew that her narrow nose, small lips, high cheekbones, slanted eyes, and grey pupils that changed colors with the sun would fuck any nigga's head up.

Chapter Two

Monica and Angela jumped in the car, headed to Ski's party. Before they could hit Baker Road, they had their shirts off and had thrown them in the back seat.

"Where do we have to stop?" Angela asked.

"Goin' out St. Croix and see what Fat Joe and Rome up to. They told me to stop by. Rome said I could come by—if I brought you."

"See, you tryin' to start somethin'. Suppose somebody else is over there and go to Allen party and tell Ray. Then I'm in some shit, and God knows I'm not tryin' to lose my man, Monica."

"It ain't even like that. We just goin' over there and smoke their weed, and then we out."

"You know Ski got weed—fuck them niggas. You just want to see Joe fat ass. I don't see what you see in him anyway."

"He's not bad lookin'—he got good hair, he dress his ass off, and he keeps weed."

"His *momma* keep weed," Angela said, correcting her.

"Don't matter. She don't care. And plus, he's sweet."

"Why you fuck that fat muthafucka anyway?"

"Because we friends like that, and he never runs his mouth. We've been friends like that since eleventh grade. I was going over there everyday after school smoking weed, and he would always hint around. Then one day I was playing with him, and he just started licking my pussy, girl, and I was hooked. He's not a bad lover. Better try you a fat, muthafuckin'-ass nigga."

"It's all right; I'll leave them to you. What about Quinn?" Angela asked.

"That's my baby. But by him livin' in Petersburg attendin' Virginia State, that long-distance shit gets hard, and Fat Joe is cool . . . my fat man." They both burst out laughing.

Monica had been with her share of guys; she was what some people would consider fast. She had gone to private school up to the ninth grade, but when she got to Bayside, she got wide open. By her junior year, she had calmed down and decided to only be with Quinn. Fat Joe was just her friend then.

Angela, on the other hand, had lost her virginity at fourteen to Monica's brother. (He was real light like Monica and had grey eyes. Girls were always crazy about him.) One weekend she stayed with Monica. He came in their room and, with their grandmother in the next room, took her virginity. She remembers the first couple times it hurt, but as it became more frequent she came to enjoy it. When Angela realized that she was just a toy to him, she stopped giving in to his secret pleasures.

She then started talking to Ski, well known and real popular, not only at Bayside, but also throughout the Tidewater area. Ski was the highschool starting running back and was shown many Friday nights on the news, scoring touchdowns and doing interviews. He held city records in track and was what people considered a track star. Not even a month into their relationship, he had girls from Green Run, Norview, and Booker T. all wanting to fight her over him. She got tired of fighting bitches for no reason, so she let him go and vowed she would never talk to any one like him again.

Then Ray came along. Very popular amongst the students at Bayside because of his wrestling skills and his muscular body; he was laid back and quiet. He was never about trouble but could hold his own. He was so sweet to her, always having sweet things to say, giving her rides to and from school when Monica didn't. They just clicked from the beginning and it's been love ever since. Angela had no real desire to be with any other guy. Ray was her love; the only love she would ever need.

"Look, girl, there's Dirt-Dirt car," Angela said.

"He fixed his little Escort up." Monica laughed. "I bet you anything Tammy and Ki over here."

"Shit, I know them bitches here. There's their momma car over there. Goddamn, girl," Angela said all excited, as if she was about to jump out her seat, "whose burgundy Lexus with the thirty-day tags?"

"Girl, that's Rome shit."

"He traded in the Honda? What he doin'?" Angela asked.

"Naw, he gettin' it fixed; it's in the shop. You know he be drivin' his brother cars."

"Who's his brother?"

"Bo," Monica answered.

Angela got out the car. "Who the hell is Bo?"

"You remember our sophomore year when they had that big drug bust, and those Lake Edward niggas got caught up?"

Angela gave Monica a dazed look.

"Remember that sports bar that was up by the Food Lion where all those hustlers use to hang out?"

"Yeah," Angela said, "we were like fifteen, sixteen years old."

"Well, the head nigga name was Black. I never met him, I just heard about him. But you know Lo from out Lake Edward, right?"

Angela asked, "Didn't he get like fifteen years or somethin'?"

"Yeah, that's him, but word is, he suppose to be co-min' home soon and shit will hit the fan. They say that when they got busted, Bo told everything to save his own ass and didn't do six months. Bo use to run hand in hand with them, and after shit went down, Bo hit the street and kept his own shit goin'. That's why he gettin' it now."

"Shit, he ain't doin' all that," Angela said, "because my cousin Quandra use to fuck with Lo, and she said that nigga was rich. I mean a-new-car-every-six-months rich."

"Well, he makin' money and he looks out for Rome. That's why Rome always dressed his ass off."

"You like that Lexus though, don't you?"

"Yeah, I do." Angela knocked on the door.

Fat Joe answered the door with a blunt in his hand. The house had about ten people inside, and the room was full of smoke.

"Where's your moms?" Monica asked.

"She had to work all night; it's my spot tonight. Why? What's up?"

"Nothin', fool." Monica made her way through the crowd and to the couch.

"Wannabe, hood rats in this bitch," Rome yelled.

"If they ain't fuckin', tell them to carry they ass home," Dirt-Dirt yelled. "Talk to me, Rome."

Rome grabbed his dick. "All these bitches know my steez, son."

"Why y'all so fuckin' nasty?" Monica asked.

"I wa'n' talkin' to you; she know who I'm screamin' at."

Angela said, "I ain't playin' with you, Rome."

"I ain't *playin'*."

"Leave her alone, Rome," Fat Joe said, "before I call Ray around this bitch."

Rome jumped up. "Ray who? Must mean Ray Mercer, the heavyweight nigga . . . because that's who you'll need to pull me out his ass."

Everyone started laughing.

"Niggas must not know where the fuck I'm from." Rome gave the crowd the LE holler, and everyone responded. Then he sat, passed Angela the blunt, and slid closer to her. "So you goin' to Hampton, huh?"

"Yeah, everything already set."

"I'll be over there with you."

"For real?" Angela was excited. Just the thought of somebody else from school going over there made her feel good.

"I got to go; all the bitches over there. I'm goin' hang with you and Monica and fuck all your friends."

"You got problems, boy," Angela said to Rome.

"You ain't goin' look out, Angela?"

"Hell no, that's fuckin' triflin'."

"I'm goin' look out, Rome." Monica got up and gave him a pound. "Put you in there with all those stupid-ass hoes. Now pass that L."

"I heard that. See, Monica my girl; Angela be on some bullshit."

They sat around drinking, smoking trees, and listening to the latest sounds being played by the 103 JAMZ. After talking about anybody and everybody—who didn't graduate or who wasn't going to college—Fat Joe finally realized the time and thought it was time to burst, so he began to clean up.

Everybody headed out the door except for Monica and Angela. Knowing how his mother was, they didn't want him to catch hell later on. She didn't mind the drinking, smoking, or the company, as long as her shit was clean when she came home.

Rome came back through the door. "Last chance, Angela—What's up?" He threw his hands up.

"I'm okay, Rome." Angela smiled. "Thanks anyway."

Rome picked up his keys off the table. "Rollin' with me, Fats, or you drivin'?"

"I'm rollin' in the Lex, muthafucka. What the hell I look like? I want to shine for the bitches a little bit too." Fats held the door for them to get out.

They arrived at the clubhouse about eleven o'clock. It was packed inside and out, young 'uns all up and down Lake Edward Drive, hanging in the streets, acting up. Monica and Angela parked the car and headed to the clubhouse.

The kid at the door had a stern look. "Five dollars a head for everybody—no exceptions."

"Tell Ski Angela out here, fool," Monica said, knowing Ski would look out for Angela.

Ski came to the door. "Monica, your charge is a hug." Ski reached out and hugged her real rough, in a playful manner. "Angela, your charge is a big-ass hug and at least one dance. Slow dance. One where I can get my freak on." He pulled her real close and tight, and hugged her, then let out a satisfying smile.

"We'll see. You know what's up" Angela said.

"Ray my man; he won't mind." Ski led them into the party.

They weren't in the party twenty minutes before Angela was ready to go. When she wasn't high, she didn't worry too much, but as soon as she got her smoke on, she became very observant and eventually paranoid if not in a calm environment. (She first tried weed her sophomore year and realized she liked the feeling of being high. She found herself giggling and smiling about everything—that's how her mother and Ken would know she'd been smoking.)

She went and found Monica who was in the corner smoking with Fat Joe and Rome, and gave her a look to let her know she was ready to go. Monica didn't mind because she was anxious to see who was at Allen's party anyway.

By the time she arrived at Allen's party she knew her time was limited. Allen's party she could enjoy— it was laid back and she knew nothing was going to kick off unexpected. Angela enjoyed hanging with the other crowd, but at times they could really get out of hand. Their idea of a good party was only if the party ended with niggas fighting or a little gunplay.

Allen's parents lived in Church Point, an exclusive neighborhood not too far from the high school they all attended. His father was an electrical engineer, and his mother was an architect. Together they made his life quite comfortable in their eight-hundred-thousand-dollar home. They allowed him to have his pool party, but he was warned that it could not get out of hand under any circumstances.

When Monica and Angela walked in the back, all eyes fell on them. They looked extremely sexy in their shorts and bathing suit tops. All their classmates came up and started mingling, except for those in the pool. Before she realized Ray was behind her, he scooped her up and took her to the edge of the pool like he was going to throw her in. She begged him not to drop her, but she saw in his eyes that it was about to happen and changed her tactics. Instead of trying to resist, she reached out and hugged him, and in a soft whisper said, "Please let me take off these shorts and sneakers and I'll get in with you."

He agreed instantly. "You promise?"

Nothing and no one was as sexy as his girl to him. He watched her as she walked over and took off her shorts and sneakers. He gently took her hand and guided her into the pool with him. His day was going well. If she hadn't showed up, it would have devastated him.

"What took y'all so long?"

She looked into his eyes. She loved when he expressed himself and asked her questions, like what she did was so important. She stood there as he held her, splashing water. She felt like a child having the time of her life.

After spending a half hour in the pool playing around, he eased up behind her. "Can we go?" he asked softly in her ear. "I know you have to be home soon and I just want some private time with my girl. Just you and me."

"Yes," she said smiling. She was really ready to go when he first picked her up. She felt her body aching for his touch, and all she wanted was to lay down, enjoy her high, and let him have his way.

"Heah, Monica," Angela yelled, "I'm gettin' outta here. I'll call you tomorrow."

Angela sat in the car thinking, while Ray went inside the Cricket Inn to get a room. *Why would he pay for a room and I only had a little over an hour to be home?*

He jumped in the car all smiles. "I know we don't have much time, but I didn't want to go somewhere and sneak like we've done so many times before. I want to take my time and enjoy you."

She sat excited like a child, feeling good about what he was feeling. They went inside the room. Without hesitation they began to undress slowly, looking at each other as if not to be the first to undress.

They climbed into bed. He began kissing her as if there was no tomorrow. She was overwhelmed and responded immediately. He lifted up, put on a condom, and positioned himself between her legs. She lay back, stared into his eyes, and lifted her legs up and back to accept him. He slowly eased his way inside of her and felt the moistness from her body—it quickly let him know that he wasn't going to last long.

She laid there not moving, just holding him tight as he bucked hard and fast like the young stud he was. She was starting to feel so good when she felt his body tense up and began to jolt. She tried to hold him, but he jumped up and hurried to the shower.

She was enjoying herself so much. She wanted him in her arms, to make love to her again. She got out of bed and went inside the bathroom figuring she would get in the shower and get him excited again. She pulled back the shower curtain and noticed his masculine body dripping with soap and water. She looked down at his thick, short penis swinging. *Just moments ago it stood up, stiff as a board.* She climbed in and stood behind him. She rubbed his back, then his chest. As she reached down to touch his penis, he turned around, rinsed the soap off his back, gave her a kiss, and jumped out. She stood there letting the shower drown her frustrations. She wanted him so bad, and he was done. When Angela finished showering, Ray took her home.

"I'll see you tomorrow," she said.

"In the evening, I got to help my father with something early. I'll call you when I finish, okay. I love you, Angela."

She pushed the car door open. He grabbed her arm, leaned over, and gave her a kiss. Again she was smiling inside.

Chapter Three

The following morning Angela woke up to the smell of breakfast cooking. It wasn't too often her mom got up before eleven on Saturday. *Why was today special?*

She wiped the cold from her eyes as she strolled to the kitchen. "Ma, why you up so early?"

"It's nine and it's not early. And I'm not your mother," Ken said. "I'm making breakfast. I need just a few more minutes. So if you get showered and dressed, we'll go shopping before anyone else gets up."

Shopping was all she needed to hear. Within minutes she had showered and was coming out the room.

Her family was sitting at the kitchen table, eating. She sat down and joined them. As she ate, she wondered if Ken was still going to take her shopping.

Her mother handed her a card. "Look, here is your graduation gift from Ken and I."

"Will you get my checkbook out my car right quick for me, Angela," Ken said. "I'll write you a check, but I'm not going to have time to go to the mall; you may have to call Monica."

"If I had my own car I wouldn't have to call nobody."

Angela opened the door and let out a scream. Ken stood there with the keys to a brand-new '96 Jetta. Angela knew this was Dr. Statton's doing. After looking in the car, around the car, she stood back and smiled as she opened her card. Five crispy hundred-dollar bills fell out. She ran over and gave Ken the biggest hug he had ever gotten. "Thank you, Ken. Thank you, Mom. I love you guys so much." Angela's eyes filled with tears of joy.

Ken felt so good to be able to give her something, and for her to appreciate it like she did . . . "Listen to me, Angela, we bought you this car so you can get to work and back and forth to school—that was our sole purpose. The payments are three hundred and sixty-eight dollars a month, the insurance is seventy-seven dollars a month. Can you afford that and the rent you're about to get into?"

"I can now, if I'm full-time, but not when school start."

"You work for me now. Your job is to go to school like you're supposed to and bring grades home to my satisfaction, and I'll pay your note and insurance. But if the grades fall or if they aren't up to par, you will quit the receptionist job, you will move back on campus, and I'll sell your car to one of my interns. Do you understand?"

"Yes, sir. I understand, sir." Angela shook Ken's hand and laughed.

She ran to the phone to call Monica. "Get up, girl. I got a car and some money, and I'm headed to Lynnhaven Mall. See you in ten minutes." She jetted out the door, happier than any eighteen-year-old could ever imagine herself to be. She thought that now she could get around, take care of the things she needed to do without worrying anyone. She wouldn't have any problem getting back and forth to work or to and from school in the fall. And now she could even drive when her and Ray went out. That excuse, "I don't feel like picking you up and then carrying you back home," was out the window. *July couldn't get here fast enough*, Angela thought. She called Ray from Monica's house to share the good news.

Ray seemed happy for her, but didn't share the same excitement. His responsibilities as her boyfriend were about to be cut down. He enjoyed picking her up from work after practice and picking her up and going out. Most of all he enjoyed her depending on him and being there for her—this was his way of keeping her under his wing. Now it was going to be just conversations here and there as she ran and handled her own business. He would no longer be able to keep tabs on her, and this worried him. He knew she wouldn't betray him and he trusted her. But he knew his girl was fine—she had a beautiful body, she carried herself like a mature woman and any man would be more than happy to take her. That's who he didn't trust.

Angela was finally moving into her new condo. (Ken knew a doctor who had purchased a condo in Willoughby, a beautiful section of Norfolk. The doctor moved to Virginia Beach and decided to rent it out. Ken found it to be perfect. *She could get to school or her job within ten minutes*, he thought.) Monica was moving with her and had plenty of help. She was inside chilling when Ray came through the door, then Angela and her help. "Heah, girlfriend. Heah, Ray."

"What's up, girl? What's up, Quinn, Rome," Angela said. "Can I get some help bringin' my shit in—all these hard-head muthafuckas standing around."

Monica's brother came out of her room, catching Angela by surprise. "What's up, Angie?"

Angela gave him a hug. *Smell good,* she thought, *and still fine as hell, if not finer, but never again.* "Monica's breakin' the lease already—they said no pets—especially no dogs in this bitch."

He stood staring her up and down and smiling, figuring maybe he could be her friend, now that her and his sister were roommates. *God she filled out beautifully and has grown to be quite a woman.* "How you been? It's been a little while."

"I'm fine. Just fine."

"Let's grab your shit," Rome said walking out the door. "I got to run." Everybody followed.

Later on Monica and Quinn sat on the couch sipping Heinekens, while Angela and Ray got her room situated. They all started talking about what they were going to do for the Fourth of July.

"Turn that down a little bit," Ray said.

"You don't like Outkast, nigga?" Quinn asked.

"They be rockin'"—Angela said—"me and you, your momma, and your cousin too." They all started laughing, and that started a long conversation about hip-hop music.

As the night progressed, they grew tired and decided it was time to retire. "Let me go make my bed," Angela said. "I'm getting tired."

"For real, girl, I'm gonna go climb in my bed as soon as I take care of something." Monica pulled out a quarter of weed and a box of blunts.

"I heard that shit, girl."

"Roll up," Quinn said, getting some extra energy.

"Let me make my bed up real quick so all I have to do is jump in. Come on, Ray, you know I need your help." Angela picked up her bag from Wal-Mart to get her new sheets, pillows, and comforter as her and Ray began to make the bed.

"Why you have to smoke that shit?" Ray asked.

"Just because you don't smoke weed, don't knock my thing. Plus, it's only every now and then."

"Yeah, right. I bet it's gonna be an everyday thing now you have your own spot."

"No, it's not, Ray, but if I decide to, I have that right—I pay these bills around here."

"And I have the right to leave."

"Whatever." Angela kept making the bed. After she finished, she asked Ray, "Are you going to stay in the room or come out and chill?"

"If you're going to smoke, I'm going to head home."

She didn't want him to leave, but she wasn't going to argue or be controlled by anyone. Her father was in Maryland, maybe Ray forgot that.

"Will I see you tomorrow?" she asked as if she didn't mind. She sat on the couch as he went out the door.

"What's up with Ray, Angela?" Monica asked.

"Nigga trippin' . . . tellin' me I shouldn't smoke. He don't know I'm fuckin' grown." Then to Quinn, "Now pass the blunt, fool."

Quinn passed the blunt. "Y'all hoes crazy." Then he rolled another.

The summer seemed so short, Angela thought; *another week and school's going to be in session.* She sat on the couch flipping channels, feeling like life couldn't get any better. It was the weekend, and after the week she had, she was trying to enjoy doing nothing. Just then the phone rang.

"Hello."

"What's up, girl?" It was Monica.

"Nothin'. Just enjoyin' the day doin' nothin'."

"You want to go to Pizzazz tonight?"

"Where?"

"Granby Street," Monica said in an excited manner. "I want to check out that club Pizzazz, where the niggas poppin' that Don and Crissy."

"I don't care; it really don't sound bad."

"I'll be home in a little bit."

Angela ran in the room to find something to wear. *For the club, I have to have a little something, something to entice the fellows, and I really don't have shit.*

The ring of the phone disturbed her train of thought. She glanced at the caller ID to see it was Ray. She picked it up quickly. "Hello."

"What you doin'?"

"Nothin'. Just tryin' to find somethin' to wear."

"You comin' by to see me?"

"I've been running all week, Ray. I figured I would just relax. You can come by here for a little while."

"Okay, I'll see you later on."

"How later? Monica and I are goin' to the club later."

"Thought you were so tired. I'll give you a call tomorrow." Ray hung up.

"Hello . . . hello . . ."

Angela slammed down the phone. "I love that nigga, but he's starting to get on my muthafuckin' nerves—acting like a fuckin' bitch. If he was any kind of man, he'd be over here fuckin' the hell out of me, so I wouldn't have the energy to fuck with anybody else . . . instead of acting like a jealous kid."

She was mumbling now and tossing things around with a little more force than usual. Then she realized nobody was there. *I am not going to be worried, not today.* She continued to look for something to wear until she heard Monica come in.

"Got any company?" Monica yelled.

"Naw, girl, I'm chillin'."

"I hope you naked," Rome said loudly, "'cause I'm comin' in." He walked into her room.

"What's up, Rome?"

"Ready to hit the club, find a little something, something."

"You look nice, Rome," Angela said.

"I know." Rome started pulling weed and a White Owl out of his pocket.

"Look at Rome, Angela," Monica said, "with his Calvin Klein gear, lookin' all good."

"Where did y'all hook up?" Angela asked.

"I was coming out of Hair Art, and he was going in Clippers, the barbershop next door. He started talking about going to Pizzazz, so I figured we all might swing out together and have a ball."

"So," Angela asked, "where you goin' to stay, Rome? On campus or what?"

"Naw, my brother got a spot in Hampton, so I'm gonna chill over there—rent-free, nigga."

"That shit worked out for ya, didn't it?" Monica put in Mobb Deep's CD. She and Angela sat down as Rome lit the White Owl, knowing how slow it was going to burn. They knew their head would be right for the club.

"CD's are over there and some Heinekens are in the 'frigerator," Monica said to Rome as she walked to her room to get dressed.

"Hurry the hell up," Rome said real low and slow as if the weed was affecting him. "Don't be like my goddamn sister."

"Shut your high ass up, nigga," Angela said.

Rome reached in his pocket and pulled out a coin. "Heads, I wash Angela back; tails, I wash Monica back—really, I don't give a fuck which one I clean." He smiled.

"Lock your door, Monica," Angela yelled out going into her room. "Nigga's bein' nasty."

Rome laughed so hard, he began choking. Then he sat down to finish the slow-burning White Owl.

Chapter Four

Rome pulled up in front of the club to check the crowd. The line was just down the building, so it was beginning to pack up. He cruised real slow past the crowd of people. He knew the two fine-ass bitches in the car made niggas admire him, and the Lex made bitches want him. He felt like the man. He was so glad Bo was letting him drive it, but it was only for a minute, only while Bo was in the rough hanging on the corner trying to get. So for tonight he thought, *GS300 do your thing, do your thing.*

They parked and went inside the club, thinking about the fake ID's getting them over again. They thought the wait would be longer than it was, but the line moved pretty quickly. They eased to the third floor. Rome leaned over to the bar to order a drink.

"You not buyin' us a drink?" Angela asked.

"Just because I drive my brother's car don't mean I have his pocket." Rome had a smirk, like he was lying.

"We didn't ask you all that," Monica said.

"Is flat *no* better for ya? Just stand there and look pretty. Stick your ass out a little and y'all will have a drink in your hand in no time."

"Look what she got on."

"Look at that bitch head," Monica added.

Angela laughed. "She could of did better than that—"

"Excuse me," a dark-skinned brother interrupted, "I'm tryin' to get a drink."

They turned and looked at him; his accent caught them off guard. They stepped over to let him pass, checking out this rude man with what seemed to be an attitude. He stood about five foot nine, medium build, slight to the slim side, and had a close cut and a perfectly shaped beard. The gear he wore complemented his physique and the occasion. His beige linen pants that tied in the front and his silk brown shirt won him points for coordination.

As the bartender sat his drink on the counter, the stranger turned to reach in his pocket and caught Monica's eye. "I'm sorry—would you ladies like a drink? Tell her what you want."

"Alizé please," Monica said.

"And you?" He stared straight into Angela's eyes. She was very attractive to him. In his mind, he'd had her before. *Or a bitch just like her.*

She stared back. His long eyelashes and sleepy eyes made her weak, but the scar on his neck and the tattoo on his forearm made her see a man that was not for her. "The same," Angela told the bartender.

The stranger pulled a small stack of brand-new money out his pocket, pulled off a fifty, and gave it to the bartender. They couldn't help noticing the thick gold bracelet that matched the chain with the iced-out medallion around his neck. He picked up the drinks and handed them to the girls. That's when they caught a glimpse of the beautiful gold Rolex with the diamond face.

It sent chills through Angela's body. *He didn't look as good as Ray, but his style and persona made up for it in every way.* She instantly took him as thug, a hustler, and she made a promise to herself that she was never going to go that route.

"Thank you," the girls said smiling.

"No problem. It was my pleasure. What's your name?" He looked at Monica.

"I'm Monica, and that's Angela. Where you from?"

"Trinidad."

Actually he was from Jamaica, but he knew they wouldn't know the difference. And, really, it wasn't their business.

"My name is Damien." He reached out to shake their hands. "It was very nice meeting you both." He looked into Angela's eyes. "Hope I see you around." He touched her on her slim waist and moved her out of his path.

Angela didn't like him touching her, but he did it so smooth, she didn't say a word.

They went to sit down and check out the crowd when this tall dark-skin brother with braids stepped up to Monica. Within minutes she was on the floor throwing down.

Angela sipped her drink and stared at her friend, trying to figure out what Monica actually saw in these thug-type niggas. Every nigga she talked to was straight hood, except for Quinn—he was a soft thug. He *played* thug, he dressed thuggish, but he was really soft.

As Angela's drink emptied, the waitress replaced it with another. "Who sent it over?"

When the waitress turned to point, the man was gone. She described what he had on, and Angela knew it was Damien. She scanned the club for him and saw nothing. Later, when she was on the floor dancing, she caught herself looking around to see if she saw him. *He wasn't all that*, she thought. *No better-lookin' than the other guys in the club, but his style . . .*

After the club, they were all standing outside. Rome had begun talking to this young lady. After his conversation got going, Angela and Monica headed to the car.

Monica got close to Rome and said loudly, "I know you not out here disrespectin' me . . . not in my face." Then she and Angela started laughing. So did the girl he was talking to and her friends.

"Girl, I'm hungry," the girl said to her friends.

"We gonna stop at IHOP on the way home," her friend responded.

"Which one you goin' to?" Rome asked.

"On Battlefield Boulevard," she said.

"Me too, shorty. I'll check you there." Rome walked off with Monica and Angela.

"If we ride way out there with you, boy, you gonna feed us," Angela said.

"For real. I'm hungry too. Goin' all the way out there behind some bitch—she ain't gonna give you none no way."

"Shit, she gonna give some to this *Lex*."

"It ain't even yours," Monica reminded him.

"By the time she find out, it will be too late." Rome grabbed his dick. "I'll be done fucked."

They reached IHOP the same time as the girl Rome was talking to did. He said, "Peep that shit."

Angela agreed. "Damn, that shit is nice."

"Sittin' on all that chrome, windows tinted. Couldn't tell a bitch shit if I had that."

Angela got out the car. "That Land Cruiser is beautiful."

The girls Rome was talking to parked beside the truck.

"Come here, y'all. Get a table," Rome said to Angela and Monica. They walked inside and were waiting to be seated.

Angela pointed to the corner. "Look, that's that boy from the club."

"Damien."

Before they could even sit down, Rome came in and joined them. "Missed out," Monica said.

"Naw, I'm goin' over there after I drop y'all off—so hurry the hell up."

"You comin' way back out here?" Angela asked.

"Her crew live out here; she lives off Hampton Boulevard."

"Be careful, boy. Don't let that bitch get you in no shit," Monica warned. "I know she probably got mad niggas."

"Why you say that?"

Angela told him, "Tellin' you to come over and she just met you. You ain't the first guy she allowed to do that."

"I know she ain't got no man," Monica added, "if she out here with her ass all out in that short-ass skirt. And her shirt's too small—bitch titties about to bust the goddamn buttons. Just don't be hardheaded, and be careful."

They had known Rome since Bayside Middle School and they had all hung out many nights before, from middle-school dances to Lake Edward house parties. And now they'd all be going to Hampton. They knew there'd be more good times to come. They also knew a lot of girls had a lot of shit with them. They didn't know her, but the way she was dressed—her weaved-in, long blond hair was put up in a french twist, and her nails were real long with airbrush designs—Monica and Angela knew the girl was fly. But fly girls can bring drama, and they didn't want Rome in no shit.

***

The girl walked over to Rome to tell him she would be home in about thirty minutes. She spoke to Monica and Angela and had a pleasant attitude. Even though they had negative thoughts about her, they could see why Rome was attracted to her. They noticed that her body was just as tight as theirs, but she had age on them. They also knew to keep her nails and hair up didn't come cheap. As the girl walked off, she took one last glance at Monica and Angela. She knew she had her shit straight, but she would give anything to have the natural beauty that Monica and Angela possessed.

As they got up to leave, Damien was at the counter paying for his meal. "Thanks for the other drink," Angela told him. "I didn't get a chance to say it in the club."

"No thanks is necessary, pretty girl," he said with a partial smile and walked out the door. He didn't even try to converse with her.

He's so short-spoken.

Angela watched as the other females tried to get his attention, but he ignored them, climbed in his truck, and backed out.

"That ain't no Land Cruiser, that's a LX450 Lexus." Rome looked at Monica and Angela. "Is Hampton goin' to bless me with one of those?"

"We'll see, starting next week," Monica said.

Angela looked at Damien's truck as he pulled off, and with thoughts going through her mind, she started toward the car. She didn't know what he did, but he didn't look as if he was worried. *But why was he by himself . . . with that truck, jewelry, and money? Why was he goin' home by himself?* She sat in silence until Rome pulled in front of their building to drop them off.

"I'll get with y'all later," he said.

"Call us tomorrow," Angela said.

"I'm goin' to page you early," Monica said, "and you better call me back."

It was Monday morning and Angela didn't feel like going to orientation. She pushed herself to the shower, threw on her sweatsuit, and ran out. She arrived on campus and looked around for Ogden Hall. She realized she was a long way from high school. She started across the parking lot in time to see Rome pulling up in his Honda Accord. It wasn't the Lex, but it was his and it was dependable.

"What's up, girl? Ready for this shit?"

"Ready as I'm gonna get."

"Where is Monica?"

"She should be here. She stayed home last night."

"You stayed home with Ray last night?"

"He came over for a little while, but he didn't stay. He was still upset about Saturday night. He jumps to conclusions and wants to act all jealous and shit. Rome, you know I ain't doin' shit, and I haven't given him any reason to get attitudes with me. I love Ray, but that shit's gettin' old."

"Tell him. You have to let a nigga know when he's pushin' you away."

"Right."

They both heard a voice hollering their names. It was Monica coming across the lot. "What's up, family?" she said smiling. Then she punched Rome. "You was suppose to call yesterday."

"I chilled out with Quanita." He shook his head up and down like a kid with a secret.

"Who the hell is Quanita?" Monica asked as they strolled into the building.

"Girl from the club Saturday."

"That's the hoochie momma name?" Angela asked.

"The hoochie is real chill. I got over there Saturday night. She came to the door in a long T-shirt. We smoked a blunt, and all she wanted to do was talk. But I actually enjoyed her company, even though I wanted to hit. I picked her up yesterday in the Honda. We went and checked out a movie and got a bite to eat. Then we went back to her spot, and she broke a nigga off lovely."

"For real?" Monica asked.

"I'm going to keep seeing her. She's a junior at Old Dominion. She seems to be pretty focused, and plus, she got the bomb shit." Rome peeked around the room. "These bitches fine as hell—I'm goin' to have a ball over here."

The next week was full of campus tours and seminars. This was Labor Day weekend and after this weekend, it was straight business. Playtime was over. Monica and Angela decided to go to the Norfolk State game at ODU. It was always the shit.

The after-party was supposed to be at Pizzazz, but they decided to ride down the oceanfront. After strolling the strip for a while, things started to settle down and they were getting tired. "I'm ready to get a bath, kick back on the sofa, and chill," Angela said.

"Let's stop out Lake Edward and get us a dime sack first," Monica suggested. "You know we need that."

They started back up Atlantic Avenue toward Fortieth Street where they were parked. As they reached the corner of Thirty-second and Atlantic, they saw Damien and another guy walking up from Pacific Avenue. They stopped and waited for them to approach.

"Hello, ladies," Damien said, "this is my brother. He goes to Norfolk State."

Angela and Monica spoke, but never took their eyes off Damien. His brother, tall and lanky with dreads, no jewels, and a different color beaded necklace, was nothing like him.

"I keep running into you. It must be meant for us to spend some time together, or at least talk and get to know one another." Damien moved closer to Angela and looked into her eyes.

"Is that right?"

"Look, I'm having a small barbecue tomorrow. It's going to start about five. Page me, and I'll give you the directions, okay? Bring Monica along. You both should enjoy yourselves."

They agreed to call and headed home. "We goin' to his cookout?"

"I don't know. I'm still kind of unsure about him; I'm not tryin' to get mixed up in any shit."

"He just asked you to come to a cookout, not move the fuck in with him. He probably got a girl anyway."

"No bullshit."

Chapter Five

"I'll see you in a little while," Angela yelled as she walked out the door Sunday morning. It was early, but she was used to getting up for the early morning service instead of waiting until 11:30. She never cared for church too much and usually got upset with her mom for making her go, but ever since her mom and Ken joined The Faith Uphold Christian Center, she kind of looked forward to going.

As she sat in church, she listened to the pastor go from Scripture to reality, and reality to Scripture. The pastor's theme was, "You don't know what God has in store." She then realized that God would not allow her life to be turned around by sending a hustlin'-ass player to stand in her path. Maybe she would meet a successful businessman or doctor like Ken, someone who would push her, stand beside her, like she had always seen him do for her mother. *I'm not supposed to be thinking about men in church. My mind is supposed to be on what blessings God has in store for me, not what man is trying to interrupt my life.*

Angela opened her condo door. *What am I going to wear today?* She tapped on Monica's door. "What the deal, girl?" There was no answer, so she knocked harder to override the sounds of the stereo coming from Monica's room. *She might have company. Usually she listens to rap, but she's playing Faith Evans.*

"Monica!"

"Yo, I'll be out in a sec." Monica's voice was low and sluggish, and Angela could barely make out what she was saying.

Angela walked away with a confused look on her face, wondering who Monica was entertaining. "I'll see you later," she said out loud. "I have to find something to wear." She looked at her Levi jeans shorts again. She knew she would be banging in them, but she didn't want to come off as a young-ass hoochie. Then it hit her, she had on a red thin skirt that buttoned up the front, red heels, white stockings, and blouse. She pulled her white top out that came down just above her waist, so her flat stomach would show. She then removed her slip and stockings so that the thin material would slide and flow with the movement of her perfectly shaped ass. Then she undid several buttons from the bottom of the skirt so a little thigh would show. Then she slid her foot into her red, open-toed sandals. "Good God." She smiled, feeling proud of how she put that together so well.

Just then Monica came out of her room.

"We still—" was all Angela could get out before Monica covered her mouth. She didn't want Quinn to know about the cookout.

Angela whispered, "Sorry. So what up, girl?"

"Not a thing."

Quinn came out of Monica's room sparking half a blunt. "How are you, Angela?"

"Fine now—since you got the medicine. When you goin' back to Petersburg?"

"In a few. My man leavin' about two. I'm going to meet him at my moms. I'm outta here." He gave Monica the blunt, kissed her, and headed out the door.

"So what's up, girl?" Monica asked.

"I'm down, girl."

Angela went to her room to get Damien's number. When she called, a girl answered, "Hello," catching Angela off guard.

"Yes . . . can I speak to Damien?"

"Hold on."

Angela held the phone, wondering if she called at a bad time.

"Yeah." The voice with the accent came through the receiver.

"Damien?"

"Who is this?" Damien sounded stern.

"Angela."

"Heah, girl, how are you?"

"Fine. I called for directions."

Damien rattled off the directions. "Got it?"

"Yes. See you about five."

Angela and Monica arrived at Damien's house about 5:30, surprised at the beautiful home. There weren't many cars in the front: the two cars he'd mentioned, a Dodge Intrepid, a black Tahoe with Jersey tags, and a Cadillac STS sitting on chrome.

As they approached the front door a young lady welcomed them in. She was a little on the heavy side, about five foot four, wide hips, and very large breasts, but the outfit she wore, she wore well. "Hello, come on in," she said.

"Thank you," Angela said. "We're looking for Damien."

"Sure, I'll get him. I'm Rhonda, Damien's sister."

"I'm Angela, and this is Monica. Nice to meet you."

"Everyone is in the back," Rhonda said, turning to walk away.

They began to follow her. When they got to the sliding glass door to go out back, it opened and Damien
appeared, acting surprised to see them. "See you found
it." He looked toward Angela. "There wasn't a problem,
was it?"

"No, you gave good directions."

"Would you like something to drink?"

"Yes," Monica answered.

"Show her where everything is, Rhonda."

"I'm okay." Angela looked at her surroundings. "I
like this."

"Let me show you around." Damien took her hand
and headed to the front to give her the grand tour. They
walked into the living room. The older-looking couch,
coffee table, end tables, and the pictures with the gold
frames hanging on the wall gave her the feeling that
the room was for show, not entertaining. They strolled
through to the formal living room and stepped out into
the dining area, which gave her a clear view of the large
off-white marble dining table with matching chairs and
china cabinet. The table was set for eight people to sit
and have a formal dinner. Damien stopped in the oval
doorway and looked back at Angela admiring his shit.
He stepped back so she could slide through and get full
view of the eat-in kitchen and family room.

Angela soon realized that Damien's home was more
extravagant than her parents'. *How could a young
man not much older than me afford something like
this*? She always heard of hustlers making money, but
she'd never met anyone who had it like this.

She watched him as he guided her into his sunken
family room with the marble gas fireplace. She tried not
to stare at him, but he looked so good. She focused her
attention back to the house. In his family room he had
dark-green leather sectional with a beautiful glass table
and the fifty-two inch Hitachi big-screen television.

"Come on, let me finish." He walked up the circular steps.

"How many bedrooms do you have?"

"Four, counting the bonus room over the garage." He entered the room over the garage. The audio system that covered half the wall was the first thing to catch her eye, then the nine-foot custom pool table that sat in the center of the room.

Damien focused his attention on Angela. *She is beautiful, but just like every girl, she's just out for the paper. No total commitment.* By her being so young, he knew she was about games and trying to explore her options. So he figured he was just going to show her a nice time, nothing more.

He held her hand and showed her the other two rooms. "This is it." He opened the door to his room. "Please excuse the mess, but this wasn't the plan. Or I would of straighten up." His accent was killing her.

She entered his room and her knees weakened. The king-sized bed had a large column bedpost that made her think of royalty. Opposite the bed, was another gas fireplace next to the sitting room, which held a love seat, chair, and small circular table.

They walked into the bathroom.

"Damn. This is the size of my brother's room."

The jacuzzi tub was large enough for four people. In the corner was a separate stand-up shower, his-and-her sinks on the other wall, and a huge closet.

This nigga home is beautiful. How the fuck did he achieve this? "How old are you, Damien?" Angela's voice sounded soft and shy.

"I'm twenty-two. Why you ask?"

"I was curious. Do you live here alone?"

"No, my brother stays here too."

She found herself daydreaming about spending time with Damien. He had her attention, but she was going to fight this. She could never see herself spending time with a hustlin'-type nigga.

"So how old are you?"

"I'm eighteen."

He laughed. "How did you get in the club?"

It was the first time she saw him smile; he was usually real stern and serious.

She smiled. "Don't ask."

He looked at her beautiful smile. *Damn, eighteen.* Then it hit him. *Maybe I can mold her into the woman I want.* He imagined her lying nude in the middle of his bed. It was picture-perfect. He didn't want to just fuck her, he wanted to make her fall in love with him, want him, desire him. Then he would have her mind and body.

He leaned back on the wall. "So what do you do?"

"I start classes at HU in a few days. I also work part-time at a lawyer's office."

"Where?"

"Off Freemason."

He smiled. "Robinson down there?"

"Yeah," she said surprised. Then she thought about a lot of young boys that went to see Robinson, local hustlers who had been caught in up in some bullshit. She could not hold it in any longer. "What do you do for a living? How do you afford this at twenty-two?"

"My father passed away when I was twelve, and when I turned twenty-one, I got my trust fund and came to Virginia. I bought this, and I opened a clothing store off Chesapeake Boulevard in Norfolk and it's doing quite well. Do that answer both your questions?"

"Yes," she said, giving him the benefit of the doubt. She still felt he dealt drugs. "So where is your girl, Damien?"

"No girl, Angela, just me."

She had a look like she didn't believe him.

"So where's your man?"

"I don't know. He's somewhere."

Instead of pursuing it, he figured he would leave it alone and just go for his. He leaned over in her ear and whispered, "I'm your man and I'm right here. Soon, you going to have to make a choice." He stood in front of her, put his hands on her waist, and kissed her on the cheek. He took her hand once again. "Come on, let's get back downstairs."

Once there, they walked to the back and stepped out onto the deck that expanded the length of the house. On both ends sat large grills filled with food. Everyone was eating and enjoying the music.

Monica was standing with Rhonda. "So who lives here, Rhonda?"

Angela waited for her to answer, to see if it matched her brother's.

"It's Damien's house, and my other brother came down to go to school. Almost everybody here leaving after the cookout; we got to get back to New York."

Monica reached out and tapped Rhonda as if they'd been friends for years. "Where is his girl? I know he got one."

"He haven't had a main girl for years. He just has friends."

Angela looked at Rhonda. "Are these all his friends?"

"No, just associates and people we know. I can say this—he had good things to say about you. I wish he could find a chill girl. Not no money-hungryass bitch. It's plenty of them out here, and all they get is played," Rhonda said as she walked away.

Damien came outside with a Backwoods in one hand and one behind his ear. Two girls came outside behind him. They sat down and began talking and smoking.

Angela looked on and actually felt herself getting jealous. She wanted his attention, the same way she had it earlier—undivided. She was almost ready to tell Monica she was ready to go . . . until Rhonda came back over with a drink and a blunt.

"Do you all smoke?"

"Hell yeah." Monica reached out.

"Who's the girls with Damien?"

"Those two girls over there are from New York. They came down for Labor Day. Pretty as hell, aren't they? Those are the two most rude bitches you ever seen. The one on the left standing up is China, and the one wearing the green top is Maria. We know them from 'Up Top.' They're mad cool; just don't get them wrong."

As Angela took the blunt and hit it, Damien looked dead into her eyes. She looked back like she had an attitude. She knew she had no right feeling like this, so she knew it was time to go. "We're going to get ready and leave."

"Already?" Rhonda asked.

"Yeah, come on, Monica." Angela headed for the sliding glass door.

By the time she went through the house and reached the front door, Damien came inside, the usual stern look on his face. "What the fuck! You just walk out without saying shit to me." He stood directly in front of her and stared into her eyes.

"Well, it seemed like—"

"I'm not talkin' to you."

Monica stood there. Didn't say another word. She could tell he wasn't playing.

"You were busy—that's why I didn't bother you."

"No, you don't just leave me without sayin' anything. That's rude . . . you understand what I'm sayin'?"

"Yes," she said like a hurt child.

"Come here; you're not leavin' now." He took Angela's arm. "You can go back in there, Monica." Then he and Angela walked out front. "These are my friends, you are my friend—I have to mingle with everyone. My peoples are leaving in a little bit.

"This new movie started Friday, and I want to see it tonight. It starts at 9:45. You can give Monica your car to drive home when she's ready, but you are mine for the evening. What did I tell you upstairs? Tell me my exact words."

"You're my man and you're right here, and soon I'm going to have to make a choice."

"Okay. Now let's go back in."

The way he came at her scared her in a way, but she liked the way he took charge—telling, not asking everything.

She went in the back and started talking to Rhonda and Monica. Damien came back in and walked over to them. He sparked the Backwoods and began talking to Rhonda.

Monica and Angela just stared, not understanding a word.

He passed the blunt to Angela and walked back over to China and Maria so he could finish talking business.

The rest of the evening went pretty fast. Before long everybody was leaving.

"Don't play with my brother, girl," Rhonda whispered in Angela's ear. "He's all I got." Then she turned and left.

How could she tell me that? Angela thought to herself. *I'm not his woman; I'm Ray's woman.* Then she gave Monica her keys to drive home.

"You need some gas, Angela. Remember, you were going to get some on the way back home?"

"Let me get my purse."

Before she could turn, Damien reached in his pocket and handed Monica a twenty. "I'm going to change," he said. "I'll be ready in a few." Then he ran up the stairs to his room.

Monica asked her, "Are you going to be all right?"

"What you think?"

"Just be careful and go straight home. Call me when you get through the door."

Angela went back inside to wait on Damien. His brother had run to take his friend back to campus, and now they were finally alone.

She decided to give him a hand with cleaning up. She started to straighten up his kitchen, but when he came downstairs—he had his shirt in his hand—her body got a certain jolt that she'd never felt before. She'd never seen so many beautiful tattoos. She quickly studied his body and ran her eyes past the scars and across the tattoos. Her body began to moisten. She could also smell the sweet aroma of his Black Jeans Versace cologne.

They stumbled around each other until everything was fairly clean, then they were out the door. They got in the LX450, and he threw in Tupac's *Me Against the World*. They jammed all the way to the movies as the weed smoke filled the Lexus truck.

Throughout the movie Angela wondered if she was going to be faced with him asking for sex afterwards. She loved Ray and didn't want to cheat on him or hurt him, but she didn't know if she could tell Damien no, or even if she wanted to.

When the movie was over he walked to the truck and jumped in, tossing a D'Angelo CD. Before they reached the condo, he hit the track so that "My Lady" could come on. Damien reached out, took her hand as the song played, and kept hold of it until he reached her front door. "I enjoyed you today."

"I did too."

He leaned over and tapped his cheek for her to give him a kiss. She did and walked inside on a real high. *Compared to Damien, the weed didn't do shit.*

Chapter Six

The next morning Angela woke to Ray ringing her phone. "Where were you last night and yesterday evening?" "I told you I was going to a cookout with Monica."

"No, you didn't, Angela."

"Well, I meant to. Look, I'll call you as soon as I get up." She hung up the phone before he had a chance to respond. Thirty minutes later, hard knocks at the door woke up Angela.

"Get the door, Angela," Monica yelled from her room. Monica opened the door to Angela's door. "Angela, that boy out there banging on the door."

Angela wiped the sleep from her eyes. "Who?"

"Ray."

She opened the door. "What the hell is wrong with you, Ray?"

"No—what the hell is wrong with *you*. You been actin' funny lately, and I want to know what the deal is."

"Ray, you need to calm down and stop yellin'."

"Don't tell me what the fuck to do. Let me know what's up right now . . . because if this is how our relationship is goin' to be, we're goin' to have problems."

"Look, Ray, I love you and I don't know why you trippin'. Calm down."

He gave her a hug. "Baby, I love you too. But we haven't been spending a lot of time lately; I just have to learn to deal with it."

"I'm going to lay back down. Why don't we get together later . . . please?"

"Can I lay down with you?" He followed her to her room and climbed in bed beside her. He slid real close to her and put his arms around her. He held her and thought about how much he cared and all he would do to hold on to her. He began to caress her body and slid his hand up her thigh, then across her stomach and up to her breast.

She moved his hand. "Please, Ray—I'm tired."

He relaxed for a minute then decided he would try again.

She sat up with an attitude. "What don't you understand?"

"What's the fuckin' problem? If you stop smokin' so goddamn much, you wouldn't be so tired. Then maybe you'll feel like fuckin' me."

"Who are you talking to?" She raised her voice. "Maybe I'm not fuckin' with you because you are weak, a weak-ass punk—"

Before another word could come out her mouth, he slapped her, and she fell to the floor, crying hysterically as if he had really hurt her.

"Get out! Get out, or I'll call the fuckin' police!"

"I'm sorry . . . I—I didn't mean to. I really am."

"Fuck that! Ain't nobody goin' to be puttin' their hands on me. Get out!"

"Ray, it's best you leave right now. I don't want to call the police, but you got to be out your mind hittin' my girl."

"This between me and her, Monica, stay out of it."

"Fuck that! You can carry your ass up out of here. Put your muthafuckin' hands on me and they'll carry you out this bitch. I'll fuck you up. But guess what—today they goin' to lock your ass up."

Monica took the phone and dialed 9 and 1.

"Monica—"

"Bye, Ray. I don't want to hear nothin'. You know if I hit this other 1, that no matter what I say, they're goin' to come out here, and I will tell them what happened." Monica hugged her friend.

Ray turned and left, and they stood there hugging each other.

Angela knew this shit was about to end and was really hurting inside. She still loved him, but that shit he just pulled was inexcusable. She still couldn't believe what just happened.

Ray rode down the street thinking about what had just happened. If he could rewind time, he would have waited for her to call him back and never went over there. Seeing that he had to face his actions head on, he wondered what could be done to rectify the situation.

He had been feeling fucked up all summer, and the fact that he was supposed to take over the family business was also bearing down on him. He wanted his own life; separate from everyone. Just him and Angela.

Since graduation his plans had changed from working in the family business to going in the military as an officer: Leave and go in the reserves now; return and be back to start school the following semester at Norfolk State University.

The following day he went to see a recruiter and got everything set to leave. The only hard thing was being separated from Angela. He wondered if she would even care. He tried calling her, but there was no answer. Feeling sick and desperate, he began talking to the answering machine. "I know *sorry* is just a word, Angela, but I am really sorry. I don't know what got into me, but I really have something to tell you. Please call me before Thursday. That's when I leave, and I need to talk to you before I go. Please call. I love you."

Angela woke up bright and early, excited about her first day of college. Everything was perfect—except for the left side of her face. It was still slightly bruised. *Thank God, he hit me with an open hand and not his fist.* Either way, she saw stars. She hardly ever wore makeup, but just a little was necessary.

As Angela entered Ogden Hall for her eight o'clock class she thought, *this isn't much different from my high school.* She wanted to see that seventy-five-to-eighty people-in-a-class shit she'd heard about.

Her instructors just spoke on what was needed and expected of them. By about noon she was done for the day.

Angela decided to go home and relax before going to work at one-thirty. She walked inside the condo and hit the answering machine. Her father had called because he hadn't heard from her and then she heard Ray. His voice and message began to soothe her mind. She listened as she thought about him leaving. *Where the hell could he be going?* Then she heard a knock at the door.

It was Ray.

She let him come in to hear what he had to say.

He took the time to explain what had him so angry and why he ended up taking his frustrations out on her. Ray continued to inform Angela of his new plans.

She was surprised but let him know she was behind him. She walked in her room to change for work.

Standing in her doorway, he watched as she stripped down to panties and bra. He eased up behind her, put his arms around her and began kissing her passionately. He removed her bra and began to caress her breasts, then removed her panties and laid her on the bed. He stood up and removed his clothes in seconds and slipped on a condom.

As they kissed again he brought himself down on top of her and eased inside. She moaned and he began to move in and out at a fast pace. Looking down at her, he wondered how he could ever put his hands on her in a negative way. She was beautiful, and loving her was all he wanted.

She opened her eyes to meet his, and relaxed her body—the picture of Damien came in her head. She began to imagine Damien making love to her and she began to move, moan, and then quickly opened her eyes to catch herself just in time, as she felt his body stiffen, and shake.

He stood up and removed his condom while walking into the bathroom. She finished getting dressed, and they walked out together.

She entered the office and figured someone had to be in love. In front of her were twelve beautiful red roses. "Mrs. Stevens, who received roses today?" Angela asked in a most professional voice.

"They came for you earlier."

"Really." *It had to be Ray wanting to show me he knew he was wrong and he was really sorry.* She hurried over and pulled out the card. It read:

> I really enjoyed your company and would love to see you for dinner. Page me and let me know what time you get off.
>
> As Always,
> Damien

She felt good; no one had ever sent her flowers. Damien sent her flowers for no reason at all; just to ask her to dinner. She sat down and got herself started on her work. After about an hour she paged Damien. Thirty minutes passed and he still hadn't called back. She paged him again, and he called back immediately.

"What's up? Look, just page me once; sometimes I'm tied up. If you do it right, then you know it went through, and I will hit you back, okay."

"All right. Thank you, they're so beautiful."

"Glad you like them. What time you get off?"

"Five thirty."

"So I'll see you then; I'll be in front at five thirty."

She kept looking at the flowers as the hours passed. *He is very sweet.*

The other night at the movies she was concerned with him wanting some ass afterwards and didn't allow herself to get into the movie. But she never even thought about him not even thinking of her like that. He surprised her, and it made her wonder why he didn't.

She tried to imagine what it would be like to make love to him. Would it be tender or rough? Fast like Ray, or will he take his time? She drifted deeper into a daze, picturing him licking her all over like she'd heard Monica and other girls talking about, but had never experienced. She thought about the conversation her and Ray had about oral sex. He'd said he would if he was married and not until. She'd vowed never, under any circumstances, to do it. The ring of the phone brought her back to reality.

"Hello. Robinson, Madison, Fulton and Williams. May I help you?"

"Hello, Angela. It's Ray"

She was surprised he'd called. "What's going on?"

"Wanted to see if you wanted to go out this evening. I could meet you at your house."

"It would have to be later; I have to finish up some work and probably won't get out of here until about eight."

"Well, give me a call when you get in."

Relieved, she said, "All right, I'll talk to you then." She was glad he called and didn't just show up trying to surprise her. She didn't want him to go off on Damien and Damien end up getting hurt.

She packed her things about 5:30 and headed for the door. Angela opened the door, and saw Damien sitting in the black truck on the rocky, uneven street. She could see the smoke in the truck, feel the bass vibration, and hear the new hot single by Nas, "If I Ruled the World," pumping through the twelve-inch "kickers" that sat in back of the LX450. She walked over and climbed in, trying not to show her excitement toward him, but she knew her wide smile and jovial attitude would easily give her away.

She felt like a child whose parents had promised Chuck E. Cheese after school. Staring at her with the remote to the radio in his hand, Damien had his back against the driver side door. He smiled, as he turned down the music and stared, amazed at what he saw. "You are so fine, and your smile makes me fuckin' weak," he said in a low, smooth tone.

She blushed as if what he said moved her, when actually it was the island accent that weakened her.

"Do I rate a hug, a kiss or something?" He puckered his lips.

She didn't know if he was playing or serious, but since she wanted to kiss him anyway, she leaned forward and kissed him.

"What you want to eat?"

"It's up to you, Damien."

"Shit, I don't know. We'll roll and spark this ganja; maybe something will come to us."

"I'll spark; you start rollin'."

He pulled off thinking she must be the coolest, baddest bitch he ever came across. She sat back, enjoying the ride and company as he rolled downtown through the expensive section of town called Gent. They drove up Colley Avenue into Park Place. She had heard a lot about Park Place and could tell the difference—as soon as he came out from the underpass, from the expensive Gent shops on Twenty-sixth Street to the outside cafes on Colley Avenue, right into the drug-infested environment that surrounded the old run-down houses and abandoned buildings.

They drove for about twenty minutes until the blunt was gone. Finally they ended up on City Hall Drive. "So what you decide?"

"You driving and I'm with you; go anywhere." She looked over at Damien as she passed the blunt. *Nice truck, nice home, and he had money, and he always seem to be in a good mood. And he never hesitated to share his weed. That was much better than hearing a whole bunch of bullshit about how bad smoking was and how it fucked you up.*

Damien pulled in front of the Marriott, and the parking attendants took the truck as he walked inside to Stormy's Restaurant.

After they were seated, they ordered drinks. "So what's up, Angela?"

"Nothin', Damien. I told you I had a man."

"What about us? I like you. Never met anyone like you so young, but yet so smart."

"I know you have a girl, Damien."

"Look, lying isn't me. All I do is chill. If I'm not playing pool or out of town, I'm at home just chillin' by
myself, and I'm tired of that. I want you there with me,
to be mine. I need someone in my life to love me and
someone I can put my trust into. I've chosen you, and
you it will be."

"What about my man, Damien? I have to play fair."

"I can love you better than any man. We can be friends,
but when you give yourself to me, it will be no game
played from that point on. You'll be all mine. When you
become mine, I won't have another man ever touchin'
you again. It will be up to you."

When he asked the waiter for the check, she thought
he was upset, or had an attitude and wasn't trying to
show it. She was attracted to Damien and loved his
style, but she loved her man. She couldn't take her eyes
off him as they left the restaurant. *He was looking so
good*. She felt good to be with him.

His style and persona made people look and admire.
He acted as if he didn't care for the attention, but wearing the things he did and driving the Lexus truck, she
knew he expected it. As his hand swung with each step
he took, she noticed the shiny gold Rolex he had on at
the club. She liked the way he shined. *It was different
than being out with Ray, who could be boring sometimes.*

She stood beside him in front of the hotel, waiting for
the attendants to bring the truck around. Just then, a
group of businessmen came out of the hotel. Two stood
beside Angela and stared her down as if she was by herself. "What is your name?" one of them asked.

Before she could answer, Damien put his arm around her and pulled her in front of him, ass to dick, body to body, and kissed the back of her neck. "You need to focus your attention elsewhere—*blodeclaat*. I'm not the one to disrespect."

Angela really couldn't understand what he said and figured the other gentlemen probably had a problem understanding too. But the tone and the statement—with no smile—was understanding enough.

He wrapped his arms around her waist until the truck arrived. "You like pool?"

"Yes, but I'm not good."

"Well, we're just playin' for fun."

They went over to Waterside, the inside mall that sat on the water, and which also included two clubs, a large poolroom, several stores, and numerous food courts. She had gotten into the game and was having fun. She'd forgotten all about Ray and the fact that she had to get up early until Damien asked what time her first class was the following day.

"Nine."

"Think it's time we go; I'm not tryin' to keep you out late until the weekend."

He drove her back to her car. Before opening the door, she paused and looked at him. *Should I just say bye, or is he going to ask?*

Damien told her, "Go ahead."

"Go ahead and what?"

"Kiss me. I know that's what you thinking—should I or shouldn't I? Angela, you can do whatever you want; I'm already yours. I'm just waitin' for you to come around. Please believe me."

"I do, Damien." She leaned over and gently kissed him on the lips.

"Let me know you got home safe."

"Okay, I'll page you."

"No, I'll be home. Just call."

She drove home floating on cloud nine, and no sooner than she was in the house, she was on the phone dialing his number. After telling him how much she enjoyed herself, she hung up and called her father's house. She went to bed with Damien on the mind and her body aching for attention, but she forgot to call Ray.

Chapter Seven

With her busy schedule, the week went fast. Thursday was here, and it was the day for her and Monica to ride and drop Ray off in Richmond. She didn't want to see him leave, but he felt it was what he had to do.

Monica and Angela came straight back, not wanting to be on the road too late. When they arrived back at the condo, they continued the girl talk they'd started on the way back.

Angela hadn't talked to Damien since Tuesday and actually missed him. He had to go to the island to handle some business and wouldn't be back until the following week. Several guys had approached her, but she didn't have the desire to date any of them, even though some were quite nice. She decided to page him since he'd told her his pager could be reached anywhere.

A girl called back. "Hello, somebody page me?"

"No, I paged Damien. This is Angela."

"This is China—I met you at the cookout. He's out of town, but I'll try and get him your message if there is one."

"Just tell him if he finds time, I would like to hear from him."

"All right. Peace, girl."

Forty-five minutes later the phone rang. The caller ID read OUT OF AREA. She picked it up quickly. It was

Damien. They talked for all of thirty minutes. He let her know he would be back in town next Thursday and that he looked forward to seeing her. She placed the phone down feeling something inside that went misunderstood. Inside, she knew that Ray was gone, and without her man being right there, she could put down her guard and let things flow.

After classes Friday she and Monica decided to go shopping. Her father's birthday was coming up, and she needed to find him a nice shirt or tie to take next weekend to Maryland. She stopped at Beecroft and Bulls, one of the men's shops known for selling quality men's clothes and accessories. As she was leaving out the door, someone pulled the door. Monica looked and kept walking, and Angela followed.

The cool, respectful sound of the man's voice made Angela and Monica turn to respond. His light-brown eyes glued to Angela. She caught him looking at her ass, and he quickly focused his eyes to hers.

Angela was stunned at the man's attractive physique, not to mention his clean-shaven face and flawless skin. "So, are you shopping for your man?" he asked.

"No, my father." She stared back into his eyes. *He's fine, and so well groomed.* He reminded her of Ken.

"Excuse me, my name is Mac, and you are?"

"Angela."

"How old are you, Angela?"

"I'm eighteen. How old are you, Mac?"

"I'm twenty-eight, and I want to get to know you, Angela. Can I?" He let the door go and stepped closer. "Tell me a little about Angela."

She smiled. "I'm a freshman at Hampton. I work every day, and I handle my own business."

"You're a very attractive woman." He reached in his pocket and pulled out his card to give to her.

She was impressed. Nobody had ever called her a woman.

"I would like to hear from you sometimes. I too have a busy schedule, but I'll make time for you. Have plans for tomorrow evening?"

Before she had a chance to think, she answered, "Not at all."

"Well, let me get your number, and I'll give you a call." He stepped over and opened the door to a S500 Mercedes Benz.

Angela stood admiring this fine gentleman in his Zanetti. The expensive Italian suit fit him like it was tailor-made. *That's probably a fifteen-hundred-dollar outfit.* When he handed her the pen, she noticed his beautiful Baume & Mercier watch and well manicured hands. She asked him, "What type of work you do?"

"I own a real estate company: Lafarras Real Estate Group, in Hampton, by Buckroe Beach. I'm going to give you a call tomorrow, and we'll finish our conversation. It was very nice meeting you." He stuck his hand out.

Angela shook his hand and was all smiles. She walked over to her car, which Monica had pulled in front, and got in.

Monica was smiling ear to ear waiting to hear some shit. "What he talkin' about, girl?"

"He say we goin' to dinner tomorrow. We'll see if he call."

Monica laughed. "*Hope* he call—that nigga was fine, girl."

"He reminded me of Ken."

"I was going to say the same thing, because he look so professional, not like the thugs that we use to, with they pants hangin' off they stankin' ass."

"That's the type of man I need in my life, a professional man who will push me, hold me down, and
help me out when I need connects."

"How old is he?"

"He's twenty-eight and got his own real estate company."

"That's the kind of nigga I need. Bet he don't smoke
weed either, girl. He probably square and shit." Monica
laughed. "Bitch got to do what a bitch got to do." They
slapped hands, knowing that what she said wa'n' no
joke.

Angela and Monica were awakened by hard thunder-
ous knocks. Angela got up and opened the door, "What
the hell, boy!" She turned to go back in her room.

"Had to take Moms to the store, so since I was up,
best to keep goin'.'"

Angela yelled, "Monica," and climbed back into bed.

"Come on, Angela and Monica," he yelled from the
living room so they both could hear him. "Get up! Let's
bounce, baby. It's ten o'clock, and it's beautiful outside. Let's go to Military Circle and get some shit—fuck
sleeping all day."

Angela yelled from her room, "Rome, you better
carry your ass home."

"I know what the fuck to do." Rome turned on the
stereo, but they didn't move. "Look, I had some extra
money, and I was going to treat you to Piccadilly for
lunch. And I might get y'all a shirt, or maybe even a
skirt—as long as it's real short so I can see something."
He laughed as they came out the room. "Oh, I got to say
I'm going to buy shit before y'all hoes move."

Monica was standing in the doorway of her room
wearing a thin, short nightie that barely covered her

ass. "Hell, yeah! Why else would we get up on a Saturday morning?"

Angela was in the kitchen pouring something to drink. "So you buyin' gear?"

"Is spendin' money the only thing that move y'all?" Rome asked, rolling a blunt. "I'm buying shit like y'all got on—that's the shit I'm talking about. So let's all get in the shower together, so we can hurry up and get out of here." He entered Angela's room.

Angela headed back to her room. "Boy, you better get out of there."

"You better call Quanita," Monica suggested.

"She's been dismissed. Looking for newer and better things. Look, if we not gettin' in the shower, then y'all better hurry the fuck up."

"Give us a few," Monica said, "we'll be right out."

Rome threw in R. Kelly's CD, *Twelve Play*, and smoked his blunt until the girls were dressed and ready to go.

They spent three hours in Military Circle, trying to find the right gear. Now it was four; time had gotten away from them. They'd run into Fat Joe and he'd promised to meet them at the condo with weed and drinks about five. When they got back he was sitting in the car, rolling up.

"Boy, don't get in trouble," Monica warned. "You don't know if these white folks being nosy or what." They all went inside to catch up on what was going on since they hadn't seen Joe in a couple weeks.

Fat Joe's moms had put in a word for him at the hospital, so he was working there. She wasn't having him bullshitting around, now that he was out of school.

Then Monica brought up the subject of Quanita. "I enjoy her," Rome said, "but I'm lookin' for something different."

"Why you change your mind about her?" Angela asked. "You use to act as if you was all press to get with her."

"Too possessive. She tryin' to keep up with my every move, fussin' 'bout my time."

As the conversation continued, Angela and Monica let them know they were taking life as it came. Quinn was Monica's main thing, but she had her friends.

Angela let them know that she was trying to deal with being alone, and that she had some other dilemmas. Nothing she would discuss in front of Joe. The last thing she wanted was some shit to get back to Ray.

As they lit the last blunt from the quarter Fat Joe brought over, they all leaned back in deep thought, wondering where their young lives were headed.

Rome got a page from his brother and had to leave. Angela, Monica, and Joe were stretched out on the couches 'sleep, when the ring of the phone woke them.

Monica looked at the caller ID. "Lafarass Group." She had a confused look on her face. "Hello."

"Yes, may I speak to Angela?"

"Hold on, please." She handed the phone to Angela, who signaled that she would take it in her room.

Twenty minutes passed, and Monica heard Angela turn on the shower. She got up and walked in her room. "What's up, girl?"

"That was Mac," Angela yelled from the bathroom. "He's comin' from his office just across the bridge, and we headed out for a bit. Iron that top for me."

Monica came out and opened the sliding glass door and lit an incense to relieve the condo of the weed smell.

Angela was in her bathroom giving herself the finishing touches, when she heard the knock at the door.

Monica jumped up to get it and looked him up and down as he entered the house. "She'll be out in a minute; you can have a seat." She went into Angela's room. "Hurry up, girl—he waitin' on you."

"I am, girl." She sprayed on some Nine West, her knockout fragrance. Then she whispered, "What he got on?"

"Black dress shorts, beige shirt, and black sandals—he's definitely good to go."

Angela came out the room, and Mac stood up. "Good to see you again," he said, leaning over and kissing her cheek.

"Thank you." She headed for the door and sent Mac into a trance. He took a second to admire her class and body.

Angela had put on a little makeup to appear slightly older. She wore some khaki-colored silk shorts that moved with the sway of her ass and a matching top that she tucked in her pants. She set the outfit off with a gold scarf around her waist and gold sandals. She was the perfect vision, and when she walked past him, the smell from the Nine West perfume had him floating out the door behind her.

He walked down and opened the car door. *What a gentleman*, Angela thought.

He wore a gold ring full of diamonds on his left ring finger and an eighteen-karat gold-and-steel Cartier watch. Which brought direct attention to his perfectly manicured nails.

He wasn't very talkative and she wasn't being out going, so they rode to Fisherman's Wharf with the relaxing sounds of Faith Evans playing. The conversation began to come alive as they sat waiting to be seated. "So what you studyin' at Hampton?"

"Mass communications. Where did you go to school?"

"I went to VCU and got my bachelor's in education, then went to Norfolk State for my master's."

"How'd you end up in real estate?"

"My father has a company in Connecticut. After I finished school, I was sending resumés out but had no luck. So I decided to try my hands at real estate until something came through, and here I am. It wasn't my plan, but it came off so well I couldn't ignore it.

"I sold real estate for three years, and then became a broker. My company is in its second year and we have revenues of over half a million, so it's coming along."

"You've done well."

"Yeah, but I'm not content in my business and I'm not happy in life." He spoke in a serious, low tone.

"Really? And why is life unhappy for you?"

"I want to make multi-millions with my business and I can't picture who I would like to share my success with. No one's in my life to share things with, to tell my day about, to just be by my side.

"I go out of town a lot—seminars and investment meetings with other real estate tycoons. Sometimes they're social dinners and formal parties. I'm tired of showing up alone. Yes, I have a busy schedule, but when I'm off, I really want someone there. Not just anybody, but somebody I could really get into. I asked God for it." Mac had a slight smile. "Maybe he sent you to me."

She smiled. "Maybe." *He's fine, successful, proper, and he shows respect.* The way he talked and the things he did made her feel special.

Dinner and conversation was going great. Mac suggested they do after dinner drinks at his house.

It was a short ride to Lafayette Shores, a very prestigious housing development in the middle of Norfolk where custom-built homes made up a gated community. *Goddamn this shit is phat,* Angela thought. *No nigga I know ain't got shit even close to this.*

They walked inside. As he strolled across the marble floor in the open foyer, she was temporarily blinded by the beautiful, but very bright chandelier that hung from the high cathedral-like ceiling. He guided her to his family room, where she noticed a smaller version of the same chandelier hanging over a deep-burgundy dining table that sat six easily.

He asked her to remove her shoes before stepping onto the plush winter-green carpet. She took a seat, and the soft bulky pillows smothered her body in comfort.

"Let me get us something to drink." Mac went over to a cooler with a glass door and pulled out a bottle of Moët and Alizé and held them both up.

"Alizé, please."

Mac picked up the remote control and aimed it for the stereo sitting in the custom-built cabinet centered inside the wall. The soft, easy sounds of jazz covered the room. It wasn't her preference, but she had learned to appreciate it by force when her mom and Ken played it. And if the right CD was on, it could be very soothing. As quickly as the thought popped in her head, David Sandborn came pouring out of the small Infiniti speakers.

Angela sipped her drink and allowed the smooth sounds to soothe her mind and body. Mac caught Angela as her eyes gently closed and she swayed her head slowly from side to side, allowing the music to take over. He eased down beside her and began to massage her shoulders and arms. Then he leaned closer and gently kissed her neck.

It felt good to Angela, so she just relaxed.

He leaned over and dimmed the lights, reached out with index finger, and touched her chin to turn her head to face him. What Angela thought would be a gentle kiss turned into a tongue swirling around in her mouth. Angela was stunned at his forwardness but did nothing. He pulled back and slowly pulled her into his arms. She leaned back, her back against his chest, legs up on the couch, enjoying the CD.

"Are you all right?"

"Yes, I'm fine. You have a gorgeous home. The African art is definitely a nice touch. Hope you don't mind me asking—but what do these homes run out here?"

"They range from two hundred fifty thousand to six hundred thousand. Mine ran me close to four hundred," he lied, knowing it was closer to three hundred thousand.

She continued to relax in his arms until the CD was through. "I think I better get ready and go; I have to get up early for church."

"Really. I attend Mt. Calvary with Courtney McBeth."

"Yes, I've visited y'all's church several times over on Popular Hall. Dr. Yeah. He's all right, but Faith Deliverance, Bishop Barbara Amos, is where I get all my strength," Angela said proudly.

"You should come visit again—like tomorrow." Mac spoke in a low voice.

She turned around to face him. "I would if you asked."

He stared into her eyes. "Would you?"

"Yes," she answered, staring deep into his.

He leaned over and kissed her gently, stood up, took her hands, and pulled her on her feet. Then he pulled her to him and gave her a firm hug. *Goddamn, this young girl feels good as hell in my arms.*

He dropped her off only to pick her up early the next morning. The service went well, and of course, as large as the congregation was, Angela saw many of her friends, and hoped it wouldn't get back to Ray. Actually she was enjoying Mac so much, her mind was free and she was enjoying life. They ended up spending the entire day, from dinner to bowling, to him having to stop at his office for some quick business. Mac didn't usually carry anyone while he handled his business, but he let her know that during the week his schedule was so hectic, it would be hard for him to get away and she might only receive phone calls. But today he had her and wasn't trying to get rid of her.

She enjoyed him and looked at him like no other guy she'd ever dated. He was a man with his shit together.

Chapter Eight

Damn! *I shoulda never laid down*, Angela thought as her alarm clock went off. She pressed the snooze button, but five minutes felt like one. She had to be at work soon and had no intentions of moving. Making it to class seemed like straight torture. She rolled over and stood up. "I got to get me some new shit." She looked through her closet. This weekend she was going to Maryland and would hit her father and Lenore up for some clothes.

She remembered a hair show that she'd seen in DC at the Four Seasons—Lenore had a big part in sponsoring it—where she got to see top-of-the-line fashions and hairstyles firsthand. She knew about two- and three-thousand-dollar gowns and hairdos that exceeded three, four hundred dollars. Whenever girls talked about clothes and hairstyles, she knew that they hadn't seen anything until they'd seen fifty drag queens strut their shit. Lenore told her, "If you really want to experience and learn some shit, keep your eyes on the queens."

Angela reached in and pulled out her pants suit and threw it on and was on her way out when Monica and Rome came in with upsetting looks on their faces.

"Why you lookin' like somebody died?" Angela joked.

"What's so funny, Angela?"

"Shut up, boy. What's goin' on?"

"You didn't hear about Dirt-Dirt?" Monica asked with a bewildered look. "He got killed last night."

"What happened?"

"Found him in the car shot in the neck. He was shot with a fuckin' shotgun. I told him to keep fuckin' with Bo. He know my brother the muthafuckin' man, but he said those Park Place niggas was giving him better prices. My brother always said he would rather be safe and stick with niggas he know, rather than try to get a deal and end up getting got."

"That shit is sad. All y'all need to stop sellin' that shit," Monica said. "That's the fifth person we grew up with out this way they found dead or has died a triflin' death."

"You right. Mo got shot on the basketball court out Lake Edward. And they found Duke and Rip robbed and cut the fuck up in Campus East."

"Then, they found Tee shot three times in the head by the dumpster, right beside the hole." Monica was referring to the dirty, man-made lake in Lake Edward.

"Everybody know that nigga, Mike-Mike, did that shit," Angela said. "And that shit wasn't even behind no drugs or money, though."

"Yeah! It was behind that triflin'-ass bitch, Pooh!" Monica said. "Now she fuckin' with Ski."

"Who haven't that bitch fucked?" Angela asked.

"Who haven't *Ski* fucked?" Rome said. They all forced a smile.

Angela had seen friends get killed, but she felt this one—Dirt-Dirt was all right with everybody. She wasn't sure where her life was headed, but she knew that she wanted to get the hell out of NW Virginia Beach. It had been hell going to Bayside, and it seemed to keep getting worse.

"We're going to his mom's house in a few," Rome
said.

"I have to get to work, but sign my name on the card.
Okay, Rome?" Angela knew better than to ask Monica.

Angela was at work thinking about the nice time
she'd shared with Mac. All the guys she met always had
that thug in them and showed it. Except for Ray. He
was more laid-back and kind.

She decided to call her girlfriend in Maryland. She
had been meaning to call, but now it was more convenient—and free. The call would be charged to the firm.

She had met Trinity the summer of '90, and they'd
been friends ever since. One summer her parents came
to their time-share at a Virginia Beach resort, and Trinity spent the entire time at Angela's house. They had
always agreed that they would go to the same college
and remain longtime friends. But Trinity decided she
wanted to attend Howard University and tried her hard-
est to convince Angela to come to DC. Angela had her
heart set on Hampton University, and neither could be
persuaded to change their mind. Then Trinity got pregnant, and that settled everything for her. If she went to
Howard she would have the help of family; in Hampton
she would be on her own.

"Hello."

"Heah, girl, what's up?" Angela asked.

"Fuck you, bitch. I don't fuck with you."

"What, girl?" Angela laughed, knowing why Trinity
had the attitude.

"You were supposed to call me last week. I bet your
ass ain't even comin'."

"That's what you know 'ho'. I'll be there this week-end." They began yelling from excitement like old friends do.

"Really? Who comin' with you?"

"Probably Monica."

"Call me as soon as you get in, girl. They got a new underground go-go club. We have to check it out."

"Sounds good—I can fuck with it. You know they don't play that shit down here. All you gonna hear on 103 JAMZ is hip-hop and R&B. None of that go-go shit in the seven cities."

"I couldn't imagine not havin' go-go, girl. But, any-way, you know I got to get to class. I'm glad you caught me. Make sure you call me when you get in. Okay?" Trinity hung up.

As soon as Angela got off the phone with Trinity, it rang again. It was Damien. He was calling to let her know he would be back in town on Thursday. He was in Tennessee at the time and was going to Charlotte Wednesday, before coming to Virginia. She soaked in every word. Angela was happy to hear from him. Not a day had past that she hadn't gone into a deep thought over Damien. Even the days she spent with Mac—he wasn't so powerful to push Damien out of her head. He couldn't get back soon enough. *What was his purpose for traveling all these places?* He was in Jamaica on vacation, *but what the hell was he doing in Tennessee?* Before she gave herself to him, they would have to sit and have a long talk.

Damien was trying to make his way back home to get close to Angela, without ever letting her know his busi-ness. How was she going to handle it when she found out that he was a hustler? He was far from the corner- or around-the-way hustler; he was connected to some major players who reigned out of New York.

**

Damien met JB five years ago and his life took a totally different turn. He was young and working the corner, slinging hard from hand to hand, serving fiends making the local niggas money. He had scraped and fought for his position. After getting in and doing his dirt, he was recognized by one of the higher-ranking moneymakers who used him as a mule for a while. But it taught him everything about trafficking drugs from state to state with little risk. As a mule and corner look-out, he was doing okay; living much better than the life he was used to.

One day while on the corner in Brooklyn, JB pulled up in his S600 and motioned for Damien to take a ride. He had seen and heard about JB through people in the hood, but now he was face to face with this true hustler. JB, on the other hand, had heard and peeped some things about Damien. Word was, "the youngster had heart and determination to succeed in this street game."

JB began to take a little time with Damien, showing him how to bring drugs in the country from the islands and then move weight state to state, not block to block. JB really never had anyone to put trust into except for his sister, Jacqueline. But in time Damien came to be not only an associate, but a trusted friend. JB brought Damien into his clique, completing his trio. These three young men worked under JB, who had schooled each of them slowly and carefully.

In just a short time Damien was going to Jamaica, making moves back to the States, with plenty of work to distribute. Damien had befriended two girls, China and Maria, two ladies who he trained well and used as mules. He would travel to the island from different lo-cations under one of his many aliases, while China and

Maria would smuggle the work through customs and usually fly into Memphis, Tennessee. The drugs were then transported to North Carolina and distributed.

JB introduced Damien to several of his associates, the ones that he was to supply. They lived and worked out of Charlotte, Fayetteville, and the Raleigh/Durham area. JB told him, "Never do business where you rest." That's when he moved to Virginia to play it safe.

Damien's position was very important, and for this he received sixty thousand a month for his role in JB's organization, a small fee for the weight Damien moved in the Carolinas. Damien began running for JB two years ago, and he made his trip twice a month. He had become contented with his life and never had any intentions of changing for anyone, not even Angela—as fine as she was.

Angela hurried home after work to shower and change before Mac picked her up for the movies. She went inside and was stopped dead in her tracks when she saw two dozen white roses sitting on each end table.

Monica told her, "Look at our new decoration."

"Who sent you flowers?" Angela asked.

"Bitch, you the only one gettin' flowers these days—don't front."

Angela's response was all smiles. She picked up the card. It read:

ONE DOZEN IS FOR THE WOMAN IN YOU AND THE SECOND DOZEN IS FOR THE GOOD FEELING YOU GIVE ME.

YOURS TRULY,
MAC

Angela's heart was deeply touched. This man, a real man, was so sensitive, and she felt she needed some sensitivity in her life. It would really make it complete.

Mac arrived at seven just as he'd said, coming straight to Angela's from his office. (He was dressed for business.) Angela came out the room and, just as she had imagined, he was dressed to impress in his olive-colored Armani suit and shoes, Chanel shirt and tie, with glasses by Perry Ellis, prescription not fashion. She felt like he could take her anywhere and she would go without a fight.

"How are you?" she asked.

"Fine. And you?" He opened the door, allowing her to step out and lock it. He walked down the stairs and opened the passenger-side door.

Angela caught a glimpse of a different ring and gold Whitnauer. She liked the way Mac came across and wanted to be in his world.

They drove down Colley Avenue listening to Mary J's CD. Angela was all into Mary. Mac could tell by the way her body and head slowly moved to the smooth, laid-back sounds.

She snapped back when they pulled in front of the Naro. "What type of theater is this?" she asked.

"It's a regular theater, but they usually show documentaries that never make it to the other theaters. They're playing *Hoop Dreams*. I hear it's very inspirational."

After the movie they went to one of the many outside cafés that lined the streets of Colley Avenue. Then they took the scenic route to Mac's house, down Waterside drive along the water.

Once at Mac's home, he poured them some Grand Marnier. The sweet, smooth taste excited her and it wasn't long before she was feeling the effects of the sweet after-dinner drink.

Mac eased over, rested his hands on her shoulders, and removed her blazer. He leaned over and began massaging her shoulders as he kissed the back of her neck and allowed his hand to slowly slide across her breast. "Let's go to my room."

"I'm not quite ready for that, Mac."

"I want to be with you, Angela," he said with sincerity. "If I can't be with you, at least stay the night and allow me to hold you."

"Mac, it's not easy tellin' you no. I know if I lay down beside you I will give myself to you, and like I said, I'm not ready for that tonight."

"Okay, I'm a patient man, but as long as you know I want you to be mine—all mine—and I will make you happier than any man possibly could. Bet on it!"

"I believe you, and I promise when I'm ready I'll let you know. To be honest, I have unfinished business to deal with; it wouldn't be fair bringin' you into my shit."

"Handle it then; I'm not goin' anywhere."

"Thank you for being understanding."

On the way home all she could think of was Ray. She had to let him know that her heart wasn't in the same place. She didn't want to tell him while he was in boot camp, but the way he acted when he got upset before, this was the best way. It would give him time to deal with the situation before he came back home. She felt so funny inside, but this was something that had to be done. He had to know the truth.

"Will we talk tomorrow?" she asked as he pulled in front of her building.

"Of course, we will. Don't think otherwise." He stared into her eyes. He knew she didn't know because she didn't fuck, but he wasn't pressed—his time was coming.

"I want to say thank you for the movie and dinner . . . not to mention the beautiful roses."

"You're beautiful, Angela, and very special. You definitely deserve to be treated like the woman you are." He got out the car and came around to open her door. She stepped out and into his arms. They embraced, and he kissed her gently on her cheek and stood back and watched as she walked up the stairs and into her condo.

Once inside she instantly pulled off her clothes and got comfortable. She rolled a blunt, sat down with a pen and pad, and began putting her thoughts on paper.

> *Dear Ray,*
>
> *I hope you are doing well and this letter finds you in good spirits, even though you're in boot camp. I received your letter and almost cried at the way you said you were being treated. You've always been a strong-hearted person, so I know you will make it. I wanted to write you because I'm dealing with a tough situation. You've been the love of my life for a long time, but these days I'm feeling the need to get out and experience different things. I didn't want to send you a long drawn-out letter because I feel it would make things difficult. Everything seems to be going fine in my life. School is exciting and it's bringing new experiences. I want to be able to explore my options without hurting you. Things are changing and I don't want to go into detail, but I don't want you coming home to any surprises. Never feel that*

I don't care or that you weren't special, because you could never be so wrong. Please know that you will always hold a special place in my heart. You will always be a friend, but you have to allow me to become a woman, learn to be a woman, and the only way is through life experiences that I feel I'm ready for now. I hope you can understand, because it means a lot to me that you do. I wish you the best of luck in your training and much success in life. Our paths will cross again and I hope to see a greater man, much greater than the one who left Bayside. I will always have love for you and you will always have a friend in me.

As Always, Angie

Angela sat there with tears in her eyes. He was her first real love, but she needed more excitement, the excitement of being introduced to new things that Mac was capable of showing her. She wanted a confident, take-charge-ass nigga like Damien, someone who possessed the capability of changing her life around. Mac was wonderful and she enjoyed him. She could relax, but trying to be a lady at all times was when the pressure began. She didn't want to embarrass herself or him and found herself watching her every action while trying to adjust to the new things in Mac's world.

Monica and Angela had the same schedule on Thursday, so they rode together. Monica was dragging, but Angela was hyped up. Damien was coming back today, and she hadn't been this excited over anything or anybody in a long time. She thought, *How could I get so excited over a nigga that wasn't even my man?*

"Come on, Monica, I have to drop this letter in the mail."

"I don't believe you goin' to do it."

"I have to; I don't have a choice. He'll just to have to understand."

"He's going to come back home in a rage and fuck up you and your men." Monica laughed.

"I don't have a muthafuckin' man, bitch, and he ain't gonna do shit." Angela climbed in the car. "I'm going to see my dad this weekend. You goin'?"

"I'm not sure. I promised to help my grandmother with some things. If she sticks with her plans, then I'm out of circulation all weekend."

"Girl, I'm going to end up taking this trip by myself."

"You do know that Dirt-Dirt funeral tomorrow," Monica reminded her.

"You goin'?"

"Yeah. Rome and I supposed to be meeting at Fat Joe house at twelve, and all of us are going to ride together."

"I can't make it; funerals aren't me. I'm going to two funerals in this lifetime—my moms and my pops. I might go to my little brother's, but nobody else's, I'm sorry."

"When we stopped through the other day, his moms was so sad, she couldn't stop crying. I had never seen his brother before, but he was there losing it. Damn near brought tears to my eyes. I felt for them."

"Death is always hard to handle, but everybody gets through it with the help of God. I been in church all my life and I know with God's help you can deal with anything that comes your way. All you have to do is pray about it." Angela's tone was very serious.

"You right, but reachin' the point of dealin' with it is just hard. I know firsthand."

Angela reached out and took Monica's hand. She knew that besides Monica's grandmother and brother, she was the closest thing to her. Monica was like her sister, and she couldn't love her any more if they were blood.

Angela's schoolwork was starting to build up and she was either going to cut back on her hours at work or give up some of her extra activities. She had a test Friday and hadn't studied at all. She wanted to see Damien, but tonight it was going to be brief. She had to put first things, first.

She left work and went straight home. Damien had left a message to give him a call when she got in. She paged him and it was taking him a minute. She was getting ready to page him again but remembered what he'd said. She didn't want him getting upset. He finally called back to let her know he would be through about seven thirty and to be ready. He didn't want to miss the beginning of *Martin.* (*Martin, Living Single*, and *New York Undercover*—those were his shows.) She let him know she wasn't going to be out long.

He told her, "Bring your books . . . just in case."

She went in her room to shower and change. She slipped on her tights and a T-shirt and her old faithful Reebok Classics, since they weren't going out.

Chapter Nine

"There's Damien, Angela."

"How you know?"

"Don't you hear the bass comin' through the walls?" Monica laughed. "Give me some trees, Angela."

"I'm broke. Better call your man."

"Who? Quinn?"

"Naw, fat-ass Joe," she said laughing, going to the door. She opened it and Damien came in. He stepped to her and gave her a hug. She didn't want to seem too eager because then he would know she missed him, so she just held him for a second longer.

Damien felt it anyway. "Heah, baby, what the fuck is up?"

"Nothin' at all." Angel smiled.

"Heah, Monica, what the deal?"

"Nothin' much, Damien. How you? Got a blunt?"

"Monica," Angela said loudly.

"She all right. I had this for us to spark on the way to the crib, but I got more at the house."

He pulled out a fat-ass blunt and passed it to her. "Watch yourself—that shit straight killer." Damien noticed the flowers in the condo. "Somebody got mad love around here."

"You don't know," Monica said on the comeback, knowing Damien wanted to know who the flowers were for. "Now we need to find somebody to love my girl like that."

"I'm trying, baby. I'm trying. Let's go; I left my truck running." He headed out the door.

Angela looked at Monica and they just smiled. Then she looked at Damien as he walked around the truck, not even attempting to open her door. *He looks so thuggish at times, not like Mac.*

Rocking his navy blue-and-white Jordans that complemented the navy blue Nautica sweats, white Nautica T-shirt, and Nautica hat that came down so low over his forehead, you really couldn't see his eyes without him looking directly at you.

They climbed in the truck and started moving to the sounds of Lil' Kim banging in the truck. "Don't act like you scared to move the way you was throwing that ass around the floor the night I met you."

"No, I won't. I didn't even dance," she said with a slight smirk.

"I thought you didn't lie, Angela." She just smiled and pumped up the sounds.

As she moved to the music in a nonchalant manner, Damien kept glancing at her beautiful face and her body. *She is so fuckin' sexy.* Every time he'd seen her, she was looking like a doll. A doll that wasn't his. It was time he had tried to control his feelings, but she made it hard and tonight she was making it damn near impossible.

He turned the music down a little. "Why the fuck I couldn't keep you off my mind, girl? The whole time I was out, I thought of you. That's not good, Angela."

"Why not, Damien?" She stared into his eyes.

"Here I am thinking about you everyday and you're not even my girl. I've never been in a situation like that. How do I handle it?"

"I can't tell you how to handle your feelings. I'm too busy trying to deal with my own."

She started to tell him about the letter, but she figured, just like Mac, he was going to have to give her time to work things out in her heart and head. The things he was saying was what she needed to hear—that he cared and that she was on his mind as much as he was on hers.

They got to the house and she thought about him opening her door like Mac, but just as quick as the thought came, it disappeared. He was already at the front door. "Why the fuck you moving so slow. Are you sick or something?"

"No, I'm fine, but I ain't in no hurry."

"Damn, something smells good. What's that?"

"My brother made some jerk chicken with beans and rice." He uncovered the pots and pan in the kitchen. "Have some?"

"I've never had jerk chicken and I hate to waste your food."

"Bring your ass in here and taste it then."

She got up thinking that he was so rude, but she realized that he spoke quickly and didn't think first. That was just the way he came across. Even when he referred to girls as bitches. She noticed at his cookout that he used it in his everyday vocabulary while talking to Rhonda and other girls, and wasn't out to offend anyone. That was just Damien, he was a real nigga, like Rome and Fat Joe wanted to be, like Rome brother Bo was, and what Mac would never be.

He pulled a piece of chicken off the bone and held it out for her. "Here," he said.

"I don't know where your nasty hands been." She opened her mouth.

He placed it in her mouth and held out his fingers. "Do you like it?"

"Yes, it's real good."

He laughed. "Then lick my fingers."

"Fool, you crazy," she said, turning and walking back into the family room and turning on the television.

"Turn that shit to *Martin*. Let's see what 'Marty Mar' doin'." She started laughing.

"I'll get us a plate in a minute." He went over to the drawer and pulled out an ounce of weed and threw it on the table. He reached for the Backwoods on top of the TV and sat down beside her.

She had never seen weed rolled in Backwoods. She was used to blunts and White Owls. "Damn, that shit strong."

"This that real shit—hundred fifty an *O*, girl."

He rolled three and lit one.

"Know what, you said on the phone that you missed me and you haven't gave me a fuckin' hug, kiss, or nothin'."

She leaned over and kissed him real slow. While he was rolling the weed, he'd taken off his shirt off and his tattoos were screaming at her to touch them. "Did they hurt?"

"Hell yeah, but I'm a man." His accent came through hard, making him hard to understand. He passed her the weed and got up to put their plates in the microwave. Then he poured two glasses of fruit punch and put them on the table by her.

By the time they finished smoking, she was feeling real relaxed and was about to starve. They talked and enjoyed each show as they ate. She was in heaven, not trying to create conversation or watching herself. She was just being Angela and it felt wonderful, especially with someone that she cared about and enjoyed.

"You better pull your books out and handle your business. Don't be bullshitting when it comes to that

schoolwork, your education. That shit is too important."

"I'm not." She went for her book, shocked that he
even cared. He got up and poured them two drinks and
lit another blunt.

"*New York Undercover* is my show. I gots to catch
this shit every week. Take off your shoes and make
yourself comfortable."

"I don't have any socks," she said.

"Hold on." He ran up the stairs and came back down
with a bag. He'd brought her a T-shirt from Jamaica
and some slippers that fit perfect.

"Thank you, Damien. That was sweet of you. I'm going to have to do something sweet for you."

"I could really use a massage. Can you handle that?"

"I think so." She leaned over and massaged his shoulders and back. Her touch was fucking him up. Her
hands were so soft and warm, every time she squeezed it
made his body weaker.

He turned to her and pulled her close as she put her
arms around him. He kissed her real slow and passionate. Kissing wasn't his thing, but she was so beautiful.
And letting their tongues touch was very stimulating.
He kissed her neck and at the same time massaged her
back. He was feeling high as shit, so he knew she was
on the same level.

As he kissed and caressed her, he felt that this was
their time and made his move. He slowly moved his
hand toward her breasts. He heard her sigh as he laid
her back on the couch, rubbed her back, and undid
her bra. Slowly he pulled up her T-shirt and kissed her
stomach. She sighed again softly from the kisses that
were now arousing her.

I said this wasn't going to happen, Angela thought
to herself, but her body loved the attention and her
mouth couldn't open to say stop.

As his tongue eased up the hairline on her stomach to her beautiful breasts, he slipped one of her hardened nipples into his mouth and began to suck gently. He flicked his tongue across the nipple, sending a sensation straight to her inner thigh, where his hand was already resting. His touch kept going higher until his hand rubbed her vagina. She squirmed at his slightest touch.

He continued and she relaxed and laid her head back, letting out a sound that let him know to continue.

"Let's go upstairs," he said, taking her by her waist and leading her to his room. He hit his switch and the light from the gas fireplace lit up the room. One hit of the other switch brought the sweet, slow, sounds of "After 7." He guided her to the bed, slowly undressed her, and pulled back his comforter for her to relax on the burgundy Ralph Lauren silk sheets.

As he stood there undressing, he stared at Angela's beautiful brown body lying on his bed. He knew he had been with mad bitches that were fine as Angela and bodies even better, but she had moved him.

He moved closer and slowly ran his hand up and down her body as if to explore it carefully looking for faults, but there was none. He leaned down and kissed her lips lightly, then each cheek. Without lifting his lips, he let his lips move slowly from her cheek, down her neck and as he kissed and gently sucked. Damien ran his tongue into the crevice of her neck, slowly positioning himself to get a full view of her breast. He lowered his head and began kissing her breast. Then in a slow motion he sucked the nipple into his mouth and began to suck firmly; his tongue flickering at a rapid pace.

Her body began to move, and he could feel the rate of her heart pick up just as her breathing became heavier.

He knew she was ready for him, but he had already
vowed that he was going to be the best she ever had.
He moved to the other breast, gave it the same attention and reached down and caressed her vagina. This
wasn't to arouse her like he played it, but to test her. He
ran his fingers across her vagina and then palmed her
breast so that he could smell the finger he ran across
her pussy. It was fresh. *Guess her momma taught her
well.* And since she did, Damien left a wet trail with his
tongue from her breast down to her vagina.

Angela's mind elevated into the clouds as Damien's
tongue worked his way past the lips of her pussy and
into its wet waiting softness. As his tongue explored
her insides, he moved so he could run his tongue from
her clit to her ass in a continuous motion. She panted
and began to get louder; her body was feeling what she
never felt before. He reached up and took her hands,
locking his hands and hers. He licked and sucked her
clit until all her mouth could say was, "Please, please,
please," as a feeling began to come over her body that
left her shaking and gasping for air.

He came up and kissed her as her arms wrapped
around him. He knew he should have gotten a condom,
but he wanted to feel her—she was his and that wasn't
going to change. He positioned himself to enter her,
and she knew it was time to tell him she wasn't on anything and he needed to use a condom. But she wanted
it to be perfect and didn't want to spoil the moment.
When he entered her, she closed her eyes and let out
a moan of pleasure. He stared down at her and slowly
stroked her to heaven. He realized that she hadn't been
really schooled—she barely moved, and her body was
real tight. But she felt so good, her inexperience didn't
mean a thing. As her breaths got louder, he got more
excited and thrust even harder. She strained to open
her eyes to see him staring down at her.

"Are you okay?"

"Yes," she said between breaths.

"You feel so good, Angela. God, you feel good." As his body started to tense, he felt the greatest feeling in the world starting to take over his body. "Are you on anything?"

"No," she said under her breaths. Her head came up wondering what he was going to do. She felt his body speed up and then began to tense up. Then all of a sudden, he snatched out his dick, laid it on her wet pussy with the head sticking up, laid his body against hers, and enjoyed the feeling of nut squirting between their stomachs. They laid there in each other's arms and cum.

"I'm sorry," Damien said, "I didn't know what else to do with it."

"Don't be sorry. Thank you for being concerned and responsible when I wasn't." She squeezed him harder.

She realized as she lay there that nobody had ever made her feel that good. He was wonderful. She wasn't going to let him go anywhere. She just hoped she made him feel as good.

He got up and got a towel to wipe them off, and she laid there as he ran the water in the Jacuzzi, with bubbles. He walked over to the bed and picked her up, sat her down inside the tub, then walked downstairs. She sat relaxing until she heard him change the CD and Maxwell came on. He came back in the bathroom and got in and let Maxwell massage her mind and body as he bathed her entire body. She thought she was in heaven; she felt she was in love. She followed his lead and started to bathe him. He laid back and let her do her thing.

It was then she realized that she was entering into a zone she had never been in. She had never been the aggressor. Ray was always fast. Kiss, kiss, and—boom!—the act was over. But Damien had taken his time and made her feel shit she hadn't felt before, so she wanted to return the pleasure.

She reached for his penis and felt his manhood harden again. "Stand up," she said. She began to rinse him off as she stared at the dick that also seemed to be staring at her. She said she would never do this to no man. *Why did this dick rate special attention? Because he made me feel so good.* She eased her mouth around his stiffening dick and began to suck with inexperienced lips, and lick with an inexperienced tongue, and each time her teeth hit it Damien jumped.

She wasn't the best and, from what Damien had experienced, far from it. But this was different. This was Angela, and he was going to accept it.

He was in heaven, and never will she ever regret it. He eased her to her feet and kissed her. Slowly he twisted her body so that her ass was up and out, which gave him easy access to slide in from the back. Her breath was taken as he entered her. She let out a sigh of pleasure. He was definitely the best she had ever had. They relaxed in the tub and held each other thinking about what had just occurred.

She cuddled up under him like he might leave. He didn't mind because he held her like she might sneak off into the night.

The next morning came quickly. Damien woke up, dick hard. He placed his dick under her butt between her legs and nudged at her. A smile came across his face as her leg lifted and invited him into the warm box that felt like no other bitch he had ever fucked.

"Damien, I have class at eight, and I still have to change."

"Okay, just five more minutes," he said without moving or opening his eyes. She sat on the edge of the bed and rubbed his back while he got in his five more minutes.

"Damien, it's that time. I also need to stop and get some breakfast," she said in a whining tone. He sat up. "Look in that top drawer," he said pointing, "and get that key with the remote on it."

She pulled it out.

"Take the truck, and I'll see you later."

"I get out of class at twelve and I don't get off work 'til five."

"I'm not going anywhere; I'll see you later. Look in the armrest and get twenty for breakfast and lunch. I got dinner. You are staying with me tonight, right?"

"Yes, baby," she said smiling from ear to ear.

When Angela arrived at the condo, Monica was getting dressed for class. Angela made a quick change, only to throw on some tights and the T-shirt Damien had brought.

"Why you rushin', girl? You got time," Monica said.

"I got to stop and get something to eat."

"Can I ride with you?"

"Sure. Come on; I'm out."

They walked down to the truck.

Monica grabbed her heart like she was having a heart attack. "Oh shit! Oh, hell naw. No, you don't got his truck, bitch. You fucked him, Angela? I know you did, but I got to hear you say it."

"No, I didn't fuck him. He fucked me, girl, and he fucked me like no other nigga have. You know most of these young niggas like to just throw it in and you don't even be wet. This nigga ate my pussy until I was drippin', then he slid in and tamed the kitty cat." Angela laughed.

On the way to school Angela gave Monica the entire rundown of the evening, then finished up on the way home after class. Monica knew this guy had her girl-friend open, but since Angela had the Lexus truck, she figured that nigga had to be open too.

Angela's day was great, except for the time spent in class when it felt as if time was standing still. She was at work when she got a call from Mac. He had gotten off early and wanted to see her. She told him she had made plans already with her mother and the only way was to come by her office.

He couldn't get by the office that evening, so he made plans to see her on the weekend when his schedule was free. She wanted to see him because he had made such an impression, but right now, she was high on Damien—that's who had her head—and when she got off, he would have her body to go with it.

Chapter Ten

She left the office headed straight to Damien's house. She noticed a white Land Cruiser with Connecticut plates parked in the driveway. She knocked.

"What you knockin' for?" he asked.

"I didn't want to interrupt."

"I heard that." He gave her a slight hug and a peck on the cheek. "I'm tryin' to finish up some business, so I want you to come in and speak, but then excuse yourself to my room for a second."

She went into the kitchen and saw the two girls she'd met before, China and Maria. "Hello, how are you all doing?" she asked.

"Fine and you?" China responded. "I see you found him," Maria added, throwing a pleasant smile.

"Yeah, he found his way back." Angela slid her hand across his stomach. "Y'all take care and maybe I'll see you later." She walked away going upstairs. *Damn, I like their style.* The diamond tennis bracelet, the rings, the long, beautiful manicured nails, the same style clothes that she'd seen in Lenore's closet, sexy, but yet conservative. She wondered if that was what Damien liked. Or did he want her to stay the same?

She heard the voice from the doorway. "What you thinkin' about?"

She turned to see Damien standing looking good as hell—new butter Timbs, dark denim jeans, and his orange RP55 T-shirt. *He must shop by the day. He always got on new shit, and whatever he wears, he wears well.*

"Oh! I was supposed to be going to DC this weekend to see my father, but Monica had something to do and I didn't want to go by myself . . . so I don't know."

"It will work out. Don't let the small things bother you. You look good today." He eased up to her and put his arms around her.

"Thank you. You not doing bad yourself." She held the medallion that swung at the end of his Cuban lynx.

"Thanks. Picked it up at the Coliseum Up Top."

"What's the Coliseum?"

"Mall in Queens with the entire first floor nothin' but gold. They be battlin' for prices."

"Sounds like the Jewelry Center in DC."

"Really, I have to check that out one day. You like jewelry?"

"Of course, but as you see it's not in the budget."

The doorbell rang. Then he heard Maria yell, "UPS truck outside."

He ran downstairs. About five minutes later, he was calling for Angela, as he said his good-byes to China and Maria, who were about to leave.

"Hold on, let me give this package to my brother," he said running up the stairs to his brother's room. He returned in minutes with smiles and a hype-ass attitude.

"What's up, girl? What we going to do?"

"It's on you, Damien. I know I have to change these clothes before we do anything."

"Want to throw on some shit to show your ass, huh?"

"Why you say that?" she asked with an attitude. "Can I ask you something?"

He smiled. "You can ask me anything, girl."

"China and Maria, their jewelry, them clothes, their nails and being fixed up all the time. Do you like that in your girl?"

"Nails done all the time—yes, I like that. Hair looking good—I demand it. Jewels—I really like on a woman, and as long as the clothes fit the occasion, I'm with it."

"What you mean 'fit the occasion'?"

"If you goin' to school or to a game, dress like that. Conservative. If you going to work, look like you look now, like you ready to handle some business. If you going to the club or if we going to a party, I want you to be the sexiest bitch up in that muthafucka—no doubt. I'll treat you like my little baby doll and dress you in real cute shit I like because I don't buy shit I don't like anyway."

"Is that right?"

"Damn right. You'll see." He headed out the door.

They arrived at her condo. "I have a TV in my room. I have to shower and change."

Damien sat on the bed and pulled out the Backwoods pack and began rolling.

Angela shut the door and put in a CD.

He continued rolling as she undressed to her bra and panties. He sat there as she walked into the bathroom, leaving the door slightly cracked. As the good weed started to sink in, he stared through the open door and thought about her sexy-ass body, how she tasted last night, how he made love to her and it was all that to him. He laid back and allowed his thoughts to interact with what he'd just seen. Along with the hydro, his mind and body was taken to a new plateau.

The opening of the bathroom door interrupted his thoughts. He sat up realizing that he had got turned on. His dick was hard as a brick. He watched her as she walked across the room to get some lotion.

"Will you lotion me down?"

"No question." He passed her the blunt and took the lotion. Then he removed the towel, and she laid across the bed. He applied the lotion slowly, then turned her over and finished up as he stared into her eyes, which began to get low from his gentle touch and, not to mention, the 'dro.

"You know I want you now," he said taking off his shirt.

She laid there as he kicked off his untied Timbs and let his jeans fall. She was so turned on by his dark skin and the glistening gold that rested on his neck and wrist. He leaned over and kissed her, and she jumped from the cold medallion touching her naked body. He reached down and let his Tommy Hilfiger boxers fall; she lifted her legs to accept him. And they fell into moments of intense sex.

Angela and Damien had just come out the shower and were getting dressed when they heard Monica come in. "Sounds like your girl got company," he said.

"Sound like Rome and Fat Joe. Them niggas ain't company; they from school. We all grew up together," she said in a nonchalant manner.

"Do they know your man?"

"No, but they gettin' ready to meet him."

He smiled, leaned over, and kissed her. *Goddamn, this bitch gettin' to me,* he thought. Never had he been with a girl that made him soft inside. "So are you going to DC?" he asked.

"Actually, it's Maryland, right outside of DC. Why," she joked, "you goin' with me?"

"Sure, I haven't been to DC in a minute."

"For real? Only one thing, I was going to stay with my dad."

"Tell you what—we'll go, I'll get a room, drop you at your dad's, and pick you up later on Sunday."

"What you goin' to do?"

"Feel like drivin'? We can leave now."

"Let me get some clothes together then we can go by your house."

"Baby girl," he said taking her hand and looking into her eyes, "let's go now while I'm in the mood. I will buy you whatever you need, from your underclothes to your shoes—I got you. Let me finish rollin' these 'Backs, and we out."

They walked into the livingroom where Monica and her company sat. "What's up, girl?" Monica pulled on a blunt.

"Not a thing. Heah, Rome, Big Jooooe," Angela said in a deep voice, punching Joe.

"What up?" Damien said, speaking to Rome and Fat Joe. "D." He gave the two guys a pound.

"We gettin' ready to go to DC," Angela said.

"Now, where's your fuckin' bags?" Monica asked.

"D said I'm straight," Angela said. She figured Damien didn't want niggas to know his real name like that. Monica smiled at Angela, and Angela smiled back. They both knew Angela had found her somebody special, a real nigga.

Chapter Eleven

They arrived in the metropolitan area around midnight. The sound of Damien talking on his cellular woke her up. She tried to understand what he was saying, but couldn't. Noticing she was awake, he held the phone down and turned his attention to her. "You going to your dad house tonight, or in the morning?"

"In the morning. I want to stay with you," she said in a soft, sweet voice that made him soft inside.

He began talking on the phone again. He talked fast and his accent was hard, making it difficult for her to understand what he was saying. Moments later they were pulling in front of a home slightly larger than Damien's and just as beautiful. She knew they weren't too far from Baltimore, because she timed herself.

"This is my cousin. Not blood, but his mother and mine came from the islands to New York together when they were young. We lived in a little spot in Harlem about eight deep in a two-bedroom hole. He moved to Jersey when we were about fifteen. Everything I did, he did, and we looked out for each other. When I came to Virginia, he came too, but he said Norfolk was a little too slow, he had to be where he could have access to the city.

"You two the same age?"

"I'll be twenty-three in December, and he'll be twenty-two in November." They walked up to the two-level, contemporary-style home.

"*Blodeclaat!*" his cousin yelled as they hugged each other like only peoples could do without looking gay.

"Nothin', man, nothin'," Damien said.

"Who's this beautiful woman?" his cousin asked.

"This is Angela. Angela, this is my cousin, Noriega."

"Nice to meet you." Angela stuck out her hand.

"No, girl," he said with the same accent as Damien. Then he hugged her as if she was family.

Goddamn, this nigga's fine. Finer than Damien and Mac, but a bit too skinny.

Noriega was a slim, dark-skinned man. His hair was like silk, and pitch-black. Noriega's father was Dominican and lived in Miami. He made his money the same way as Damien, but through a different connect. His father dealt strictly with heroin and would get it to Noriega by different means, and Noriega would distribute it to his peoples in Baltimore, DC, Phili, and back in Jersey.

Damien and Noriega never dealt with anyone in New York anymore. They said once they got out, they weren't going back. They still went to visit their peoples, but it was only for a second. Even though Noriega had much more paper than Damien, you could never tell. He wasn't materialistic. He wanted nice shit and had nice shit, but never extended himself to look as rich as he really was. Nevertheless, he always respected Damien's hustling skills from the street to the penthouse, and Damien had the same admiration and respect for his cousin.

"Come on in and have a seat," Damien said to Angela as he walked to the kitchen.

"Ya hungry or ya tired?" Noreiga asked. "You can't be both—not in this bitch. 'Cause it ain't shit in here to eat. So if you're hungry, we got to go out."

"Starvin' cousin," Damien said with Angela seconding the motion.

"Salone," Noriega yelled from the bottom of the stairs, then back into the den. "As soon as she gets dressed, we out of here. It's Friday too." Noreiga's lady, Salone, walked in wearing a long, emerald-green, silk robe, with matching slippers.

Damien thought she was a goddess; Angela thought she was a model. She was tall, slim, very petite frame, but beautiful.

"This is Salone," Noriega said. "And this is my cousin Damien from VA and his girl Angela."

"Hello," Damien and Angela said simultaneously.

"How are you? It's a pleasure to meet you both." Salone spoke with an accent that made Damien weak in the knees.

Damn! This bitch is beautiful. Where the fuck she from? Damien thought.

"Get dressed. We're going to find something to eat. And show Angela where they're going to be sleeping at tonight."

Angela and Salone walked away.

"And bring my boots I had on down." Noriega looked to make sure the girls were gone.

"Goddamn, D, that bitch phat as hell, and fine. With class too. Respect, respect."

"Naw, cousin, you always did fuck the baddest bitches comin' up, but you outdid yourself." Damien shook his head.

"I do all right." Noriega smiled, ready to tell his cousin his girl's credentials. "She from France. D, I hooked up with a French bitch, man. Got a degree from Howard in political science and works as a translator. I sent her ass back to school for her masters, but I'm gonna marry her ass before she graduates. Bitch not gonna get my paper and fly away. I'll have to move again. Bitch will make my body count begin to rise in the South." They both began laughing.

By now they were talking with such a hard accent that if the girls came up they would really have to listen to get the words.

"I'll drive." Noriega handed Damien the Backwoods to spark. He opened the door.

Angela eyes widened at the thought of how well Noriega lived. *Family with money*, she thought.

Damien gazed at the new E300. "When you get this?"

"That's her shit. Can't ride in that, because we can't smoke in that." Noriega opened the door to the new black four-door Tahoe. The boys jumped in the front, letting the ladies know they had things to discuss. They turned the music up just enough to enjoy the Backwoods and good conversation without being heard.

"She got any friends?" Noriega asked in his hard Jamaican accent.

"Roommate." Damien smiled. "Picture Salone at eighteen with a body like Angela." They gave each other a pound.

"I'm comin' down soon. Salone friends are all studious and shit. Bitches got degrees out the ass, makin' good money, got they own shit, and ain't been fucked in months. Next time you come in town, bring some fly shit; I'll turn you on to these hoes. Invest your money in them—it will always come back to ya."

"All right," was all Damien could say with a spaced look on his face.

"Yo, man, I know you not lettin' that shit from Richmond fuck with you still. Don't do that shit, cousin," Noriega said, getting real serious.

"Go to Big Bob's," Salone said over the music.

"You want Big Bob's or some shit in the street?"

"Just grab some shit in the street. Where we hangin'?"

Nore decided to check out some of the Jamaican clubs that he knew about. He didn't hang out much, but with his cousin Damien by his side, he knew the night was going to be all right.

After a long night of partying, Damien and Angela were awakened by the smooth sounds of Maxell coming through the walls. They strolled downstairs to catch Noriega and Salone embraced, dancing around as if they were in another world.

"Turn down that damn music. Where the hell you think you at?" Damien said with Angela by his side smiling.

Noriega and Salone jumped as if they forgot they had company. Damien and Angela began laughing hard because they had scared the couple.

"You two are crazy," Salone said.

"Make a nigga grab his shit—you know I'm fuckin' paranoid."

"We have to go to the mall." Damien picked up the ashtray with the half-smoked Backwoods and lit it."

"Hold on, we're going also. Then we can stop at Big Bob's to eat and I can find something to wear to the game," Salone said. "You know Howard and Hampton play today, don't you?" she asked as they headed for the stairway to change.

"What you goin' to do?" Damien asked.

"I have to meet Lenore at one at her shop." She stood waiting for his response.

"Then I'll drop you off and then get with you tomorrow."

A look came over her face that let him know he'd said the wrong thing. Maybe not the wrong thing, but it wasn't what she wanted to hear.

"Angela, what do you want me to do?"

"I want to go to the game if you goin'," she whined.

"How in the hell are we gonna do that?"

"Go to the mall, come back and change. Then I'll go to the shop with Lenore and either she can drop me back off or you come back and get me about five." She said it like it was nothing.

Who in the fuck feels like doin' all that? "All right then, that's what we'll do." He looked at her and promised himself that that beautiful smile would remain there forever.

When they returned from the mall and breakfast, they showered and all met on the back deck by the pool. "I'm gettin' ready to drop her off at her people's salon. I'll be back."

"Where's the shop?" Salone asked.

Angela told her, "Up near Georgetown, off M Avenue."

"I'll drive you," Salone volunteered, "then I can do some shopping."

They walked the girls outside to the car. Damien reached in his pocket and handed Angela some money. He put his arm around her neck and pulled her close as they walked. "You can do some shopping too. See you later." Then he kissed her, and they were gone.

Noriega and Damien had run out shopping. Damien wanted to pick up a gift for Angela before she returned. When the girls did return, they never knew the boys had run out because they were sitting in the same spots on the deck, sparking Backs and sipping Henny XO.

The girls were gone a little longer than expected. When Noriega heard the door, he yelled from outside, "Where the fuck y'all been?"

Salone screamed, "We'll be ready in a few minutes," and went up the stairs.

Moments later they returned ready to go. Angela asked, "What you waitin' on?"

Damien and Noriega turned to see three of the most attractive young ladies standing behind them.

Trinity had met Angela at Lenore's shop after getting her hair done. They shopped a little, and Trinity decided to go to the game also.

"Trinity, this is my friend Damien and his cousin Noriega. This is my girlfriend Trinity."

"Nice to meet you," they said as they both tried not to stare at her, but it was hard.

Trinity was shorter than Salone and Angela, standing five foot two, with long, dark, beautiful, healthy hair hanging down her back, cut to a point like a lion's mane. Her skin was flawless—dark and smooth. She wore a white outfit: pants with a drawstring in the waist that was loose that came down just past the knees, and a matching top that came down just below her breasts, leaving her pierced belly button, tight waist and flat stomach exposed. The top was loose enough for comfort, yet snug enough to show her braless, firm C cups. The thong she wore allowed her ass to jiggle with every movement of her body.

Damien and Noriega looked at each other and gave the eyes as if to say, *Only God knows what I'll do to that bitch. Only God knows.*

Noriega walked away and talked to Salone. "We're outta here in a minute."

Damien looked Angela up and down slowly. "Baby, I like—goddamn, baby, your nails fuckin' me up; I like that shit." He smiled.

"I was hopin' you would."

"I got something that's goin' to set that shit off." Damien reached over, getting the two wrapped boxes off the table. She opened one. He reached inside and pulled out a diamond tennis bracelet. The gold glittered as it went on her left arm. The other box contained a nice gold chain that now brought some well-deserved attention to her slim neckline.

By this time Noriega and Salone had returned. Noriega handed Damien another slim box. He opened it and took out the gold Movado watch and placed it on Angela's right wrist. She stood there shocked, heart racing with happiness.

"That's real nice, Damien. I hope you taking good care of my girl," Trinity said. "She couldn't stop talking about you."

"Shut up, girl . . . tellin' my business."

"I hope she can't. Now I know I'm on her mind too." He and Noriega looked at the ladies walking out the door, looked at each other, and shook their heads, knowing their girls were nice. But Trinity's shit was tight—that shit that would make a nigga dig in his pocket quick. All was said without a word.

Damien smiled and focused his attention back to Angela walking out the door. *Damn, she phat as hell. I know muthafuckas goin' be tryin' to holla.* He slapped her ass to let her know that those new Calvin Klein's were fitting—and because he could. She slapped his hand and leaned into him. He put his arm around her waist and their lips met. Then their eyes. So many words were said in a split second. And they got in the truck and were out.

Chapter Twelve

After the game Angela went out to her father's house to spend the rest of the weekend. Trinity stayed with her so they could talk and catch up on old times.

Trinity asked Angela, "So did you enjoy the game?"

"Hell, yeah. Anytime Hampton beats Howard, it's a glorious day."

Trinity turned on the radio. "You crazy as hell, girl. I see your daddy still got his little girl's room sitting here."

"I'm still his baby girl," Angela said without thinking, "you know how they are."

Trinity, whose father was never there, grabbed her bag. "Naw, I don't, but I'll survive."

Angela started looking around, then went in the closet and pulled out a small fan. "Girl, I need something to blow this smoke out." Angela lifted the window and set the fan in a position to blow the weed smoke out the window. Then she threw a towel down at the door and rolled up a Back and lit it. She inhaled and passed it to Trinity, who turned her down.

"You wouldn't have to go through all that if you fucked with this—" Trinity pulled out a small bag of coke.

"Naw, bitch, you do you." Angela pulled on the Back a little harder, allowing the smoke to fog her mind. She had seen girls and guys starting to fuck with that shit out the way, but it wasn't for her—weed and liquor were her only desire.

"I was goin' to ask you how you been keepin' the weight off, but now I see."

"You crazy, girl. I just started fuckin' with this about six months ago. I got my shape back when shit got tight as hell and school was almost a thing of the past. I was around here having a hard-ass time. Then 'you know who' got locked the fuck up, and then I was really fucked. Then one day I was out walking, trying to deal with my frustrations and some niggas rode up on me, and guess what they said and did?"

"What?"

"Now I'm at the lowest point in my life, Angela." Trinity's eyes started to water. "And they rolled up three deep in a Cadillac—new shit, girl—and two of them held out about three grand in each hand and said, 'Bitch, you got some big titties and a big ass—if you toned it up and lost that belly, I would give you three grand just for you to dance. Might give you five to fuck. But guess what, this is all you get until . . .' and that nigga threw a hundred on the fuckin' ground and they peeled off laughin'."

"What you do?"

"Picked up that hundred, bought my baby some food and shit, and took the rest and joined a gym.

"Got in there and met this girl. She'd seen me in there for about two weeks and told me if I kept it up, I could get a job with her. We became close and she started bein' my personal trainer. Within three months I was looking like this. And within four months I was dancing like this." She stripped, removing her top and skirt, and began dancing.

Angela, high and shocked at Trinity's new life, sat staring at her girl's every move. *Damn, this bitch got skills like the girls I seen on TV.*

"Dancing pays all right up here, but I go to DC or Baltimore and do private shows and I get that three thousand. Them niggas said it, and now I do it. I'm straight, my baby straight. I'm still in school and I even got money to put on the books for 'you know who.' And all he got to say to me is, 'Who you fuckin' for money?'"

"Who are you fuckin' for money?"

"I ain't had no dick since that nigga got locked. One day I'm gonna tell him that it ain't the niggas you got to worry about—it's these pussy-eatin' bitches."

Angela stood up. "What!"

"Don't knock my thing. You do you, and I'll do me . . . like you said."

Angela frowned. "Girl, you lost me."

"Like I said, Angela, it was the lowest time in my life and she just came in, being my friend. Then we got close and one night it just happened. Only thing is, she always do me and will never let me touch her."

"Bitch just eat your pussy?"

"Yeah, I just lay there and she does shit to my body no man has ever done or can do. Afterwards, sometimes I feel funny, but I enjoy it when it's happening. I enjoy her when she's around, and when I get horny, I look forward to her doing her thing. I know I can't fall in love with no bitch, but I can't see no other nigga—except for Tite—runnin' up in me, skeetin' all in me and all over my sheets. So until he comes home, and only God knows when that will be, I'm goin' to play on the other side of the water."

"I'll stick with dick, girl. I will stick with the dick." Angela handed Trinity a shirt.

"Yeah, but you can get some of this money, girl; you got the body for it."

"I work. I got my peoples, and Damien handles his."

"You just said it—*his*. Girl, you better get his and whoever else's you can get, because niggas just want to get their dick wet. Please tell me you got another nigga and you ain't open on this non-talkin', knotty-head-ass, Jamaican nigga."

"Girl, you know I keeps me two, three danglin'." Angela laughed and gave Trinity five. "Got a nigga name Mac. Fine, real estate muthafucka with dough—couple-hundred-thousand-dollar-home dough. Ain't gave him no pussy yet, but I felt that nigga dick layin' all on my thigh, beggin' to get in. I controls my shit—don't get it fucked up." They gave each other five and laid there in silence.

It was noon and Damien was headed out to get Angela. Noriega wanted Damien to stick around and check out his business deals. He and Salone were going to Chicago to check on a club venture, and he wanted Damien in on it and to bring Angela along. But with school and work, that wouldn't be possible. Damien talked about the possibilities, but gave no definite answer.

After a little while, Damien was on his way to get Angela and head back to Norfolk with a new business venture on his mind. After arriving at the condo and taking in all her bags, he decided to break out. She had work to do before class and some shit to tell Monica about the weekend.

That evening Angela and Monica were looking at the *Jamie Foxx Show*, eating popcorn and sipping Alizé when the phone rang. "It's Mac," Monica said, covering up the phone. "He's been callin' all weekend."

Angela came to the phone. "Hello. How are you?"

"I'm fine. How was your weekend?"

"Fine. Just did a little shoppin' with my dad and step-moms. I always have a great time in Maryland."

"If it's not too late, I would love to stop by and see you."

She wasn't really up for company, but it had been quite a few days. "Sure, I'll be here."

"Is he coming over?"

"Yeah, for a few. I'm not going to be up late."

"Yeah, yeah! Now finish tellin' me about his cousin."

"Girl, the nigga is fine. Real dark and jet-black, wavy hair, with real pretty skin. Gots plenty dough—baby is paid," she said with excitement in her voice.

"Do he have a girl?" Monica asked.

"Yeah, and she's very attractive. Look like a fuckin' model. Slim like a model. But you can tell her shit is tight. Bitch from France, but went to Howard. She a together girl; I like her.

"Damn, the good ones always got a bitch in the cut. Don't matter . . . she better keep his ass up there because I still wouldn't mind meetin' him. Shit, I got a man."

"Never know. He might just come this way . . . you never know."

Then a knocking disturbed the girls' conversation.

"I'm going to bed," Monica said. "I'll see you in the morning."

Chapter Thirteen

Mac came in and sat down with Angela. They sipped Alizé and talked until the late hours. He wanted to stay with Angela, but she didn't think it would be a good idea. After explaining to her that he really missed her company, all he wanted was her next to him to hold in his arms. That would definitely make his night. She finally agreed and they went in her room and went to sleep.

The running shower woke Mac. He wanted to make love to her so bad. All night long, every time she brushed against him, it made his body cry for hers. After she came out of the bathroom fully dressed, he got up to wash his face. She walked over and hugged him. She couldn't resist; he looked like a Greek god, standing there in his silk bikini drawers. Her body moistened as she felt his dick rise for the occasion when he pulled her close to him. She wanted him and last night it took all she had not to give in. In his arms she felt so secure, so overpowered, she wished he would have been a little more forceful and had just taken her, instead of always coming across like the perfect gentlemen.

"So will I see you later?" she asked.

"I'll do my best. I have an appointment that I know will run until late, but I really want to spend more time with you, so I am going to do my best." He headed for the door.

***

It was now November and the last couple months had flown by, and being with Angela had been glorious. Mac had never met anyone like her. He couldn't explain the feeling he got when she was in his company, but inside he knew she was the one. And the excitement that came out of her when she was introduced to something new made him long for the opportunity to show her the world. He pulled the French doors open that allowed him to step outside of the master bedroom and stood on the balcony of his two-story brick home, staring out over his covered pool while the brisk breeze came across his face. It was a week before Thanksgiving and Angela had invited him to have dinner with her parents at their home.

He turned and walked back inside. He moved closer to the bed, staring down at the two empty condom packages. Then he focused his attention to Angela's bare body lying on his California King. He and Angela had shared many special evenings, but last night was special.

He sat down on the bed and rubbed her back, reminiscing about the night before and how he could hear the smile in her voice when he told her the limousine was coming to pick her up at seven. When the limo arrived she was to get the wrapped gift box out the back and it would be her attire for the evening. He had personally gone out and bought her a navy blue, velvet evening dress by Carol Little.

The limousine then took her to his home in Lafayette Shores. When she walked in, he had the mellow sounds of Najee playing throughout the house as the chefs and servers waited on them. He wanted Angela to feel like royalty in his castle; to be served a gourmet dinner prepared by one of the finest chefs in Hampton Roads.

He'd brought several dozens of roses, red and white. He had rose pedals sprinkled from the front door to the bedroom and on top of the hot water that filled his Jacuzzi.

After dinner they slow danced. As their bodies intertwined, he felt something. Something different. He picked her up and carried her to his room. He slowly undressed her and took her hand to guide her to the Jacuzzi where he bathed, and then made slow passionate love to her. He started at a slow pace, but with the condom on and the water, he could barely feel her wetness, but he kept going until he was dripping sweat in the hot, steaming water. He moved her to the bed and dried her off, taking the massage oil that he'd purchased from Victoria Secret and slowly began applying it to her body. She allowed him to take every toe and finger into his wet mouth, before he buried his face into her vagina. He took in her every move, her every sound, and fell in love with the sounds and her love noises. He lifted himself and climbed on top of her. He entered her and didn't last fifteen minutes before he found himself climaxing, even with the condom.

He had to get her home so she wouldn't be late for class. When he pulled in front of her condo, she said, "Last night was beautiful. I've never been treated so special. Thank you." Nervous the other might happen to pull up, she never felt comfortable sitting in front talking with Mac or Damien.

"Close the door a minute," he said. "Have you ever been skiing?"

"Once . . . when I was eleven." She remembered when Dr. Statton took her and her mom to Masanutten.

"During the Thanksgiving holidays, I would like you to accompany me on a ski *slash* business trip. Some business, but more recreation."

"Sounds exciting. I would love to." She leaned over and kissed him and proceeded to get out the car. *Damn, a ski trip sounds exciting and romantic.*

One more day of this shit and then my vacation begins, Angela thought as she turned in her test paper. She wondered if Damien was going to help her study. *He could be so helpful sometimes.* She remembered how helpful he was the other night. He was supposed to meet her at the condo when she got off.

When she arrived, him and Monica were inside smoking, with Tupac blasting out the speakers. They all sat watching *Moesha, and Malcolm and Eddie*, getting lifted before deciding to order Chinese food.

As Angela and Damien went into her room, she was feeling tired and groggy. He decided to help her wake up and, boy, did he wake her up. They did their thing and showered. When they came out, he sat up with her, drilling the material into her head.

Angela was walking across campus on her way to take her final exam when she felt somebody's arm wrap around her.

"Heah, baby," Rome said.

"What's up?"

"Not a thing. Just ready for the weekend."

"I know what you mean. I'm going skiing and plan to have a ball."

"With your family?"

"No, me and my friend, Mac. He has a condo at a resort, and we're spending the weekend in Colorado."

"Enjoy yourself but be careful; I don't want to see you hurt. I'll see y'all tomorrow night. I'm coming through," he said, running off to holler at another girl.

Angela continued across campus to the bookstore in the plaza when she saw Damien's truck parked at the Burger King. She didn't want to go over by the truck and see him talking to another girl—that would really fuck up her day—but she couldn't see that happening. She walked over to where he was and Damien was sitting on the passenger side talking to a girl standing outside the truck. She stood there in her tight Levi jeans, black Nine West boots, short black leather and long micro braids.

The girl's real cute, Angela thought. She could feel the jealousy rising in her. She knew how bitches were and she knew Damien. *He was a catch—he carried himself well and had that phat-ass truck—any 'ho' be glad to get their hooks into him.*

She made her way over to the truck. The young lady turned and looked at her. Damien turned to see who the girl was staring down and saw Angela standing there with a look in her eyes to cut.

"Can I talk with you?" she asked in a sharp tone, not being too polite.

"Yeah, hold on." He turned to finish his conversation.

Angela never moved. She just stared into the truck at Damien.

"Look, it was nice meeting you," Damien said to the girl as she walked away. Then he got out of the truck.

Angela watched as his winter-green Timbs hit the pavement and he stood in front of her with his green Phat Farm hoody.

"What's your fuckin' problem, Angela?"

"Why you out here with that bitch all in your face . . .
like you just don't have no respect for me?"

"My brother stopped over here, and she came to the
truck and started talkin' . . . not that I have to explain
myself."

She started to say something.

"Shut up! I don't have time for this jealous shit."

She put her hand up to his face. "Whatever."

He grabbed her left arm and took a firm hold of her
chin with his right hand. Then he pushed her against
the truck, putting himself up against her so she couldn't
move. "You know who you fuckin' with—I'll split your
muthafuckin' skull and not think 'bout it. I'm not the
one. You better get your shit right. Now carry your ass to
class or home." He pushed her and got back in the truck.

She walked back to her car with tears in her eyes. "I
don't have to put up with this shit," she yelled as she
headed back into the Hampton Tunnel. "He didn't
have to grab me—simple-ass muthafuckin' Jamaican. I
need a real man anyway, not a drug-dealin' punk. Fuck
you!" She yelled coming out the tunnel onto the bridge.
She had told her mother she was going to stop by but
decided instead to get herself together and go straight
to work.

She was at work hating him, but every time the
phone rang, she wished it was him. It seemed like the
longest four hours, and he still hadn't called.

The phone rang again. "Hello. Robinson, Madison,
Fulton, and Williams."

"Hello, Angela. It's Mac. How's your day goin'?"

"Fine. Just tired, and my day still not finished."

"Thought I might see you later," he said.

"I'm kind of tired, but I'll call you when I get home."

She stopped by her moms before going home and got there just in time for dinner.

"I know you're going to eat."

"No, I'm not really hungry."

"Sit down and eat something. I don't care if it's a piece of corn bread, but you have to eat something," her mother said, fixing her a plate.

They sat down and started to bless the food. Her little brother was holding her hand, squeezing it and playing. She looked at him and smiled. *You're something*, she thought.

"Amen," they said together when the prayer ended.

"You know I want you here early Thursday to help out. Your friend still comin'?" her mother asked.

"Yes. He asked me to go to a ski resort with him this weekend. Business and fun."

"I don't agree, but you have to make your own decisions now. Where is it anyway?"

"Colorado Mountains," Angela said low.

Her mom looked at Ken. Ken just looked at her. He knew Thursday's dinner was going to be very interesting.

The next morning Angela got up in a foul mood. Here she was, getting ready for a long weekend in Aspen, and she wasn't excited. (Mac had come over the night before and showed her pictures of his deluxe, picture-perfect, mountainside condo in Snowmass Village.)

She went to her only class of the day to take a test. She scrambled to stay focused, but her mind kept wandering off, thinking about what she was going to say to Damien or how she was going to say it. She strolled around with a knot in her stomach that was keeping her from even thinking about eating. All she wanted was to be in Damien's arms again and for things to be back to normal. Eventually, she buckled down, finished her test, then went home.

When she arrived, she found Mac sitting in front of her house. She forgot she told him she only had one class that morning. Angela really cared for Mac and enjoyed his company to no end, but he wasn't who she wanted to see.

"Hello, Angela." He opened her car door so she could get out.

"Hello, Mac. How you doin' today?"

"I'm okay."

"Mac, I don't mean any harm—nor do I have anything to hide—but I don't like unexpected visits. I would rather you call before coming over. I make my mother call and she pays the rent, feel me?"

Mac had a confused look on his face. "I don't see the problem."

"There isn't a problem," she said in a soft, sweet voice, "but next time, please call first."

"Okay, I'll hit you up first, if that's what you want."

They walked inside while he talked about how excited he was about the weekend and how good it was going to be to see the guys from his fraternity and investment group.

"I came by because we need to go to Ski World and get my baby prepared for the slopes."

Angela put her things up and they headed out the door. She listened to him talk about the great time they had the previous year.

As he ran down the scenario, he noticed she was in another world. "Are you all right, Angela?"

"Yes, I'm fine; I just have a few things on my mind."
Angela felt she could open up and discuss anything

with Mac—he wasn't just somebody to fuck; he was her friend. But being on the outs with Damien was bringing her down, and she had to figure out a way to deal with it.

They arrived at Ski World and she began browsing at the skis, ski suits, hats, goggles. Together they picked out the necessary things and she tried them on to be safe. They had the counter filled, she couldn't believe the total. This is when she realized how expensive the sport was.

She watched to see if Mac was going to pull out the fat knot like Damien, but he reached in his wallet and threw down his gold VISA credit card. He didn't even have fifty dollars cash in his pocket.

"So is there anything else you need?"

"Long johns."

He smiled. "Thermals."

"Whatever."

"Let's go by Coliseum Mall. Then I can drop this offer off on this house that I received today."

By the time Mac was dropping her off that evening, she saw the familiar cars in the front. Then she spotted Monica and Rome holding bags from The Package Store. They gave her a hand with her bags. Her and Mac said their good-byes, and he was out.

"What the hell is all this shit?" Rome asked.

"My girl goin' to Aspen," Monica told him. "Bitch goin' to hit the slopes."

"You ballin', ain't you, shorty?" Rome asked. "Got a nigga with a LX 450 Lexus and then this nigga pulling up with the big-boy 500." He grinned. "Wonder I can't get on."

"And poor-ass Ray just couldn't cut it when it came to the major players," Monica said.

"It's not even like that, y'all."

"Bullshit. Who the fuck you think we are? You and Monica both know that if them niggas ain't have no paper you'd still be fuckin' with Ray boy. His brother told me and Joe you wrote that nigga a Dear John letter while he was away—that shit wa'n' even right."

"It ain't your fuckin' business anyway, Rome," Angela said opening the door.

"I don't give a fuck. I'm going to speak my mind. You don't run shit here. Fuck I look like—one of those yes-niggas you fuck with?"

"Why you arguin' with Rome, girl . . . actin' like he yo' goddamn man. Fuck him."

"Naw, fuck both of y'all niggas. Better straighten out *your* act."

When they walked in the living room, Angela realized that they had other company. *Monica and Rome must have already been inside and ran to the store.* She brought the smile back to her face as she greeted everyone. "Hello, everyone," Angela said to Fat Joe, Quinn, and Monica's brother. "What the deal, player?" Angela hugged Monica's brother.

"Nothin' at all, baby. Angela, this is Kim; Kim, Angela." He turned to expose his friend. Angela shook her hand. The girl was tight as shit—nails done, hair done, eyebrows arched, and was wearing an outfit that complemented her body well. Angela didn't expect anything different from him.

She went into her room and laid her things on the bed. She looked at the time on the watch that Damien had brought her, and thoughts of him began to fill her head. The feeling came in the pit of her stomach again. If she didn't straighten things out with him, she wasn't going to be any good to no one. She picked up the phone and dialed.

"Hello, hello."

She tried to catch her voice. "Damien there? This Angela."

"No, he left about an hour ago. Page him; you might catch him."

She hung up quickly and began paging him. She waited three minutes (it seemed more like fifteen) and paged him again, putting 911 behind her code.

He called back. "What up?" he said, as if he wasn't pressed to talk.

"Where are you?"

"Why?"

"We need to talk." All she heard was silence. "Please, come by for a minute, so I can talk with you. Please . . ."

Angela was sitting in the front talking with her company when a knock came at the door.

Monica opened the door, and he caught eyes as he came in. "Let me take your coat," she said.

He handed her the big, puffy, "bear" coat, which matched his bear boots.

Angela looked at her nigga and smiled. She knew her man was always styled to impress. She looked him up and down, from his Pelle Pelle jeans to his Pelle Pelle shirt with Marc Buchanan down the sleeve. The long chain that hung down on his stomach let muthafuckas know he wasn't from VA—that was some Up-Top shit niggas was on.

"This is D, everyone. These are all my friends, and that's Monica's brother and his friend, Kim."

Kim stood up smiling, and they embraced. "How you been, D?" She shook her head like, *I know your name.* "It's been a while."

"I'm straight, and you? What you doin' here?"

"I go to school at Virginia State. You have to come check me out." Then she hugged him again, and they continued talking.

Angela looked at Monica.

When D broke away, Angela walked to her room and gave him the eye to follow. She closed the door. "How do you know her?"

"She from Up Top. Her peoples live on same block; we go way back."

"She act like y'all real close like that."

"Actually, we just knew each other from Up Top, but two years ago I was in Richmond for a minute and chilled with her and her girl. We all became real tight, but that's history. "What's up?"

Their talk soon escalated to an intense discussion. That's when Damien threw up his hands and said, "I have to go." He came out and got his coat and asked Kim to walk him down so she could get his number. Kim came back about twenty minutes later.

Angela looked as if she had an attitude with the world. Damien had her fucked up, and she wasn't in the mood for anything. She went into her room, as her company sat around getting fucked up, playing cards, looking at the Wayans brothers.

"Is she okay?" Kim asked.

"She'll be a'ight," Monica said. "Just upset."

Kim got a blunt and walked over and knocked on Angela's door. Angela was lying across the bed, her eyes red with despair.

Kim sat down beside her. "Can I talk to you girl-to-girl?" She lit the blunt. "I know Damien from way back. He was always a wild-ass nigga. Niggas was shook when he came around; plus, his peoples were known to wild out." She passed the blunt.

Angela sat listening, soaking in all the inside shit on her man. To her this was a dream—somebody just telling his story.

"What I'm about to tell you is between you and me. Never mention it, please . . . because he'll hate me and it will fuck up the relationship I have with him."

"Promise. I'm just tryin' to learn this nigga."

"Damien grew up fast, just like all the other kids on our block—everybody chasin' the dollar bill. Most of the guys who started hustlin' either ended up gettin' got, or in jail. Somehow, Damien and his cousin—I forgot his name, black-ass, fine nigga . . . Well, anyway, they blew up in the hood.

"Once he had money, every girl out our way wanted to fuck him, and he had his share. Then he met my cousin Annette. They kicked it for a while and then she left for school—Virginia State. He decided to move to Richmond. I came to Virginia State and was going to stay on campus, but he and my cousin insisted I stay with them. She kept accusin' him of fuckin' around all the time, but then one day he came back early from a trip to New York and walked in on Annette fuckin' two scrub-ass niggas that he was sellin' to."

"Fuck he do?" Angela passed the blunt.

"Nothin'. He left and went to New York. About a month later, they were all at McDonald's on Broad; regular hangout. Him and his cousin pulled up and started blastin'. Four niggas got killed, and my cousin got caught in the crossfire. That was the last I'd seen of him. After all this happened, I was sittin' home about a week later and Damien's cousin came to me and let me keep the car, saying that he'd paid it off. He gave me money for my rent for two years.

"I know they never meant to kill Annette so I never blamed them; I blamed it on her lifestyle. Damien told me that whenever a girl start accusin' him, this pops back into his head and he sees another problem. He knows how it feels to be betrayed, so when you start trippin' and accusin', you push him away. I could tell by his conversation he cares about you, and I will tell you you will not find a better man. But you have to trust him and put some faith into him. And I promise you that nigga will be all that and more." Kim threw her hand up for a high five.

"Thank you," Angela said, and they hugged each other and went out to join the fun.

Angela could now see why her jealousy got that nigga hot. She knew she'd talk with him, but not until after the holiday weekend. She prepared herself for the days to come. *It was going to be great*, she thought. *A very romantic weekend with Mac.* However, she still had to get through the next day's dinner.

Thanksgiving dinner took a turn for the better. Angela's mom's biggest concern was Mac's age. She even went as far as asking Mac what his interest was and why he was dating such a young girl. Mac kept his poise and explained that when he and Angela met his intention was strictly a friend-to-friend relationship, but over the weeks they had become much closer. Now, he just wanted her to enjoy some of the finer things in life that he'd been enjoying by himself for so long.

He won over Angela's mom, but Ken wasn't so easy. Ken let it be known that Mac was too old and had games up his sleeve that Angela's head was not ready for. "She needs to talk to someone closer to her age," Ken argued. And going away so far with this guy was out of the question in his book. But deep down he knew her mother would have the last say so because Angela wasn't his daughter.

Before the end of the night, Mac and Angela had Ken and her moms behind closed doors in a big disagreement. Ken never even came out to say good-bye.

"He doesn't believe in this trip," she said, returning to the den. "Mac, my daughter's safety is in your hands, and please bring her back the same way you leave here with her."

"I promise you I will; you have nothing to worry about."

"Mom, I'll be okay; don't worry."

"I know. Just be careful and be smart. I love you." Then she held her daughter in a tight embrace, as if it was her last time holding her.

Chapter Fourteen

"That was a'ight. I'm glad you called and invited me."

"I'm glad you here," Salone said. "Noriega seems like a different person when you're here."

"He does seem to smile a little more," Gwynn added. "He's usually very direct and hardly ever talks, but I saw a different Noriega today."

"So, Gwynn, how long you been living in DC?" Damien asked.

"About three years. After going to school in the East, I decided to go back to California and finish graduate school. After I received my master's from UCLA, I knew the East Coast was where I really wanted to be, so here I am."

"So have you regretted your decision in any way?"

"Not really. I left a good man in Los Angeles, but he didn't want to leave. We tried a long-distance relationship that lasted six months before I called and his new girl answered the phone. You know how the rest goes."

"I've been there, but you can't let a bad relationship keep you down." Salone excused herself and went upstairs to see what Noriega was doing.

"I haven't let anything keep me down. I jumped into my work and let it take over my life. I've grown from an administrative clerk for different political organizations, to a job in the Pentagon. I've dreamed of the life I live right now; nothing could make it better."

"So you have a new man, someone to come home to every night? A nigga sittin' in the crib, waiting for you to come home so he can massage your feet, wash your back, and hold you through these cold-ass nights in DC?" Damien walked over and poured himself a glass of Rémy XO.

Gwynn looked at Damien as he fixed his drink. *Damn, he's a good-looking guy*, but she felt he was too young.

It was just a few months before she turned thirty. She'd been in DC for three years and hadn't dated anyone, except for the white Congressman who owned the condo under hers. She and Salone had been friends for a while, and seeing neither one of them really hung out, they both put a lot of time into their work. But Salone came home to a strong black man every night, while she sat alone in her lavish two-story condo.

"No, I don't have a man in my life doin' those things, but I'm all right."

"Then you lied to me . . . because something could make it better—I could make it better." He smiled as he took a sip of his drink and stared into her eyes. He had just met this woman today and was feeling her.

"I didn't lie; I'm contented with my life, Damien. I don't need a man to make my life complete."

"I know you don't, but when you leave, I would like to see how you live, go over and keep you company. That a'ight?"

"Why?"

"Because I want to spend some time with you. Maybe I'll massage your feet or even wash your back."

"What?" she asked, even though she'd heard him.

Damien smiled. "Nothin'."

Just then Salone came downstairs. "We're going to play Scattergories. You ever played, Damien?" Salone set up the game.

"No, but I'm with it. Willin' to learn." Damien looked at Gwynn. "You goin' to teach me what you know?"

She just looked at him and smiled. "You're too much." Then she said to herself, "Maybe I need to consider showin' you where I stay."

Noriega caught the last of the comment. "Goddamn! How long I been upstairs, Salone? D making moves on our guest and shit."

They played card games until the wee hours then Gwynn and Damien broke out.

The next morning Damien was on his way back to Norfolk. He drove down Interstate 64 listening to Notorious B.I.G., and as "One More Chance" played, he thought about the video and remembered how he used to ball in the club, him and his peoples, buying out the bar. Then as the chorus came in, *Biggie, give me one more chance . . .*

His thoughts went to Angela. He was upset with her for the way she played herself out at the school, but he missed her. He'd had a good time with Gwynn but wasn't pressed on what she had to offer. If he was broke and needed the help of a woman, he would've looked at her in a different way. But he had plenty dough—*fuck what a bitch had.* He knew he had to be happy and that's what Angela brought to the table.

He forgot he'd told her that he was going to New York, so he figured it would be better to wait until Sunday and give her a call. Then he could have Saturday to himself, maybe go to Pizzazz. If he ran into her, he could tell her he just got back. Here he was trying to figure out how he would explain shit to her and they were on the outs. He'd never had to explain himself to no girl. *What the fuck?*

He leaned over and removed the CD from the deck. "I Don't Want To Be A Player" by Joe was playing on

103 JAMZ. He listened to the words and remembered how he used to be. Now, Angela was the only thing on his mind. It was then he realized that he loved her.

"It's freezin' out here, Mac. Where's the car?"

"Right here." He opened the door to the Mitsubishi Montero Sport, and they climbed in.

Angela had her hands between her legs, trying to get warm, and the cold leather seats were not helping. She looked over the snow-covered land and took in the beauty of it all.

Mac couldn't find a black radio station, so he threw the Mary J CD into the changer. While rolling to their destination, Mac pointed out different landmarks to her and, at the same time, tried to give her pointers about being on the slopes.

"This is Snowmass Village." Mac came to a stop. "Welcome to my winter getaway." Mac had a slight smile. He knew this shit had her mesmerized.

Angela stared in amazement. She never figured this place would be so beautiful. It was lit up, bright and beautiful. It reminded her of Waterside, downtown Norfolk, but instead of restaurants and clubs, this was a resort. It wasn't just the building, but also the snow that covered the open windows, window seals, the grounds and the mountains that left her speechless.

"Here we are, baby," Mac said, opening the door to the condo.

"Oh my God!" She dropped her bag at the door and walked around slowly, looking at the white leather furniture, with the base that held the glass tables, and the fireplace that was already burning with a bearskin rug lying in front of it. She walked into the bedrooms—two master suites with king-size beds—and the view could not be put in words. "I have to get a picture . . . because there's no way I could ever explain this to my peoples."

Mac reached in his bag, took out his camera, and began snapping.

Angela was like the perfect model, standing in front of the fireplace, lying on the rug, standing in the windowsills, holding two bottles of champagne and allowing Mac to snap away as if he was a professional photographer. She was never going to forget this.

"I have a meeting later on. Then I have a short meeting Sunday before we leave, but all the other time is ours—you and I, baby." He took her into his arms and laid her on the bed. He'd been wanting to take her in his arms since they were on the plane.

She was feeling him and wanted him just as bad as he wanted her. She had the picture in her mind of him laying her on the bearskin rug and making love to her until she begged him to stop.

He undressed her slowly and stepped back, as if her beauty stunned him. She lay there watching him undress. He removed his T-shirt and leaned over and kissed her. Then he reached down and removed his shorts and guided his hard, throbbing dick inside her.

"Where's your condom?" She jumped up as if he'd burned her with something.

"I forgot them, and plus I feel it's time we started trusting each other. You are mine, Angela, and I love you. You not going nowhere and neither am I—I'm done with those things."

This nigga think I'm that caught up in the fuckin moment. "What about me gettin' pregnant, Mac?"

"I'm not going to cum in you, girl. I ain't tryin' to go there." He held his hard dick in his left hand and reached for her with the right.

"No, Mac, I'm not ready to take the chance."

"I would have to go to the store, Angela. I promise I won't. Put your trust in me this one time," Mac pleaded; "don't spoil the moment."

"No, I can't see it. I'm feelin' you, but I can't, baby."

"Fuck it, I'm not goin' out now," he said, getting dressed.

She ignored him and reached in her bag and pulled out her thermals, slid on a T-shirt and relaxed in front of the fireplace.

He put on his clothes and left.

She sat there wondering what he was thinking. She had never been with any man without a condom, except for Damien. She didn't even know why she allowed him, but he had somehow gained her trust and, over the months, never came in her. She turned on some music and poured herself a shot of Rémy. She didn't care if they made love or not, she was relaxing and enjoying herself.

Her mind drifted to Damien. Since she had started fucking him he would be romantic sometimes and set the mood; other times he would be *like I want you right now,* pull her to him, lift skirt, pull down pants, whatever. He would take charge and fuck her like a wild dog in heat. And she actually liked that, never knowing what to expect.

Mac came in hours later running to change. "You can go get you something to eat; I'm going to be tied up for a couple hours," was all he said before going out the door. She walked downstairs to the restaurant and got a bite to eat then returned to the room to wait on Mac. She sat staring out the window, wishing like hell she had some weed. *If Damien was here, I would be a high as bitch and wouldn't give a fuck what we did, if anything at all.*

***

Mac came in and got himself a drink. He sat beside her on the couch. "You ready to hit the slopes?"

"It's all on you, baby." She tried to soften him up, not wanting the vacation to sour.

"I'm sorry about earlier, I just wanted you so bad and the thought of stopping fucked my head up. I hope you're not too upset at my action."

She walked over to him and straddled him in her panties and T-shirt. "You have condoms now, and I'm not upset."

Mac lifted her straight up and laid her on the bear-skin rug. He lifted her T-shirt and began massaging her breasts as he ran his tongue across her nipples. He took off her shirt and pulled her panties down and stood back staring at her body glistening from the firelight. *Goddamn, this girl's body is a fuckin' dream. I will never let this shit go. She will be mine.* He undressed again, laid down beside her, and pulled her on top of him so he could stare into her eyes and enjoy her beauty.

He gently put his hands on her hips and moved her like he wanted her to move. She relaxed and let him guide her until she saw his eyes close and his body extend. He squeezed her hips, and she kept moving her inexperienced body back and forth. Then his body began to jolt, like he was having a seizure.

She enjoyed the gentleness that he shared and the tenderness when they made love. He was so attentive, but she had never cum with him. Only during oral sex.

He laid there exhausted. She sat on top of him, waiting for him to get up, flip her over, and fuck her until sweat dripped and her pussy squeezed at his dick for more. But he wasn't Damien—being aggressive and rough wasn't him, yet she wouldn't mind if he fucked her correctly.

***

Within an hour they were on the slopes. Angela was definitely an amateur, but with Mac's skills and help, she was skiing like a novelist by the end of the evening. Later they sat in the windowsills, sipping on Baileys and coffee, looking at the snow that fell slowly on the slopes and trees. She stood up and made herself comfortable between Mac's legs. He hugged her and kissed her neck. She was all he wanted; the woman he loved.

They got dressed and walked down for dinner, joining four other couples that they'd skied with earlier. They had soups, lobster, and steak, and popped bottles of Dom with dinner. Mac's friends all had money and mostly discussed their next meeting, arguing about where it was going to be. After dinner they all sat around the fireplace, drinking champagne and sharing lies, and everyone was having a great time. Especially Angela. She'd finally fallen into the groove of these old heads. But she wasn't used to the champagne, and it wasn't long before Mac was taking her to the room and calling it a night.

When Angela woke up the following morning, Mac had already gotten out to attend his meeting and finish up his business with his colleagues. After his return they hit the slopes again, did some last-minute socializing, and headed back to the room.

"This was a great weekend, but it ended too fast. I really enjoyed this, and I really like skiing.

"We'll come again, baby. Real soon."

Chapter Fifteen

They arrived at the Norfolk International Airport that evening, got into Mac's Benz that was left at the airport, and he took Angela home. She threw her things on the couch and collapsed. "How was it, girl?" Monica was ready to hear every juicy detail.

"Light a blunt, bitch, and I'll tell you everything—startin' with this nigga wantin' to run up in a bitch 'raw dog.'"

"Oh shit! Talk to me, girl." Monica lit the blunt. She couldn't understand how her girl made it the entire weekend without smoking. "Did you take any pictures?"

"Yeah, but they won't be ready until tomorrow. We have to go to Wal-Mart about noon. I'll probably pick them up before I go to work." Monica passed the blunt to Angela and she took a long drag. The smoke went down the wrong pipe, and she began choking, but quickly got herself together. "Monica—I almost forgot—Tuesday, I want to go see your doctor and get on the pill or talk to someone about that shot shit you get every couple months . . . something."

"No problem, girlfriend. How much sex y'all have while trapped in snow? I know you two got mad busy."

"Actually, we only fucked twice. I didn't cum all weekend, but I still had a ball."

"Is the nigga that weak, girl? All he got is the Benz—rich-ass nigga with no fuck power." Monica wasn't smiling.

"He gots rhythm, but he just acts like he can only dance to one song. Damien, now, he's the muthafuckin' deejay and he keeps goin', and goin', and goin'."

"Just like the energizer bunny."

"Just like he got batteries in his ass. By the way, did my baby call?"

"No, but I saw him in Pizzazz Saturday, lookin' fine as hell, rockin' Versace shit, bitches all in his face."

"He see you?"

"We talked for about twenty minutes. He bought drinks and shit, but he never asked about you. Didn't even mention you."

Angela sat confused and heartbroken. She cared for Mac and enjoyed his company, but she loved Damien and wanted him to be her man, all hers.

The week was going fast. It was already Wednesday, and she hadn't heard from Damien. She had paged him several times and even called his house, but there was no response.

Meanwhile, Mac was calling everyday, but he was working and wasn't trying to see her until the weekend.

But she wanted to hear from Damien. She couldn't take it anymore, so when she left work she went by his house. He wasn't there so she taped the letter she had written at work to his door. She had to get a response. All she wanted to do was tell him sorry and then fuck until he begged her to stop.

The next night, she and Monica were looking at *New York Undercover* when the phone rang. They looked at the caller ID. "It's not coming up," Monica said.

Angela jumped up to answer the phone. "Maybe it's Damien." It happened to be Quinn calling from Richmond. He and Monica talked awhile then said their good-byes.

After the conversation with Quinn, Angela went in her room and laid across her bed, listening to the quiet storm. She kept beating herself in the head for wilding out on Damien. She started picturing Damien fucking the girl by the truck. The girl was cute and her face was plastered in Angela's head. Angela was feeling sick. She wanted to get up and just go ride by his house and see if his truck was there. She tried to fight the knot that was balling in her stomach. She climbed under the covers and fought to hold the tears back. At that moment nothing in the world mattered.

Just as she was beginning to doze off, the phone rang. She knew it was for Monica so she never bothered to get it. After the fifth ring she reached over and picked it up. "Hello," she said, not even trying to get her composure.

"What up, baby?" The island accent brought her to her feet.

She had so much to say and didn't know how much time she had, so she decided to talk fast. But when she opened her mouth, she couldn't put it together. "I'm sorry, Damien. I am. I just felt like I had gotten stabbed in the heart and I let it get the best of me. I'm sorry, baby. Please understand." Then out of nowhere, "You said I was yours and you were never letting me go," and she burst out crying.

"Shut up, Angela. That shit is yesterday, and today, my love, is a new day. So shut the hell up with that shit." He said it like it was nothing.

"I'm just coming back from Up Top. I'm coming through the Hampton Tunnel right now. You going home with me, or you want me to call you when I get home?"

He could have gone down Route 1 and across the Chesapeake Bridge, but he'd been missing the shit out of her, and this would put him right at her front door. He had business to keep him occupied through the ordeal, but lessons had been learned and it was time to "dead this shit."

"Yes, I'm waiting in the doorway. Hurry the hell up, please." She hung up the phone without giving him a chance to respond.

Monica opened her door and saw her throwing on her sweats, T-shirt and Reeboks. "Where you goin', girl?" Monica figured it had to be Damien. She could see her girl had been crying, but the happiness that sat on her face was slowly erasing the tracks of any tears.

"That was Damien; he on his way," Angela said through a thousand smiles.

"You weren't this excited when you were on your way to Aspen—you really care for this nigga, huh?"

"Girl, this week has been hell. I been tryin' to get through this bitch. When I was in Aspen, I felt he was tryin' to find me, so I was able to keep goin', figurin' I had the upper hand . . . that he was chasing me. But when I got back and he hadn't called, then you saw him and he didn't even ask about a bitch, I've been fucked up ever since. I don't think I ate three times this week." She walked over to her girl and stared her in the face. "I care for Mac; I love Damien. I love him, Monica. He gives me a feeling that . . . I can't explain it." Angel hugged her girl.

"Go hug your man, then kiss your man, then fuck the hell out your man and let him realize what he been missin' for the last week. Don't forget what Biggie said, girl: *If they head right, Biggie there every night.*"

They both laughed. Then they heard the bass from Damien's truck.

"See you tomorrow, girl," Angela said.

"Be careful, Angela. Love you, girl." They smiled at each other as Monica watched her girl until she reached the truck.

Damien jumped out the truck, and she fell into his arms. He hugged her like he didn't want to let her go. They jumped in the truck and headed to his house.

"Heard you was in the club Saturday."

"Yeah, just had to get out for a second, you know? Where the fuck you was?"

"At my mom's. I've been there since Thanksgiving. How was your Thanksgiving?"

"Fine. I spent it with Noriega and Salone."

"That's it? Just you three?"

"No, she had a girlfriend over." Damien said it like it wa'n' shit, knowing her mind would wander.

A streak of jealousy shot through Angela, but she instantly caught herself, realizing if she wasn't on the outs with him, she probably would have been in DC.

They arrived at his house and walked through the door. As soon as he sat the things down, he pulled her to him and threw his tongue in her mouth. She placed both arms around his neck and sucked his tongue. Damien threw both hands in her sweats and palmed her ass. In one quick motion they fell against the wall, and he pushed her panties and sweats down to the floor. He slid off the clothes and sneakers as her body lay pinned against the wall, then he grabbed her left leg, lifted it and threw his wet tongue across her clit.

She jumped. Then as he buried his tongue into her pussy; she relaxed her head back on the wall. He licked and sucked as the juices ran down his chin. He never thought about stopping because the sounds that she made pushed him. When she was pushed over the edge, she let out a soft scream, gripped both sides of his head with her hands, and allowed her body to fall into ecstasy and fold into him. Before her body was re-energized, she found herself "on the steps," raw dick entering her from the back. She tried to move with his every movement until he began to speed up and fuck like a wild horse. The harder he went, the wetter she got. His body began to shake and jolt, then he collapsed on top of her back.

The next morning when Angela woke up, it was too late to even try to make it to class. She went to the bathroom and showered. When she returned Damien was staring out the window. "Those are for you." He pointed at the two boxes on the dresser. "When I was Up Top I was thinking of you, and this is to say that I really care."

She opened the boxes to find a 2ct diamond baguette bracelet and three Greek key bangles. She saw the diamonds in the bracelet and could only imagine what it cost. She'd seen the bangles in the shop in DC and they ran a thousand dollars apiece. She walked over and hugged him. "This is beautiful, and I don't know how to say thank you. Words aren't enough."

"Words along with your actions is all that need to be said. Just continue to show me love. I'm not use to really expressin' myself, but just take my actions as a way of sayin' how I feel."

"Is this saying that you love me?"

"Not exactly, but it's sayin' that I really do care," Damien said as he walked to the shower.

He came from the bathroom hype, as if the shower had given him life. "What you gonna do today?"

"Whatever. I have a hair and nail appointment to-morrow afternoon." She knew she couldn't keep going to DC to get her shit done, so she decided to give Monica's hair stylist a try.

"I have some friends that I do business with that's comin' in town tonight. We supposed to meet for drinks later, so you're goin' to have to run home and get some clothes. Now is good, then we can come back and just do nothin'." Damien began to think about the thirty-minute drive and corrected himself. "Why don't we just go to Greenbriar Mall and get you some shit for today?"

"Either way, Damien, house or mall, I can find something both places." She smiled.

In the mall Damien saw two girls with fly, short cuts. "Them bitches got they shit cut like yours."

"You right. I need to ask who did they shit. At least I can say I seen the girl work, instead of just takin' a chance."

"Ask 'em."

Angela hesitated, so Damien yelled out and the girls came back. After introducing Angela as his girl, he asked where they got their hair done.

"The House of Rica on Granby Street," said one of the girls.

"Ask for Fred," said the other. "He's high as hell, but he's the fuckin' bomb."

After coming out the mall, Angela called to see if she could get in, but he was booked solid. "The soonest I could get you in is next Friday," Fred said.

Angela figured the wait would be worth it. After talking with him, she remembered him from her church and realized he had the reputation for being the shit, not only with the hair, but also designing and sewing.

***

Mac was upset. He'd been calling for a week and kept missing Angela. Monica told her that sometimes he was calling first thing in the morning and that he realized she hadn't been staying at the condo. Monica added, "He even stopped by one evening and was questioning me about your car being here and you wasn't."

That's when Angela pulled up. They got into a heated discussion about her now-so-busy schedule, when actually Damien was getting all her time.

Damien had dropped Angela at the hair salon after getting her nails done. When she finished, he was sitting in the parking lot, waiting for her to come out. He wanted to ask her to go to Jamaica with him, but he knew she had school and he would be gone at least a week. She came out of the salon and got in the truck. He always examined his girl from head to toe every time he saw her. He noticed the new outfit and all her jewelry. He noticed the 1ct Marquise diamond baguette ring that matched the bracelet he'd bought. And the new Michael Anthony diamond watch that he knew he didn't buy. "Nice watch and ring."

"Thanks. My mom and dad gave it to me," she said without looking at him.

(The other evening Mac took her out for dinner at the *La Galleria* on Great Neck Road for dinner. As usual they were dressed for business, and when he picked her up, he came with flowers and gifts. Those were the gifts. She just forgot to leave them at home.)

She kept talking to get his mind off the jewelry, but his conversation was short and direct. She could tell something was wrong. She continued to talk until they arrived at her condo. "When are you coming back?" she asked.

"Next week. I'll call you from the island. Angela, look—I'm not one to act like the jealous kid, and this has nothin' to do with jealousy, but I will let you know that I'm not comfortable with your gifts."

"I told you my parents gave this to me."

"Look, I'm not sayin' you're lyin', but your parents never gave you expensive gifts like that before. That's a hell of a place to start. Do you know what that ring and watch cost?"

"No." She wondered where he was going. "It was a gift."

"The same way you don't know what those bracelets cost that I gave you. Angela, I'm going to say this and then I'm done with it—that ring cost almost as much as those bangles, and all three bangles cost over three grand."

Her eyes widened.

"That watch cost almost as much as that bracelet, and it ran fifteen hundred. Now you say your parents bought it, but if they didn't, anybody buyin' gifts like this will come to light. All I can say is—don't get caught in the crossfire; it's a dangerous place to be." Damien looked deep into her eyes as he spoke. He left wishing she was telling the truth, but knew she wasn't. *Whatever she's doin' in the dark will come to light.*

Angela walked into the house knowing she had slipped. She had been seeing both Mac and Damien for almost four months and, with their complicated schedules, it was going fine. But she never wanted Damien to get suspicious; he was her love. But she enjoyed Mac's company also.

Angela saw Monica at the door with her bag. "Where you goin'?"

"Girl, I told you I was going to Petersburg this weekend to see Quinn."

"Yeah, that's right. You have a safe trip." Angela hugged her girl.

"You better be safe." Monica knew how crazy guys could get, and her friend didn't know the game like that.

"Girl, I'm okay. Damien just left headed for the islands and Mac will be here at nine. We gonna look at the entire *Godfather* tonight. I was going over his house, but since I got the house to myself, I guess I'll chill the fuck out."

They said their good-byes, and she lit the blunt, trying to get her head right before Mac arrived. Then she heard a knock at the door and, thinking Monica had forgotten something, she opened it, wearing nothing but her panties and opened blouse. She was shocked to see Ray standing there. He grabbed her and pulled her close.

She gave him a half-hug and pulled back, holding her blouse together.

"No need to hide it," Ray said smiling. "I've seen it all before. How you?"

"I'm fine." Angela stared at Ray. *The Marines had turned him into a man*, she thought. He was clean-shaven just like Mac, but had lost the boyish look. The baby fat was gone; he had bulked up, showing his now cut physique. He had on sweats and a T-shirt that read *USMC* across the front.

"When did you get home?"

"Just came in and I wanted to drop off this and let you know that I'm going to stop through later so we can sit and talk. I got to go now; I'll see you later." Staring at her, he kissed her cheek and handed her a box. She looked better than when he left—the makeup, the nails, and the beautiful jewelry she wore made her look like those fly-ass bitches that he always thought was all about money. Money he didn't have. But he still felt that he had Angela and that they just had to talk.

Angela opened the box after Ray left. He had bought her an eighteen-inch Figaro chain. She sat it on the counter to give back to him. She knew it didn't cost much. *It's the thought that counts.* He looked good, but he wasn't her interest and she had to return it. All she had to offer to him was her friendship.

Mac arrived about nine thirty. She opened the door to see him dressed in a suede suit by Dolce and Gabbana, some crocodile-skin boots, and holding two pizza boxes. He handed her the pizzas.

"Make yourself comfortable."

He kicked off his boots and laid his suede coat across the barstool.

"I see you decided to go back and get them."

"Yeah," he smiled, "I figured I'd treat myself to an early Christmas."

Angela walked over and took his hand. He had on a stainless steel Rolex on one arm, a platinum 5ct diamond baguette bracelet, and a platinum 2ct diamond ring. She stared at Mac thinking he was that man any woman would want. She remembered the day she saw the jewels at the jewelry store in Hilltop, an exclusive shopping area in Virginia Beach. He'd walked into one of the jewelry stores and each piece that he'd looked at cost over eight thousand dollars. Made her wonder just how much money he had. At this moment this nigga was shining and that shit had her going. "Treat yourself well, huh?"

"If I don't, who will? But I still got plenty love for you, and I will always treat you just as good—believe that." He smiled and shook his head up and down, staring at her.

"I heard that! And the answer to your question—*I'll* treat you good. Maybe not to that extent, but to the best of my ability." Her voice was soft and sweet.

"I know you will, love. I know you will."

Mac pulled the *Godfather* sagas from the Blockbuster bag, and she sat down beside him to enjoy the pizza and the movie. As the evening progressed she relaxed in Mac's arms. Her only worry was she didn't want Ray to come back. She fell asleep in his arms until the late hours, and they went into her room and climbed in bed.

The following morning Angela was awakened by Mac's soft, wide lips on her neck. She snuggled her ass against his dick. He was just kissing her, but she wanted some. He kept kissing her back as his hands roamed across her breast. Her nipples hardened. He reached over, pulled the condom out his pocket and slid it on. She lifted her leg, and he grabbed his dick and slid inside entering from the back.

He began stroking slowly. *This bitch ain't tight as she was in Aspen—like she been fuckin'. Or is it because she so wet?* His mind began to wonder as his pace speeded. He couldn't picture her fucking another nigga, but it was fucking with him.

He didn't stop until he finally came. He laid there holding her, with thoughts bouncing off his brain. Finally he realized that he couldn't worry about simple shit like a kid. *If she was fuckin' up, it will come to light.* "I'm goin' home to shower and change. You want to go to Williamsburg?" Mac asked getting dressed.

"I'll be waiting." She got out of bed to go over and rub his chest.

He sat his shirt down and hugged her beautiful, naked body when the loud knock disturbed them.

Her stomach dropped and began to churn. She walked over and threw on a T-shirt. *Please let it be somebody sellin' something, please God.* She walked out to the front door while Mac stood in her doorway in just his boots and pants.

Angela opened the door and there was Ray standing in the doorway. He stepped in as Mac was putting on his wife-beater. Ray had seen the Benz in Monica's spot, but he didn't want to believe that another nigga was in the crib with Angela.

"What you doin' here, Ray? It's just a little past ten." Angela asked as if Ray was just a friend, hoping he would follow after he saw she had company.

"I have to have a reason to come see my girl."

Angela's breathing quickened at his response and her stomach tightened when Mac's hand touched her shoulder and pulled her back to him.

"So who did you say you were, partner?" Mac asked real calm as if he really wanted to hear it again.

This can't be happening, Angela thought.

Ray said, "I'm her boyfriend—who the fuck are you?"

"What's goin' on, Angela?" Mac asked. "You need to talk to your little friend?"

"Yeah, Angela, do you need to talk to your little friend?" Ray spoke in a little squeaky voice imitating Mac. "Need to carry yo' ass with that gay shit."

"You need to chill, partner. And, Angela, you need to start talking before both of y'all get fucked up in here." Mac's voice was cool and calm, but his insides were boiling. *The dark was coming to the light and this bitch better start talking.*

Angela's churning stomach went away when she heard Mac's comment. Angela moved Mac's hand from her shoulder. "Who you think you gonna fuck up?"

Mac turned to her with a surprised look. *She got this nigga hollerin' she his girl and gonna get smart because I asked her to explain. This bitch playin' me for soft.*

Then, all Angela saw was darkness. The unexpected open-hand slap to her face buckled her knees. Mac jumped back and caught Ray in the jaw, but the punch never affected Ray. Mac began to throw a flurry of blows at Ray, but Ray kept coming until he went down, scooped Mac up by his legs, and slammed him to the floor.

Angela was screaming for them to stop. Mac scuffled to his feet still throwing blows to get Ray off of him. When Ray tried to slam Mac again, Mac waited for him to bend down and quickly stepped back and kicked him on the side of his head, which sent him slamming into the wall. Several blows to Ray's head sent him to the floor. He balled up in a knot, trying to fend off the kicks and punches.

Angela ran over and grabbed Mac when she saw the blood pouring from Ray's head. Ray saw the light of the open door and scrambled out on his knees and began running down the stairs, leaving nothing but a trail of blood.

Mac slammed the door when he saw Ray scurrying out of the parking lot. He turned to Angela, who was standing there crying. "Fuck that cryin' shit. You gonna play me in front of that nigga. I ask you something and you gonna get smart." Mac came toward her. "You think I'm one of your fuckin' buddies or something," were his last words before she felt the blow to her forehead. It sent her over the back of the couch. Before she could hit the floor, he grabbed her by her neck and with both hands, lifted her little body off the ground. Her feet were swaying back and forth as her breathing was slowly being cut off. "You wanna be smart? Be smart now. You wanna play? No bitch plays Mac." He threw her through her room door, and she fell to the ground in tears.

She was no longer feeling the pain of his abuse, she was too scared. She jumped up and dove across the bed to her phone and tried to dial 911. She had only gotten to dial the 9 when she felt something go across her back that stopped her every move. She tried to scream but nothing came out. She thought he had drawn blood, but it was his crocodile belt he'd snatched off and took across her back.

"Mac, I'm sorry. I'm sorry. I won't do it again, I promise." Angela tried to get away.

He grabbed her by the T-shirt, twisted it in his left hand, and pulled it until her arms were extended over her head. Then he pushed her head and neck into the bed and pinned her down. She fought but couldn't move. Like a helpless child he beat her naked ass with the belt until she stopped fighting.

Angela cried like a baby. "I won't do it no more! I had written him a letter; he's my ex-boyfriend! My ex!"

The belt continued across her butt and legs. She had given up, thinking the torture would never end. Then it did. He grabbed the back of her neck and pushed her face into the pillow. "Don't you ever—I mean, ever—turn against me. You belong to me, and don't ever put the next muthafucka before me. Do you understand?"

Mac stepped back, put on his belt, and grabbed his shirt. "Maybe you need some time to yourself." Mac stared at her on the bed, balled up, shaking, and crying. He felt proud of himself. He knew that he loved her and this was going to make for a smooth relationship. He had put his foot down and let this young girl know who she was fuckin' with.

He left her on her bed crying hysterically from the pain and in tears from fear. For hours she couldn't move. She was feeling as if all her security had been ripped away.

When Monica came in later that evening she saw the wrecked house and dried blood on the wall. "Oh my God." She ran to Angela's room. Angela was lying covered up and still shaking. Monica went over and touched her. When she pulled back the cover and saw the welts that ran from her girlfriend's back to her thighs, she let out a scream. Tears began to form in her eyes. She picked up the phone to call Angela's parents.

"No, don't call my house."

"Then I'm callin' the police. Who did this—that sorry-ass Jamaican? Those muthafuckas think they can do what the fuck they want. I never liked his muthafuckin' ass anyway."

"It was Mac," Angela said crying.

Monica looked at her in amazement, like she couldn't believe what she'd just heard. "Fuck that shit! He gots to pay for this shit, one way or another." She dialed 911.

The police arrived, took a report, and demanded Angela go to the nearest hospital. While at DePaul, two other officers were called in by the doctor. They picked Mac up at his home in Lafayette Shores.

While being held downtown he attempted to call Angela several times. Monica denied all his collect calls. She finally accepted one. "What the hell could you possibly want, son of a bitch?"

"Put Angela on the phone."

"What the hell she got to talk to you about? Something is wrong with your ass."

"Fuck you! You tell her when I get out—" was all he got out when Monica hung up on him.

"You need to get a restraining order against that nigga—he really crazy."

"What was he yellin'?"

"Something about when he gets out, but you know he's not coming by here."

The phone rang again. They thought it was Mac but realized it was coming from Ray.

"What the fuck do you want?"

"I need to speak to Angela."

"No, you don't. Your punk ass started all this shit. Then you ran your bitch ass off while she stayed here fightin' your battles. Don't call here no goddamn more, boy." Monica slammed the phone.

"You need to tell your parents."

"No, then my mom be actin' all funny and shit. I'll handle it. I'm gonna go to court, and he'll pay for this shit." Angela was scared and kept thinking about the five minutes of horror that was threatening to turn into a lifelong nightmare.

On Monday Angela was still in no mood for school. The incident really had her nerves fucked up. She never thought a man in his right mind could do that to a woman. Especially not the ones she picked. *At least the police would straighten him out.* She was standing in the kitchen washing up dishes when the phone rang. She picked it up expecting Damien.

"Baby, I need to talk to you."

"I have nothin' to say, Mac; I just want you to stay away."

Mac could hear the tension in her voice. "Look, Angela, I let them bitches get in your ear. Listen— and I'm goin' to say this one time—you are mine. If you act like a child, I'm goin' to whip your ass like one. I hope you remember. Now cut out the bullshit."

"Stay away, or I'll call the police."

"Fuck the police! I got one of the top attorneys in the state on retainer. Think I give a damn about the police?"

Then she heard the knock at the door. She was glad somebody was going to be there with her. She opened the door and there stood Mac. She tried to close the door, but little force on his part got him inside. He grabbed her from the back and hugged her. "Relax, relax, r-e-l-a-x," he said slowly. "Baby, I love you; I wouldn't do anything to hurt you."

"You already have, Mac. After all this, I just want you to let me go. Just leave before you get into more trouble."

"What you goin' to do—call the man again? You can call then, soon as I get out, I'm comin' back. This shit can go on forever . . . because you will be with me. Who's gonna give up first, huh?" He eased her over to the sink. He held her with his left arm and, with the palm of his hand, cocked back and slammed it into the back of her head, forcing her face into the dishwater. The force slammed her teeth into her tongue, and pain shot through her mouth, now filled with dishwater. She never saw it coming. Terror shot through her body. He lifted her head, still having a firm grip on her neck. "Now, who's your fuckin' man?" he asked; his mouth pressed against her ear.

She was scared, confused, and didn't know what to do. "You are, Mac . . . you're my man." Her voice trembled with fear.

This turned him on. Just last week she had him so fucked up and emotional, but now he was in control.

She felt him reach down to unbuckle his belt. The
fear of what she'd gone through gave her a burst of
energy. She spun around, bringing her elbow across
his face, knocking his head back far enough for him to
loosen his grip. She began kicking and throwing blows,
fighting for dear life.

He was out of control. The quick punch to her chest
left her gasping for air. She dropped to her knees, but
her every hope was snatched from her body when she
felt the brown, leather belt wrap tight around her neck
and snatch her to her feet. "Please, Mac," Angela cried,
"I love you, baby. I do. Don't do this." Angela tried to
get her hands between the belt and her neck, but the
more she tried, the tighter it got.

Mac guided her body against the wall. He twisted the
belt around his hand and was pushing her around by
her neck. "Show me some love, Angela. Show me some
love." He pressed his body against her ass, undid his
pants, and let it drop to the floor. "Get those tights off
and open up," he said real calm.

"Mac, I'm beggin' you . . . let's go in the room. Not
like this. I'm not goin' to fight you."

Her begging turned him on. He stood behind her
poking her butt with his hard dick. "Angela, listen carefully—if I got to tell you one more time, I am going to
rip that extension cord off the blender, drag you into
the bathroom by your neck, strip you down, throw you
in the shower, and fuck you up royally. Try me!"

Her prayer for Monica to come home or for anybody
to knock at the door went unanswered. She leaned
down and removed her tights, opened her legs, and
elevated her ass.

Mac was full of smiles as he entered her, never letting go of his firm grip on the belt wrapped around her
neck. "How you feel, baby? How you feel?" he asked,
slowly sliding in and out of her.

A blank expression on her face, Angela fought back every tear. "Good, baby. Good."

Mac's pace increased as he moved closer. He pressed her against the wall, dug his fingers into her stomach, and pounded in and out of her like a wild animal. She felt the release of the belt on her neck and felt his body shut down as he came inside her. "Did you enjoy it, baby?" Mac removed the belt from around her neck and acted as if nothing was wrong or different.

She stood motionless, in a daze and staring straight ahead, the side of her face still pressed against the wall.

"Angela, I love you, and nothin' is goin' to keep me away. But you better believe if you try and lock me up again, I'll be back—on campus, at work, here. I'm not sure where I'll catch you, but I will. And, I promise you, your family won't be able to recognize the remains. Don't ever go against me, baby. I really hope you understand. Now I'll call you later." He leaned over, kissed her on the cheek, then walked out the door.

Angela stood in the kitchen with her pants laying beside her, barely able to move, with cum running down her leg. She began crying, wondering what the hell she had gotten into. *No man in his right mind would act like this, and the police couldn't do shit. And if the police couldn't do shit, then my parents wouldn't be able to do a fuckin' thing either.* She made her way to the bathroom and fell in the shower, allowing the water to run on her body until there was no more hot water. She threw on her robe and laid across the bed.

The phone began to ring. She wanted Monica to come home. "Yeah," she said with no strength or enthusiasm.

"It's Ray; we need to talk."

"No, we don't; I'm done, just like the letter said."

"Angela, we were happy. I know things didn't change like that in a few months. Has it changed? Do you love that nigga, or what?"

"You'll never understand. Don't call or come here again, or I'll change my number," were her last words before hanging up. She felt nothing but hate and resentment for Ray and Mac. Even her only good thoughts for Damien were slowly fading away, figuring it was just a matter of time before that fantasy life fell through.

The last week had been hell and torture and Angela saw no way out. She needed a friend, a male companion, strictly for his friendship and had no one.

The phone rang again. Angela started not to answer it but prayed it was Monica on her way home. Monica wanted to see how her girl was doing since she had to go to the library and would be late coming in. Angela tried to handle the situation by not thinking about it, but her ordeals were heavy on her mind, she had been violated and controlled.

And this muthafucka feels he can do it whenever, like I belong to him.

She walked to the front and turned on the TV. Sitting in the room she felt as if she was going to lose her mind. She was looking at "In the House" when she heard a loud knock at the door. The knock scared her to death as she balled up on the couch. *That door was not getting opened until Monica came home.* The knocking continued. Then she heard a familiar voice. She eased to the door. "Who is it?"

"Open the door, girl," Rome said. "What the hell you doin'?"

She opened the door. Rome saw a look that he hadn't seen on Angela's face since he'd known her. He walked inside and shut the door. Her back was turned to him. "What the deal, girl?" Rome walked up behind her.

She turned to him and fell in his arms and began crying. He waited for her to calm down and asked again.

"Nothin'."

"Look, Angela, don't tell me nothin'. I know you and this ain't you. Now what's going on? You know me and you know I don't fuck with nobody but my brother . . . so your shit is between me and you. Understand?" Rome sat her on the couch.

"Rome, right now I just can't talk about it, but I need a friend like you wouldn't believe," she said with tears in her eyes." "Okay, okay, but you promise to talk to me soon."

"I promise," she said as he put his arms around her and held her. She lay her head on his chest and was fast asleep, feeling "oh, so safe."

Chapter Sixteen

Mac called again and no one answered. He slammed down the phone in anger, not with Angela, but with himself. *She was a great girl, and I fucked up again.* She had shown him nothing but love, and here he was acting like the controlling man his father was when he was coming up. He had seen his father control his mother, his sisters, and his life until he was able to stand alone. He looked around his beautiful home as he poured himself another drink. All the anger he had built up was coming out, and he was striking back in a manner he'd been accustomed to.

He went into his home office and sat at his computer. He leaned back and took the bourbon to the head. "Fuck you, Dad! Fuck you! I have my own shit now. I'm successful now, and I don't need you or your fuckin' approval." Mac screamed at the top of his lungs as he threw books across the room and kicked over the end table. He went to his desk drawer and took out his .45. "Touch me again, muthafucka. Put your muthafuckin' hands on me again and I'll do your ass in." He fell to the floor and went into a tantrum, thinking about the abuse he was a victim of for no reason. So many times his father had made him strip down, get in the tub, and beat him with a leather strap, extension cords, race-track pieces. Anything that left welts and stung like hell.

Mac remembered all the times his father forced him to eat soap just for speaking out of turn or not saying "excuse me." His father wanted him to be scared of him and he was. Until he reached thirteen and received his brown belt from Curtis Bush karate studio and had won competitions to go to a state championship. When he got there the guy favored his dad in looks and build. Mac stood across from him and saw his father. Without hesitation he almost killed the guy, with all the built-up anger and confusion that was in him. He vowed that the next time his father tried to abuse him in any way, he would stand firm and show him that he was no longer standing for it.

That day had come. His father came into the house after a long day of work and a few beers. He walked into their two-bedroom apartment, where Mac slept on the couch and his sisters shared a room. It was summer and it was hot as hell. He was laying on the couch, trying to catch the hot air that the fan blew around the room. He wasn't really asleep, but acted as if he was to keep from putting up with his dad's nonsense. He heard his father scrambling through the drawer and moments later, felt something go across his back that seemed to cut him deep.

He jumped off the couch, holding his back, listening to his father yell. "Didn't I tell you not to leave water in the goddamn sink? Dumb ass!" As his father raised his hand to swing again, Mac came off with a flying kick that sent his father slamming against the wall. They locked up, and it was then that he realized that his father had come from the school of hard knocks and he was just a pupil.

He took a real beating. His father held his neck in a choke hold until his mother ran out. Mac was gasping for air. All his energy was being drained from his body as he fell to the floor throwing up everything he'd eaten. His father ended up putting him out, so he scrambled in the streets, trying to make it until winter, when he returned home. The abuse never stopped.

Mac layed drunk in the middle of his floor, staring up at the ceiling slowly turning. He stumbled to his feet, sat down in his chair at his desk, and removed his gun from the desk drawer. He stared at the black-handled, squared-off Glock. He put one in the chamber and put the barrel to his head . . . then in his mouth. Mac had tears in his eyes as he contemplated taking his own life. He knew he would never be able to cope with his life's past.

"Damn!" He slammed the gun on his desk. This was the third time he'd been this close to taking his own life in ten years. He reached in the drawer and pulled out a half ounce of cocaine. He poured four grams on the table and made it disappear just as fast. He strolled to his bar and poured another drink. Sitting in his chair with Angela heavily on his mind, he leaned back and drifted off to sleep feeling sorry for himself and Angela. His head was messed up, but he was trying so hard to deal with life and couldn't see living it without Angela.

Angela woke up to the movement of Rome. "Where you goin'? What time is it?"

"Three thirty. I was just trying to get comfortable."

"You can lay across my bed," she said as she headed to her room with Rome following her. They laid across her bed, and she closed her eyes, her mind, and fell into a deep sleep. Neither of them ever said a word.

***

The morning came fast. Monica got up and saw Angela's door still open. "Get the fuck up—class starts in a few."

Rome jumped up. "Goddamn, I'm runnin' late fuckin' with y'all hoes."

"Spark a blunt, nigga, before you run."

"Here." He passed them some weed. "I gots to get to class." Then they heard the door slam.

Monica rolled the blunt and walked in Angela's room. "So how you feelin' today, girl?"

"Fucked up and still scared, but I'm goin' to class."

"Well, at least the welts are gone off your legs."

"Yeah, I'm glad they took pictures or nobody would believe me. But look at my fuckin' neck—that shit hasn't cleared up."

"You'll be all right; that's not that visible. You are a strong one. So what's up? You and Rome buddy-buddy like that."

"No, but he's a real friend; he's mad sweet."

"Yeah, I know." Monica passed the blunt to Angela. "He's very sweet."

After smoking they went to shower. Angela went through her closet. She didn't want to wear anything Mac had bought but noticed that most of her winter shit he'd given her. She pulled out her Liz Claiborne pants suit so she wouldn't have to change for work. The Nine West boots set off the suit, and she was out the door.

When she arrived home later that evening, she came in to find five dozen roses. *Monica must've brought them in when she was home earlier.* She heard a knock and began to panic. She grabbed her Mace from the kitchen drawer. If any foolishness kicked off today she was not going to be overpowered. She put the Mace in one hand and a long knife on the cabinet beside the refrigerator. She opened the door and there was Mac standing there. She knew if she tried to shut him out she would end up like she did the day before, and she wasn't trying to go there. *There's no tellin' what this crazy muthafucka might do.*

Mac walked in, and chills swept through her body. She was scared as hell of this man and trying not to show it. She stared at him, keeping her distance. He was in the kitchen, and she was right by the door, ready to burst out. He stared at her. "I want to explain, Angela . . . I have a lot of problems I'm dealin' with—and that's no excuse for my actions—but I can't change it; all I can do is apologize and promise it will never happen again. I love you like you would never believe, and when that guy said he was your boyfriend and you sided with dude, I lost it. I didn't mean to but I did. And I'm very sorry I hurt you.

"You just don't know how sorry . . . but my jealousy kills every relationship I ever been in and I had told myself not this one, but—" He threw both hands up.

"You say sorry, Mac, but you hurt me. And the trust I had in you is gone. I just don't understand."

"I'm not goin' to talk you to death. I just hope you find it in your heart to give me another chance and to forgive me. I love you.

"I was goin' to carry you shoppin' Saturday and get you some things, but things got out of hand. So here's something to pick up a few things. I'm goin' to give you some space because I know you have some thinkin' to do." He laid two grand down on the counter and left.

Angela still had so much hatred for Mac. She went from being scared to hating him, but as she looked around at the flowers, it softened her. The sight of the hundred-dollar bills made her want to run him down and say, "Fuck your money! Stay away from me!" But when she grabbed the money, she thought out loud, "Damn . . . what a way to say good-bye." *He was dead wrong for all that he'd done and the way he handled his shit, but Ray was the real cause of all this shit.* She saw Mac had a very bad temper and could get real crazy, but the nigga that just left was the nigga she was fascinated by.

Angela clenched the wad of hundreds. "What the fuck?"

"Monica, hold up so I can walk with you." Rome was out of breath from running across campus to catch up.

"Come on, boy. I got to run."

"So what's goin' on with Angela? I've never seen her like this."

"Well, right now she needs a friend, not a nigga tryin' to fuck." Monica gave Rome an uninviting look.

"Shit, what the fuck I look like? I'm tryin' to find out if it was big-ass money with the Lex or cool poppa with the Benz."

"Simple-ass nigga with the Benz. That muthafucka whip Ray ass and sent that bitch-ass nigga runnin'."

"He did what? I guess the Marines can make you look like a man, but if you bitch, you bitch."

"That's not it. After he beat Ray ass and he took off, then that nigga fucked Angela up too. Beat her ass."

The words rolling off her tongue cut Rome. A serious look came over his face. He played and joked with Angela and Monica, but they were his girls and he had mad love for them both. "Know what, man—that shit fucks with me, and if she was my peoples, I would step to that nigga. But she fuckin' that kid and I can't get in that shit; she'll end up hatin' me."

"You right . . . because yesterday I saw flowers and shit that he sent. In a minute I'm gonna start thinkin' Angela like that wild shit. Especially if she keep fuckin' with him after this shit."

"Where's 'Big Money'?"

"In New York, I guess. He'll be back later in the week, but he better stay away. That crazy bitch be done fucked him up too." Monica knew her friend had got herself in a bad situation and felt for her, but quickly realized that all she could do was stand with her, no matter what her decisions were.

Monica arrived at the condo just in time to catch Angela before leaving. She was dressed as if she was going to a business luncheon: the long leather cover, the tight Anne Klein skirt suit she'd picked up on one of her many shopping sprees.

"I know that ain't who I think it is downstairs," Monica said with an attitude.

"Don't start."

"'Don't start? Don't start'? Fuck you mean, Angela? That shit that nigga did ain't normal, and if you let him get away with it he's goin' to end up hurtin' you real bad."

"No, he ain't; I'm just goin' to dinner. He has some things to discuss, so I'm goin' to dinner after work and then I'm comin' home. I'll call you from work."

"Look, Angela . . . Damien will be back soon and then he may come by. Then what? You gonna let Damien walk up on some bullshit like you did Ray so 'Crazy' can beat his ass too."

Angela walked out knowing her girlfriend was right, but she realized that she was caught up. She didn't want to see Mac beat Damien like he did Ray. Ray, she never meant to see him get hurt, but Damien was her real love, and it would hurt her more to see him hurt over her unfaithfulness. She realized that she was going to have to tell Mac it was over, regardless of the outcome.

She came downstairs and Mac was standing outside to open her door. They rode down the street with tension in the air, but as the sounds of Monica flowed through the car, her mind began to relax.

"I never knew she sang like that. Her CD is nice."

"My girl got it and this song is the bomb," Angela said.

Mac leaned over and turned the volume up, then relaxed his hand on her leg through the split in her skirt.

She jumped at his touch and looked in his eyes. It was the first time she realized how sneaky his squinnted red eyes looked through the clear Perry Ellis eyewear. She reached down and placed her hand on top of his. It seemed as if she was just returning his affection, but it was to keep his hand in place so he wouldn't be sliding it where he shouldn't. He tried to move his hand, and her grip became tighter. She was beginning to feel uncomfortable. "Relax, Mac, and enjoy the ride."

"What's the problem?"

"No problem; I just want you to chill."

"What you mean 'relax'?" He put his hand back on her leg.

"You really need to stop, Mac . . . like I asked." She tried to remove his hand. His grip tightened on her leg. He grabbed a piece of the skirt and balled it in his hand. "You want me to rip this muthafucka off—I'm talkin' to you?"

"No." She was scared of his reaction. She was trying to be a big girl, but she was really scared of this nigga, who seemed to have two personalities.

He released his grip and rubbed her upper thigh and slid his hand back down to her knee. "As much as my girl turns me on, she don't want me to touch her—what kind of shit is that?" He pulled in front of the lawyer's office. "I don't ever want to hear that shit again. Now you have a nice day, and I'll be back in a few hours to get you; I have a surprise for you at dinner."

Angela got out of the car and walked into the office confused. She didn't know if she was to call the police so he would stay away, or call her mom and get some advice. The police didn't do shit last time and her mom's involvement would just create more aggravation. *Mac definitely ain't scared of the police and there is no way to protect myself from him.*

The situation disturbed her. *How could any man just flip personalities like Mac did?* She didn't know what to do. She picked up the phone to call Monica and straighten everything out with her friend, but to her surprise, Monica told her that Damien had stopped by and was curious why she didn't drive to work.

"What you tell him?"

"That you were hangin' out with your mom and she dropped you off. I think you better call him because he might try and surprise you and pick you up."

"Let me call him; I really don't need to piss him off. That muthafucka was trippin' comin' here, girl, touchin' me and shit. I told him to chill, and he caught a serious attitude.

"What he do?"

"You know how niggas try to be all rough to intimidate you. He's out of control."

"Well, you better catch up with Damien before he comes up there and Mac do some crazy shit to you and him."

"I know what you mean." Angela hung up the phone and paged Damien.

It was close to the time she got off and her stomach was starting to churn. She called Monica back.

"Did he say he was comin' by here?" Angela asked as soon as Monica answered the phone.

"No, he didn't say, but he insinuated that he might. Oh yeah, he had this black muthafucka with him. Fine as hell, girl."

"Probably his cousin. Look, I'll call you back; the other line ringin'."

"Hello, Madison Robinson Williams and Fulton. May I help you?"

"I'm sure you can if I want you to," Damien said.

"Heah, baby, where are you?" She was so excited to hear his voice but was still troubled with the thought of him coming by and running into Mac.

"I'm on St. Paul's, making a right on Monticello. How were you getting home?"

Before she could answer Mac walked through the door, stood in front of her, and blew a kiss, as if not to disturb her.

"Did you hear me? How you gettin' home?"

"Friend of mine." She was praying he would say okay and change his direction since Monticello was only six blocks away.

"Well, call her and let her know that I got you."

"That won't be necessary."

"Why? What's the problem? Talk to me, Angela."

"I can't right now."

Mac was staring her in the face and realized she was talking to another man.

"Oh, you can't, but you will. I'll see you in a minute." Damien hung up the phone.

Angela hung up the phone slowly, waiting for Mac to say something. "Now I'm just your friend. Can't talk in front of me." Mac assumed it was Ray on the other line. "So you still fuckin' with him?"

"No, it's a friend of mine I hadn't seen in a while and he was stoppin' by to see me." Angela could see the change in his eyes. The same look he had when he hit her before.

"Well, he can see us and talk to us if he's just a friend."

"Please, Mac . . . he's just a friend I haven't seen in a while, so why don't you and I get together another time? I'll call you later, I promise." She was about to cry.

"Hurry and get your shit before one of these lawyers have to read your will. Tryin' to change our plans— bitch, you must be crazy." Mac stared as if he wanted to tear her head off.

She began gathering up her things as he stared with hatred in his eyes. She heard the bass from the truck even before the doors opened. Mac opened the door for her to walk out. She locked the door, and they began to walk to Mac's car just as Damien was coming down the rocky street. He jumped out the truck as they headed to Mac's car. "Let me speak to my friends and then I'm comin'," she said, turning to walk toward Damien.

"If you embarrass me by doin' that, I will embarrass you twice as much." Mac spoke under his breath in a stern tone. It stopped her dead in her tracks. She quickly remembered the last time he hit her.

"What up, girl? What da deal?" Noriega yelled from the truck.

She just waved and focused her attention on Damien walking up. Her stomach turned into a knot as he walked up and hugged her. "What up, baby?"

She gave him a half-hug.

"Yo, Nore," Damien yelled toward the truck, "my girl don't want to hug me in front of her colleagues." Damien assumed Mac was one of the attorneys, seeing he was dressed in the three-button wool suit by Armani.

Noriega jumped out the truck and walked over. Mac stared at him as he listened to the sounds of the new butter Timbs scraping the rocky street.

"Hello, my name is Mac." He said and extended his hand to Damien, and they shook hands.

Mac introduced himself again and held it out toward Noriega.

Noriega left his hand hanging in mid-air and turned to Angela. "So you hangin' out with us tonight?"

"Naw," Mac said, "she's goin' to be hangin' with *me* tonight."

"I'm not talkin' to you, son; I'm talkin' to her." Damien stared into Mac's eyes.

"Well, I answered for her. Now get in the car, Angela." Mac opened the door.

She was scared and confused.

"Look, I don't know what the fuck is goin' on"—Damien grabbed her hand and pulled her to him—"but you will explain later. Now go get in the truck. Right now." Damien pulled her toward the truck, putting himself between her and Mac.

"Bitch, you tryin' to fuckin' play me." Mac slammed the door and stepped toward Angela.

Before he took a second step, Damien scooped his ass up and slammed him on the hood of his car.

Mac's hands found Damien's throat, but the cold steel against his temple quickly brought him back to his senses.

"*Blodeclaat*! You know who you fuck wit'? No man test me." Noriega let Mac feel the butt of the 9 mm, and blood flowed from his head as his body fell to the ground.

Mac saw darkness as he held his head, but kicks from Noriega's Timbs and Damien's Gortex sent his head slamming against the side of the Benz until whimpering sounds came out as he folded up in pain.

"*Moniskunt*! I'll kill ya, ya ever cross me again." Damien's accent was so hard not even Angela could make it out.

"Fuck around and lose yo' life, boy." Noriega shook his head as they walked to the truck.

Angela watched the incident, and even though Mac had treated her badly, she still felt no one should get a ass-beating like they had just given him. But for some reason, inside she felt a little relief, even though she didn't know what was in store.

"Hurry up, man. You know I'm on paper," Noriega said. They rode toward Damien's house without a word being spoken.

Angela's stomach was still tight. She didn't know what to expect of Damien once they arrived at his house. She quickly remembered the conversation she'd had with Kim and realized she was riding with two killers. And she was worried that Mac might hurt Damien.

They arrived at the house and went inside and found seats. Damien walked in the kitchen and rolled a Backwoods.

Noriega could tell she really wasn't used to the shit that just went down. "You all right, Angela?"

"I'm okay," she said in a soft, uncertain voice.

"You all right, cousin?" He held his hand out for the Back.

"I'm goin' to be if this girl don't fuck around and make me kill her ass."

"You goin' to be all right. Just talk it out and it's going to be okay. Heah, Angela, what's up with your roommate?" Noriega asked.

"You have to talk to her."

"What's the number?"

Noriega picked up the phone as Angela gave him the number to dial. Angela knew her girl would be glad to hear from him.

The movement of Damien grabbing his coat brought her back to her present situation. "Come on," Damien said, "let's go for a walk." He headed out the door.

They walked in silence for about two minutes before any words were said. "So . . . talk to me, Angela."

"What can I say, Damien?"

He stopped and turned to her. "Look, don't fuck with a nigga and please don't get your shit split playing stupid. I want to know what the fuck is up—and don't lie to me."

She began to explain her relationship with Mac, excluding their trip to Aspen and quite a few other intimate details. She did her best not to lie, to just leave out the things that could get her knocked the hell out.

Damien knew there was more to the story, but the only way he could find out was back at the lawyer's office. And he wasn't about to talk to him. He thought about it and realized he had to do one of two things—let her go and just don't fuck with her no more, or love her the way he'd been doing and hope she learned her lesson.

As they approached the house he looked at her walking with her head down and staring at the street. She looked so innocent in the eyes, so beautiful, but she was so naïve he wanted to take her in his arms and just protect her from the world.

"Damien, I'm sorry. I've made mistakes before, but I really regret this one. I love you more than I could ever explain in words. I just don't want to be hurt."

"Hurt? I travel state to state, making moves, trying to live a comfortable life and, at the same time, trying to make sure my cap don't get peeled or I don't get caught up. Then lately, when I go out of town, no matter what I'm going through, all I do is think about you and getting back so we can be together. It brings a smile to my face and gives me a reason to come here. You're special, but the shit that happened today can't be happening. It could have gotten real bad real quick. Then what?"

She had nothing to say. She was stunned at what she'd just heard. She wanted to hear, "I love you, Angela," so bad, but it never came.

Noriega was on the couch getting lifted when they walked back in the house. The sounds of B.I.G.'s "One More Chance" was pumping through the system.

Damien and Angela looked at each other and smiled.

"Can I have one more chance?" she asked, only moving her lips.

"Hell, no. No more chances here." Damien threw her the keys to his truck. "Look in the back of the truck. It was for you, but now I'm gonna give that shit to Monica."

Angela walked outside and returned carrying two Nordstrom bags. She took a black leather DKNY sports coat out. "Damien, this shit is the bomb." She gave him a hug. She opened the other bag and realized he had picked her up a pair of black boots to match. "Thank you, baby. I love them." She tried them on.

"I guess we crew again, huh, Angela?"

"Be quiet, Noriega." Angela walked in the kitchen. She wanted to get away from that conversation. What she really had on her mind was showing Damien exactly how much she missed him and how much she appreciated him thinking of her while he was away. She eased behind Damien and put her arms around him and rubbed his chest.

He turned to her and kissed her long and slow. "Maybe we need to go upstairs."

Before she could answer, the doorbell rang.

"Open the door for my babe," Noriega said to her.

"Oh, that's your babe." Angela walked to the door, smiling. "What about Salone?"

"We broke up—tell your cousin."

"I was wonderin' why I didn't see her."

"Yeah, right. I heard that."

She opened the door. "What's up, girl?"

"Nothin'—my ass almost got lost. It was light the last time I came out here. So what's going on? Spark it up, my niggas." Monica sniffed the aroma in the air.

"Here you go, baby." Noriega passed the 'dro rolled in Backwoods.

Monica looked at it and started smoking.

"Monica, your boy told me to open the door for his babe."

"Really? He didn't tell you? We established that earlier." Monica smiled and sat down closer to Noriega than people just meeting would sit. They began to go solo on the Backwoods.

"I'm hungry as shit, cousin, what's up?"

"What you tryin' to eat?" Damien asked, rolling another Back.

"It's all up to you, baby." Angela moved close to Damien.

"What you want?" Noriega stared into Monica's slanted grey eyes. *This bitch is fine as hell.* There was no doubt in his mind that he had to have this. Just the thought was making his dick jump.

Monica had taken off her coat to reveal a tight beige sweater that was cut low in the front, and a black pair of Levi's that looked as if they were painted on.

"Tell me your pleasure, girl, and I'll make it happen. Anything."

Monica stared back at this dark-skinned, wavy-haired, handsome black man. She knew he was talking about restaurants, but wished he would widen the selection. Then she could tell him what would really please her. "I like Pargo's and it's not too far."

"Pargo's it is then, baby. I like your outfit too, girl. All you need is the leather coat, a gold chain to go right there." He rolled his finger from her neck to her cleavage. "It would definitely set shit off."

"You can set shit off anytime you like—I wouldn't be mad at you." They were about two inches apart, talking in codes to each other, but leaving it open to the imagination.

They ended up at Pargo's in Greenbriar. After dinner they sat and had drinks until the restaurant closed. They all left feeling real nice from the blunts and alcohol.

No sooner than they were in the house, Damien rolled some smoke and walked over to where Angela had taken a seat. "I want you bad as hell, come on," he whispered into her ear.

"What you goin' to do, Monica?" Angela asked.

"I'm goin' to spark this with my man, then I'm goin' on home."

"Well, I'll see you in the morning," Angela said, as she and Damien made it up the stairs.

Damien went in the room and took off his boots and T-shirt. He undressed down to his Tommy Hilfilger boxers.

Angela undressed as Damien lit the blunt. He watched while she stripped down to her burgundy bikini panties and grabbed his T-shirt and threw it on. She went and put on the Mary J CD and walked over to the bed.

He stood over her and passed her the L.

She took two long drags and passed it back. As she began to kiss his chest and stomach, he leaned over toward the ashtray and almost dropped it as her mouth eased down on him.

His knees buckled as she began to satisfy him orally. "Goddamn, Angela," he said, his hands massaging her shoulders, "I got to feel you right now baby."

She leaned back and elevated her hips so he could easily remove her panties.

He leaned over and entered her. When he felt himself about to cum, he started to pull out, but her legs locked him in and he came inside of her, collapsing on her shivering body.

Angela rubbed his back. "You okay, baby?"

"I'm fine. Why are you shaking?"

"Why you think? Feelin' you cum inside of me just took me over. I never dreamed it would give me a feeling like this."

"Why did you let me do that?" Damien looked into her face with a serious expression.

"I'm on something now; I got on it for you. I knew pullin' out was gettin' old. I love you, Damien. I really do." Angela got under the covers and laid down as if she was 'sleep.

He lit the Backwoods and laid back. Thinking she was 'sleep, in a very low tone he said, "Girl, I love you too, but I'll never let you know how much."

With her back turned and eyes closed, she smiled, knowing no other man could make her happy as she was at this moment.

The next morning the rapid ringing of the doorbell woke her up. "Damien, someone's at your door." Angela walked to the window. "It's the UPS truck."

"Go downstairs and sign for it," he said, sleep still in his voice.

When she went to the door she realized her car was still parked. Her girl had decided to stay the night. *Noriega probably begged her to stay.*

She walked in Damien's room and opened the box, thinking it was a gift or something he ordered. She dumped the contents on the bed, and he woke up.

"I told you to sign for it, not open it."

She stood there with her mouth open. She had never seen so much money at one time. She found it strange that it was wrapped in Saran wrap. She watched him count it with quickness and finesse; she could tell it was something he was used to doing.

He handed her twenty hundreds. "Put that in your purse; you will never need nothin' from nobody. If I don't give it to you, then its not meant for you to have. You understand what I'm sayin'?"

"Yes."

"Was my peoples up?"

"No. My car still outside."

"I heard that." *Bitch was all on my cousin dick. She wouldn't have left if he gave her money for a cab.* It didn't surprise him. Since they were young, girls always loved Noriega—even when he was broke. After he got money, he had to beat bitches off.

He walked to the kitchen, and Noriega came out. They gave each other a pound, smiling. Noriega asked, "So what's up, cousin?"

"Not a damn thang," Damien responded. "You tell me, kid. Shit!"

"Young girl got it goin' on; I'll be back down here real soon."

"I wouldn't steer you wrong."

"So what's up with that shit from yesterday? Bitch-ass nigga." Noriega opened up the pack of Backwoods.

"She said it was nothin', that he was an ex that had been buggin' out on her."

"Shit . . . niggas don't just act up over a bitch unless they fuckin'—don't act like you stupid." Noriega stared Damien in his face.

"Yeah, I know, but people make mistakes. I care for her Nore and I have to give her the benefit of the doubt."

"Look, D, she's young and she has to learn, but I can see she got you all open and shit. But I'm not tryin' to see my peoples get in no shit behind no bitch—I don't give a fuck how fine she is. If you love her like that, then you need to stay in her ass. Living like we do, last thing we need is to bring attention to ourselves. You know what I'm sayin'?"

"Yeah, you right."

"A'ight then. Handle that shit like you from Brooklyn, player. You know how we do—BUC! BUC! BUC! Lay a nigga down." Noriega had two fingers extended out like a gun.

"What y'all talkin' about?" Angela asked as her and Monica entered the kitchen.

"Guy talk," Damien told her. "Some things aren't meant for your ears."

"Must be talkin' about us."

"That's another way of tellin' us none of our business," Monica said.

Damien put his arms around Angela. "Never that, baby."

"I was talkin' about y'all." Noriega lit the Back. "I was talkin' mad shit."

"I believe that," Monica said. "Probably tellin' Damien how smooth you were and how you coax me into spendin' the night. But little do you know I knew I was plannin' on stayin' *before* we went out for dinner. You know your black ass too fine and sexy." She rubbed her hands across Noriega's bare chest.

"Oooo," Angela and Damien said as if she had gotten his ass.

Angela watched her friend with Noriega. She could tell she really liked him, but she knew he had a girl.

Even though Monica had a man, he was nothing like Noriega. Quinn was nice and he looked good, but *he* did the chasing; Noriega was fine, nice, secure, spoke with much confidence, and had money that Quinn could only dream of. And if he wanted, he could give her girl anything she thought she wanted.

Angela looked over at Noriega. She could see how her girl could very easily get open over this nigga. They always loved thug-type niggas. Her mind drifted to Tupac videos and remembered how crazy they used to act whenever they would see him. Damien had tattoos and she found him madd sexy, but Noriega had tattoos on his chest, across his stomach, and both arms, and when he pulled a glass out the cabinet, she noticed that he had "RUDE" on one tricep and "BOY" on the other in Old English letters. His body was sculptured just like

Tupac's. She just hoped he didn't end up like the late Tupac.

She knew eventually her girl would catch feelings and be hurt by Noriega, but *that was part of life.* "Niggas be thinkin' they players and shit," Angela said.

Monica smiled at her. "They don't know we already know."

"I know I'm hungry," Noriega said.

"For real," Angela added.

"I want seafood. Crab legs," Damien said.

"Nothing's open until eleven." Then Monica added, "Let's do this: Let's go to our place so we can change and carry our ass to class. Then we'll come straight back to the condo, where y'all will be waiting, and then we'll go to Red Lobster."

"Sounds good to me," Noriega said. "Then I don't have to be away from my girl too long." He kissed her on the cheek. Then he passed the Back to Damien and went upstairs.

Damien hit it and passed it to Angela and headed upstairs.

The girls kept talking as they finished the half-lit Backwoods.

"Thanks, girl. I'm glad you said that."

"No problem. You know I have to look out for my girl. I know you would be worried about that simple-ass muthafucka comin' over and trippin' after what you said happened yesterday. Goddamn! I wish I could of seen that shit. I would have been hollerin', 'Beat his ass! Beat his bitch ass!'" She could hardly get it out, from her and Angela laughing so hard.

"Do you have to go to work today?"

"I called them and said I needed some study time; they're really understanding."

Talking about Mac brought thoughts of him. Angela knew he had problems and that he was no longer the man for her, but he'd introduced her to several things that would never be forgotten. *One day, maybe, he could be a friend. A very distant friend.*

It was a week before Christmas, and Angela hadn't seen Mac since the incident outside the lawyer's office. He had tried calling, but she refused to talk to him. He even showed up at her door one evening, but without hesitation she dialed 911 and he never stuck around.

Now here she was getting ready to go into the courtroom for the charges she had against him. She had already tried to get the charges dropped so she would be done with him, but new laws changed that "dropping" shit.

As she entered the courthouse and saw him sitting on the bench in front of the courtroom, the hurt and pain that he'd put her through began to resurface.

She tried to ignore the fact that the nigga still looked good in his black slacks, black silk shirt, tie, and sports coat. He was the cleanest brother she'd ever seen. *How could someone so fuckin' fine be so mean and disturbed?* She stopped and their eyes met. She'd forgotten what this man did to her when he stared into her eyes and pulled her close. Mixed emotions ran through her, but her focus was easily snapped back when Monica grabbed her arm. She was so glad her friend had come along so she wouldn't have to face the situation alone.

They sat down and waited for the court doors to open. Moments later she saw an elderly, well-dressed white gentleman come in and take a seat next to Mac.

She thought she had seen this man before—Steve Decker, one of the most powerful lawyers in the Hampton Roads and well respected by judges and prosecutors. She'd seen him meet with lawyers at the firm in which she worked. His reputation preceded him.

After a long session, Mac walked out of the courtroom with a warning, and one stipulation—that he stay clear of Angela.

Steve Decker made the situation seem like a domestic dispute that got a little out of hand, but nothing serious.

Angela was upset because of the lies and projection that his lawyer used to defend Mac, to make her look like a young whore that got caught fucking around on her man. But what else was she to expect? Mac was high on the social ladder and rubbed elbows with big heads throughout the city of Norfolk. He ran in circles with the likes of Ken and his associates.

Growing up in an upper middle-class neighborhood, she'd seen the importance of education and professionalism. Different neighborhood gatherings that her mother and Ken held or attended always opened her eyes to the lifestyle she wanted.

Mac could give her that life and the status. He was someone to be admired by all. On the other hand there was Damien, young and powerful in his own way, and he probably had more money than Ken and Mac. But the way he made her feel could not be compared.

"I know I was told to keep my distance, but I miss you," Mac said as she walked down the courtroom stairs behind Monica.

"The hell with you, Mac. What you did to me and in that courtroom was inexcusable."

Monica told him, "You need to carry your ass before I make a phone call."

"Okay, Angela, I fucked up. I made a big mistake. Do I have to pay for it forever? If you give me the chance, I'll make it up. I never thought being without you would have me so fucked up the way I've been." He eased closer where she could see the water in his eyes. "Please, just allow some time for us to talk. Please?"

Angela began to feel for him. She began to weaken as he preyed on her emotion.

"I'm not goin' to crowd you or try to put you in an awkward situation, but if you find it in you to talk to me, please call. All I ask for is conversation." He walked away.

She walked with Monica in silence. This was the first in a month that she was in a confused state of mind over him. She loved Damien, but Mac was the type of man all her peoples would admire and accept with ease.

"Don't fall for that shit, girl—I know when a nigga ain't shit."

Angela never spoke. *With a fucked up life, who was she to give advice?* Noriega playin' the shit out of her; Quinn hadn't been home in months; and Fat Boy was fuckin' whatever moved.

"What time you plan on comin' back, Angela?" Angela's mother was frustrated at her daughter's actions.

Angela continued out the door, ignoring her mother's calls.

Angela was tired and her head was banging like she'd been hit in the head with a bat. She got in her Jetta and quickly drove away. She stopped at 7-Eleven where she could get something to relieve her migraine. It was cold out, and she never expected to run into anyone, but just as if it was a hot summer's day, the young thugs that she'd grown up with were still hanging on the corner, forties in paper bags and blunts passing from hand to hand.

As she opened her car door, a pretty new fire-bird pulled up and parked beside her. A young man jumped out eager to get her attention. "Hello, Angela. How are you?"

"I'm fine, Ray. And yourself?" She tried not to ignore him but didn't really give a damn.

"You lookin' good these days. What you been doing with yourself?" He was hoping she would say something; giving him an invitation to pursue her once again. *She's fuckin' gorgeous. Irresistible. Definitely not the girl I left behind.*

She had transformed into a fly-ass young woman.

He noticed the new-found jewels that rested on her fingers with the freshly designed airbrushed nails. She wore a hat with fur around it that hid her short cut, but brought out every feature in her beautiful face. She'd put on a pound or two, but the extra weight filled the black Parasuco that had her looking phat as hell and leaving nothing to the imagination.

"I've been taking care. Can't and won't complain."

Before he could say anything else, Ski and Quan came walking up from the crowd of niggas on the corner. "Fuck is up, Angela?" Quan asked.

"Nothin' much. Been a minute," she said, knowing he probably just came home.

Ski yelled, "Angela, drop us off up the street."

Quan opened her back door. "We'll hit you off."

Ray asked Ski, "You don't see me talkin'?"

"Fuck you, nigga. Better carry you' ass. I heard about you." Ski remembered him getting beat down and running. *To lose a fight is one thing, but to let another nigga run you without a gun was the act of a bitch.*

***

Ray walked in Ski's direction. "Who you talkin' to, son?"

"Yo, Ray," Quan called out. "This ain't the time . . . and I'm not gonna to say it twice."

Ray knew Quan was a young nigga throwing rocks at the penitentiary, that he'd been hustling since middle school and was known for holding heat and having the heart to put something in a muthafucka quick. He walked in the 7-Eleven without another word being spoken.

"So what's up, girl?" Ski asked as they drove away.

"We suppose to meet Rome. His brother Bo havin' a party later . . . invitation only. You goin'? He just bought a fat-ass house with a pool out Bellamy Woods."

"Yeah, Rome said something to Monica. I haven't seen him in a minute."

She sat hitting the blunt they had rolled as she pulled in front of Fat Joe's building.

Rome and Fat Joe pulled up minutes later, just as she was leaving. He blew the horn for her to back up then parked and jumped in her car to talk.

"Almost didn't recognize you. That's your brother's new car?" Angela asked, referring to the black GS300 Lexus.

"Naw, that's mine."

"Oh, everybody else doin' it—why not you, huh? You're being stupid; you have too much to lose, Rome."

"I'm a'ight."

"I thought you were smarter."

"Look, I don't need the fuckin' lecture," he said loudly. Then he added softly, "I need a girl who understands me. You don't care."

"What you mean by that?" She stared at him.

"Ever since that night I stayed with you and held you, I haven't been able to get you off my mind. I feel we should spend more time, and you can get to know the other side of me. But you want to keep fuckin' with those knucklehead-ass niggas."

"That's my business, Rome, not yours."

"Fuck that! I'll make it mine and do both those niggas. Fuck them! Niggas ain't from around here."

"Listen at this. I don't believe you."

"Yo, shorty, that's how I feel." Rome got out the car. "I never want to see you hurt again, and if you're with me, I'd know you're taken care of.

"Look, my brother's party is tonight, and I want you and Monica to come as my guest. Page me and let me know what's up." He shut the door and left Angela sitting there for a second, wondering what just took place.

Rome was supposed to be like a brother. Where did this come from? She shook her head, smiled, and drove away.

Rome entered the apartment with a serious attitude. "Y'all niggas finished that package?" he asked Quan and Ski.

"Yeah." Quan handed him fifty-five hundred for the "big eight" he had gotten on consignment.

They counted money, made plans to meet later, and they all left.

Joe had already paid Rome, so all they had to do was go meet Quinn in Richmond and get his. Then he'll be ready to see Bo again. His brother was giving him kilos of "soft" (powder) for 17,000, and he was selling nine for 5,500, which was giving him five grand a week, nowhere near what his brother was getting. Bo was moving five kilos a week; one he gave to Rome.

Rome had learned a lot from his brother. For as long as he could remember, Bo hustled and made much paper. After the clique he ran with went down a couple years back, Bo became the man. For a while he had to serve out-of-town kids to get back up, because cats in the hood thought he was wearing two faces.

After his clique got locked up, Bo walked away without doing any time. To hear people talk . . . they said that when the Feds scooped him up, he squealed like a bitch against his own man, the nigga that brought him in the game, Lo. The same nigga that took him from poverty to the mainstream. Word on the street was that Lo put a 20,000 mark on Bo, but after two years, it was forgotten about by some. Bo was supposed to be living on the low, but after a period of time he felt he was untouchable. He never really got Lake Edward niggas in his corner again, so he threw his brother out there, who had built a tight clique. Rome was handling his and making a name for himself.

Rome and Fat Joe were on their way back from Richmond when Rome's pager went off. It was Monica and Angela telling him to pick them up for the party, seeing Damien was in Jamaica and Mac was keeping his distance, but calling the house like a crazed schoolboy begging for love and another chance.

Rome scooped them up, and they headed to the party. Once they arrived they couldn't believe their eyes—on the table in the dining area was a bowl of cocaine, and beside that was a bowl of 'dro for the rolling. Just for company.

Angela noticed there was just as many whites as blacks, but everybody was partying as one. Halfway through the night, Angela was looking for Monica when she entered the back room and saw her girl bent over, snorting lines of coke through a hundred dollar bill that someone had handed her. She looked up.

Angela could barely see her girl's pretty grey eyes.

Monica expanded her hand to give the rolled bill to Angela and signaled for her to do the two lines that were still on the dresser.

Angela thought twice and figured it was the holidays and she was going to have a good time, so she indulged. The coke took her to a new plateau. Feeling refreshed and like they were ready for anything in the world, they partied till the wee hours of the morning.

They woke the next afternoon feeling drained but no side-effects, except for the shits. Angela had gotten a small sack before the night ended. She threw it on the table in front of Monica.

"I guess we know how we startin' this here day," Monica said.

"Shit! You know how the fuck you started the week-end, so keep it poppin', nigga."

It gave the girls a quicker and smoother high than weed. The girls had a new thing.

"That was a hell of a party, kid." Rome pulled shrimp out the refrigerator.

"Bitches were everywhere and ready to serve niggas with the quickness," Bo said, "and you all in that short face."

"Bitch is bad though, right?" Rome smiled and gave his brother a pound.

"Give it to you, she's nice. But will she pull your back when you really need her?"

"In time she will, son. Promise you that."

"Do your thing, kid. I'm feelin' you. But remember one thing—use them hoes before they use you. Them bitches is treacherous." Bo walked to the front door.

Rome watched his brother as he strolled around in his silk boxers and wife-beater. He had always looked up to him because he maintained.

Their older sisters had looked out a little when they were younger, but now they could barely take care of themselves. They were living at home with moms and were headed nowhere. One had two kids and the kid's father was doing five years. The other had three—the oldest child's father got killed hustling; the other was locked; and the youngest kid's father didn't even acknowledge he had a kid.

Bo had always kept his nose clean, except for when he got caught up a while back fucking with that clique that owned that sports bar: Black and them niggas that were headed for destruction from the beginning. He was now laid back, pulling in mad paper, living like a "Big Willie." But he was not only taking care of himself, but his moms, sisters, and they kids.

He used to take care of Rome, but that was history. Rome was used to having his own and was determined to rise to the status of some of the biggest ballers to ever come out of Bayside, like Tremaine, Big Lloyd, JunePune, Pimp, E, Lo, or, the most notorious of all, Black.

Black was compared to Ninno Brown. He built a name, schooled his little cousin, Lo, and Lo in return schooled Bo. Lo was doing time, and word on the streets was that Black was doing life. Some say that he got caught up in DC and was killed. Rome didn't know what the truth was, but whenever they talked about big-time hustlers that came out of the Hampton Roads, his name was always mentioned.

Rome wanted to make a name. Wherever he ended up in life, he wanted to be known. He wanted ghetto celebrity status, not just neighborhood notoriety. "What you getting into?"

"Go to Lynnhaven. I need to finish up this Christmas shit. Why? You swingin' with me?" Bo asked.

"Yeah, I'll show you the Rolex I want." Rome laughed.

"You get your Rolie when you've paid some fuckin' dues. A Rolie carries a certain amount of respect, and as you know, respect is earned, not just given." Bo stared into Rome's face and gave him a pound. Bo knew Rome was smart, but trouble wasn't him, and in this shit, you had to be ready for both sides.

Rome knew what Bo was talking about—the-other-side-to-this-street shit. He knew Bo had damaged many niggas during his soldier days and wouldn't hesitate to destroy a nigga today if he had to. He never had to prove himself like that because Bo gave him his start on a platter and the money started flowing. "Ain't shit respected but this right here." Rome clutched his pocket, showing the knot of money through his jeans.

"Yeah, that do get mad respect." Bo smiled. "You ain't lyin' there, kid. You ain't lyin' there."

Chapter Seventeen

"Merry Christmas, Sissy. Get up. Come open your present, Sissy. Hurry up!" Angela's little brother yelled.

Angela looked at the clock. It was seven. She knew she was going back to bed. She put on her robe and took her brother's hand. He pulled her to the family room by the brightly lit Christmas tree that was near the fireplace.

Her mother and Ken came into the room. "Merry Christmas, family."

He hugged everyone individually, then collectively. Her brother picked up a present and began to open it. "Hold on," Ken said. "You know we pray and thank God for this day before anything. Now join hands and bow your heads.

"Dear Heavenly Father, the first, the last, the Alpha and the Omega, the one from whom all blessings flow, as we bow our heads on this joyous day, we raise praises for all the good things that you have stored upon us. We stand here as a family, thanking you for the opportunity once again to come together and thank you for your many blessings. We thank you for another Christmas that we all have lived to enjoy the love, happiness, and prosperity that you have supplied upon this family. We cannot thank you enough, but we will continue to give you praises. So we ask you to continue

to bless us and watch over us as a family and then individually. We ask this of you in Your Holy Name."

They all said, "Amen," and began opening the gifts
they'd bought for each other.

Angela eased to the kitchen and called her father.
She hadn't spent a Christmas with her father since her
parents got divorced. She missed her dad at times like
these. Even though Ken always did all he could to make
the holidays a family thing, no matter how sweet he
was, he still couldn't take the place of her father.

After talking to her dad and Lenore and wishing
them a Merry Christmas, her spirits were lifted and
this precious day was off to a great start. They were listening to Christmas music and sipping hot chocolate.
Ken was enjoying a cup of coffee mixed with several
shots of Baileys.

A knock at the door disturbed the family.

"Angela," Ken yelled from the foyer.

Angela walked out, and to her surprise, Mac was
standing there, looking gorgeous as ever, with a gift in
hand. She wanted her step-dad to excuse them so she
wouldn't have all her business out.

"What are you doing here?"

"I came to see you, baby. I know we're not on the best
of terms."

"No, we're not on *any* terms. Too much shit come
with you, and I'm not with it no more."

"I made my mistakes, Angela, but I'm gettin' life
together and I need you with me." He moved closer to
her.

She stepped back.

"I see you need more time to yourself. I guess I
should be leavin', huh?" He sat the box and the card
down.

"Whatever." She noticed the new black drop-top CLK Benz sitting in the driveway when she opened the door.

He stepped out the door and turned to her. "I love you, Angela, no matter how hard you act. I know you still love me. See you soon."

She shut the door. *How the fuck he going to come around here unexpected and call me out on Christmas?* She walked in her room and got her purse. She needed something for her head, and her peoples definitely wa'n' allowing her to spark no weed. She locked her door and laid two lines out on the dresser. One up each nostril. "Goddamn!" She shook her head. This new shit was no joke—straight to the head. She was now ready for anything. She walked back to the family room, where her family was still chilling around the fireplace.

After the day got going she began wondering about Damien. She missed him. She got dressed in one of the pants suits her mother had given her. She was on her way out the door when she noticed Macs gift and cards. She unwrapped the box to reveal a long, red Anne Klein dress coat.

"My God, that's a beautiful coat," her mother said.

"It is nice, isn't it?" Angela almost felt bad about the way she treated him. She opened the card, and her mother watched the sadness come over her face as she read it.

I'm Sorry Playing ball, running wild, no worries Things a child should do. Beatings, molestation, feeling insecure Things that I went through Family vacations, loving parents, nothing but love and affection. Things I conceived in my mind Poverty stricken projects, abusive father, making it on my own. Why was my life so unkind As frustrations were taken out on me. Didn't they hear me say, I'm Sorry.

Now my childhood is gone and I stand as a man Still facing the past everyday, the best I can I never know what my future holds Stay strong, get help, lean toward God A strong black man chooses his destiny These are all the things that I am told No one knows how many times me and the problem has come Face to face and all I've done is cried. Strength comes from you and I have to have you in my life. If I fail again, I want you to know that I have really tried. Another mistake in life and again I have failed.

I say I regret it once and I say it again Didn't you hear me say, I'm Sorry.

With much sincerity,
Love Mac

She passed the box and card to her mother, asking her to put it in the room, and walked out the door.

She arrived at Damien's house and strolled in with her gift in hand. "Heah, baby! Merry Christmas." She gave him a hug.

He seemed to force a smile.

She came in to find his brother and sister relaxing on the couches.

Damien began to open his gift. "Thank you, Angela. I really like this. I'm sorry I didn't pick you up anything, but I'm not a holiday person. Growing up, Christmas was just another day, and now I look at it the same way—just another day. For special ones in my life I show my love all year; I don't need a holiday."

"It's okay. I'm just so glad you're here and I have the opportunity to spend this day with you. That means everything." She leaned over and put her mouth on his ear and whispered, "The best gift is yet to come; you have to unwrap it upstairs."

"I'll see you all later." Damien took Angela's hand and walked upstairs. When he walked in the room he scooped her up.

She yelled as he slammed her to the bed and crawled on top of her. She spent the majority of the day loving him.

The day passed quickly, and the evening, even faster. Damien was asleep and was awakened by the sweet kisses and touches of his love. "Happy birthday, baby." Angela stroked her hand up and down his back.

He lay there motionless as if he was still asleep, enjoying the soft, sensuous touch of his lover. Nothing in the world ever felt so good and made him totally relax to a state that nothing mattered. Today was his birthday, and to him, his birthday meant more than Christmas.

"I hope you didn't make plans for today," Angela said, "because I have the day already planned out, from breakfast to breakfast."

Damien knew that he had made other engagements, but if she wanted to celebrate his birthday with him in some laid back, unforgettable kind of way, then so be it. He was hers from breakfast to breakfast. He turned over on his back. "So what's the plan?"

She moved in closer, laying her head on his chest and her hand on his stomach. "We're going to start the day making love to each other, then breakfast will follow. Catch an early movie, then we will go to an undisclosed place. And that's where we'll be until breakfast time tomorrow. Can I have the entire day?" She began to kiss his neck and chest.

"I did have a few things to do," he said real slow.

"Is that right?" She ran her tongue slowly across his nipples. She could feel him starting to get aroused. She reached out and took him into her hand and stroked him gently again. "I can't be with you all day?"

"Ummmmmmmmm, Angela," was his only response.

She climbed on top of him and guided him inside her. He let out a sigh of satisfaction, and they began to fuck like crazed animals for five minutes.

Then his body began to shake, and he squeezed her to him so tight, her breath was taken away. She started to get up.

"Don't move, don't move."

"You still leavin' me today?" she asked, relaxing in his arms.

"Actually, I have to run to Carolina, but you can ride with me."

She began to smile. That was all she wanted to hear, even if they did nothing. As long as she was with him.

After a quick shower and breakfast, they were on their way. Damien had asked Angela to drive while he lay back, relaxed, and rolled blunts while traveling down 85 South headed to Durham, NC.

They arrived at the home of one of his colleagues. She kind of figured he was in the business also when she saw the phat-ass Acura that sat in front of the condo, sitting on dubs.

Damien pulled the 9 mm out from under the mat, put one in the chamber, and slid it into the Chanel purse he had picked up for her in DC.

She looked at him confused.

"It won't be needed, but it's better to have it and not need it than to need it and not have it."

They got out the car. She pulled her bag on her shoulder and watched as he slid on his Avirex jacket that matched his jeans. She knew her man was on and was turned on by just being with him.

As they went inside the condo, a tall, light-skinned guy with curly hair showed Damien mad love. He stood about six foot three and was very muscular. She sat down as the two men went into the kitchen. From her vantage point she could see the money and coke being pulled from the cabinets. This made her nervous, but at the same time, it was exciting her.

Moments later she and Damien were out the door headed to another associate's house. When they arrived, Angela's mouth dropped at the sight of the man's beautiful home. The older gentleman stood in front in a Dickies jumpsuit. She realized that one of the arms to the jumpsuit was just hanging. She was curious about what led to him losing his arm. He stood about six feet with a very large frame, 300 pounds easily. The older gentleman's head was full of grey, and his beard held the same color. It was thick and neatly trimmed and had a very distinguished look.

"What happen to his arm?"

"Long time ago in New York, he was part of the 1940's heroin epidemic in Harlem. Some say he owed money, some say he had skimmed off the top, but they took a bat and beat his right hand and arm so bad, it had to be amputated. He's gotten along good over the years without it." Damien took the gun out of her purse and placed it back under the seat. He pulled the bag from the back, and they headed to the porch where the older gentleman was standing.

"What you say, young 'un? Look like you in good spirits and seem to be doin' well. Who's this beautiful lady?"

"This is Angela."

The older gentleman hugged Angela around her neck. "Come on in, young 'un."

They went into the living room and took a seat on the antique furniture. A woman who appeared to be in her forties came in. Her hair had silver streaks in it, which convinced Angela that she was at least in her fifties, but her style was that of class and elegance.

"Heah, Daddy, can I get you and your guest anything?"

Damien quickly jumped up and hugged the lady when he noticed her presence. "Hello, Aunt Mable."

"Good to see you, Buttons," she said to Damien. "You really have to come and visit more often."

"Yes, ma'am. I try, but the store keep me so busy. I'm trying to build a base so I can live like Uncle John in my later years." Damien pointed to his close friend. Because of their age and the respect he had gained for John over the years, he gave them titles. Calling them by their first name wasn't for him; he wasn't old enough.

"Put business first and your future will fall into place, Buttons. Remember that," she said walking off.

"Take this, Mommy." John handed her the bag Damien had given him.

"So how long you here for, young 'un?" John asked Damien.

"On my way out now." Damien stood up. "It's my birthday and she made plans, so I'm heading on back to VA."

They walked outside to the car. Damien stopped and stared at John's new deep burgundy Cadillac Deville with the leather white interior and chrome Cadillac rims on which the Vogues sat.

"Uncle John, if you ever get rid of this, I got first dibs."

"I keep that in mind, young 'un." John smiled and showed his gold crowns.

Then they got in the truck and made their way. "They seem like nice peoples, Buttons," Angela said smiling as she drove away.

"The best. I want my life to fall just like his. Aunt Mable and Uncle John been together since they were in high school. Now they're in their fifties and still going strong. He's an old hustler, but now he has stores, real estate, and own an after-hours club in Raleigh; he's pretty much straight for life. They've traveled all over the world, and I really doubt if he wants for anything."

"Do they have kids?"

"Yeah, he has a daughter in California. She's an air traffic controller. She went to Hampton too." Damien smiled, thinking about the coincidence.

"Really?"

"His son went to Morgan State in Baltimore. Uncle John was paying his tuition, rent, and sending him dough to live, and that nigga was fuckin' with that shit. So Uncle John cut his ass off. He decided to stay up there. Far as I know he still up there strung out on heroin."

"Damn! Some just don't realize how good they have it."

"Yeah, they really don't." Damien stared at Angela and smiled.

"What?"

"You know what? You got it the same fuckin' way."

"My parents ain't got money like his."

"Yeah, but they doin' all right. They pay your tuition, and they pay your rent. What?"

"And I plan on takin' advantage of it like I'm doin'—I ain't gonna fuck it up."

"I'm gonna hold you to that shit. You can believe that, baby!"

The early movie was out by the time they arrived at Columbus Theaters in the downtown Virginia Beach area. The matinee had already started, so Angela talked him into going to Barnes and Noble and having a cappuccino until the next show began. He wasn't crazy about it, but this was her thing—she'd planned this day, and he was going to allow her to guide him through it.

They went inside, and she picked up the *Cycle* magazine because of his love for motorcycles. She got herself an *Essence*, a table, and two cups of cappuccino. After looking through the magazine, Angela could tell Damien was getting restless. Then she remembered a magazine that she'd seen at Mac's house. She went over to the shelf and brought back the *Robb Report*. He began to look through it. Moments later, when she glanced over at him, the magazine had his full attention. When it was time to go Damien brought the *Robb Report*. He had already filled out the card for a subscription.

After the movie they ran by her condo and retrieved her night bag. When they arrived at the Virginia Beach Resort, Angela had already made reservations for the room and dinner at the four-star restaurant inside the resort, Tradewinds. Tradewinds gave them an astonishing view of the Chesapeake Bay and the relaxing mood of an ocean front café.

Dinner was fit for a king and the atmosphere of candlelight and soft music set the mood for what was to come. After a few drinks, they made it back to the room. While Damien stood on the balcony collecting his thoughts, Angela was in the bathroom running water for his bath. She asked him to undress and come into the bathroom. He sat there wondering what would make a woman treat him in such a way. He knew money was what kept most women going, but it was more than that. The style and money may have gotten her attention, but it wasn't money that was keeping her there, making her do the things she did and treat him as if he was the most important thing in the world.

Angela, young and outgoing, was learning fast. She'd met many girls at Hampton and, listening to girl talk, realized that a woman handled her business like a lady but also took care of her man. She knew making him feel like he was her world would either make him take advantage of her or give back and show her the same love. Damien showed her the same love, and it brought the best out of her.

She took the cloth and went over his body, bathing him slowly and thoroughly. He leaned back and enjoyed every second, thinking that no man had a love like his. After drying him off and applying lotion to his body, she went to her bag and pulled out a pair of silk boxers with Christmas designs. Then she escorted him to the couch, removed an already rolled blunt from her purse, and lit it. She passed it to him and excused herself to the bathroom. Minutes later, which felt like an eternity to Damien, she returned wearing a short white silk see-through robe. Damien's eyes widened as she allowed the robe to drop and reveal the most perfectly shaped body in a white thong with little elves and Santas on it, with a matching bra.

When he noticed the new tattoo Angela had gotten—she had a set of tiger paws going up her leg that ended at her kitty cat—his hormones took off. He stood up and picked her up. She wrapped her legs around him, and they fell on top of the bed. The embrace lasted till morning.

The knock at the door woke the two, and Damien opened the door to retrieve the room service that Angela had filled out and put on the door. He uncovered the food and looked over at his girl. *She is incredible.* All he needed for his life to be complete. He pictured Uncle John and Aunt Mable, then himself and Angela. A smile came across his face; he felt something he had never felt. *This shit here is real.*

"Angela, get the phone," Monica yelled from her bedroom.

Angela didn't respond.

Monica got up and went to her room and opened the door, but she wasn't there. Then she heard noise in the bathroom. "Angela."

"What, girl?"

"Get the phone; you know I have company. You need to get the phone or turn the ringer off."

"Stop cryin' all the fuckin' time."

"Just get the phone." Monica left out of her room.

Angela rushed to the phone, thinking it was Damien in New York for the weekend. "Hello," she said in an excited tone.

"How are you today?"

"I'm fine, Mac. How are you?" she asked in a nonchalant manner.

"Were you expecting someone else?"

"I was in the shower. You're going to have to let me call you back."

"We haven't talked since Christmas, and I figured you would of call by now. How did you like the gift?"

"It was nice, but I don't want you buyin' me anything else. Matter a fact, I really can't accept it."

"Well, I gave it to you from the heart, so I can't take it back. Angela, you don't seem to understand—I'm not and I can't let you go. I love you."

She hung up the phone. The more she pushed him away, the more aggressive he was becoming. The phone rang again. She picked it up quickly and answered with an attitude. "Hello." Her tone was loud and forceful.

"Who you talkin' to? That's not the way you answer the phone."

"I'm sorry. I thought you were my moms callin' again."

"You all right this morning?"

"Yeah, I'm okay. Now I'm really okay," she said with a smile in her voice.

He smiled too. "Are you?"

"I'm gettin' so attached to you, Damien. When you're here I want to be with you, and if you aren't, I'm missin' you to no end."

"I can relate, baby, but you realize that business has to be taken care of if I plan any future for me and you, right?"

"Yes." Then the phone beeped. "Hold on, please."

"Yes," she answered with attitude.

"Don't hang up on me, Angela."

"I'm on the other line."

"Fuck that! I know it ain't that young-ass punk," he yelled.

She clicked back over to finish talking to Damien. Her good mood jumped back up when she realized he would be home New Year's Eve, but she knew it was time to handle Mac, who was really getting out of hand.

Angela came into the living room with Quinn and Monica. "I'm going to call the police because Mac keep trippin' and I can't take it, Monica."

"Well, Monday morning we'll go downtown and let them know. That's one nigga you could have left alone," Monica said, "but we'll handle it."

"Where your friend, Angela?" Quinn asked.

Angela remembered that Damien told her never tell anyone about his whereabouts and when he leaves out of town. "He's in DC."

"See Quinn's new car?" Monica asked.

"Little somethin'-somethin'." Quinn smiled and put on his Ralph Lauren black leather jacket to go with his black Lugz.

"Leavin' already?"

"Yeah, I have to get back to Petersburg; I got mad shit to take care of up there."

They walked outside. Angela was surprised to see his new black 325 BMW. "Damn, Quinn! This shit is nice." Angela looked at Monica, who was smiling ear to ear. Her man was rising on the social ladder. He was turning into one of those guys that she had always admired and now she had one of her own. She was so glad she got Rome to put her man on and was proud of Quinn. And despite all of her unfaithful actions, she really loved him.

Quinn pulled in the Hampton Club complex. This stop was mandatory before going back to Petersburg. He walked up to Rome's apartment and was invited in. Quinn noticed the dark-skinned guy sitting in the chair smoking a blunt. Quinn spoke, but the guy gave no response. Rome had walked to the back bedroom and reached deep inside the mattress and pulled out a

whole brick all ready cooked for Quinn. Quinn placed
it in a Food Lion bag, stuck it in his pants, and they all
walked out.

Rome and Quinn were talking as the stout, dark-
skinned guy followed. Quinn signaled for shorty in the
passenger side to get in the driver's seat. As she got out
and walked around to the driver side, Rome stared in
amazement—he didn't think Quinn had it in him.

"Damn, nigga! I like that."

"She's nice, right? She got three roommates. They all
live in a big-ass house in Petersburg right off campus.
And, son, all them bitches bad."

Rome was still staring into the girl's eyes. She wore
no makeup, but she was the finest dark-brown shorty
he'd ever seen. Her coal-black, wavy hair was just
slightly darker than her skin, but she filled the jeans
with the widest hips and phattest ass he'd ever seen.
All he could do was rub his dick off this one. "I'd pay
for some that ass, son." He knew Monica was Quinn's
girl and wanting this bitch was no disrespect since she
was just something on the side. And far as Rome was
concerned, there was no better way to play.

"Y'all niggas need to get up to Petersburg. It's like
that all day. Holla at a nigga." Quinn gave Rome a
pound.

Rome and his new partner got in the GS300 and
drove off. They'd been talking. This guy was trying to
get Rome down with him. The kid was in his junior
year at Hampton University, from Philly. Him and his
peoples had a lucrative business bringing bricks into
Hampton and Newport News.

Rome noticed Sincere on campus, first fucking with
cute bitches, then fucking with niggas with phat whips.
He wasn't flashy—jeans, hoody, and Timbs was his
normal attire. One of the girls that Sincere had been

fucking started liking Rome. Sincere didn't care; it was his way of meeting another baller. It wasn't many cats who had it like Rome did, so he felt good to hang with a nigga who had what he had. It felt good fucking with new niggas, meeting new bitches, and balling out of control.

One day he even asked Rome to get down with him and his peoples, but Rome let him know that he only fucked around with the cats he'd been dealing with forever, but he was still cool and if anything changed . . .

Rome dropped Sincere off and headed to Norfolk. This felt like a night for clubbing, but not by himself. He swung by Angela and Monica's condo to see what they were up to. "Sound like a Pizzazz night to me. What's up?" he said, entering the condo.

"You got us?" Monica asked.

"Why bitches always yellin' that shit. I know y'all got money."

"Not the point," Angela told him. "You heard my girl—do you got us?"

"Yeah, but y'all got to meet me. I'll call before I leave my house." Rome sat down and rolled the blunt.

Monica handed him a small bag containing a couple grams of coke. He sprinkled some onto the weed and rolled it. The "yes-yes" had their eyes bloodshot red. They kicked for a few until Rome had to leave and catch Kappatal Kuts before going out.

Angela pulled on Granby St. The line was around the building with no parking anywhere in sight. "I am not parkin' in no garage tonight."

"There's Rome talkin' to some nigga."

They pulled over, and to their surprise, the dude was about to pull off. Angela lucked up and got a close spot.

They kicked it for a moment until Sincere strolled up. He knew security; he showed a little love, and they all walked inside, still having to pay, but without waiting in line.

Sincere walked to bar on the first floor. He signaled to the bartender that Rome and the ladies were with him, and four glasses appeared on the bar, filled with shots of Rémy. The four made their way past the laughter of the Comedy Club on the second floor and found a table on the third.

"Thank you," Monica said.

"My pleasure, shorty," Sincere said. And to the waitress who made her way to the table, "Cristal and four glasses."

The girls looked at each other as if to ask, "Who is Rome's new friend?"

"Damn! My fault. Sincere, this is Monica and Angela, my sisters. This is my man, Sincere." Monica and Angela glanced but tried not to stare. But this dark-ass nigga, rockin' braids that some bitch had freaked for him, had the girls wondering who this nigga was, showing them mad love.

They began to talk and converse, but kept getting interrupted by the different ballers and players coming up showing what some would consider love. But it actually was respect to Sincere. Rome was curious because he knew his status could blow, hanging with a ghetto celeb.

Monica and Angela just liked the attention they were receiving from the onlookers, standing around watching the waitress pop the champagne and pour four glasses, and then sit the rest on ice.

Suddenly two girls came speeding to the table, followed by another pair. Sincere stood up and received a bundle of hugs. "Yo, Rome, this is Kay-Kay and Reva, my sisters from the crib.

"And this is Seri and Star," Reva said. "They from the spot too."

"Germantown hoes up in here," Sincere joked.

"You don't know, better ask somebody," Kay-Kay said smiling.

"So what's goin' on at Norfolk State, ladies? Why don't I buy you all a drink and y'all tell me how things are going."

They walked over to the bar, with Sincere leading the way and his arm around Seri, as the other three followed. Seri was light—what you call yellow. She had light-brown hair and was a real pleasure to look at. Not to mention, her forty-DD's pushed up for the world to see, but not at all trashy . . . in no way.

"Goddamn, Kay-Kay," Rome said loud enough for only Angela and Monica to hear as they sat at the table with their eyes on Sincere and the Philly girls.

"Go get her, player," Angela said.

"He scared. Nigga don't want no pussy, An." They both started laughing.

"No rush. No rush," was all Rome said as he watched Kay-Kay's ass swing side to side in the snug-fitting polyester pants. The tight-fitting shirt with buttons only at the top revealed her pierced belly button and hairline, which gave him an instant hard on.

They saw no more of them until the club ended. As Rome walked with Angela and Monica to the parking lot, Sincere came up behind them, "Ladies, it was nice meeting you both. I hope we see each other again.

"Yo, Rome," Kay-Kay said "what's up. She wants some breakfast—I got Seri—come on, nigga."

"Shit . . . nigga, you know I'm down. Let's go." Rome turned and said his good-byes to Angela and Monica and burst. He had to see what the young Philly girl was 'bout it.

After leaving IHOP, Sincere and Rome took the girls back to their house in Merrimac Landing, where the four young ladies shared a four-bedroom home. After thirty minutes of blunts and more conversation, Rome and Karen retired to her room.

By the time morning came, Karen felt she had a new man, and Rome would tell her no different. The young girl from Philly had him open with her style and graceful movements, and having that bomb-ass body and the skills to go along definitely didn't hurt.

Chapter Eighteen

Angela felt like a weight was taken off her shoulder when she left the courthouse. The court told Mac to stay away. Now, she had taken another restraining order out against him. *Once papers were served, he would be out of her life for sure.*

"How can somebody so fine be so fucked up?"

"It goes back to that nigga childhood. He says the way he was brought up and his household did it to him and that what makes him act the fool sometimes. I feel sorry for him, but I can't take care of a grown-ass man, you know what I mean?"

"Shit! I know, girl, but we learn from all our mistakes. All of them."

"Well, we made enough for '96, and all we can do is pray that '97 brings about a change for the better."

"It will, starting tomorrow when your man gets back. What we gonna do tomorrow night anyway to bring in the New Year?"

"Whatever. Long as I'm with my baby." Angela smiled.

Just as Angela was thinking of Damien in New York, he was doing the same as he explored the diamond district. He didn't get her anything for Christmas, but after all the love she'd shown him, he had to let her know it wasn't in vain. He knew he had never had a female express herself the way Angela did, and he never wanted to see himself without her.

After meeting with JB and finding out that things were real good on the business end and his future was in no jeopardy, he went out to find her a little something. While riding through Manhattan, he pulled down his sun visor and the two pictures of Angela fell in his lap. He knew he had a beautiful girl, a very precious jewel that any man would be glad to have on his arm.

He studied one from head to toe, from the fly cut she wore, to the sexy Donna Karan sandals. The second picture was more recent—he was standing there, looking like the Big Willie he was, as she leaned into his arms, her arm around him and her left hand resting on his chest. He imagined the soft touch of her hands and the way she took the beautiful, freshly airbrushed nails and lightly ran them down his back as he made love to her. "Wow! Goddamn, girl," he said out loud to himself.

He went into the district to find her a ring. Something to say, "I love you, and I'm not going nowhere." He put the pictures back above the sun visor. He knew he would need some help, so he scooped his sister Rhonda, who had the taste to help him pick out the perfect ring.

Angela pulled in front of Monica's house. "I'll be back in about an hour; I'm going to my peoples' house."

"You gonna tell your moms?"

"Yeah, I really think I need to now; plus, I want her to meet Damien tomorrow—that's who I'm goin' into the New Year with, and he's going to be a permanent part of my life. It's time she met him. Monica, don't forget to page Rome and see if he has some candy, and you know we need some weed.

"You got money?"

"I told you to call, didn't I?" Angela pulled off.

Angela walked into the house to find her mother packing her lunch for her three to eleven shift. "Heah, Ma."

"What you doin' today, Angela? Surprise to see you. I saw Ray's mother at Farm Fresh. She said that you can still give her a call."

"All right."

"Where you comin' from?"

"I had to get a restraining order against Mac."

"What?" Her mother stopped what she was doing.

"That's why I wasn't tryin' to see him Christmas. He decided he wanted to hit and control me. When he first did it, I cut him loose.

"Lately I've been talkin' to this guy, Damien, and one day Mac come to my job and tried to do the same thing, but Damien was there to straighten it out. I really care for Damien, Mom, but Mac won't leave me alone. So I went to the courts today."

"What the police say?"

"They're goin' to serve him the papers, and then if he comes near me, he'll be picked up."

"You be careful, baby; some men are really crazy—I mean really crazy. Why are you just telling me this? I want you to start sharing things with me; I am your mother. Okay?"

"You're right, Ma."

"So when I'm going to meet this Damien character?"

"Tomorrow I'm going to stop by." They hugged and left out the house together.

***

Angela picked up Monica, and they were on their way to Fat Joe's house, where him and Rome were chilling, smoking, looking at "Rap City."

Afterwards, the girls headed back to their condo to waste the rest of the day on another level. The ringing of the phone in the late hour woke the young ladies up. It was Quinn in the car, telling Monica to open the door. The girls had passed out and left the television watching them.

Quinn's knock at the door was Angela's good night signal. She went in her room and paged Damien. He never called back, but she never knew it. She was dead to the world.

The following afternoon, New Year's Eve, Monica and Angela were still in the bed. The loud bass from Rome's Lexus brought Angela to her feet, thinking it was Damien, but she knew by the rattling of the car it wasn't him. *His truck didn't rattle.* The knock at the door had her questioning herself. She ran to it, and to her surprise it was just Rome and Fat Joe coming up the stairs.

She quickly ran in her room to put a robe over the oversized number twenty-three Bulls jersey she had on. It revealed a little too much. (It was Damien's and reeked of his Curve cologne; the reason she wore it.)

"I thought y'all were Damien. Need to get all that rattlin' fixed—shit don't sound good."

"Fuck you talkin'?" Rome ignored her comment. "Hell y'all doin' tonight?"

"We talkin' about gettin' two bitches and goin' out Waterside and checkin' out the fireworks."

Angela yelled out in the direction of Monica's room. "We goin' out Waterside tonight?"

"Down for whatever."

Rome asked, "Who here with her? Quinn?"

"Yeah. But I have to see what Damien has planned; I'm sure he's down."

"We headin' to the mall to pick up some shit," Joe said. "What you gonna do?"

"I'm chillin', waitin' on my man."

Rome asked her, "You always play fair like that?"

"I do . . . when my man play fair with me." Angela had a devious smile. "Which mall y'all goin' to anyway?"

"Coliseum," Rome told her. "Bring yo' ass. I got you on a T-shirt or something, if you help me pick out something nice for my new babe."

They jumped in the whip and began roaming. They started at Coliseum and ended up at Chesapeake Square. By the time they dropped Angela off it was dark, and she was wondering why she hadn't heard from Damien.

She showered and changed. The plan was to meet Fat Joe, his friend, Rome, and KayKay down by the Bank of America building downtown. Just as the clock struck ten, Angela began to worry.

"If he don't show, just swing with me and Quinn."

"Thanks, Monica, but I ain't tryin' to be the third wheel. Y'all go ahead. If he comes, I'll meet you'll down there."

"You sure; you know it's not a problem?" Quinn asked.

"I know. But tonight I want to wait on him."

When they left Angela lit a blunt and put in a CD, Tupac's *Me Against the World*. She listened to the lyrics and realized for the first time why this man was a legend and why her man also was a thug for life.

As time slowly crept away she realized he wasn't going to make it. But she understood he was a busy man and, the way he lived, anything could come up. She had gotten a bottle of J. Rogét for her and Damien to pop open for the New Year. She got the bottle and sat on the couch. Just as she was beginning to accept the disappointment and prepare for a night of loneliness, she could feel her body tremble from bass. Then the sounds began to become clearer. She jumped up and ran to the door. As she opened the door, she saw the new butter Timbs, untied and the tag still dangling, hit the top step. By the time his body hit the doorway, she was in his arms, full of joy.

He squeezed her—she knew he'd missed her by the way he'd taken her breath with his embrace— and they shared a very passionate kiss.

She stared into his eyes with the biggest smile. She looked down at her watch and saw it read only eleven-fifteen. "Can we go to Waterside?" "

It's on you; I'm with you."

She really wanted to be with her crew, but fine as her man was looking, she almost said, "Let's just stay the fuck in."

"You look cute, baby." Damien admired her DKNY jeans, Nine West boots, and the leather he'd gotten her.

She knew his style was thuggish and she liked it. So when they walked to truck she never commented on his camouflaged suit, new Timbs, and Phat Farm T-shirt that was set off by the iced-down medallion swinging from his neck. Instead she just admired him for him. *Fuck the occasion.*

They headed downtown. Damien felt this would be the perfect time to give her the ring . . . as soon as the fireworks went off.

They joined Angela's friends. Everybody was standing in the cold, bouncing around, trying to stay warm as the skies roared and lit up from the fireworks. They all popped champagne and hugged their significant others.

Damien reached down in his side cargo pocket.

She smiled a big smile when he pulled the 3ct diamond solitaire from the box and placed it on her ring finger.

"This is to say that I promise never to leave you and that we are a team until the end." Angela eyes began to water. She never knew she meant that much to him.

He leaned over and hugged her tight. "I love you, Angela. That, I promise you, will never change."

Angela was shocked to hear those words. She just squeezed him harder and cherished the moment.

After an hour of celebrating and gulping down champagne, everyone went their separate ways. Angela and Damien ended up back at the condo with Monica and Quinn. They decided to play a few hands of spades until the early morning before retiring to their rooms.

After intense lovemaking, they fell asleep, snuggled and cuddled in the each other's arms.

Angela had heard the phone ring earlier that morning, and the noise from Monica and Quinn in the living room didn't allow her to go back to sleep. She walked out into the living room, while Damien was getting dressed. "What's up, girl?"

"Nothin' at all. Mac called here three times demandin' to talk to you."

"Fuck him! He need to carry his ass and get a life. Tell me this—how can a man as fine as him and with the money he has turn into straight bitch?"

"Angela, you really need to be careful because the way he acted on the phone and his past actions really shows me that he is disturbed."

"You right, but I think he has too much to lose to do anything crazy crazy; plus, I'm not intimidated by him no more."

Damien came out the room and put on his coat, and Quinn grabbed his, knowing it was his chance to burst. They walked out and went to the LX450 and BMW parked beside each other, neither noticing the drop-top Benz parked across the street.

Damien opened his truck door and heard a voice behind him say, "Who's Big Willie now, muthafucka?"

Three shots rang out, and Quinn tried to jump in the Beamer.

Angela and Monica heard two more shots. They ran to the door and ran outside. As they ran down the stairs in time to see Mac's black Mercedes speeding out the parking lot and onto Ocean View Avenue.

Both girls ran to their man's side, screaming hysterically.

"Somebody, call 911," Monica yelled as she took Quinn's hand. "Hurry up!"

Quinn lay motionless on the front seat of his car with a gunshot wound to his chest and his stomach.

Angela stood there crying out of control.

Neighbors came out to see what was going on. Angela looked down at Damien lying in the puddle of blood that turned his army fatigues and Phat Farm shirt into a bloody mess.

Norfolk police was quick to arrive, along with the ambulance and rescue squads. They moved Monica and Angela out the way, and the girls sat on the curb, comforting each other. They watched as they took Quinn out the car and placed him in the ambulance. Monica got in and rode to the hospital with him—he wasn't moving but was still alive.

Angela stood watching as they placed a white sheet over Damien's body. Her entire body began to shake, and her legs gave away. She sat balled up on the wall as the detectives approached her to take a statement. She let them know it was Mac.

Afterwards, she went inside to call Noriega. It was the only number she had for anybody in his family.

A little later, the phone rang. Monica was crying to a point you couldn't understand anything she was saying. "Slow down, Monica . . . please."

"He's dead. He died in the operating room," Monica said through her cries.

"I'm on my way."

Angela got her keys and rushed to Norfolk General.

As the clock struck twelve New Year's night, Angela and Monica rested on the couch in complete silence. All you could hear was the whistling of the cold wind blowing in off the Chesapeake Bay. Monica was staring into space with a blank look on her face, and Angela couldn't stop the tears from flowing. She just wanted to sit and drown her sorrows in the leftover champagne and snort the coke that they had stashed away.

Monica's grandmother and Angela's parents had come over to persuade the girls to come home, but they knew they had to deal with the situation themselves and needed each other, not anybody who wanted to point fingers and ask a lot of questions.

The knock at the door scared both girls. They jumped up instantly, staring at each other to see who was going to answer.

Monica eased to the door and peeked out. It was Noriega and two of his soldiers. When he walked in they both hugged him as if they never wanted to let him go. They stepped back, and Angela burst into tears.

Noriega stood there in his camouflage outfit, new butter Timbs, and an Azzure T-shirt, a long chain hanging down to his stomach. "So did they get the kid?"

"Yeah," Angela told him. "They went to his house and never found the weapon. He probably threw it in the Bay when he drove over the Hampton Bridge."

"A'ight. That means he's comin' out on bail." Noriega looked at Angela. "I need you to show us where he lives, okay."

"Time to show these VA niggas how we get down in Crooklyn," one of the soldiers said.

They rode out for her to show him where he lived and then got a ride back home.

Next time she heard, Noriega had gone back to New York to help out with his cousin's funeral arrangements. Damien's funeral was being held on Saturday at Woodward Thompson Chapel on One Troy Avenue, Brooklyn, and Quinn's was being held on Sunday at Fitchett Funeral Home on Liberty Street in the South Norfolk area.

Meanwhile Mac was released on $50,000 bond. Police thought everything was drug related and didn't put any emphasis on the case.

Angela and Monica left Friday night for New York. When they arrived there, she was surprised not to see Noriega.

Saturday came and the funeral was harder than the girls expected. Angela took it harder than some of Damien's own family, but Noriega showed up to help pull her together.

After the funeral they all met at Damien's mother's house. As Angela approached the home, Rhonda dropped her plate and grabbed Angela and slammed her to the car.

Monica grabbed Rhonda, and Kim slapped the shit out of her, yelling, "Get your fuckin' hands off her."

"I told you, bitch. I told you don't fuck my brother up," Rhonda yelled between cries. "Why? I told you." And she fell to the ground, losing her breath and screaming.

Kim held Rhonda, trying to comfort her as the tears streamed down both their faces.

When the girls climbed into the car to leave, Noriega walked over and hugged Monica. "You be strong, baby, and everything will come together. I'll be callin' to check on you soon."

Then he eased over to Angela and stared into her eyes. She didn't know what to say or do; her eyes watered as they embraced. A tear fell from his eyes, as many began to flow from hers. "Look, my cousin had mad love for you. Don't allow the circumstances to fuck up your life. Keep your head up and keep going. If you need anything, don't hesitate to call. Be strong and put it behind you—it's over. Revenge is the sweetest thing in the fuckin' world," he said with a smirk.

Angela just stared, knowing what he meant.

They arrived back in Norfolk with just enough time to change and get over to Quinn's "set up." When they pulled in front of the house and made their way to the door, they caught looks as if they were the ones who murdered him. Upon entering the house, his mother embraced Monica showing her love. His father never spoke, he just turned and walked away.

Quinn's brother just stared with hatred in his eyes before all hell broke loose. "My brother lost his mutha-fuckin' life over y'all—simple-ass bitches!—and you got the audacity to show up at my mama house. All this fucked up shit in the world and he loses his life behind some nasty-ass hoes." His eyes filled with tears.

"Shut your mouth and go in the room, Aaron," his mother said.

Aaron had only said out loud what everybody else was thinking.

"Monica, honey," she continued, "I know things were not your fault, but you know how brothers and family who don't have God in their life can react. I'm sorry." She touched Monica's hand.

"I just wanted to come by and give my condolences. I'm sorry for what you have to go through. I really am. I'm going to leave, though; I don't want to build any-more tension than I already have." Monica hugged her again and made her exit.

As she was leaving, Rome, Ski, and Fat Joe came up. "Y'all a'ight?" Fat Joe asked.

"We will be as soon as they lock that simple mutha-fucka up," Angela said.

Rome told her, "Ya musta just got back."

"Yeah. About an hour ago."

The guys began to smirk. They were surprised the girls hadn't heard. "Locked up?! That kid who shot Quinn and your boy is dead."

"What you talkin' about?" Angela asked.

"They found the guy burned to death in his drop-top Benz. On the news they said he'd been shot twice, then his car was soaked down with gasoline inside and out, then torched. He was burned beyond recognition."

Monica and Angela looked at each other. They both knew Noriega had handled that shit like a real nigga—A LIFE FOR A LIFE.

Chapter One

"**O**utta this muthafucka. After four years of this solitude shit and livin' in this big-ass jungle, it's time for me to carry my ass." Black stared at himself in the mirror with a feeling of satisfaction inside—JB's facial expression as those two "nines" exploded in his face was all he needed to get back. "Who in the hell would of ever thought I'd catch that bitch nigga comin' out of Junior's, of all places? I been hustlin' these triflin'-ass boroughs, from Uptown to Brooklyn to Queens, for years and had no idea when I'd come across this nigga."

The nine shots to the head were strictly for Junie.

That muthafucka had no reason in the world to leave my brother on the side of the road with two in his head. He didn't live like that and he didn't deserve it.

"But I got him, Junie, and he knew it was me." Black's eyes watered from his past haunting him again.

Four years ago when he left, he left VA knowing the consequences if he stayed. (That Saturday night when Boot got killed and the Feds came kicking in doors kept playing over in his head.) With his crew in custody, he had only one choice: burst.

He was happy as hell when he saw Poppa pumping gas at the Exxon after all that shit kicked off. He hadn't seen Poppa in about five years—he'd been doing a bid for a malicious wounding charge.

Black had looked out for Poppa a couple times before he got locked, but nothing that would make him feel Poppa owed him anything.

He came up on Poppa and they embraced. "What the deal, Black?"

"Mad shit, kid."

"Heard you the fuckin' man, son. We catch all that shit Upstate."

"Well, did you catch when the Feds were comin' . . . because you should of called me? Shit just fell. They made a sweep and everybody fell." Black had a spaced-out look on his face. He was lost. No D, no Lo, no Junie, no moms.

"Whatever you need, son," Poppa said with a serious look on his face.

"I need you to get me the fuck up out of here—Philly, Jersey, New York—it don't matter."

"I don't have a car. This my mom's shit, and I only been home three days, Black. I don't even suppose to be leavin' the state."

"Fuck all that gay shit, Poppa. You still that same hungry-ass, young nigga that just came home and need some dough. What you gonna do? Check it—all I can offer right now is this Rolex and bracelet; after you drop me off, you can have the whip." Black knew he'd just made the right offer.

Poppa looked at the Integra and the jewels and knew he had no choice. The jewels, he could off and get dough to get on his feet, and the Acura Integra with the stash box was a blessing in disguise. Not only was this going to be a come up, but somebody had to step up and handle Black's business in his absence. "Drop you off and I'm out, Black."

"Let's go, son. We got to get the fuck outta here." Black wanted to get to New York, where he knew it would be impossible for him to be found.

Most niggas who got in trouble went to New York, but usually ended up back in VA because they couldn't cope with the streets in the big city. But that was Black's last worry. He was a hustler and he knew he could hustle any muthafuckin' where. Nobody wa'n' gonna tell him he couldn't get no money. He was built for this shit.

Poppa dropped his mom's car off and, without a word, jumped in with Black and headed for Interstate 264.

They reached Richmond and veered off on 95N; they both knew the Chesapeake Bay Bridge was a no-no for a fugitive.

Black sat back with no facial expression. His whole life was over in a flash. He had to build anew.

Poppa dropped Black off and gave him a number. "You can always reach me here. Black, I promise you, nobody will ever know you saw me, or what's goin' on. I'll let you know everything that's goin' on in VA. Just call." Poppa prayed that Black would remember this. That would be his ace in the hole.

"All right, Poppa. You are my only connect to VA. Hold me down." Black got out the car in front of the old two-story home.

They gave each other a pound, and Poppa was out, headed back to VA.

Black walked up to the door. It had been a while. But these were his peoples, so he knocked.

His cousin, Leeta, opened the door. "What you doin' here, Black?" She opened the door and hugged him. She knew from going down South to visit with her crew that her cousin was the man and all she had to do was say his name and it opened doors. She knew too he didn't fuck with New York. If he came in town it was always to Brooklyn and they would only get a phone call.

Now he was in Hollis, Queens and she knew some-thing was up even though he came across as a laid-low type nigga without a lot to say.

"Who's that at the door, Leeta?" Her dad came down the stairs and pulled the door open some more. "Boy, come on in here." He pulled Black in. "Edna," he yelled to his wife of forty-five years, "fix the basement. Earl boy here from Virginia."

"How long he gonna stay?"

Shac looked at Black, looked into his eyes, looked outside and saw no car, looked at the floor and saw no bags.

"About as long as his daddy did when he came here in a hurry many years back." His voice faded up the stairs. Shac knew the scenario—get in trouble down South; run up North till shit die down.

"Nobody's to know I'm here, Leeta." Black looked at his cousin.

"A'ight, I know you done fuck up. What you do? You can tell me." She smiled at Black. All she really wanted to know was how long he was going to stick around because she knew all he needed was a guide around Queens, and this VA nigga could get it.

She knew he was still a fuck-up, and all the bad things they said that the other side of her family was into, but it made no difference to her, she looked up to that shit.

"So where Curtis? He still hustlin'?"

"He do . . . a little bit, but he workin' some job now too. But he can still put you in."

Black hadn't been in Queens a week when he decided JB had to go. Even though he was his main supplier for years, all ties were broken. Things were bad, and the only way they could be corrected was "somebody had to be outlined in chalk."

He knew JB always visited his sister, Jacqueline, and remembered Junie saying where she lived. The rest wasn't hard—she was still driving the same BMW.

He followed her into her building and raced up the flight of stairs, waiting on her as she waited on the slow elevator. She never noticed him as he slid past her in the black hoody.

She entered her apartment and before she could shut the door, Black forced his way in quickly.

She jumped back and reached in her purse, but Black busted her in the head with the butt of the gun.

She dropped everything and stood there, only the wall holding her up. "I don't know what's goin' on, Black. I don't get in my brother's affairs."

"Bitch, my brother dead and that's all you can come up with. Fuck is you sayin'? He walked closer to her and caught her with a left jab that put her head through the plaster and a right uppercut that laid her ass out.

Darkness hit her.

When she came to, she was laying flat on her stomach, butt-naked with her hands and feet duct-taped.

She turned her head to see Black sitting in the chair holding an iron. He plugged it in.

She began to squirm and tears began to flow. It wasn't much more she could do with the rag in her mouth.

He turned the iron on high, sat it down, and walked over to her. He rubbed her hair and looked down at her. "I need to know two things: your brother's phone number and where he lives." Black moved the rag from her mouth.

"His number is 718-555-4444, and all I know is he lives in Manhattan," she said, talking fast.

"I just wanted to see if you were goin' to lie, and you did. Don't forget I know all that," he said, not really knowing.

"I'm sorry," she said through breaths. "I'll tell you."

"Too late, girlfriend." Black stuffed the rag deeper into her mouth. He turned up her stereo then he picked up the iron and snatched it out the wall. He took the extension cord and began to whip her as if she was a child.

She cried, and her body jumped with every forceful swing that cut her skin as he let out his immediate frustrations on this bitch that got his brother caught the fuck up.

"You thought this shit was a game. You thought your brother had this shit all on lock." He grabbed her feet, flipped her over, and placed the iron in the crease of her pubic hair. Right where her legs came together. "I hope you recognize right from wrong in your next life, and wherever you end up—heaven or hell—tell 'em, 'Don't fuck with Black, that nigga from The Lakes.'"

Her body jolted from the pain. He let the iron go as the foul odor of burnt flesh and her body losing control hit him in the face. He reached for the belt she had and wrapped it around her neck and pulled tightly as her wiggles slowed and her body went limp.

Now JB will feel the pain for the rest of his life, just like me. Black eased out of the apartment.

A year and a half had passed and making money in Queens was for real. Curtis had gotten killed, and Black caught two bodies, trying to survive in the game. He was used to the killings and the murders, but this borough they call Queens was a miniature DC. Niggas was dropping like flies, and he really couldn't see why . . . because they wa'n' gettin' it like that.

After that second body he left Queens, and made his way over to his Uncle Les in Harlem. Living Uptown was like no other place. Harlem was wild and took no "shorts." Cats were organized. They made paper up and down Lennox and Seventh Avenue like it was a real business. Black eased in and found work—Les had put him in with some cats as his nephew—but he was still a nobody and that's how he was getting paid.

He was a lookout for a while and thought niggas might give him a chance, but he soon realized that if these cats didn't know you since P.S. 180 you got nowhere. So he waited for the right opportunity, and his role went back to stickup kid.

Stickup quickly became murder.

Black quickly burst from Harlem, feeling like New York was closing in on him. He left so fast, he never knew that his Uncle Les paid for his bodies with his life.

Black ended up in Wilmington, Delaware, playing the streets, fucking with the strip clubs, and seeing the money potential in this new town.

This is where he ran into Polite. (Polite was in the car with his cousin Curtis when they got shot up.) He was in a wheelchair now, in Wilmington, doing his thing.

Polite had a spot over in Roosevelt Projects in Brooklyn. He ran with a team of niggas that had several blocks locked. He and Black clicked, and Black became his legs. He told Black, "After that bullshit, I'm only fuckin' with my peoples from Brooklyn."

Black stayed in Brooklyn and earned the ranks of lieutenant, only reporting to Polite. Polite tried to make him a soldier in the organization, but Black quickly let him know he only killed if he wanted a nigga dead, not because the next nigga was too scared to put in work. Polite understood.

Polite was moving much weight in Brooklyn and Wilmington. Life was all right, but the bulk of his money didn't come from drugs.

Before the drugs, it was credit cards and checks.

Not personal checks, but company checks and company credit cards. Since they moved easier down South, Polite would send Black down to NC and SC to work the credit cards and check scams.

The idea was to get bitches to use the cards. As long as the card was signed on the back, they wasn't supposed to ask for ID. Buy from one store and return to another. Company checks were deposited. A seven-grand check would clear three grand in three days and the rest two days later. This money was always good, and this was when you got your gear right.

Polite had a gold mine in Wilmington, and Black was part of it. Whipping a 2001 GS400, Black was living well, but wasn't where he wanted to be. So he began to call Poppa. Poppa would meet him in Raleigh when he went down for other business so he could kill two birds with one stone. Black would give him a brick and he would pay next time around.

Poppa knew the day would come. He'd been keeping Black abreast of everything going on in VA. Black knew Bo, a nigga he put on and taught, was running everything, but this muthafucka snitched on him and Lo to save his own ass. They never caught Black, and he was still wanted. He knew Lo got fifteen years, had done three, and was home almost a year and was scrambling. He also heard that his brother D was in Charlotte with Chanel, but they had bounced to Atlanta. He knew Chanel was always going to hold D down, but what was D doin'? Poppa had said something about promotional shows.

***

Polite and Black sat out in front of Applebee's on Flatbush in the black-tinted Range Rover, checking everything coming from the mall on Fulton. Making a U-turn in front of Junior's, something caught Black's eye and got his adrenaline running. Black couldn't believe his eyes as the baddest bitch in Brooklyn parked her Lexus truck and walked over and got in a black Tahoe.

A nigga jumped out and hollered at his man, as the woman got in the truck. Black couldn't believe his eyes, it was JB. The one nigga that had his life on hold, the one he always looked over his shoulder to check if he was there. Here he stood four cars away.

"Yo, Polite, get ready. Crucial move."

Polite became alert. He knew one thing about this VA nigga—he was ready and prepared for anything. And once in action, the thought of turning back wasn't an option. "What's the deal?"

Black pulled off slowly, following the Tahoe. He moved through traffic so he could position himself two car lengths behind. JB never even suspected the black Range.

"What you gonna do in all this traffic?"

"Fuck this traffic and fuck these New York niggas." Revenge was already in Black's eyes. He looked at Polite. "I'll meet you in Wilmington tomorrow. Jump over here niggas and use your gadgets." Black pulled back his leather FUBU coat and removed his "nines," put one in each chamber, and jumped out the truck. He walked at a rapid pace as all the other people did on the street and shortened his steps as he reached the driver side of the truck and looked JB in his eyes.

JB's eyes widened and terror covered his face—as did glass and hot bullets. Bullets pierced through the windshield and ripped through not only JB, but also the beautiful passenger that sat beside him holding his hand like lovers out on a Sunday cruise.

People yelled and began scattering. Black disappeared into the crowd and never stopped or looked back until he was able to sit down on the train. His heart was beating at a rapid pace as a feeling of satisfaction filled his entire body. He placed his head in his hands and thanked God for giving him the opportunity to close a bad chapter of his life.

Chapter Two

It was early, and Black had beat the sun up, something that happened often because of his sleeping habits. He looked up at the building that towered over him, the Fort Greene Projects. *From Forty Projects in Queens to 142nd St. Uptown, I done stomped all over this muthafuckin' jungle and made my mark.* He stared in the mirror, "VA nigga, what?" he yelled. "Muthafuckas don't know where I come from—Lake Edward, nigga; LE, baby—niggas better recognize."

He took a long, deep stare into the mirror. His eyes were naturally low, and you could hardly see his pupils. His dark skin barely allowed his perfectly trimmed beard to show. The hardness in his face came from many years of playing the streets.

"Aaron Lee Brooks, better known as Black." He stared into the mirror, thinking of a new alias. "Aka Strong." He smiled as he closed the door to the apartment and carried his bag, which contained all his belongings—two pair Timbs, two pair jeans, green cargo pants, four T-shirts, and his three-quarter length field jacket.

He jumped on the Brooklyn-Queens Expressway and headed the hell out of Brooklyn. He'd destroyed bodies and lives during his stay in New York—two in Queens, three Uptown, two in Brooklyn, and one in Wilmington.

The Delaware body was the only body that actually bothered him, because that shit was over a bitch and not business. He lost count of the bodies he left in the seven cities in VA and Richmond.

For every nigga he killed it had just gotten easier. Easier to see the terror in a nigga's eyes, and seconds later, watch the life slowly slip out of his body then be able to stand and say, "That's my work. And for any man or woman that crosses me or try to stand in my way of this dollar, will experience my work." *It shouldn't have to be like that.*

Black traveled down 495S and made his exit, headed toward Hilltop on the west side, one of the projects that was flooded with drugs. The only other projects that came close to as much drug activity was Riverside on the northeast side of Wilmington. There were other projects, but the money wasn't flowing like these two.

Black remembered when he first came, Polite was on the scene making dough, but the respect he was getting was next to none. He had a nice team of money-making young 'uns, but the real money and survival game came from the man with brains, and mad heart. Black brought all that to Polite's organization, and took him and his team to limits they only dreamed about. Now, after all this time, Polite's organization was on point and booming.

They had learned a lot from each other, but Black's stay up North was over. How was he going to tell his man, captain of the team, that he was never going back to New York? Polite still didn't have to say yes, but Black was going to throw it at him. And under no circumstances was he giving up those two bricks that sat in the stash. He was done with the boroughs of New

York and this bullshit-ass town they called Wilmington.

Black pulled into the projects. Young lookout niggas
let Polite know Black was coming before he reached the
house.

Polite was out front when Black pulled up. As always
he had on the fly shit, sitting in his wheelchair. He
smiled as his comrade parked the whip and jumped out
the GS400 Lexus, shining like the sun.

He knew Black was the reason his finances tripled
in the last year. Since he brought Black in to run everything under him, money stopped coming up short.
Niggas was paying on time and his weight had gotten
up tremendously.

Black never played with the workers or even had
conversation for them. "Finish your work and be on
time with the money" was all he demanded.

"What up, P ?" Black gave him a pound.

"You know the deal, Black."

"Strong. My name Strong," Black said sternly to let
Polite know that changes had been made since he last
saw him moving through Brooklyn at a quick pace after
murdering that nigga.

Polite had a new respect for Black; he'd seen Black
handle many situations, but what he did the other
night made him realize that Black was one of those cats
you read about in the *F.E.D.S.* magazine or *Don Diva*
that was still free and on the streets.

"A'ight, Strong. What the deal, baby?" Polite knew
niggas changed their name for one reason—to kill the
other name completely—so he never questioned the
change.

Strong stood over the once tall young man. He remembered when he first got to Queens how Polite and
Curtis would take on any two cats; two on two for any
amount of money.

"Gotta burst on me?" Polite prayed he would hear something different.

"Let me holla." Strong moved behind Polite and began pushing him from listening ears. "My business in New York is done. I gave New York four years of my life. The streets of New York saved me, taught me, and brought me back to life, but I've dreaded every minute."

Polite looked back at him. "Every minute?"

Strong smiled."Not every minute."

"I know damn well. 'Cause we can ask Sandra or Monique."

"Bitches been good to me, but you know me.

"This what's up—I got peoples in VA waiting on me; peoples in Carolina. Those credit cards and checks ain't the only thing poppin' in that tri-city area down South. Now, I'm not tryin' to stop any of this flow, I'm sayin', 'Expand.' Right now Rell and Rico are buyin' twenty kilo each. You come in and you are buyin' ten. If you buy ten more, all of your prices go down and everybody makin' more money. Right now you're slowin' them down."

"Another ten! Whoa, Strong!"

"Lot of work only in the beginnin'. Give me two to three months and I'll be moving ten ki's a week."

"You can't leave me hangin', Strong," Polite said like a sad kid.

"I'm not. You got Li'l Wayne in Brooklyn that's ready to step up; he's put in mad work and it's time. He knows the job.

"I'm gonna get everything set up down the way and I'll be back here. Plus, you got peoples up here while I'm gon' to hold you down . . . without a question."

"Kev and Kev," Polite said.

"Hell yeah, I know Kev is a live wire, but he will listen to you and I know shit won't happen while I'm gone. And Kev, you think all he want to do is play ball, smoke, fuck, but believe me, nigga, he gonna make sure he get that money first. Always."

"One thing, Strong," Polite said with a crooked smile, "you right, but Kev gots to get the fuck up out of here. He cut a kid up last night."

"What?"

"Yeah, over a fuckin' bet."

"That PlayStation shit," Strong said, disgusted.

"Yeah, I'm tryin' to get him back home."

"Queens?"

"Naw, man, our peoples from Ten-a-key—Memphis, Tennessee," Polite said, proudly reppin' his home.

"That nigga said that tattoo meant Making Easy Money Pimping Hoes In Style."

"Straight pimpin', nigga. You don't know." Polite smiled.

"Well, I'm gettin' ready to make moves. I'll carry him to VA. I got two of them things in the car. I'm goin' to VA, then to Carolina. He on his own after that."

"So when you plan on seein' me on them things?" Polite asked quickly, not really concerned about the money, but agitated that Strong could only carry Kev so far.

"Two weeks tops; aimin' for one."

"You got two of my things. I'm lettin' you burst and set your own thing up, and you can't do me this one and make sure my cousin get home safe and help us set up shop down there?"

"And what, nigga? Oh! Hell naw. I don't know shit about way down South."

"You ain't know shit about New York, but you played the concrete jungle like it wa'n' shit. I'm goin' down there in a minute; I just need my backbone and my legs down there with me." He smiled at Strong. "And don't forget, nigga, when you left VA somebody looked out for you. I know ain't nobody suppose to know and I didn't ever think I'd have to use it—but don't forget I use to fuck with your cousin Leeta, nigga, and you know pillow talk is a muthafucka. Now go get my cousin from Shana house, then carry yo' ass to VA and get your crown. You never know, you might can use his ass down there. Then I'll meet y'all in Memphis later and finish up business. But for now, he got to get the hell out of here. And since you takin' my shit and bouncin', I don't think I'm asking too much." Polite looked at Strong in his eyes. They both knew the tightness they'd shared—the streets had brought them as close as two niggas could get.

Strong pulled in front of Shana's house. Kev could barely make out the driver as he came out the apartment. As he approached the car cautiously, he checked his waist for security; his four extra pounds that he never left the house without.

Strong saw his actions and rolled down the window so he could make out the image through the tint. Last thing he wanted was to lay this young 'un down over mistaken identity. "Hurry up, shit—pretty muthafucka."

"Shut the hell up, nigga." Kev tried to pull his sagging jeans up and hold his bag. "You know I had to lay this dick down before I left . . . show a bitch how a pimp get down." He closed the door, laughing.

"Bitch cryin' 'cause I'm leavin'. Say she comin' to New York to see me. Bitch, I ain't goin' to New York, I'm carryin' this dick down South. I ain't never comin' back to this little, dirty muthafucka." Kev laughed so hard, he had tears in his eyes.

"Knock that dirt off your shoes, nigga."

"Ain't no dirt on these, fool. These fresh white ones out the muthafuckin' box."

"Can't go wrong with a fresh pair Uptowns. Never go wrong. What's in the bag?"

"Drawers, cosmetics, two ounces of raw, and my 'nine.'" Kev said it like it was nothing. "Oh and two ounces of that good green and hundred of those B's. See what those niggas and hoes know about that Ecstasy.

"I know this phat-ass shit got some secret hole or something."

"No doubt." Strong helped Kev to open the stash. "We out," he said and pulled off, headed toward the Delaware Memorial Bridge. "And roll the fuck up, you already high."

"Goddamn, it's a beautiful day. Sun shinin', skies clear, little chilly, but I'm straight." Kev passed the Wild Rum Backwoods.

"Yo, Shana did your braids?" Strong checked out the design she had freaked in Kev's head.

"Yeah! She nice."

"Don't you got two strikes, son?"

"Yeah! And I was lookin' at number three before I got in this Lex and brought my ass." They both smiled at the convenient escape.

"Got to hold that shit down, kid. You just turned twenty-one and I know you've done some wild shit in your life time and I know you done seen some money, but you ain't seen shit yet, son. And you getting ready to do life over a gee and John Madden." Strong had a frown on his face as if to say, "Are you out your mind?"

"It wa'n' John Madden; it was NBA 2000."

They both began laughing knowing it was a wild move as the twenty-inch chrome rims carried the GS400 down 13 South.

"Yo, Black, you right."

"My name Strong. Anybody call me Black know me and my past—that's a major threat, Duke."

"True. True." Kev thought about changing his name. "I ain't no killer, Strong. I caught a felony for beatin' a nigga down. I didn't know he was a diabetic. And the nigga last night, I been knowin' that nigga for years. You wouldn't believe it, but when I heard he died this morning, it fucked with me. Every nigga I've killed keeps poppin' in my head. At night a nigga be 'noid. I mean scared. Nobody knows how I fight with those fuckin' demons. That's why I stay high, stay drunk, stay rollin' off that Ectasy. If I'm not fucked up, I'm ballin'— that, or I'll lose it." Kev stared straight ahead in a daze.

Strong handed the cashier ten dollars for the toll to cross the Chesapeake Bay Bridge.

As Strong came off the Chesapeake Bay Bridge, a reality check hit him hard. *These are dangerous streets and my presence need not be known for the moment.*

The bridge ended and North Hampton Boulevard began. He made a left on Diamond Springs Road, heading toward the notorious Newtown Road. "This is LE, baby. All those apartments right there is Lake Edward West; all those townhouses behind that shopping center. See the hair salon, New York Hair Design, Beads and Bangles, Beauty Supply Store—check out that shit." Strong was taking in the changes.

"Nigga, stop actin' like this shit ain't hood. You got the Chinese spot, check cashin' spot, dollar store, Jamaican restaurant—this shit straight hood." Kev laughed out loud.

Strong made the right on Baker Road. He knew he was home. "Over here on the left, you got Lake Edward too."

"Damn, you basically got a little city of row houses." Kev smiled, realizing the potential that this little city had.

Strong never responded in no way. His mind floated back to his peoples and family. Riding by where Auntie used to live fucked him up.

As he crept past his moms' court, his heart dropped. Moms was holding the door while Auntie and Tony T carried bags in the house. His eyes watered; he knew family was everything and everything he had ever done was for family.

Kev never saw Strong's emotions behind the tinted Cartiers. Strong kept flowing through as he caught eyes focusing in on the new Lex rockin' New Jersey tags. "Young niggas hangin' on the corners not doin' shit; not getting' a goddamn penny."

"Broke as hell. We passed about sixty niggas, only ten look like they workin'."

"Shit's about to change; the bullshit is over. Yo, nigga, there's my cousin Lo. That's my ace, god-damn!" Strong wanted to jump out and hug the nigga and tell him everything was going to be all right. But he had waited four years. *What was a couple more days, if it meant sticking to the plan?* "Lo and Mike Mike." *What the hell were they doing on the corner?*

Poppa had already said Bo shitted on Lo when he came home—no dough, no work, nothing. Just a "fuck you, nigga"—after Lo put him on.

"Yo, them cats starin' real hard."

"Who? Mike Mike and Lo?" Strong smiled, showing his four gold crowns that rimmed out his front teeth.

"This what I'm talkin' 'bout, son."

Strong pulled by the packed basketball court that sat right in the middle of the notorious projects. "Don't get hype now, nigga; it's not playtime, and plus you have to get to Memphis."

"Yeah, but not today and not tomorrow." Kev was going to show Black he needed him right here.

The girls out LE were nice; young girls about sixteen and looking like twenty. Black watched him act like a kid in a toy store.

"These bitches phat as hell, and they ain't wearin' shit. Like they don't know it's fifty degrees out this bitch."

Black wasn't impressed—nine out of ten times either he, Lo, or Dee, had fucked their older sisters, momma, cousin . . . somebody.

"See the cat with the 540 BMW over there with all those gay-ass niggas around him? That's Bo with the bald head and his man, Nat. They runnin' LE right now. That's the same nigga that turned on me and snitched on Lo. I hope that nigga run was good." Strong turned his attention to some other cats. "See those niggas over there with the 4Runner, Jag, Q-45, with all the young hoes over there being grown. Those niggas from Carriage Houses right around the corner; it's not really a project, but you got mad Section 8 out that bitch. So you know how the story goes—momma don't got it, young niggas gon' get it."

"What about them niggas?" Kev asked, plotting on the niggas in his new surroundings.

"As they say, nigga, ride or die. They'll get a call from Strong and ride, or they'll meet Black and die. I don't give a fuck. I'm back with a vengance, and this is all my money. I got something for all these niggas.

"Let's go get a room and call Poppa."

"Who's Poppa?"

"That's my link, baby. He been eatin' off my plate. Bo goin' through about ninety ounces a week. Poppa only movin' half of that but risin' fast off clientele that Bo was missin'—Damn! That's my little nigga. See dude with the black Cadillac Escalade. Nigga name Javonne. Poppa said he was comin' up, usin' the same style as me. See him by himself, with only bitches around— that's what I taught that nigga. He don't fuck with nobody. Do his own thing . . . in and out of town. True hustler. Poppa say he movin' about a brick a week. One call and he'll be gettin' that brick right here."

Chapter Three

Strong headed to the interstate after showing Kev all the clubs that sat off Newtown Rd: Picasso's, Par 5, and VA's finest, Shadows, where all ballers ball. He headed downtown to the Sheraton. He wanted to run shit as they did in New York. If he could get these slow-ass niggas to respect the game and respect the chain of command, he could put Lake Edward housing on a big-city level and this run would be real sweet. He arrived at the Sheraton and called Poppa.

"Yo, who this?" Poppa yelled over the music.

"Strong."

"Who?"

"Turn the fuckin' music down."

"What the deal, Black, man?" Poppa asked, catching the voice. "Call the number back to see where I am . . . room 412 and bring dat, a'ight."

"One," Poppa said, knowing the number was local. *Was Black home or just a new cell*? He strolled to the caller ID on the cell and found the number and pressed send. "Y'all niggas, shut the fuck up—I can't hear shit," Poppa yelled to four guys standing around his Ford Explorer.

"You don't tell me shit. You from the other side anyway. Carry you' ass back to East Hastings, nigga." Mike-Mike passed the Grey Goose to Lo.

"Tell 'im, Lo."

The four guys were all laughing.

Lo took a swig of the Grey Goose. "That nigga know Buc. I'll burn his ass up quick." Then he hit his "deuce deuce" of Heineken.

"Fuck y'all laughin' at? Who the fuck is you two niggas?" Poppa looked at the two cats hanging around. "Better go on before niggas get spit on—this is fuckin' business." Poppa's face was expressionless.

Two of the guys eased away and began stepping. They knew of Poppa's reputation; the nigga stood six feet, dark-skinned and looked ruff all the time. He wore a gritty look on his face as if he was aggravated at the fact you were looking at him. His hair was cut in a short 'fro, that looked good coming out the barbershop, but it didn't get touched again until the following week. No comb, no grease, just a dry 'fro with a hellified "edge up." His baggy jeans and XXXX white T didn't do much to hide his two-hundred-and-ninety-pound frame. Conversation was minimal, and his patience was shorter than that.

Poppa was Lake Edward born and raised. His peoples had moved twice, trying to get away from the clutches of Lake Edward that kept sending young men to the penitentiary and to an early grave. Plaza and Atlantis Apartments, farther in the beach, were short stays. Not only was he still in the streets, but now he was around niggas he didn't know, and that was beef within itself. Soon they found themselves back on East Hastings. Poppa didn't care—he loved LE; LE respected him. And he was quick to let a nigga know that LE was where he rest.

When he got older he took the moves as a way of meeting new niggas from across town. Poppa would disappear for months, then resurface, go away for a year, then resurface.

It didn't take long for everybody to realize he was trouble. But he just wanted to be like all the legendary hustlers that came from LE: Big Chris, Reese, Cadillac, Black. Everybody dreamed of rising to the status of Black before his team got scooped, or Cadillac, before he started sniffing dope and robbing niggas to find himself laying face down in the gutter in the back of LE on the Norfolk side.

"Hello, hello." The voice brought him back to reality.

"Yes, where is this?"

"Sheraton downtown. Waterside."

Poppa hung up, and a smile came across his face. *This is what I've been waiting four years for. This dough I'm getting is peanuts to what Bo tearing off.*

Bo always slept on Poppa because he knew Poppa didn't know nobody to score weight, and his connect was always straight. Poppa, on the other hand, never killed Bo because of Bo's stability. Bo had learned from the best, one of Black's lt. So he rode along with Bo and plus he kept himself out of the limelight, and still made a living. But if this was the call that he'd been waiting years for, sorry, nigga, but you gots to go.

"I'm out, niggas," Poppa yelled to Lo and Mike-Mike.

"Drop us off on the other side," Lo said.

"I'm tired of this walkin' shit. I'm gonna get me a Lex with 20's like that shit we saw earlier," Mike-Mike said.

"Fuck that nigga shit. You suckin' his dick like that's your man. I done been through them shits—fuck them niggas' shit."

"You *use to have*, always talkin' that 'use to' shit, and your ass been walkin' since you came home." Poppa and Mike-Mike started laughing.

"Fuck you, son," Lo said.

That let Mike-Mike know he was getting to Lo, so he started up again. "Simple-ass nigga talkin' about when Black come back they gonna do this and that. Always talkin' about what you *use* to have. Now you a broke-ass nigga who drink and stay fucked up like me. That's why you my boy." Mike-Mike hugged on Lo. "But you know Black either dead or locked. He probably locked—that nigga was off the muthafuckin' chain."

"One day, nigga. One day!" Lo said, leaving it alone.

Lo felt bad inside. He was making a couple hundred a week. (Helping Auntie with the rent and taking care of his kids was leaving him "ass out.") Selling what Poppa fronted him was hard because his clientele wasn't what it used to be and he needed real weight to confront the niggas he did know like that. So he stayed scrambling. Nobody knew, but the hopes and dreams that Black would one day appear out the blue was the only thing that kept him looking forward to another day. To find out Black was dead or locked somewhere would have crushed his entire world, and for saying that shit, anybody else might've found themselves stretched the fuck out. But Mike-Mike and Poppa were fam. Close as childhood friends could get.

Poppa knocked on the door to the hotel room. Strong opened the door and signaled for him to come in. Poppa was used to Black getting straight to business and being out. This time was different; he seemed a little more relaxed. Poppa came in and handed Black a bag, and Black passed it to Kev.

"Kev, this is Poppa—my man and definitely part of the fam. A friend of ours." They all laughed as Black imitated the Italians. Even though it was meant as a joke, Kev got the picture.

"Poppa, this is Kev, my little brother." Poppa looked at Kev. He knew Black only had two brothers, Dee and Junie, and Junie was dead. So if he referred to this young 'un as his brother, he was to be accepted, trusted, and not to be fucked with.

They gave each other a pound and sat down.

"So what's the deal, Black? Tell me something good."

"Strong—Black is dead; nigga from the past—call me Strong. If Black show up, it's just like the Grim Reaper poppin' up." Kev laughed while he licked the Backwoods.

"This is what's good, Poppa—I'm here now and it's my time to fuckin' shine. Right now we been movin' a brick here and there, but you got clientele now. How many bricks Bo movin'?"

"About two a week . . . with the help of those Carriage House niggas."

"So after those niggas gone, they'll be lookin' at you for those things. I got to move ten of those things a week; my weights has got to come up. You along with Lo and Kev are gonna lock down LE again, the right fuckin' way."

Kev pulled on the Back and smiled, knowing Black had just included him in his plans to come up and he wasn't going to Memphis no time soon.

Black began putting things together in his head. A few more contacts and shit would be flowing like talking about it. "I just need y'all to hold down LE . . . because that shit's a gold mine. Everything will be ran out of there."

"It's a lot goin' on out LE," Poppa explained. "Different niggas doin' different shit."

Kev told him, "All that's goin' to change. If it don't come in a blue valve, then it's not sold. We not tryin' to control the city, just get our share."

Poppa listened. *Evidently Black had been talkin' to him about the entire plan.*

"I'll spend the next week settin' up shit, and then it's on. Where niggas fuckin' around at tonight?"

"Shadows," Poppas said. "Real niggas and the fake-ass ones be up in there. But if niggas movin' weight and tryin' to shine, they in that bitch."

"Well, that's the muthafuckin' spot," Kev said. "Somebody gots to get on this head."

"Tomorrow we goin' to sit down and I'll lay down the plan. So you and Lo come by here tomorrow, and we'll get this shit poppin'. Especially with this nigga, Bo." Strong stared at Poppa.

"Gotta watch that nigga, Black—I mean Strong. He came a long way; he won't be easy to get."

Black looked at Poppa and smiled, showing his gold crowns. He stared at Kev and nodded his head toward Poppa as if he didn't believe what Poppa said.

"When it's time for that nigga to be touched, he'll be touched with no muthafuckin' problem—believe that shit." Kev pulled on the Backwoods and stared at Poppa. *I'll touch your ass too, nigga. Fuck these VA niggas.*

"So the bag straight?" Black asked.

"Forty-six, exact."

"My man, I'll probably be at Shadows tonight. Come through; bring Lo. Yeah, I been meanin' to ask you— seen Carlos?"

"Yeah, man," Poppa said slowly, "Carlos be wildin' out. You don't see him that often because he on paper. Niggas say he sniffin' too."

"Coke?"

"Naw, that 'boy'! Say that diesel got him on a robbin' spree. Last I heard he robbed Tooty, his own fuckin' cousin." Poppa started laughing but tried to hold it in. "He ran up in his own cousin shit, made his girl get butt naked, lay flat, and robbed her."

Strong and Kev started laughing; Kev, because he just heard another wild story, Strong, to keep the hurt from shining through. *Carlos was his boy and he shouldn't be living like that.*

Black knew, outside of the business, many issues had to be addressed. First things first—find out what's going on with Dee; he needed his big brother to hold him down, and he needed Lo on the street close by. Poppa had held him down, but Poppa was not blood.

On top of all that shit, he had two kids that he hadn't seen in four years.

Chapter Four

The last eight months of Angela's life had brought about a drastic change. She'd just had Damien's son (he was murdered seven months ago) and was finding out what it was to struggle.

After getting pregnant and quitting school, her parents cut her off. Now she and her two-month-old baby were living with her cousin in a two-bedroom in Norfolk. Her car needed tires, a tune-up, and gas, and she was down to her last forty dollars.

Thank God her moms bought her baby anything and everything, but their relationship changed. Their conversation was short, with how she fucked up her life usually ended up being the topic. But her moms was right down the street and didn't want Angela leaving him with just anybody, so she made herself accessible.

Angela had just dropped him off and was walking into her apartment. Her cousin April was sitting in the living room drinking with a friend.

April was five foot nine with a medium frame, had brown skin and an athletic body with small breasts (about a B-cup). She wore a short cut that fit her slim face and was sitting with a butch-ass-lookin' bitch, who was wearing Timbs and a sports bra to press her titties down. "What you doin' tonight?" April didn't even give Angela a chance to set her bags down.

"Why you askin'?" Angela asked with an attitude.

"I need a little something on the rent, cuz. It's been two months and I haven't ask for shit. But I know what you doin' and you can give me something."

"Fuck is you talkin' about, April?" Angela didn't appreciate her bringing this shit up in front of company.

Truth was April hated Angela even though they were cousins. Angela had always had better opportunities in life and never took advantage of those easy roads. Even when she was shining in the streets with her ballin' friends, she never showed April love until she had nowhere to turn.

"Word is that you out there shakin' your ass for money. Glad you got your shape back real fast so you can use that money-maker, huh." April sipped on some Henny.

Angela could tell she was fucked up, and her little girl-freak friend seemed even more laid back. Even though April opened her house to her, Angela still thought she was funny and all about money, and just wanted to put enough dough away and get the hell out on her own. Just her and Li'l D.

"Before you say shit, hit this blunt." April held the blunt out for her.

Angela turned from her room and took it.

Angela had started doing private parties with Monica, but when it came to sex, she hadn't had a man in almost a year. How the fuck she got here, she didn't know. She figured she needed money and Monica was doing it. *So why not?* she thought. And she was getting dough, as she would tell it.

Angela was only doing parties across the water in Hampton and Newport News, to miss the local niggas she went to school with. She had done several parties, but it had been a minute. *How did April know?*

***

"Girl, I haven't danced in a while."

"You dance?" the other girl asked, like she didn't hear the conversation.

"Not like that."

"This is Shannon," April said. "We've been friends since middle school. She was living in DC, but she back now."

"Nice to meet you." Angela felt relaxed—no, higher than usual—after hitting the blunt. She poured herself some Belvedere.

"Your girl gone, ain't she?" April asked.

"Who? Monica?" Angela had a confused look.

"That bitch doin' more than dancin'. Niggas say she fuckin' for the money now."

Angela took a gulp of the Belvee and looked down. She was hurt. That was her girl, but she had started lacing blunts with crack, then moved to smoking right out the pipe. That was a knife in her heart. "Who said that shit?"

"Bitch, that shit true. She smokin' that shit too. Niggas out the way say she suckin' dick and all that. You better stop fuckin' with her. You ain't had no dick in a year and about to be called a trick."

Shannon smiled and looked at Angela. "It's been that long? So all you do is dance?"

"That's it—just dance. As soon as I get enough to get my own, I'm outta here."

"Carry your ass then." April looked at Angela. "You too fuckin' prissy any goddamn way."

"So you still dance?" Shannon asked again.

Shannon and April had laced the blunt with PCP, and they hit lightly and passed quick. April wanted to get her cousin and passed the blunt back to her.

Angela made the front of the blunt turn bright red and held it—she was taking in way too much.

After gulping down her drink, she began to head to her room. She stood up and the room began spinning. Suddenly she lost her balance, and Shannon was right there to catch her.

"Damn, this shit good. I'm going to get a shower."

Shannon looked at April and threw her hands up as if to ask, "What's up?"

"I'm going to bed." April smiled and walked to her room.

Angela walked to hers and pushed the door. Through a slight opening in the door, Shannon, who sat rolling another blunt, had a clear view of the mirror and stared as Angela removed her clothes and grabbed her robe and made her way to the hall bathroom.

"Hit this right quick!" Shannon told her.

"Shit, I can't stand up now." Angela took the blunt and hit it hard twice before walking to the bathroom.

Shannon sat down and poured herself a drink, waiting patiently until Angela returned. Then she passed the blunt to Angela as if she'd been smoking all the time.

Angela smoked and sipped until she sat nodding off like she was on heroin.

"So what's going on with you, Angela?"

Angela began talking with Shannon.

Shannon knew a little about Angela from what April had told her and kept steering toward her past to try and play on her emotions.

Angela was on a high she had never experienced, and as she began to talk, depression and sadness took over her mind and thoughts. Her eyes watered as she talked with Shannon.

Shannon reached out and hugged her and watched as Angela's robe began to gap and unfold. "Go ahead to bed," Shannon told her. "I'll check you tomorrow."

Angela stood to walk in the room, and Shannon followed, holding her arm to assist her.

"Girl, I'm fucked up." Angela fell across her bed, not moving.

Shannon kept talking to her and nudging her to see if she was awake. After five minutes Shannon knew she was out. She slowly pulled Angela's robe off in the dim lights and began rubbing her. Shannon couldn't believe the perfect figure that was lying beside her had a two-month-old baby. She kept rubbing her hands across Angela's breast, knowing that when her nipples hardened she would respond to what she had in store for her.

Angela felt the hands, but with the dim lights, the laced weed, and the alcohol, her judgment was impaired. Her blurred vision and the close cut of the silhouette brought thoughts of Damien. "Damien," she murmured.

Shannon took Angela's dark nipple into her mouth. Then she took her other nipple between her fingers and, at a snail's pace, massaged them both with her tongue and fingers.

Angela began to let out sighs as she tried to gain control.

Shannon let her hand slide down Angela's stomach and rest on her lower stomach. She unhurriedly took her fingers and massaged Angela's clit. The wetness allowed her long, slender middle finger to slide into Angela's warm, moist vagina. Shannon massaged Angela's spot until her body tightened around her finger. Shannon smiled as her experienced fingers roamed in and out of Angela, and Angela's legs began to open. Shannon eased down and placed herself between Angela's legs. She gradually began rubbing her tongue up and down the inner lips of Angela's vagina, then across her clit. Then she leisurely and lightly sucked, flicking her tongue around.

Angela's moans got louder, and she reached down and grabbed Shannon's head.

Shannon pushed her tongue deep into Angela's tight, hot box. Her lips covered the rest of her hole, and with no air being able to escape, she forced a gush of hot air into her vagina.

Angela's almost lost it when it was done repeatedly.

Shannon reached to the foot of the bed and strapped something across her pelvis as she greedily licked and sucked at Angela's pussy. She eased up and planted a sloppy kiss onto Angela lips before guiding herself between her open, waiting legs.

After cumming several times, Angela's head began to clear slightly. She lay there in Shannon's arms confused. She wanted to say get the fuck out and slap her dike ass, but Shannon's touch felt better than good.

The morning came quickly. When Angela opened her eyes, Shannon was standing over her, looking like that butch bitch she saw the night before when she came through the door.

"How is my girl doing?"

"Fine." Angela answered as if talking wasn't in the plan.

"You did a lot of talking last night. I want you to get your car together and get yourself together. Get some new thongs and bras"—Shannon reached down and got

Angela's panties off the floor—"this tacky shit here ain't the fuckin' answer." Shannon tossed the panties on the bed. Then she handed Angela five hundred, kissed her lips, then left.

Angela lay there fucked up and confused, but figured she'd come to a conclusion later; right now she had five hundred dollars.

Two months had passed and for once in a long time, Angela felt like she had peace of mind. Her and Monica were cool again, and that bullshit April was kicking was just that—some bullshit.

Angela didn't agree with anything beyond dancing, but she couldn't say shit because Monica didn't agree with her so-called friendship with Shannon.

Monica had become all business, and her street game was coming together, hooking up with a clique of money-making bitches, whereby all parties and engagements were set up by Queen Bee.

Queen had built a rep. If she put you down with her team, she made sure you got money and demanded that you carry yourself like a lady. That you carried yourself like money. Queen took no shorts, and, whatever a nigga desired, she had a girl for ya.

But Monica always turned heads, and this way of life was no different and it was working. She had a new used SC300 coupe and a one-bedroom condo, just to let bitches know she was handling her own.

Her crazy night-running and still trying to take classes was no joke and had begun to take its toll. Her new party drug had become something to help her cope with life—she had fallen into sniffing an eight-ball a day and not missing a beat.

Angela reminisced about their last conversation.

***

"So how's little man?"

"He's fine. With my moms and his uncle."

"Your little brother growin' up, huh?"

"Yeah, so what's the deal—is this dancin' shit gettin'
you up?" Angela asked, cutting to the chase.

"Hell naw. Just gettin' me by."

"Is these niggas still payin' you well to suck dick and
fuck?" The shit Angela had heard was fucking with her.

"Is that bitch payin' you well to eat her pussy?" Monica knew her friend got a raw deal, but so did she. And
at this point in their life, neither could really smile or
look each other in the eye.

"I don't eat pussy; I can't even touch her. Talk what
you know about, dick."

"I don't got time for this, Angela. Sometimes I believe you mad because our lives switched. We still
peoples, Angela. And I'm gonna tell you—you need to
find a man. Somebody you can chill with. And he'll look
out for you and my nephew. Instead of you and that
nasty bitch bumpin' pussies. What the fuck you get out
of that anyway?—Naw, don't tell me! Fuck it, it's your
life."

"I got more respect for myself than to sell my body.
What I can't get dancing, I guess I won't get it. Talk your
ass off. I even heard you fuckin' with Rome brother, Bo.
You done stepped into the big leagues, huh?"

"Every now and then we hook up—that nigga got
dough. If I do fuck, niggas come off a gee or better.
That's how Queen got us livin'. Broke niggas can't fuck
with it; fuck what you heard! Do your dike-ass bitch got
it like that?" Monica moved closer to Angela. "'Cause
I ain't slowin' down for nobody who can't hold me
down."

"Later, girl. Stay up." Angela watched her girl shit on her life. Her mind drifted to thoughts of Shannon. She wasn't able to defend her against Monica. *Why?*

Ever since this new relationship, Angela hadn't spent much time with her friends. She ran into Rome and he was telling her that his brother was kicking it with Monica, but he was in a big hurry to go meet his workers, as he put it, trying to sound like he was the big man.

Rome had escalated up the rankings in the hood. Ski and Quan was moving mad weight, and Fat Joe had started selling powder to some of the employees at the hospital. Rome's little clique was making him plenty money, but everybody new Rome's brother Bo was the man.

Angela got home and Shannon was already there waiting. Once inside she noticed Shannon wasn't her usual self. "What's up with you?"

"Some shit happen in DC earlier in the week and it's not safe to go back. So my sister is moving to Atlanta. I'm going to need to go down there for a while."

"What's 'a while'?" Angela's heart weakened. *Just like a nigga, a bitch come with more shit.*

"My sister knows this guy that bounce at a club down there. He say the club is very exclusive—them ball-playin' niggas and real ATL ballers. You just have to get licensed or some shit and the money is there."

"You want me to go to Atlanta?"

"Why not? Starting over in a new place may be what you need." Shannon knew she could show off this bad, young bitch that she'd turned out.

"When you leavin'?"

"Within a week."

"Shit, I got to talk to my mom, but I'm going. ATL, here I come—fuck with it," Angela said in a loud, hype voice; so many things going through her head.

Angela knew her mother wa'n' going to take the news well. But this was her life, and all the shit she'd been through in VA, she needed a new start.

Even though Shannon was talking about dancing, Angela heard that Atlanta had mad opportunity for black people and that the job market paid well. Dancing was a start. But she felt like she had more in her and it was time to get her shit on.

Angela went to see her moms, and just like she thought, she went through the ceiling.

"You not takin' him anywhere," her mom yelled. "You don't know what the fuck you want to do with your life. You headin' for a life of destruction. And what the hell is in Atlanta?"

"Opportunity and a new start. Mom, you know what I've been through. It's hard here. Maybe I need to get away and get a new start. If it don't work, I can always come back."

Her mom began to cry at the thought of Angela and her new grandbaby so far away.

Ken came from the bedroom. He'd overheard the conversation, especially when their voices got louder. He walked in and hugged her mother. He looked over at Angela. "So is your mind made up?"

"Pretty much."

"If you stay, we'll help you get a place," her moms said through sighs.

"Y'all just don't understand—I need this."

Angela's mom rose up and got her purse. She walked over to Angela. "Look, you do what you think you need to do, but you leave Li'l D here until you get your shit straight."

Angela stood with a lost look on her face, but she knew it would be much easier with just her and Shannon.

Eventually she agreed. She sighed sounds of relief as she made it back to her car. "Atlanta, here I come," she said, pulling out onto the Boulevard.

Chapter Five

Poppa leaned back in the leather seat on the passenger side as Lo pulled the GS400 in front of Mini Italia in the Newtown Shopping Center. He was in deep thought, wondering what the hell Bo wanted—Bo was still getting his dough. Poppa knew he wasn't going to say shit about the side-money being made, as deep as his pockets were. *And I ain't even started shinin' yet*, Poppa thought. He looked over and saw Bo's LX470.

"Let's go see what this nigga want," Poppa said, even though he knew he was the only one going in to talk with Bo.

Poppa knew Black—no, Strong—was back and what he wanted was going to take power moves—bullets were going to fly, and some would have nobody's names on them.

Mike-Mike and Lo followed Poppa to the entrance of the pizza shop. Poppa gave Rome and Ski a pound as he walked past them to sit in the booth with Bo.

The other four guys stood outside, involved with their own conversation. "So you comin' up, Lo; that shit phat," Ski said.

"Comin' up, nigga? I been here before; just my time to shine again."

"Hell yeah, just gettin' it back, nigga—better ask a muthafucka." Mike-Mike popped the top on the Heineken and bounced around hype as hell, expressing mad energy.

"Mike-Mike crazy, out this bitch drinkin'," Ski said.

Rome said, "Naw . . . that shit stupid. He be done made the police come over this bitch and fuck with niggas—I ain't got time for that dumb shit."

"Fuck you, nigga. Police ain't fuckin' with you. Who the fuck are you? Oh, you the *brother* of the man." Mike-Mike turned the Heineken up and downed a quarter of the "deuce-deuce."

Lo and Ski laughed.

"Pooh butt-ass nigga," Mike-Mike added.

Rome took offense to the remark but tried to play it off. He thought of punching Mike-Mike, but that would disturb business for his brother. That would make Bo flip. "Who are you, nigga?—a leech. Don't do shit, just hang around." Rome knew Mike-Mike never did shit and Lo always carried him.

"I fuck too, nigga—my girl *and* your girl. Don't forget I really know your girl."

Lo knew he was really getting ready to fuck with Rome, because he did go out with Rome's girl before.

"I know you went out—that's no secret; you was beggin'—but you didn't fuck. Don't lie on your dick, Mike-Mike."

"Never will I lie on my dick, son. I didn't fuck, but I ate her. She let me eat her two times, so next time you eatin' her, ask yourself or ask her, 'Am I doin' a better job than the mighty Mike-Mike?' She'll know what it mean." Mike-Mike held up his hands then downed the rest of the Heineken.

"You need to get control of your man before somethin' happen to him."

"Ain't nothin' goin' to happen to him. He a'ight—believe that." Lo stared Rome in his eyes, letting him know there was a difference between a hustler and a killer.

Rome played hard, but he knew Lo's credentials. He'd heard horror stories about him and Bo. He didn't want to bump heads with Lo because he knew he wasn't built like that, but he banked on Lo not wanting to bump heads with Bo. That's what made him feel like he had the edge—Bo was still the man and that's how half the niggas in the Beach was eatin', including most of the cats out The Lakes.

Poppa sat across from Bo. Bo, never a bullshit nigga, knew something was up. Poppa had been fuckin' with Bo for over two years, and after that big bust his associates had to go through, it took him almost a year to clear himself and eight months to get back. So he respected him for what he knew and the hustler he was, but Bo had snitched to save himself. Now four years later, the niggas he fucked were back and in a strong way.

"So what the deal, Poppa?"

"Coolin', tryin' to hold it down."

"I'm comin' straight at you—you was doin' a little on the side and I knew it, but you movin' mad shit without me, from what I hear."

"I ain't doin' no more than I been doin'—a brick here and there; I'm just breakin' it down a little more. Couple of young boys on this side of LE got potential. I put them on since all they were doin' were hangin' around the studio rappin', not gettin' shit, but young 'uns turn out to be hungry."

"So you buy that kilo from me, and I'll front you the same; you can front them and more dough is made for us."

"You gettin' yours, Bo. This is me. I'm a'ight."

"Naw, nigga, it ain't a'ight."

Poppa stared at Bo.

Bo stood up.

Poppa stood up.

"The way I see it," Bo said, remembering the tags on the Lex, "you done got comfortable with the New Jersey niggas. You know goddamn well them niggas come to the other side with that shit. My pockets gettin' weaker, and these young niggas doin' it with your help. You rollin' with Lo now, like he your boy. With y'all Jersey connect Lo talked you into, you and him takin' this shit back. Nigga, please . . . Lo can't run this—he ain't Black, and you ain't ready."

With no facial expression Poppa said, "I ain't tryin' to shine; I just want to get mine and eat."

"But it show through your team. I know Tech and Dundee scoring from you. Young boys comin' up and I know it's you, son."

"Them niggas work. I don't know who they fuck with. Wish I could pull them my way." Poppa knew those was his young money-making niggas, but they didn't want to fuck with Bo's snitchin' ass.

Real niggas out the way didn't want no part of him, except to rob him.

"I'm gonna leave it alone for now. Just don't forget who holdin' all this down. Don't forget who brought all these Beach niggas out the fuckin' drought and who put your ass back on your feet."

"You the one, Bo. Much respect." Poppa gave Bo a pound.

"You goin' to go in with me and sponsor this basketball team for the Lake Edward Hoop It Up? Only got a couple months before June."

"I'm straight. Got a squad," Poppa said, exiting the shop.

"Heard that, kid. I'm out. Holla!"

As everybody walked off, Bo and Lo made eye contact and never uttered a word. Rome and Ski jumped in the truck and sped off.

"Fuck that nigga talkin' 'bout?" Lo asked.

"I'll holla." Poppa was in deep thought and didn't want to discuss too much in front of Mike-Mike. He was chill and could be trusted, but when he got to drinking it was no telling what he'd say or do.

Mike-Mike said, "Drop me off Uptown. I'm going to my baby momma house."

"Sit the fuck back, Buc . . . before I tell Poppa how Rome was gettin' ready to fuck you up."

Poppa smiled. "He was gonna fuck him up, Lo?"

They dropped Mike-Mike off out Ingleside and figured to head downtown and catch up with Strong.

"Nigga know we gettin' ready to take over his shit. Talkin' 'bout, he can tell by the way niggas shinin'. Talkin' 'bout you—and I don't know how the fuck he found out Tech and Dundee score from me. Them niggas don't even shine like that."

"Shit, they came to the courts the other day in a new white Tahoe with thirty-day tags, new '99 joint. Black-ass Dundee was laid back, braided up, pushin' the Tahoe like he the shit." Poppa smirked at the thought. "I thought they were putting that money away for a studio. All Tech do is ball, make money, and spit lyrics."

"That's it—write and spit. He gonna make it. Nigga smart, him and those Street Fella niggas, damn!" Lo pulled the CD out of the side-door pouch. "Check this shit. This is Ashy Knuckles, Hannibal, Young Hop, Pop G, and Guttah did the beat. This is the hottest shit I've heard."

They sat listening to five of the hottest niggas to
come out of Tidewater and nobody had gotten signed.

"Goddamn, that shit hot," Poppa said.

"Yeah, hot as it comes." Lo turned the music down
with the remote. "And niggas don't even fuck with each
other no more; niggas actually think they can come up
on they own. Young 'uns need some real guidance."

"You right. Some guidance on life and business, not
burnin' a nigga ass up. That's part of life too, nigga.
That's part of life."

Black and Kev were inside lounging. It was still early
in their world. Poppa told Strong about the meeting
with Bo. Strong had rushed in and was slowly carv-
ing his piece back into the city. Poppa was shaping his
team and slowly building his position so, when Bo was
gone, his team would be the link to the street. And he
had Tech and Dundee. Those niggas had no idea how
large they were about to come because every worker
would be coming to them, and Poppa would be the
man, holding the title, "captain."

"Roll up, Kev," Strong said.

"Already ahead of you," Kev said smiling, with his
fronts in. He had been by Strong's side since they hit
VA, and he knew he would lock Memphis down the
same way. "Check this out—I got some cats comin'
up here, two niggas I've known for a while. Friends of
mine. They from Bowling Park but been hustlin' down
the block forever. Another nigga I know, friend of mine
from out Norfolk, he run through Norfolk and Portsmouth. Between the three I figure to move at least six
bricks a week. That means it's four bricks for the family, for you and friends of ours."

Strong had already made close to two hundred thousand in the three months he'd been back. Now it was time to really get shit poppin'.

"Poppa, your price will be twenty-one thousand a brick. I'm sayin' it now, so when I start talkin' amongst friends you know. Understand!"

Poppa knew the regular street price was twenty-four. He figured he'd sell his halves for twelve thousand, and quarters for sixty-five hundred. Take another brick and break it down. *Goddamn*, Poppa thought, *I'll see four to five off at least two bricks a week*. He knew Lo was going to move the other two. "We gonna set up LE like a fortress. Fiends from everywhere welcome. There's four entrances to LE. We'll have an apartment and row house, entering off Newtown Road, and two young 'uns keepin' watch. Let cats know every time po-po come in. Another joint on Baker Road so you can work and see popo enter at the light. Get another joint in front of 7-Eleven in Brandywine and Wesleyan and a row house on Blackpoole with the garage. Put two young 'uns out there on the corner of Baker and the Drive. The fourth and last is the easiest and the biggest outlet in the back of LE at the rail that separate Norfolk and the Beach. Gots to have a spot back there on West Hastings. We'll spend about eight thousand a month on cribs, but that ain't shit. Y'all will give the niggas titles and they will all play their position. Everybody gonna eat and eat well; this gon' be a strong and safe work environment."

"So how you plan on gettin' these cribs?" Poppa asked.

"Buy the row houses and rent the apartments. All that's covered. Y'all will have the keys in a couple weeks."

***

Lo knew what all that meant. Black talked all that business shit, but he knew Black was about putting that raw on the streets and ballin'. Only one nigga handles his business and money: D.

A knock came at the door. Lo jumped and put his hand in his waist. Kev jumped and put his hand behind his back. "Calm down; it probably them cats I spoke on."

Strong opened the door, and two dudes walked inside.

"What up, my nigga?" The guy came through the door, giving niggas pounds, then grabbed Strong, showin' love.

"What up, Black?" Mont smiled. It was good to see a nigga that had been hustlin' as long as he was and still shining like he on top.

"They call me Strong now, Mont," Black said sternly.

"A'ight. I'll call you goddamn Saddam, long as the numbers right."

Everybody laughed.

"This my brother Grip."

Grip gave Black a pound and threw his head up at the other niggas.

Mont and Grip was going to hold down the NE side of VA Beach. That left the SW side that connected to Chesapeake and NW side that connected to Norfolk for Poppa, Lo, and Kev to hold down.

"When we hook up, this is a taste of what y'all will be fuckin' wit." Strong threw a bag on the table.

Mont picked it up, put some on his fingernail, and touched his tongue. He knew his powder. When most niggas was hustlin' "hard" like his brother, his clientele was white folks. Mont was a thug to no end. No secret about where he come from—gold in his front, loud when he talk, almost intimidating because of his five foot eleven, 280-pound frame, looking like he ate weights. He started lifting when he first started getting locked up. He never stopped getting in and out.

His brother Grip was slightly taller, slightly smaller, but cut as if he ate weights also. He wore house shoes and white T, while Mont rocked all that designer gear.

Mont handed him the bag.

Grip took his nail and scooped some. "What this shit stand?"

"Maybe two. I suggest one," Strong said.

Grip sniffed it and lifted his head. Then he stuck out his chest and shook his head. "A one, nigga; be real." Grip stared at Black.

"I don't care if you put a six on that shit, long as you give me twenty-three thousand, five hundred a brick— five hundred for your smart-ass mouth."

"Come on, man," Grip said smiling, "you can do better than that fuck."

Kev told him, "Fuck what, nigga? This ain't no bargainin' table."

"I just made it one, muthafucka."

"Twenty-three thousand, five hundred, muthafucka. Done!"

"Twenty-three thousand, five hundred, and it will stand two, guaranteed." Strong tried to gain control of the situation. He was depending on these niggas' dough. They were going to buy three bricks a week, seventy gees a week like clockwork. Niggas wa'n' livin' like that these days.

Another knock came to the door, Strong peeped through the peephole and opened the door.

In walked two cats. One was a young boy, and the other looked about Black's age. Young boy was wearing a Rocawear jean suit with butter Timbs. To set it off, he rocked a long, white gold necklace and bracelet. The other cat was a husky nigga with a 'fro, wearin' Levi's, Polo shirt, white Reebok Classics, no jewels, and when he spoke he showed two gold fangs.

Strong turned to everybody and said, "This my nigga, Speed."

Poppa's head snapped in his direction as did Lo's; they both had heard that name before. This nigga was a true street legend, and the treacherous shit he'd done spread throughout Tidewater.

"What the deal, Mont?" Speed gave him a pound.

"Not a thing. Same old shit. When you start fuckin' with this shit here? I thought you only fuck with 'boy' (heroin)?

"This shit is in demand too—I fuck with the money. You ain't tryin' to share, nigga. Make a nigga come and take y'all block." Speed smiled a wicked smile toward Mont and Grip. They knew he was serious, but they smirked it off.

Speed turned toward Black. "So what the fuck you got, Black?"

"Strong. They call me Strong now, Speed." Black was firm, to let him know he wasn't joking.

"I don't know Strong; I know Black and that's who I supposed to be meeting. Now go get him."

"These joints twenty-three, five apiece. This is it." Black handed him the packet.

Speed handed it to the young boy. He took a twenty out and did a one and one then shook his head, looking in Speed's direction. "Thorough, son. Whoooo!!"

"How many? Three?"

"Next week."

"Yeah!" Black was hoping Speed got down. Lot of cats didn't fuck with him because they were scared. He had a hell of a reputation and was somebody you didn't want to go against.

Black stared into his eyes as they negotiated. Speed had the upper hand because he knew he could flip the whole bird and get quick money.

Heroin was his thing, but he had folks, and he loved the hustle, the grind, the streets, and doing dirt was in him. That's why Black was trying to bring him in. He knew in no time he could get Speed buying four and five bricks. He had the money and he knew the people.

Black knew he was a dangerous nigga who had mad bodies and never got locked. What Speed didn't know was that Black's count was running neck and neck, and one more would make him no difference.

Speed agreed.

After burning a couple Backs and pouring some Henny, niggas broke out. Poppa, Lo, Black, and Kev still remained in the room.

"A'ight, Poppa, Lo, y'all know Bo plannin' to get y'all. If he don't, it would really surprise me, so let's hit him. Time to handle this shit."

"If you don't get Rome too," Poppa said, "he gonna come back."

"No, I got plans for Rome first. Then his girl. Then Bo will fall. Feel me, Lo?"

"No doubt, fam. Please, let's do this."

"Look, if I say, bring me a nigga, however you have to do it, bring me the nigga alive and bring him to Balview, out Ocean View. It's a house that sit up on a hill. Got a basement and all. Eight thirty-two is the house number—don't forget . . . because I need Rome soon as possible. One other thing, Lo—call Dee and find out where he at. We out of here tomorrow. I need my brother."

Lo knew already. He knew Dee was going to lose his mind, just like he did when Black and Poppa came up in the poolroom. That time, he thought he'd seen a ghost, until he rubbed his eyes, focused in, and realized it was for real. And when Black handed him the keys to the Lex, he knew his cousin was back and this was not a dream.

Mike-Mike didn't have shit to say that night. All he knew was that his man was back on top—new whip, new gear, and a different hotel every night. After four years, the good life had made its way back around.

Strong, Lo and Kev broke out the next day, headed up 58 to 85S. Six hours later, they pulled in front of a cute ranch-style home in the city of Charlotte, NC. Strong hadn't seen Dee in four years, and his stomach was sick from excitement. Once Dee was by his side, he could find peace of mind on some aspects of the business.

He saw the Mazda Millennium in the driveway. They parked and knocked on the door.

"Who is it?" the voice asked. She pressed her eye to the peephole. "Black," she yelled, trying to get the door open. She couldn't believe her eyes. She stood there, her eyes wide and her mouth open.

"How you, Chantel?" Black asked.

"Fine." She gave him a big hug. She had nothing but love for this man. She reached over and hugged Lo, who she'd only seen once since he'd been home.

She had love for Black, but she knew from his attire and the tinted black S500 with thirty-day tags that he was back and getting money.

"Dee not even here. He's in Atlanta handlin' business. He's down there more than he's here."

"What he doin'?" Lo asked.

"Promotin' shows. Bringing artists to Atlanta. Not doin' bad either. He just catch attitude when niggas try and shine and act like they the shit. He say he hate caterin' to these fake-ass niggas tryin' to play gangsta." She laughed.

"Why don't he do shows here in Charlotte? They say the money here since y'all got the pro teams and shit. Ain't this where all the money at?" Lo asked.

"Dee don't like it here either—he say Charlotte ain't shit, but a good place to live when a nigga retire."

"That's Dee," Strong told her. "Got his own way he see shit."

"He's a spoiled-ass nigga with a bad attitude. He just want shit his way and he ain't gonna do shit he don't want to."

"I don't know. I think some of that's changed. The way he struggled these last couple of years, he will do what he don't want to." She made it seem like Dee was getting soft. Black didn't like the comment but realized that Chantel had the right to say anything she wanted.

She'd been through hell with Dee. One time he got fucked up with another bitch and the girl died, and everyone looked at Dee as if it was his fault, even though he was left fighting for his life. Chantel had taken a leave of absence from her job in Charlotte and came to Virginia to take care of this nigga, then took him to Charlotte when she was no longer able to stay, but continued to nurse him back to health.

"No, he don't have to do shit he don't want to and he will be all right." Strong didn't give a fuck how she took it. "You got a number to reach him?"

"Yeah, 770-671-****. And if you miss him, Ken-Ken can reach him; his number is 404-323-****."

"Ken-Ken from Kappatal Kuts?" Black said to himself out loud.

Lo said, "That's the only Ken-Ken I know that he would fuck with."

Chantel looked on as they all climbed in the Benz and drove off. *Black still that cool, black-ass, money-chasin' nigga.* She knew her life was about to change.

Why was her stomach turning? Why did she feel uneasy? Black was home. Wasn't that good?

"This suppose to be the shit," Lo said as 85S changed from a two-lane highway to a six-lane.

"ATL, dirty muthafuckin' South," Kev yelled. "This where niggas from Memphis come and ball."

They searched the radio until the banging sounds of Outkast came pouring through. Black picked up the cell and pressed one—he had already programmed Dee's number in his phone.

"Who is this?" Dee answered.

"What up, man? Where you at?" Black asked, as if they'd talked earlier.

Dee knew the voice, but this couldn't be—his brother was gone, locked up, like so many people said. Others said and wished he was somewhere dead, but Dee hoped and prayed that neither was true. His hopes and what seemed like a fuckin' dream sat in the back of his head. His life had been fucked up for the last couple years. He was bowin' down and fuckin' with nothin'-ass niggas, compared to the niggas he'd fucked with in the past. He fell to nothing, fuckin' with bitches and really truly depending on them. Then these niggas he was getting money with was fuckin' him and lookin' down on him as if he was some needy, beggin'-ass nigga. But Dee had no choice—it was either get down or drown. Many days he wished God would allow him to never wake up. He prayed for it, but it never happened. And by the grace of God, he was still here for his brother's return.

"Oh my God. Yo, son—what the fuck?" Dee yelled, the eagerness bringing tears to his eyes. He never thought he'd hear this voice again. "Where you at? VA?"

"Naw, Duke, I'm tryin' to find you. Me and Lo on 85 South, headin' into Atlanta."

"Hell yeah!" The anticipation made his stomach turn. Dee tried to give directions, but the words came out scrambled. "Look, stay on 85 South and take 285 toward Decatur and Stone Mountain. Then take I-20 toward the DEC and get off on Candler. Make a left and then you'll see KFC on the right. Pull in there. Hurry up, son." D yelled like an excited child.

"One." Black smiled and looked over at Lo, laid back, sipping on the pint of Hennessy he got before leaving Charlotte.

They pulled in the KFC parking lot, and Black instantly noticed the '94 740iL sitting in the parking lot, looking run-down and dirty, with a dent in the driver side door. "I thought I told him to sell that, Lo?" Black said, thinking out loud.

"You did. He hard-headed, always want to do what the fuck he want to do," Kev said, repeating what he'd heard earlier.

They all laughed as they got out the car.

Dee climbed out on the other side of the BMW.

"I'm tired of this shit." He planted his feet on the ground. "Fuck niggas hit my shit and kept goin'."

"Hit my shit and kept goin'," Black said as they embraced. "Told you to sell that shit."

"I needed something to drive."

"Yeah, it could of came back on you. Gotta listen sometimes, man," Black whispered as they hugged, so it could only be heard by him.

"So what up, nigga?" Dee punched Lo.

"You know the deal, cuzzo." Lo and Dee embraced.

"You back on yet, nigga?" Dee asked.

"Like you wouldn't believe, fam. Couple more steps and we'll really be back."

"Who dis nigga? Gotta be fam, if he rollin' with the clique." Dee looked at Kev.

"Kev, man." They gave each other a pound.

"So welcome to the ATL home of Jermaine Dupri. This shit is off the hook, Black."

"His name Strong now," Lo told Dee.

Dee laughed. "Strong, Black, whatever. Nobody don't know you down here."

"Is that about to change? Is the ATL ready for Strong . . . because I know goddamn well they ain't ready for this VA-bred, LE-raised, muthafuckin' Black." Everybody started to do the LE yell. Even Kev, who was loving VA about right now.

"So what you got goin' on here?" Strong asked.

"Promotional shit. 3E Entertainment—that's the company name. Doin' this shit, the object is to get in with the local radio personalities and you in there. This deejay here is Frank Ski. He runs the city. If he say it's bond, it's bond. His word is law like the Buda Brothers.

"Then they got this girl, Mama Chula, who's just like the girl Chris Caliente on 102.9. If they deejay the party, it's packed because of their name and reputation. These clubs here hold more people, and if you do a show you got five million niggas to promote to. How can you lose?"

"A'ight, I hear you. Now what would it cost to bring one of those rap niggas out?"

"Yo," Kev said, "we can't talk about this somewhere else? This shit don't look all that hot; let's get the fuck out of this parkin' lot."

"For real. I don't even know where the fuck I'm at," Lo added.

"Shit, I'm ready to put something in the wind and start rollin'," Kev said.

"Fuck you know about rollin', nigga?" Dee asked.

"Roll with the best, nigga." Kev pulled a small bag containing several Ecstasy pills.

"What kind you workin' with? Let me see one."

Kev handed Dee the bag.

"Aol, D & G, 007, tweety birds. I see, son, you got plenty. Let me see what these D & G feel like." Dee popped one and handed the bag back.

Kev reached in the bag and popped one before putting them back in his pocket. "Yo, kid, that's twenty."

"A'ight, I got you," Dee said. "Roll with me and twist one up."

They climbed in the car, headed north on Candler Road. By the time they reached South DeKalb Mall the trees was in the air and Fifty was blasting through the speakers on a Clue mix-tape.

"Thought you would have it on one of these stations playin' that Down-South bullshit."

"It's a'ight sometimes, but some of that shit is a headbanger. I got a six-disc changer—Jiggah, Mr. Cheeks, Mobb Deep, Foxy, Jaheim and Clue, son." Dee pulled on the Backwoods. He turned into an apartment complex much larger than the one in VA, but not bigger than The Lakes (Lake Edward).

Dee jumped after Kev, while Strong and Lo found a spot. They followed Dee to the second floor, where they went inside a spacious, two-bedroom apartment and sat down. When Strong and Lo saw Dee put his key in the door, they knew this was his shit.

"Roll up, somebody," Dee said, going into the kitchen.

Lo had already grabbed the remote and turned on the TV and started fuckin' with the stereo.

The bedroom door opened, and out walked a shorty in sweats, bra, and wife-beater. "Hello," the dark-skinned girl with shoulder-length hair said. She walked to the kitchen.

They all looked in her direction in time to see her extremely phat ass jiggle with every step through the sweats. She hugged Dee and turned around with her arm around his waist.

"This is Tricia. Tricia, this is Kev, Lo, and Black—I mean Strong."

Her eyes widened. "Your brother? It's like I know you, Black. Nice to finally meet you. You too, Lo." She turned to Dee and placed both her hands on his stomach. "I'm goin' to take Krystal to my mother's; I'll be back about nine." She kissed him and walked into the other bedroom.

Moments later she returned with a little girl. "Krystal, that's Uncle Strong, Lo, and Kev," Dee said. "That's my muthafuckin' family and yours too."

The three-year-old just looked.

Strong looked at the cute little girl and thought of his own. He also noticed the look in Tricia's eyes when Dee spoke or hugged her. *What was going on here?*

Dee locked the door when she left. "Shorty a'ight." He looked at Strong.

"We can see that. She got peoples and I mean peoples that look like her, phat as hell just like that? Goddamn!" Lo said.

"He ain't lyin'," Kev said, laughing on the low. "And that shit startin' to kick in too."

"That's how they come in the ATL?" Lo finished off his Hennessy. "We got to go to the liquor store before it close; it's almost nine."

"You ain't in VA, nigga. These liquor stores don't close early like that."

"Where Tricia from?" Strong asked. "I know she from Up Top."

"Jersey, son."

"I know. I been up there with that shit for four years; I caught the accent."

"Damn, let me call her and tell her to bring some Henny and Alizé so we can sip on some thug passion. She'll drink that too."

"Me too," Lo said. "That's my shit."

"Bitch drink. You don't mix shit with Hennessy, bitch-ass niggas." Kev laughed. "Thought you hung with troopin'-ass niggas, Strong?"

"Tell 'em, Kev. Fuckin' up the Henny—I don't know them muthafuckas."

Tricia came in about ten. The time had flown by as they sat around catching up on everything and everybody. Tricia decided to call it a night. She knew the boys had to catch up on a lot of things that she wasn't entitled to hear.

Dee excused himself. He went in the room to shower, but Tricia had other plans.

"I need some help going to sleep," she said walking into the shower.

They hugged, kissed, washed each other, and dried off. Dee laid her back and raised her legs. He'd been fuckin' with Tricia for three and a half years. He didn't only know how to make her feel good, but he knew how to make her cum.

And tonight she came quickly. She was out before he could clean up, throw on the Polo jeans, new white T-shirt and Timbs, and squirt on some Black Jean Versace cologne.

"Let's roll. I know y'all niggas ain't tired. Atlanta don't shut down at two on Thursdays. Let's go finish talkin' business, then we'll catch dessert."

They all jumped in the 500 with Dee driving. He adjusted the seat and was admiring the wood grain. *Goddamn! This is a fuckin' car.*

They jumped on 20 East, headed back into Atlanta, to 285 North to GA400. He kept the Benz floating for about twenty minutes, which only felt like ten by the time they reached Exit 5, heading into Sandy Springs.

Dee turned into some townhouse type apartments. "Come on." Dee opened the door. The condo had three bedrooms. Dee closed the room doors and walked into the kitchen. Off of the kitchen was an office. "This is my office, son. This is where I put my deals together." Dee stopped in his tracks, looked at Kev and whispered, "Damn! I feel good as shit."

"Nigga, I'm over here about to jack my dick if I don't get around some ass," Kev said. "Can we make some money down here, kid?"

"No doubt. I know mad bitches that get down. Next trip down, everybody rollin','" Dee said. "Get shit rollin'."

"Shut the hell up, nigga, talkin' yo' ass off," Lo said.

"Well let me finish talkin' about this business shit," Dee said, directing his conversation to Strong.

"So how you makin' money right now? Who financin' this shit? How much you gettin'?" Strong asked all at once.

"I'm gettin' like twenty percent of the profits, usually around five to six thousand. Niggas Ken-Ken know, VA cats, down here doin' their thing."

"Can I smoke in here?" Kev lit the Backwoods.

"Yeah, but go in the room on the left. She don't like smokin' in her shit. She don't like it around her daughter; plus, she a substance-abuse counselor."

"She need to come out here and go to work," Lo said. We all started laughing and walked in the room.

"This my room."

The room contained a couch, a chair, TV/VCR, and a smokeless ashtray. Lo and Kev stayed, and Strong and Dee walked back to the office.

Black saw that Dee had a computer, scanner, printer, and fax, all the necessities to run a business. "So this is all the promotional shit? You in with the radio peoples?"

"And I'm makin' all the connects and gettin' invites to the big parties. Ball players, rap niggas, their managers—I go straight to the source. I have special guests show up at parties. I make niggas thirty gees, and I walk away with five."

"That's why I asked how you was livin'? Five gees every couple months, girl in Charlotte, bitch in Decatur . . . Who shit is this? And where the fuck we at?"

"Vianna, and we in North Atlanta."

"You got three bitches, the car look like shit, but it's still rollin', yo' gear half-decent—not off five gees every couple months."

"There's a kid down here from VA. He live on the West End. He had niggas comin' down, makin' company checks off big corporations, and even printin' credit cards by the same big company. We would get bitches to deposit them, hit them off, and pick up some change. Dude sister work for Bank of America. She get him credit card numbers and his man make up the credit cards, Visa. Sign it and they aren't suppose to ask for ID, but you know how that goes. That's why I try and get my shit in a bitch name—them hoes get away with murder. Buy today, return tomorrow. Shit ain't steady, but nigga got to do whatever.

"I was fucked up, son. Chantel gave me money to get down here. Vianna gave me dough earlier to take care of some shit. Gots to give that shit back Saturday.

"I got a show tomorrow downtown, 201 Courtland. Local cat you never heard of, but he went gold down here. Cat live in Florida now. Special guest Big Boi from Outkast. Shit will be pack. Thirty thousand will be made."

"It's some money down here . . . street money?" Strong asked. "Because VA is locked and I'm gonna come through Carolina and then Memphis."

"Memphis?"

"I'll explain when we go. Right now I need you to come to VA and set up everything, work houses, stash house, company shit. Do your thing tomorrow for those niggas, and we out early Saturday."

Dee didn't know exactly how established Black had gotten, but after Black laid his entire plan down, Dee saw the light.

"Black, fuck Atlanta. This is a place for livin'. Do dirt in VA, SC, NC, and even Tennessee. Let me do my thang here, and we'll take this promo shit to another level. It's a lot of clean money here, and to be a millionaire in ATL is a man's muthafuckin' dream. Let's make it happen, son."

"Well, tomorrow's show is the last show you will do with niggas outside the family. From now on we'll finance our own shit. If thirty thousand come in this bitch, it's ours—fuck them niggas. So next time a show is done, it's being brought to you by Triple Strong Entertainment."

Dee thought about his brothers—Junie, D, and Aaron, three strong cats. They gave each other a pound.

"Tomorrow's a new day, Dee. Beginning of a new life." Strong smiled at Dee. "Last run was all right, but this time we going to shine amongst the stars, my nigga."

"Amongst the real stars. Believe that." Dee smiled.

"Feel that 'X'?" Strong asked.

"Hell yeah. I need some trees." Dee went to the room with Lo and Kev. "Pass it, nigga."

Kev was laid-back, fucked up. Lo was still sipping on the fifth of Henny and had just tooted up damn near a gram.

"Don't get dead now; we out in a minute." Dee pulled on the Backwoods, passed it to Strong and made his way to the other room.

"What up, baby?" He jumped on top of Vianna.

"Stop. I'm tired. You know I can't go back to sleep when you wake me up."

"I don't give a fuck," was Dee's response as he ran his hand from her arm to her leg and to her ass and gently massaged it.

"I said no, Dee."

He pulled the covers back and slapped her on her ass. "Come meet my peoples. Throw something on."

"Meet who? And I know you aren't smokin' in my den."

Dee was Vianna's man for three years. When she first met him, he treated her like a queen. She was from a well-to-do family of six, and he was a street nigga from VA, running from a past that took her over a year to find out about. He was hard and harsh at times, but when he loved, every moment was like a fantasy slowly being played out.

He got his money in the streets and swore he was never getting a job, and on top of that he stayed high— two things she said would never be in her life. Yet this nigga had a key to her house and car. Dee ran the streets a lot, and it did leave her lonely. If it wasn't for her girlfriend, she would've lost her mind a long time ago.

"I'm smokin' in the room. My day been goin' good; don't fuck it up with all that bullshit, god-damn!"

Vianna sat up in the bed, her eyes watering as she spoke. "I was just sayin' I don't like no street people comin' here smokin' and—"

"Look, love, have I ever brought anybody to your house since I met you in the three years I've been fuckin' with you?"

"No." She wiped her face.

"If I smoke, don't I go in the room?"

"Not all the time." She stared into his eyes.

"Lately I have, but look my brother and cousin out there."

"Black and Lo?"

"Yeah. Slip something on." Dee stared at her golden brown legs and small, manicured feet sticking out of the purple silk shorts with matching top. He grabbed her by the back of her long, black, curly, wet hair, pulled her head back, and kissed her gently on her little lips. "Hurry the hell up." Then he poked her and said, "Brush your teeth—your breath fuckin' me up," before he returned to his peoples.

They all walked to the den. "What up, Kev?" Dee asked.

"Here, nigga." Kev passed him another X pill.

They turned when they saw the beautiful figure appear. She had brushed her hair back in a ponytail.

"What up, baby? This Black, Lo, and Kev; fellas, this is Vianna."

"How you all doin'?" She opened the refrigerator. "Would y'all like anything?"

"Naw, we all straight," Strong told her.

Then Lo said, "Shit, got any turkey sausage or something?"

"Hold tight. We goin' by Krystal's on the way out." Dee picked up the keys.

Kev looked at Strong. *Damn, that bitch fine. Hope she got some peoples.*

"So where you from, Selena?" Lo asked.

We all smirked, thinking this nigga stupid, calling her the girl from the movie.

"I'm from Texas, but I've been in Atlanta for a long time."

Kev asked, "So what, you Mexican?"

"Mexican and black, baby."

"I thought your ass was Filipino," Lo joked.

We laughed, and she had a look of curiosity on her face.

"If you were in New York people might think you Puerto Rican," Strong explained. "In VA we grew up with Filipinos, not Mexicans."

Vianna stepped in front of Dee. "You comin' back tonight?"

"It's up in the air. Showin' these niggas the ATL."

"Call me." She kissed Dee. "I'm gonna say goodnight. Hopefully, I'll see you all tomorrow or today. Nice to meet you, Kev, Lo, and I'm happy you're back with your brother, Black." She reached out and grasped Black's hand. She knew the deal, this was the brother of the man she loved.

Vianna had faith in Dee, but she'd heard enough "if Black was here" stories every time his back was against the wall. She walked into the room, fell into deep thoughts, then drifted to sleep.

***

"Spark up," Dee said.

Kev lit the Backwoods and coasted onto 85S. After riding for about ten minutes, they took an exit and went past the bus station.

"Where we goin', fam?" Lo asked.

"Can't you see, fool?"

Everybody hyped up when they saw the bright lights that read MAGIC CITY.

Lo, in ignorant form and fucked up, sipped on the Henny. "This shit packed. I hope we ain't have to walk a country mile or GA mile—whichever one longer."

Black, nice from the Henny and weed, was nowhere near fucked up, and Dee and Kev just felt real good in the car, talking their ass off.

Dee pulled up in front, parking the car in VIP. Security walked up. "What up, Dee?"

Dee jumped out and put a fifty in his hand. "Put my name on the list for tomorrow; other niggas got that baby." Dee walked away. They knew him from promoting the shows, but balling and handing out fifties, it was like WHO DAT NIGGA?????

Dee knew he wouldn't be there long. Strip clubs wasn't Black's thing. One thing Black didn't know was these bitches got naked. There was forty naked bitches walking around, titties and ass everywhere, different shapes and sizes, and they carried themselves like ladies with a sense of self-worth, even though butt-ass naked.

Kev had two beautiful-ass, naked bitches giving him a dance fit for a king. In an hour he'd spent two hundred; Lo, about eighty. Dee had given two girls twenty dollars apiece and spent his time talking, hollering at two girls he knew, on some business shit.

Strong had given two shorties fifty apiece. They'd talked and danced for him the entire time without hesitation. When they were leaving, they broke their neck to give him their numbers. Dee knew then that Strong would be coming back.

Lo asked Kev, "Get any numbers?"

"Hell naw. I gave them bitches mine; they gonna call me later."

"Them hoes ain't callin' you, fool. They got your money to carry to the mall. Bitches gonna be in Lennox tomorrow with your dough." Dee laughed along with Lo and Strong.

"Them hoes gonna find a way and call my long-distance number; I'm from Memphis, nigga—I was born a pimp." Kev got in the Benz.

They pulled off toward Peachtree.

Dee leaned over to Strong. "How we livin', son?"

"Real good, and my plans is for us to be millionaires in this fuckin' game, son—within six months."

"Get a room down here?"

"Get a *suite* down here, nigga."

Dee and Strong were sitting in the room talking when the phone rang. It was about 4:00 A.M. Lo was on the couch 'sleep, and Kev was sprawled across the bed.

Lo jumped up and handed Dee the phone. "Yo, Dee, tell them hoes where we at."

Half an hour later, four of the baddest young women walked in. Two was sniffing with Lo, and two was smoking with Dee and Strong. Kev had invited them over and they couldn't wake him up. He was out.

Chapter Six

Poppa turned on to Lake Edward Drive. *I hope they don't have no roadblocks out here today, checking shit. Thank God.* He turned on E. Hastings and stopped about fifty yards from where niggas was making their dough.

He took the paper bag that contained twelve grand. "It's straight, right?" He looked over at Dundee.

"No doubt, baby." Dundee, most of the time mistaken for having a look as if he was runnin' game, spoke in his low, cool voice. "This shit is gone, man; we need more." Dundee said it like he was complaining.

"In just a second, you'll have all you need, then we'll see what the fuck you gon' do."

"You already know I'm ready, son, or you wouldn't be fuckin' with me." Dundee smiled, gave Poppa a pound, and jumped back in the truck with Tech who was already on E. Hastings.

Tech looked at the guys that crowded the corner. "Look at all these niggas, son. I gather it's about thirty niggas out here, and three makin' money—need to clear this shit out."

"Let a couple bodies drop and we'll see the difference in the morning." Dundee palmed the gun that sat in his waist, a reflex action that came with the talk of murder. "But you drop a nigga who the shit, think he bad, and got mouth. Don't kill Pee-Wee—he gettin' it out here— or Scotty—he keeps Pee-Wee under control and keep his mind on money."

"And that nigga Rome serve both of those niggas," Tech said. "So it's only one way to get them to come our way—ask 'em."

They both started laughing as they drove off in the white Tahoe and threw up peace signs at the young cats on the corner hanging out. Some of the young boys hollered they name.

The rundown row houses, dirty sidewalks and parked cars made the road seem real narrow for two cars. As Tech and Dundee approached Lake Edward Drive, Rome, Ski, and Fat Joe were turning on E. Hastings in Rome's new Ford Expedition. Rome's eyes caught Tech's; Ski's eyes caught Dundee's.

Dundee began quoting:

"Come with me, Hail Mary
Nigga, Run quick see, What do we have here
Now, do you wanna ride or die?"

"Hold tight," Tech yelled. He tried to grab Dundee, but it was too late. He was already halfway out the truck. Tech then slid his hand under the armrest and gripped the chrome .45.

Rome slammed the truck in park and, in one swift motion, opened the door, and pulled his nine. He began shooting, shattering the Tahoe's front windshield.

Dundee came from the right side of the truck and shot Rome in the shoulder. Rome's gun fell.

Ski had positioned himself out the passenger side window and ended up catching two from Dundee, the bullets ripping through his head and neck.

Rome, meanwhile, had fallen on the truck, and two more shots from Dundee's gun left him lying on the cold pavement.

Dundee looked down at Rome, never bothering to pay attention to the LX470 that was behind the big Expedition. He felt the bullet shoot through his arm as Bo let off shots from the two black nines he held tightly, one in each hand. One gun fired shots through the windshield of the Tahoe, the other in the direction Dundee ran, until he disappeared into the back alley.

Bo ran up to his brother. Blood covered his abdomen, thigh, and shoulder, but his eyes were still open. "Come on, baby. Please hold on."

Fat Joe jumped out the back. He'd been down on the floor from the time he saw Dundee. He looked at Rome on the ground gasping for air, then over at Tech sitting up in the driver side of the Tahoe. Even after nine shots to the head and chest, he never slumped over. Niggas say he loved that Tahoe.

Bo yelled, "Fuck you doin', Fat Boy?"

Fat Joe looked at Ski and grabbed his stomach, throwing up.

The police sirens drew closer.

"Fat Boy, go get some help, muthafucka!" Bo kicked the truck hysterically.

"Somebody already called 911. I'm out—I just came home last week." Fat Boy went to stand on the sidewalk, his body trembling.

Dundee ran inside, holding his arm. "Goddamn, this shit burnin'." He grabbed the phone and dialed Poppa. "Yo, shit just popped off out the Lakes. Don't go out there. I'm headed over to Bayside."

Poppa heard the doorbell ringing and knocks banging in the background. "What happened?"

"Hold on." Dundee reached under his couch and pulled out his shotgun. He pulled his curtains back and saw Teisha, his baby momma.

"You drivin'?"

"Yeah. What happened?"

"I'll tell you in the car. Let's go to Bayside."

"Poppa!" Dundee climbed in the Honda Civic.

"Yeah. Talk, nigga!" Poppa said impatiently.

"Me and Tech was out the Lakes after you dropped me off. Rome, his clique, and Bo blocked us in and jumped out. I got a couple of them, and I think Tech, Rome, Ski, and Fat Boy dead. I don't know. Bo had two burners blastin' on me and I barely got away."

"Fat Boy and—" was all Teisha could get out her mouth before Dundee signaled for her to shut up.

"A'ight," Poppa said. "I'll holla back." Poppa knew he would catch the real story later out the Lakes.

"Now what was you gettin' ready to say?"

"I was tryin' to tell you that Rome ain't dead and Fat Joe was in the back on the floor. He didn't get touched. Ski dead, Tech dead, and the house next to the end, on the right, the lady's son got hit while playin' PlayStation. One of y'all niggas shot through the window. His momma was out there screamin' until the paramedics had to calm her down. They out there saying that the lady saw you and know you, and was talking to the police."

"I didn't shoot through no windows, and I didn't jump out first—fuck her! That was Rome punk ass."

"Don't matter. I just want you to know what Poppa gonna hear out the Lakes, so get your shit straight." Tiesha was young, but she knew guys died everyday. And she didn't want her baby daddy ending up dead.

She reached the emergency room.

"Why you didn't park?"

"I got to get home—my moms babysittin'."

"Park the fuckin' car. You goin' with me; yo' momma will be a'ight. I'll give her something later, shittt!"

"You gonna stop talkin' to me like you fuckin' crazy. You coulda got one of your other bitches to bring you up here." She got out the car.

"Keep talkin'. You in the right place to be runnin' your mouth—they can admit your ass real quick."

"You can call me later with all that bullshit you talkin' . . . 'cause I'm goin' home—you ain't admittin' me no-where, muthafucka."

He put his good arm around her neck. "Shut the hell up. When I'm done, I'm gonna call you to come get me, so stay by the fuckin' phone."

Chapter Seven

Dee woke up to Tricia pushing her ass against his dick. *Damn*, he thought. He had just fucked when he came in. He knew them niggas had a good time with them shorties after he'd left them at the hotel and took the drive back to Tricia's crib. He felt like chilling, but he knew he'd be leaving for VA soon and wanted to give her some time.

After taking that Ecstasy he wasn't only ready to get freaked, but he was ready to suck titties, eat pussy, suck toes, lick ass. He smiled and put his arms around her. He was glad he had her to come home to. Vianna would've woke up, fucked, but no freakin'. And the thought of going to Chantel's house at three in the morning tryin' to fuck was out of the question.

Tricia was different. She appeared to be ready all the time—maybe not all the time, but he couldn't remember her ever telling him no.

The movement of her full, soft ass on his now-hard dick had him starting to move himself. He reached down and rubbed her thigh and ran his hand to the back of her left knee, and the left leg came up, giving him the perfect position to slide into a world that felt like a fantasy. He'd never felt a woman so soft, her body melted into his while he squeezed her in his arms.

***

Tricia didn't have the schooling and degrees that Chantel and Vianna had, but she had common sense and could relate to a man's struggle and mistakes. She also knew that the small things mattered, like cooking, bringing a glass of water, keeping a clean house—everything to make a man feel like a man. And she worked full-time and raised her daughter, never missing a beat when it came to him.

He pulled her tighter as his body began to let loose.

She pressed her ass against him and squeezed her pussy to drain him of every drop, then turned to him and kissed him. "I love you."

For Dee it was hard. He loved Tricia and Vianna, but his feelings for Chantel went much deeper—you could say borderline unconditional.

Tricia walked to the bathroom and returned with a wet, warm bathcloth. She wiped his dick thoroughly as he laid back happier than life.

His brother was back, he had a show tonight, and he had the support and an abundance of love from three strong, black women that made him feel like a king; women that any man in his right mind would kill for.

He leaned over and pulled his phone off his pants to call the hotel.

Kev answered the phone. "What the deal?"

"Nothin', fam. Where Strong?"

"In the bathroom."

"Tell him I'm headed back that way."

"A'ight." Kev walked to the bathroom. "He said drive the Beamer."

"A'ight, one!" *Why the fuck he got me driving that old-ass, raggedy shit? Got a new Benz and I still got to fuck with that shit.* Dee complained, but nothing had changed—when Black said do something he had his reason and meant what he said.

Dee showered and got dressed. Tricia had to be to work at nine, so they left out together.

When Dee arrived at the hotel, Black was in the restaurant eating breakfast.

"So how much we need down for a new Beamer? And how much a month?—I know you checked."

Dee smiled and said quickly, "Eight thousand down and trade-in worth twenty-five thousand, leaves us financing fifty thousand."

"Don't smile, nigga. We ain't got no real dough yet, but let's ride and look at one."

After eating they climbed in the car and shot up to Sandy Springs.

Dee had already checked out a new one with the dreams of getting two shows back-to-back and making the ten gees. Then the next move, without hesitation— put it all on the whip. Dee learned early that the status you put out there for self could put you where you needed to be; the rest was up to the hustle in your ass.

They pulled up to the BMW lot on the corner of Roswell and Abernathy. "Check that shit out, second from the left." Dee pointed and smiled.

They walked over to the BMW.

"What up, my brother?" the car salesman said, walking out with keys to the deep-burgundy 750iL, V-12. See you made it back."

Dee asked, "Same deal still on paper?"

"Ready! Pass me some dough and the title and we're in business."

Dee got the title out the car, and they walked into the office for Mike, the car salesman, to do the paperwork.

After about half an hour, Mike returned. "All I need is to call your job and get verification and some recent pay stubs."

Strong looked at Dee, hoping his brother was still on point.

Dee picked up the phone and called Vianna at work. "Hello."

"Yes, Ms. Gonzalez, this is Arthur DeAndre Brooks. I'm trying to purchase a vehicle, and they need job verification and a copy of my last paycheck voucher. I have a fax number."

"Dee, I'm tied up right now," Vianna said. "I'll do it in a little bit."

"Yes, I need that done ASAP, thank you."

"Dee, I can't, right now."

Dee got up and stepped outside of Mike's office. "What the fuck! I can't really talk in the office. I'm up here now gettin' ready to get my shit and you jivin'. Goddamn! Take twenty minutes and do this please."

"All right." Vianna slammed the phone down.

Selfish-ass nigga. When he need me I'm suppose to jump, but when I ask him, he always too busy or broke. And he know this shit takes more than twenty fuckin' minutes.

Dee and Strong were outside sitting in the four-door burgundy whip, sitting on aluminum rims, with a slight tint.

"So where you find out about dude?" Strong asked.

"Through you, nigga. You remember that nigga Ant from Portsmouth you use to fuck with back in the day?"

"Ant? The only Ant I know fuck with that diesel."

"Run with that nigga Lou from Tidewater Park. Well, I seen him at the strip joint. Kicked it a minute and the nigga was pushing a new 745il, and those shits ain't even hit the fuckin' streets. Got him a mini-mansion down here and everything. I got the nigga number."

"Gotta holla at him before I get out of here. He mighta came up. Really came up. Shit . . . I use to serve his peoples. He always been a hustler. Run hard. Last I heard he was sniffin' boy and robbin' niggas."

"Shit!" Dee said. "He must be robbin' a lot of niggas, because dude livin' well."

By this time Mike came out and let them know everything was a go.

Dee and Strong pulled off the lot in the new '99 BMW. When Dee pulled onto GA400 and punched it. "Hell yeah, nigga! Love you, man."

"I know, nigga. Let's get Lo and Kev. Go get the 500 and get to the mall. I can tell you need some new shit." Black handed Dee two stacks of hundreds and fifties equaling up to about five gees. He knew his brother had been through hell; scrambling around just like he was in New York. "Take care of your business here, man, so we can get outta here tomorrow. Find Ant number too."

"You got gear? That shit tonight at 201 Courtland is dress, son."

"I'll get something, but if Lo and Kev can't get in with Timbs and jeans, you know they ain't fuckin' with it."

After leaving Lennox Mall, Lo and Kev wanted to check the Underground that they'd heard so much about. Dee had to go handle business for the show, and Strong strolled along.

"Slow down, son. I got proper ID, but I ain't tryin' to use it."

"Bet. Just enjoyin' this shit. Damn near forgot how this feel. I got to pick dude up at the airport at seven, and this traffic gettin' ready to get fucked up."

Dee got on the phone and called Tricia. "Can you get off early today? Look, go home and I'll pick you up in twenty minutes."

When he arrived Tricia was pulling up in her '88 Dodge Aries, with smoke coming from under the car like she needed to be stopped. She saw Dee driving the new 750 BMW, and a wide smile came across her face. She climbed in and poked her lips out for Dee to kiss her.

Strong and Dee both knew public affection was a no-no, but Dee kissed her anyway.

Strong knew this bitch had his brother. *Why not? He seemed happy with her.*

Dee turned into the Jeep lot.

Strong shook his head smiling. "Dude said with your credit and job, you could get that blue joint with a *G* down, right?"

"Yeah." Tricia smiled from ear to ear.

They got out and walked inside.

Thirty minutes later, Tricia was leaving the lot with thirty-day tags, looking fly as hell in her new, little four-door truck.

"I got the show tonight; I want you there. Here's five hundred. Get you something nice. Real nice. Show niggas who this VA nigga really is. Oh, and get some shit for the crib so I know y'all all right while I'm gone. I'm out tomorrow."

The wide smile disappeared. She knew her man was on his way back up and there was no way she could stop the hustle. She knew from past experiences, when you fuckin' with a street nigga, it's dough, the streets, and you—in that order.

Dee and Black headed toward the airport to pick up the night's featured artist.

"Yeah, on paper this nigga cost fifteen gees, but he used to hustle in VA back in the day with Dre. You know dude in the wheelchair from Up Top? So you know I hollered, got in contact with his manager. Half that.

"One day I want a phat-ass crib here. Then I can take niggas by the house. Real niggas we know. Most niggas in this lifetime don't even know I got a brother."

"I'm about that paper, Dee. It's always been 'get this money and have a good time,' but now it's 'get this money carefully and smart, then live good.' I know Ant got that diesel."

Dee told him, "We don't fuck with that shit—goddamn heroin!"

"Yeah, I know. I just want to holla."

"I hear yah. I already made that call. He'll be at the club tonight."

Strong gave Dee a pound. As always they were on the same page. "This ain't a bad city; it's relaxin', and it feels mad peaceful."

"Man, I thought I was the only muthafucka that felt that shit. This shit is relaxin' as hell. Like you ain't got a worry in the fuckin' world."

They arrived at the airport and picked up the artist and his manager. Dee had reserved them a suite at the same hotel they were in.

"This one wasn't bad," Dee said walking into their suite.

Kev had hooked his PlayStation up to the hotel television and was smoked-out, and Lo was tooted up and sipping on that Hen-dog, playin' NBA 2000.

"Usually niggas flow with an entourage and need a thousand things. All that nigga asked for was a bottle of Moët, two boxes of Dutch, and an ounce of that good green and he straight. And he'll leave for the club when we head out for the club."

"How they goin'?" Lo asked. "They got any ice on."

"Bitch niggas better get they ass in a fuckin' cab." Kev looked at Dee and pulled out his bag of X. "Yo, big brother, how you feel?"

"Good, son, but I'm about to get better." Dee took one with some orange juice.

Strong passed him the Backwoods.

Dee took a long drag, "Usually I rent a limo, but it's only two niggas. And what's better than pulling in front of the club in a new 740 and a new 500?"

"Yeah, but I've seen some shit down here."

Dee told him, "And you ain't seen shit. Wait 'til to-night. Niggas comin' out with it. See, in the ATL you got ballin'-ass niggas battlin' with those music niggas and those professional ballplayin' niggas. Everybody tryin' to live like they got ballplayin' money. But a lot niggas got dough."

"Should be plenty of bitches for every muthafuckin' nigga who want to fuck, all these gay-ass niggas I seen," Kev said. "Me and Lo went roamin' around today; we seen gay-ass niggas everywhere.

"ATL got the largest population of gay black men. They come in packs. They say that some gay niggas like to act like thugs. They put gold fronts in they mouth, loose jeans on and white T's, like they playin' thug, but all along they want to pack meat in they ass. Kev, please tell me you don't pack meat. Oh Lord!" Dee yelled out, laughing along with everybody else.

Dee looked at Kev seriously as Lo and Strong looked on. "Check this, little brother. I want to tell you two things, and remember your big brother told you this. One—always be yourself. Fuck the world if they can't adjust. If those bullshit fronts were you, they would be permanently attached. Two—never fuck with a bitch who can't do shit for you. I mean, really hold you down and got her shit together. Fuck with shorties that got credit, credit cards, bank accounts and good credit, not those bitches who let niggas in their past fuck their shit up with cars and cribs. Hoes like that, you know their past and where they been. So what type of bitches you think you gonna attract with those bullshit fronts in your mouth? Nigga, I will never tell you nothin' wrong. Promise you that."

Dee went to shower and get dressed. When he returned he stepped wearing beige slacks, dark brown Cole Haan's with a gold buckle, and a dark-brown button-down. He changed his clear eyeglasses to some slightly tinted Ralph Lauren framed glasses.

"Now, what kind of bitches am I gonna attract?" Dee grabbed the Backwoods and gave Kev and Lo a pound. "Hurry up, Strong. Got to get to the club so they don't fuck up my money.

Strong came out wearing black, wool, pleated Coogi slacks and a black Coogi sweater and some black square-toed Prada shoes, set off by a stainless steel Breitling timepiece, not to mention the clear, platinum-framed Gucci glasses.

"Somebody, pop that nigga collar," Lo said.

Dee looked at Strong, thinking how his little brother done stepped the club gear up.

"I clubbed a little in the city," Strong said, checking his gear.

"These niggas jigged the fuck up," Kev said without his fronts, smiling and revealing the prettiest set of white teeth.

"I got on Dickies, new white T and new Timbs— shit, I'm dressed," Lo said.

They headed over to the club. When they pulled in front of 201 Courtland, the line was already forming. The artist jumped out of the S500 driven by Dee. Strong was in the back chilling, sipping on Henny XO, and smoking that Gandi the artist had requested.

The artist's manager decided to roll with Lo, wanting a toot before his night got popping.

Dee felt good. Not only was he in control of the night's show, but this was the last time fuckin' with niggas outside the family.

"Yo, I forgot to tell y'all something," Dee yelled over the music.

They all leaned in.

"Being it's so many gay niggas down here, it's an abundance of females. They always outnumber us— this shit gonna be off the hook."

Security tapped Dee on the shoulder and talked in his ear.

Tricia was there with two friends. They all had the fellas' attention when they flowed in. Tricia walked up and hugged Dee.

"Heah, Strong," she said smiling.

She continued, "This is Lo, Kev, and Strong, and these are my girlfriends, Kay and Sheronna."

Black stared over at the back room where the artist was relaxing. Lo was bouncing around with two Heinekens.

Kev stared at Dee. They were both feeling the X. Dee cut his eye at Kay, telling Kev that he probably could, knowing Kay liked pretty-ass niggas.

"Let me get y'all a drink," Kev suggested, and of course, they agreed. "We'll need to get a bottle and pop some champagne so the head can get right."

"Tell them to bring it to the table," Dee said as he guided them to the back room that had couches, tables, and its own bar.

As the club began to pack, four females walked to the front, cutting line. "Don't act like you don't know who the fuck I am—I got most of y'all niggas money in my pocket," Peaches said. Her crew started laughing.

Dee saw them and signaled for security to let them through.

"What up, Dee?" Ecstasy asked.

"Coolin', baby," he said kissing Ecstasy, Peaches, Star, and Diamond, four of the baddest bitches ATL had to offer—faces perfect, bodies perfect, nails, hair, and feet, all done to perfection.

Dee met these girls when he started doing shows. They worked at Strokers, a gentleman's club. They had approached him, letting him know for any stars that wanted real women, they were his connect and he always got a kickback.

Out of nowhere Ant came strolling up, hype, giving security and the owner pounds. He gave Dee a pound and stared down the clique.

"Do me a favor, Ant—see the girls to the back so they can meet the artist. Yo, Black in the back too."

All these bitches had tight bodies, Dee thought, *but not one of them had shit on Tricia.*

Everybody who had VIP was in the back room behind a rope—Lo, Kev, Strong, Tricia, her friends, the artist, Peaches and her crew, the investors and their team and their girls. For every bottle the investors bought, Lo and Kev got a bottle with Strong's nod. The artist lit a Dutch, which triggered a chain reaction. The investor team lit up, Kev lit up, and the party began. The artist's manager told the girls that Kev had that shit to get you "rolling" and Lo had that "soft." Before long the VIP was banging.

The investors wondered who these cats were. They could tell Strong was the money because of his attire, style, and how Kev and Lo ran shit past him.

Two of the girls who were supposed to be working the artist, Diamond and Star, made their way over to Strong and Ant as they kicked it about Tidewater and the early 90's.

Ant saw the investors and his team order four bottles of Moët. He called the waitress who was taking Lo's order. "Bring two bottles of Cristal for me and my man, some glasses, twenty shots of Henny, ten 'thug passions' for all these hoes, and ten Heinekens."

Lo signaled for the waitress to cancel his order.

"Show these Southern muthafuckas how VA niggas get down." Ant gave Strong a pound.

"They don't know." Lo let out the "LE yell," rolling his tongue with the *L* and letting the *E* flow. Then he took his T-shirt and wrapped it around his head like a turban.

Strong knew he was now fucked up. *No matter where you carry a Lake Edward nigga, he'll be LE to the heart, 'til he ain't breathin' no more, never steppin' out of character for nobody.*

Dee came back to the VIP followed by Ken-Ken. They grabbed glasses for the champagne. "You remember my brother Strong," Dee said, allowing Strong and Ken-Ken to give each other a pound.

Ken-Ken swore his name was Black, but he knew his face and reputation. Him and Ant knew each other from school, growing up in Portsmouth, and Ken-Ken knew his reputation. Ken-Ken didn't hustle, he was a barber and a cool-ass barber, known for cutting all the hustlers' heads and was a made middleman, fitting in and never responsible for anything.

Dee grabbed the L from Kev and introduced Ken-Ken. "This is my cousin Lo, and this my little brother Kev."

"I ain't know you had another brother."

"He was too young then; now he think he grown, hangin' with the big boys." Dee punched Kev lightly in the chest.

"How you feelin'?" Kev asked.

"What?" Dee had a wide grin.

Kev reached in his pocket and pulled out his bag.

Dee grabbed two. "I want shorty to try this shit at least once."

Kev handed him another one. "Give this to Kay for me."

Dee pulled Tricia away from the crowd. "You a'ight?" He passed her the Backwoods.

She hugged him. "Yes, I'm wonderful."

"Things gettin' ready to get much better. Hold me down, and I'll always play fair and be here."

"You never have to worry." She stared into his eyes. Her tongue ring just took sexiness to another level.

"Yo, try this."

"What is it?" She took it from him.

"X—so you can say you tried it and you won't ever try this shit with nobody else. I wouldn't give you shit to fuck with you."

"They were takin' them earlier. Kay and Sheronna wanted to try one too."

"Well, Kev said to give this to Kay. Give it to her on the sly—no more freebies." Dee watched Tricia walk away, and the way her ass shook with every step. *Goddamn*!

Dee was standing beside Kev in the crowd while the artist put on his show. Kev told him, "It's some hoes in here."

"It's like this everyday all day and night in the ATL," Dee replied. "But you know, hoes or not, Strong can adapt to any environment. The nigga changes with the times. He has no choice." Dee looked around for his brother. He knew Black was wanted by the Feds and had been running a long time. That's why he never questioned Black about the way he wanted to handle things, like his own security, and anybody that jeopardized that, without a question, would rest forever.

Tricia, Kay, and Sheronna came up. Tricia stood in front of Dee, allowing her ass to rest on his lap as she danced to the artist.

Kay hyped her up and egged her on, both high off the weed, drunk from the thug passion and champagne, all while rolling off the X. Kay stood in front of Kev with her jeans so tight, Kev saw every curve in her perfectly shaped ass.

Kev touched her waist and pulled her to him. He knew she was on it, he had to make sure nothing else pulled him in. She was phat to death, and with him rolling and her rolling, the touches between the two became very arousing and intense as they moved around as one.

Dee knew the deal—Tricia kept turning around, talking about how good she felt. Dee tried to hold his eyes open and calm his racing body down. *Damn! I feel good as shit*, he thought.

The artist finished, and they escorted him out the door. The 740 made the escape back to the hotel, carrying Kev, the artist, and his manager, followed by Peaches and her team. They got to the hotel, Dee and Kev headed to the suite after giving pounds to the artist and his manager.

Moments later, there was a knock at the door. Kev jumped up, and Dee laid a magazine over the 'dro he was getting ready to roll.

"Who the hell is that?"

"Strong and Lo wasn't leavin' the club, right? Ain't we goin' back?" Kev walked to the door.

"Yeah! I'm goin' back, then I'm headed to the Dec and catch up with my baby."

"With-my-baby, gay-ass nigga."

Dee knew he sounded soft, but he was talking about Tricia and didn't give a fuck.

"Yo, it's those hoes," Kev said in a low voice.

"Who?" Dee walked over and peeped through the hole and opened the door. "Fuck y'all doin' here?"

"They ain't doin' shit. Just chillin' one-on-one and Star said she had to tell Kev something."

"Fuck you got to tell my little brother?" Dee said as he finished rolling. "What y'all get out of them niggas?"

"Thirty-five hundred." Diamond gave Dee fifteen hundred. "Ecstasy and Peaches in the suite gettin' tip money."

"Y'all did good. Five hundred apiece for comin' to the club and makin' a nigga feel like he famous and shit." Dee lit the Backwoods.

The night was a success. He'd made forty thousand and he'd pocketed eight gees and he made money with his girl clique. They always hit him off and showed their appreciation for letting them in on the stars he brought in. He never worried about them cheating him, because they knew for a nigga to get four bad-ass bitches in Atlanta to replace them was easy as picking up the phone.

Diamond moved closer to Dee. "I'm tryin' to get my tip."

"Girl, you better double up on Kev," Dee said seriously.

She rested her body against his, then grinded her pelvis against his dick.

He ran his hand down her back, slowly down her spine, to the nape of her back. He rubbed the thin, soft material that clung to her ass to reveal every enticing curve. He felt the thong and followed it from the top until it disappeared into the crack of her ass. His dick was instantly hard.

She backed up and removed the dress and stood on the bed in just the lavender thong. She turned around and began to make her ass jump. She then faced Dee on her knees, pointed her finger, and signaled for him to come closer.

He approached her.

She unzipped his pants and pulled out his dick. She ran her tongue across the tip.

He thought he was going to scream.

She slowly took it in and sucked like a pro.

Dee looked over at Kev, he was putting on a condom getting ready to throw something in Star, who had her knees planted into the couch with her red ass high in the air, exposing all her love, which gave Dee's dick some extra stiffness.

When they finished tricking, they threw the girls two hundred for their tip. They burst out and headed back to the club, where Lo and Strong were in the front by the 500 with two shorties.

"We headed to Tricia's. I got to go find my baby Kay." Kev pulled up by where Lo and Strong were chillin'.

Strong smiled. Lo was sitting in the passenger side, head laid back, eyes shut, fucked up.

"Yo, we out nine o'clock," Strong said.

"Bet. I'll holla," Dee yelled.

Kev threw up the peace sign headed toward Decatur.

They arrived at Tricia's. Candles were lit up and she had just gotten out the shower.

Kay was on the couch smoking. "Where the fuck you was with my man?" she asked Dee, grabbing Kev's hand.

Dee and Tricia started laughing.

"We'll see y'all in the morning." Kev smiled and went out the door. Kay lived in the same complex.

It was nine o'clock on the nose when Kev and Dee pulled in front of the hotel. Lo and Strong were already ready to go. "Gotta stop at Vianna's, and we out."

"Following you."

They left and ran by Vianna's. She was up cooking breakfast while her child looked at cartoons, already dressed.

"What's going on?"

"Fine. I'm going to Northgate Mall, then I'm going by Barnes and Nobles down the street to find a couple of children's books and pick up my book club book of the month."

"What type of bullshit y'all readin' this month?" Dee asked.

"Actually, we're taking a different turn, instead of the norm. Somebody suggested we try one of those street novels. The girl said it was 'hard' street—you might enjoy it, something you might relate to, 'cause I can't. It's called *My Time To Shine* and it's about the streets of Virginia."

"Fuck readin'—somebody need to write a book about
me and my family's life and the hell we been through.
That's a goddamn story. Best fuckin' seller. I'll look at a
movie, but fuck readin' shit."

"Do you know how you sound?"

"I don't give a *f-u-u-u-c-k*."

"I'm also going to stop by my job for about an hour.
Are you gonna be here when I get back?"

Dee looked at her hating that he had to leave. She
was being sweet, not fussing and that's when she had
his heart.

"Naw, I got to go to VA."

She looked startled because she knew VA was off
limits, he had his moms there, but he was in and out,
never a day. "How long?"

"Couple weeks. Putting some things together." He
reached in his pocket. "I need to put this in the business account." He gave her two gees. "And this is your
two hundred and eight hundred for you to buy yourself
something. He pulled her to him and hugged her.

She squeezed him tight.

"Walk me out?" Dee turned to her daughter. "And
you be good."

They walked outside.

She saw the Beamer. "Ummm, oh! When were you
going to tell me? Damn, that's nice. So my baby doin'
his thing." She moved closer. She knew this was Black's
doing. She just bowed her head and said a silent prayer.
She hugged Dee and whispered in his ear, "I love you.
Please be careful and call me soon."

"I will, and you be good." He started up the 740.

"You know you don't got shit to worry about," she
said with an attitude as if he'd said something real stupid.

Dee didn't ever worry about another nigga getting no pussy. It took him a second to find out she really fucks off her emotions, so another man never crossed his mind. Women were another story.

Dee met her four years ago, but she had chosen an alternate lifestyle. They were friends and they did business together, but the last three years something clicked and she was all into him, but she always said if it didn't work out she was going back to "The Life."

He watched as she made her way back to her door. "Boy, you just don't know."

"Naw, nigga, you fuckin' your pimp game up. You really care about your girls; you ain't no playa." Kev laughed.

"You right about that, my nigga. You right about that."

Three hours later they pulled in front of Chantel's house. Dee walked up and went inside. "Y'all, hold tight. Let me make sure she straight.

"Chantel!"

"Heah, baby?" She wrapped her arms around him. "You have company with you?"

"Yeah, my peoples."

"Hold on. Let me go put on something." She put down her books and went into the bedroom.

Chantel was the woman—strong, confident, and sexy as they come. He watched as her large breast moved in slow motion through her shirt and her nipples got hard and poked through. He could feel his soft penis begin to erect.

He looked as the T-shirt clung to her full, low-cut panties. Her body was not soft, but toned, her breasts large with thick, dark nipples.

He went to the door and signaled for them to come in. He walked into the room.

She had removed her shirt and was leaning over to come out her panties. Dee grabbed her, hugged her and gave her a kiss.

She kissed him, then pulled away and got in the shower. "How things go last night?" she yelled loudly from the shower.

"Fine. I came off a'ight—five gees."

"I heard that. You know you got shit to take care of. You got two tickets and a fine that gots to be paid. You charged six fifty on the VISA and we need to put that four hundred in the mail like yesterday for your child support—before they pick your ass up. All that come to about twelve hundred."

"I got that."

"Well, big money, you got five hundred for my maintenance? It's time. I need four hundred for my credit card bills and a thousand for shopping." Chantel laughed. She spread more lotion on her body.

Dee walked over. He put lotion on his hands and began spreading it on her back.

She turned around.

He took her large breast in his hand and placed her nipple in his mouth.

"Stop, they in the livin' room."

"So? they ain't in here."

"Dee, you better—"

He laid her back and put her clit between his lips and sucked, his tongue flicking across her clit lightly. Ten minutes of strong sucking, licking, flickering, heavy panting and she was squeezing his head between her legs.

He eased on top of her, allowing his dick to slide into her soaking wet, extremely warm pussy. He closed his eyes in ecstasy without being on Ecstasy. He pumped in and out with a feeling that you only get from new pussy and love.

She moved her body with his every stroke. As her body began to climax, she brought her legs up and back so that his strokes would rub against her clit, her vagina grabbing at his dick, pulling.

His body began to tremble, as the greatest feeling in the world raced from his feet to his head, and went numb.

They got dressed. Dee laid three thousand on the dresser—all the money he'd made. He knew this shit was coming back, running over. He had to handle his shit and make sure she was okay before he burst.

Chantel smiled. She knew this was the work of Black. Dee never had no extra, not like this . . . except for when she met him. Now she was getting ready to lose him to the streets again and she couldn't take it.

"I got to go to VA."

She knew this was coming.

They walked outside. She spoke to the same team that had knocked on her door two days ago.

Strong held up her book. "So how much longer?"

"Another year and a half and I'll have my doctorate."

"Bachelor's, easy; master's, real hard. This shit here is a whole lot of writing. Sometimes I want to say fuck it, but I came too far."

"Don't we know," Dee added.

They all walked outside.

She shook her head at the new BMW with Georgia tags.

He gave her the keys. "I'll be back in a couple weeks. You know I'll call you." He kissed her. Then they climbed in the 500 and were out.

"I know she get lonesome down here by herself," Kev said.

"She work and go to school full-time. She don't give or take out too much time for nothing else . . . including me."

Dee loved Chantel more than anything. She had proven she would be there through anything, but she never catered to his every need. But she was always there.

She dished sex out as if it was a bill, once a week if that. But he understood. She was caught up in her studies and work, *but goddamn*!

Even though Vianna and Tricia were wonderful women, Dee felt without Chantel, his world would definitely crumble. He couldn't make it without her and didn't want to try. She inspired him, gave him that "get up and go," and the thoughts of giving her the world was what kept him striving hard all these years. Her dreams were his; his dreams were hers—she was his world.

Chapter Eight

Where the fuck is Shannon? Angela stood in front of the MCI Building in Alpharetta, GA (some say North Atlanta). This was the third time this week she'd been late. *She knows I want to go home before I go to the club.* Angela began to walk up the sidewalk in the heels and hot pants suit. *This is some bullshit.*

She came down here with Shannon, but she got the money together to get the apartment, dancing. Now she got this job during the day. *Shannon's not doing nothing, but running her car in the fucking ground. I know she's going to give me that "got-caught-in-traffic" shit. I'm going to start keeping my shit. Then she'll really be stuck.* Then she saw her car pull around the corner. She climbed in.

Shannon headed toward 400S. As they made their way down 400, the traffic was bumper to bumper. "I ran into that shit, tryin' to get to Exit 9."

"Should have left earlier. You got more time, and I'll be drivin' my own shit."

"Come on, chill." Shannon put her hand on Angela's leg. "You hungry?"

"Yeah!"

"What you want?" Shannon was talking like she had money.

Angela noticed the new sweatsuit, sneakers, and headband and the bulge in Shannon's pocket. She reached down and grabbed it. "Where you get this?"

Before Angela could get it out, Shannon slapped the shit out of her. "Bitch, don't you ever."

Angela yelled, punching Shannon.

Shannon grabbed her hands, trying to stop her— *Bam*!!!!! They ran into the back of a Chrysler Concord.

"Now look what you did. What the fuck we goin' to do?" Shannon yelled.

"What the fuck am *I* going to do? I'm the one that got to get to work," Angela said with tears beginning to fall down her face.

Traffic began to back up. They got out the car to assess the damage. There was no question about whose fault it was—Shannon received a ticket, and the car was towed away.

Shannon and Angela were dropped by the tow company closer to home. Then they caught a cab from a wreckage company off I20. The cab cost twenty-two dollars by the time they got to their apartment on the West End.

Angela walked in her door. "How the fuck am I going to get to the club? I'm late, but I damn sure can't be a no-show, I'll get fired."

"We'll catch a cab and figure out all this transportation shit later."

They arrived at Strokers at nine, two hours after Angela was supposed to be on the floor at seven. She quickly changed, tooted her two lines, and headed for the floor, wearing light-green, skin-tight shorts that left over half her ass hangin' out.

She strolled out and glanced around. Many had their money in hand, giving her the signal. She caught glimpse of a fifty and the knot he tried not to expose. She eased her way over. Her large firm breasts barely swayed, but her ass bounced with every movement. She began to dance sensually and removed her shorts.

By the time she left that table, two hundred was made off two songs. *Those were real niggas.*

Her night was about to end when Shannon pulled out a twenty, and Angela came over and began to dance.

Shannon knew she had Angela, but she knew Angela came from a man's world and she always had one. But she made her feel for a woman—that she knew would be in Angela forever. She also knew Angela was about dough. She looked into Angela's eyes as Angela stared back slowly moving her body to the music. Shannon loved the twenty-one-year-old young woman she turned out. She was all Angela knew about the life, and she was planning on keeping her ass in eyesight and locked down.

Angela slid her pants on, gathered her money, headed for the dressing room. A dark-skinned brother grabbed her hand. "Please dance for me?" he said, holding out two fifty-dollar bills.

She could see the gold crowns on the four front teeth. In just that one sentence, she also knew he wasn't from GA.

She began to dance.

Shannon stared. *When her time was up she always flew off the floor. Why did this nigga catch her attention? How much did he give her?*

Angela couldn't keep her eyes off him. She looked at the tattoos that ran up his forearms. It had been a long time since she'd even desired a man, but this cat's vibe was real. She looked at the guy that sat in the booth beside him. She'd seen him many times in her two months there. He had even tried to take her out, talking about he was VA's finest in the ATL. She never entertained their conversation; she never entertained anyone's conversation—especially the other bitches that always tried to get at her. *Ant—that's his name, but who is this guy beside him?*

"What's your name?" the guy asked.

"Champagne."

"Fuck that—what's your name?"

She blurted, "Angela," before she knew it. She'd never told anybody her name because it was all a game.

"I'm Strong." He passed her a card with his numbers on it. "If something happens to this card for any reason, remember Triple Strong Entertainment. Call information. Leave a message, work number, e-mail or something."

Angela looked at him.

"I'll be here until tomorrow, then I'm out. And if I were trying to fuck, I would offer you a couple grand and skip the bullshit."

Strong was back in ATL. He'd come down to handle some business with Ant. It took them almost two months before Ant decided to pull him in. Strong got his enterprise popping with the backing of Polite, and things were running well. Strong's plan was to try and find Bo's connect, so Poppa could control all of that. But Dundee had set off shit and things were off the hook, but with Dee handling the apartments for lookouts, and the real estate out Lake Edward for stash spots, a fortress was being built.

Poppa had runners, workers, and "watch out" niggas all reporting straight to him, Lo, and Kev, who had learned the land.

Strong was bringing in the weight, and it was getting moved fast. Mont and Speed were working out perfectly.

Poppa was having problems trying to put his people on the other side since Rome got shot up. Bo was on a vengeance. When Dundee set off the gunplay, it left three people dead, but left Rome fucked up. He could no longer stand on his own. He had to use the help of handicap tilts. No longer the young man he used to be, he couldn't control his bladder and walked around wearing a bag. It fucked Bo up every time he saw his brother.

The day he picked up Rome was a glorious day as they left Norfolk General Hospital. He pulled in the front as they rolled his brother down. He had hired a home-care nurse to sit in his home and take care of Rome. Rome sat on the passenger side in silence. Bo knew it wasn't much to say. This was something Rome was going to have to come to grips with. He'd lived his life avoiding shit like this, but now he got caught up early in the game and it was tragic. It hurt him to see his brother like this.

As he pulled out of the hospital parking lot, he never paid the men in black suits with bowties any attention as they approached his truck with the *Final Call*.

"Would you like the *Final Call*, my brother?" the guy in the Muslim suit asked.

"Or some incense or oils?" the other one asked the passenger.

"Naw, I'm a'ight." Bo didn't want to be bothered.

"Can you make a donation, my brother?"

Bo reached in his pocket and held out a five for the guy. He never expected for the guy to grab his arm. When he realized what was going on it was too late— out came the nine that sat in the pack of *Final Call* newspapers—to his neck.

The second Muslim opened the door, picked up Rome, and threw him in the back, not giving a fuck how he landed. Rome let out a groan as he tried to adjust his twisted body.

One was in front with his burner on Bo, and the other Muslim climbed in the back with Rome.

They made Bo drive to a undisclosed location in the Industrial Park. "Shut off the engine, put your hands on the steering wheel." The guy secured Bo's hands to the steering wheel tightly.

They tied Rome's hands; his legs weren't much help to him at this time. Then they placed them both in seatbelts and secured them. Right about the same time a tinted-out, charcoal-grey 300M pulled up.

Black stepped from the car. Bo's already shaken stomach was now about to turn over. Piss trickled down his leg, and he clenched his ass tight, to control his bowels.

"So what's the deal, baby?" Black walked toward the truck and smiled at Bo.

"Come on, Black . . . I thought—I thought—"

"You thought I was never comin' back. You thought you had shit under control. You thought you could fuck me and it was never comin' back on ya. But you thought the wrong thought, partner."

Lo walked up.

"You was my man, Bo, and right now I can't even say anything in your defense. You fucked everybody that ever tried to do something for you."

Up pulled a black 929, tinted-out. Poppa got out the passenger side while Dundee parked. Dundee sat in the car (he finally got a chance to see the infamous Black). He was riding this nigga shirttail and he knew this cat was legendary.

"Bring that, Poppa?" Black asked.

"Yeah," Poppa said.

"Pop the trunk, Dun." he said as he approached the trunk. He pulled out a red gas container.

Bo eyes widened with fear.

Rome began to breathe hard. "*Uhh! Uhh! Uhh! Uhh!*" This was some shit he could have never imagined. He looked into Poppa eyes. "Please, Poppa, I never did nothing to deserve this. Come on, Lo. Oh! God. Help me!" Tears ran down his face.

Poppa walked over to the truck. They both began to yell as Poppa poured gas into the truck on Bo's lap, on the door, to the floor, soaked the seat around him. Bo began to go crazy, trying to break away from the steering wheel, but he was secured well. Them fake Muslims did their part and were long gone.

Black lit his already rolled Backwoods.

They watched as Poppa approached Rome's side and began pouring gas into his lap, floor, door and soaking the floor. He threw the container on the floor between them.

Rome was still crying and praying. "Jesus, please help me. Jesus, please. I'll be a child of yours forever, if you help me! Please, Lo. Please, Lo." He turned his head in Lo's direction.

"Better keep calling on Jesus because he's the only one that can help your ass now." Lo took a sip of the Hennessy.

Black looked into Bo's eyes. "This gay-ass, snitchin' muthafucka, sittin' here with slobber runnin' from his mouth and tears on his face, cryin', 'Oh God! Oh, Black! Oh, God! Oh Black!" Black took a long pull off the Back, then flicked it inside the window.

The lower part of the car burst into flames. The screams ripped through Poppa, but he stood there.

This shit was an act of a beast. No man barbecues another human being, Dundee thought. He stared in amazement as their screams turned to sighs. This was a savage act, but Bo was a snitch and, inside, everybody out there knew this shit should have been done a long time ago. Dundee had nothing but respect for this nigga that now headed up the team.

Lo turned the pint of Hennessy up to his lips and gulped. Then he took the bottle and threw it, busting Bo in his now-cremated head. "Have some Henny, son—you had a good life."

They climbed in the whips and were headed back to The Lakes to claim their home.

In the three months Strong had been in VA, he moved over eighty kilos of cocaine through the seven cities. He was moving about six ki's a week, but for the last two weeks, ten bricks were being pushed out the door. He had a slight problem within his organization that had to be addressed. He'd seen Dundee at the mall in Hampton. Dee had gotten Strong a house in Hampton, away from it all. Before leaving VA, that was far, but after chilling in ATL, it wa'n' shit, as long as you had a nice whip.

Dundee came to him like a real hustler with respect. "I've only seen you a couple times, Strong, but I know who you are." Dundee gave him a pound.

Strong knew he was feeding this nigga.

"Can I holla at you a second?"

"Sure. Holla!"

"I'm movin' three bricks a week, some through my LE, some to my peoples in Carolina."

"What part?" Strong had some bad experiences with Carolina cats.

"Well, I'm from Elizabeth City originally. But I been out The Lakes since I can remember. My cousin's down

there gettin' like I'm gettin' it, but they can't stay supplied. They are movin' from Elizabeth City, goin' to Raleigh, Durham, Greensboro, and Charlotte. I can move
five a week through them—they ready to buy—but I
don't have it to buy and Poppa won't, or can't, front it.
Which leaves that money I could be gettin' danglin' in
the wind."

"I understand," Strong said. "I'll get back at you."

Dundee walked off not knowing if he'd done the right
thing. *But how was he going to get back, he didn't
have my number?*

Strong sat there thinking he had made over four
hundred in three months. He was giving Polite fifteen
gees for each brick, getting twenty gees or better. Here
Ant was getting ready to give him twenty bricks for
two hundred thousand and give a kilo of heroin for
seventy-five thousand and a street value of one hundred eighty thousand.

Strong told Polite to see if he could match the love,
but it wasn't possible. Strong even asked him if he
wanted to come in and they get forty ki's.

Polite was ready for the move but said he still had to
get to Memphis.

Ant yelled for another girl to come dance as Angela
made her way through the door.

"So it's on, my nigga—VA niggas gettin' it," Ant said.

"How can you do it, though? How?"

Ant leaned over. He'd known Black a long time and
he knew the nigga that sat in front of him was real. "I'm
in bed with some Africans. I was in the wrong place
at the wrong time, or you might say right time. I saw
some shit go down. Africans was doin' a deal and the
muthafucka cut dude hand off. They sliced his head in

half and left the machete there. Pulled out burners and popped two more cats. I had left the 750 in a garage. I took off thinking I was straight. Two days later, cats are at my house. When I come in—the house I had then was nice but secluded. No cars, no idea—muthafuckas ask who am I. I know I'm gonna die," Ant looks at Black. He had Black's undivided attention even though fifty of the finest dancers in ATL were within inches, naked.

"Before I knew it, I was hemmed up with a wire around my neck, cuttin' my shit. Rippin', man. Then I told them, 'I'm from VA. I hustle heroin.' I had half a million in the garage and three ki's in the stash in the car. They got the heroin and the money . . . and let me down. They ask me about the muthafucka I dealt with and pulled us in. Now I'm a millionaire in this shit. They have unlimited supply of soft and that diesel. So let's get you rich and me richer.

Strong couldn't complain; he was getting ready to come off, but still had to move this diesel.

Chapter Nine

Angela walked in the door. Shannon followed her, complaining about the attention she'd given Strong. "Know what . . . you are gettin' sickenin'!"

"Now I'm sickenin'? Why is that now? You tore up my car, I'm sittin' here trying to figure out how I'm gettin' to work in the morning and you talkin' about a nigga." Angela went to the room to undress and to take a shower.

"I been watchin' you dance for months now. You never give anybody the time of day, nor do you take numbers. Where is the card anyway?" Shannon went through her things.

"Know what, Shannon . . ." Angela stood in front of her nude. ". . . we came down here together. The girl I met in VA was lovable and comforting. Now I don't need comforting—I'm past that—I need love, support, trust. Somebody to help me up and get myself together so I can bring Li'l D down here. And now that my car is fucked up, you're hinderin' me. Instead of tryin' to figure out how the problem is going to be resolved, or how I'm goin' to get to work and back to the club, you here wildin' out, throwin' my shit, and actin' like a fool."

Angela shook her head and walked into the shower. She allowed the water to wash the sweat and filth off her body. She could hear Shannon hollering. Shannon's babbling came closer. Then she heard the bathroom door open.

"Why you blamin' me for your faults? You aren't perfect, and you wrecked your shit, bitch. That's why your own cousin help me turn your ass out. I have been here for you when nobody else was, when you were runnin' around here fucked up because you had two muthafuckin' niggas killed for nothin'. Because you wanted to be a fuckin' ho."

Angela turned off the water and pulled back the curtain. "Now I know how you really feel."

"You bein' smart." Shannon stepped toward Angela and grabbed her hair.

Angela grabbed Shannon by the throat, but the force of Shannon pulling her hair slammed her to the tub. Angela began swinging.

Shannon got two grips on her head, trying to push it under the water in the slow-draining tub.

Flashbacks of Mac overpowering her, pushing her head underwater, came back to Angela, and she dug her nails into Shannon's face and eyes.

Shannon let go, and Angela's hands were swinging wild. Shannon's fight soon became a scramble to get away. She busted out the bedroom with Angela on her ass.

Angela slipped on the wet floor, coming up only to grab the iron, twirling it, barely missing Shannon's head, and leaving a large imprint in the wall. She heard the front door slam.

Angela fell on the bed, trying to catch her breath. "God, why am I going through this bullshit. Why?"

She grabbed her robe and went to run some bath water. She needed to sit in the tub and relax. She turned off all the lights and lit two candles. As her body hit the hot steaming water, she let out a long sigh. She held the phone in her hand. She wanted to call somebody. Her best male friends were dead.

Her heart fell as she thought about the day Monica called and told her about Rome. She had flown home to see him when he got shot up, and was lying in the hospital. There was no coming back when they found him and his brother damn near cremated. Her girlfriend, Monica, she just didn't want to hear her drama, and Trinity was another story.

She didn't know anybody in Atlanta, except for the people she worked with, and that was business. And she didn't really fuck with none of the dancers, except for one. She thought about the number 678-424-XXXX.

"Hello," the man's voice answered.

"Dream there?"

"Don't no muthafuckin' Dream live here. Dream worked at the club; call down there."

"Can I speak to Felicia?" she said with an attitude.

"The phone, Fee—it's one of those dike-ass, trick bitches you dance with," her friend said.

"Hello," Dream said.

"What the deal, girl? It's Champagne." Her and Angela had talked a few times, but not that often.

Dream was like her—she had another job and just danced strictly for the dough, not trying to get caught up in the money.

"Heah, girl! Sorry about my friend."

"See you kind of busy?"

"Hell no, girl. Just got out of the shower and he gettin' ready to carry his ass to work. That's why he mad. Got a job and still broke. I'd be mad too." Dream laughed.

"I just wanted somebody to holla at."

"Where your girl?"

"We fell out big—she left."

"That's why I don't get down with bitches. I've heard those hoes put you through more shit than a nigga. At least a nigga got something I can play with."

Her and Angela talked about twenty more minutes. "A'ight, Fee. See you tomorrow."

"Definitely. I go on at six, and Angela, take it for what it's worth—the life you livin' is a controversial life; if you want it to get better, get a man."

Angela climbed out the tub and dried off, thinking about what Dream said. She lotioned down and wrapped her head. Then she fell to her knees, something she hadn't done in a while, and began to pray. *It had to get better.*

The sound of the alarm clock scared Angela. Usually it was set for music, but somehow it ended on alarm. "Goddamn, I just laid the fuck down." She walked into the living room to see if Shannon was there. *I guess she found another bitch to lay up with.* She did want to know that she was all right. She reached for the phone and dialed 301-497-XXXX.

"Hello," Lenore answered.

"Heah, Lenore, can I speak to my dad?"

"Yeah," he said.

"Heah, Daddy. I miss you."

"What happen, baby?"

"I wrecked my car."

"You all right? Did you report it to your insurance?"

"Yes, yes. But I need to get a rental."

"Talk to Lenore. She'll send you something. Take care. I got to run."

"Dad, I also need a two-hundred-dollar deposit . . . because I'm not twenty-five."

"Damn, baby. Let me see what's up. Call me on my cell at noon."

Angela got dressed and headed to the Marta. She was going to have to ride to North Spring Station and catch the bus to MCI. *What the hell am I gonna do?*

She sat at her cubicle making calls, not being productive at all. Her mind was on her car, Shannon, and that fine, black muthafucka named Strong. *Damn, that nigga look good.* She was confused. She had strong feelings for Shannon, but she wasn't looking at her the same way. Her mind was running a thousand ways. Fuck it! She figured she would deal with one situation at a time.

She called her insurance company and found out she had rental coverage. She decided to still let her dad Western Union her some money. And Enterprise Rentals was going to pick her up at five to take her to pick up the car. *One problem down.*

Then she looked at Strong's card—Triple Strong Entertainment. She wondered if she should call. She looked at Strong's number: 757-292-XXXX. *What! Seven five seven. That's the crib. He got to be from VA. That's why he was with Ant.* She dialed his number.

"What the deal?"

"Hello, Strong. This is Angela." She hoped he caught the voice.

"Champagne?"

"Yes. I prefer Angela, if I'm going to be social."

"Me too. Talk to me. What's up?"

"Just callin'."

"No, you ain't just callin'. What time we gettin' up? You at work?"

"Yeah. I go to lunch at twelve thirty."

"Where you at?"

Angela took it into her own hands to give directions. "GA400 to Exit 9. Go right, second light make a left, straight down on the right. I'll be out front at twelve thirty. MCI Building," she said feeling funny inside, but hoping he said he would be out front.

"See you, cutie." Strong never gave her a chance to respond.

"Damn, he rude," she said to herself. She walked back to her desk smiling.

It took twelve-thirty forever to come. Angela looked in her hand mirror, checking herself. She adjusted the skirt that stopped just before her knee, smoothing out the blouse that was on the outside of her skirt, but stopped just past her stomach. Her heels gave her a walk that demanded eyes focus on her.

She walked out and glanced around. *Damn, I didn't even ask him what he was driving.* Then she saw someone arrive. She caught a side glance and knew it was him. She walked over to the rented Cadillac.

Strong had flown in and rented a whip.

"Hello."

"What's up?" Strong said.

"Good to see you again," was Angela's response.

"So what you feelin'?" She checked Strong out. She expected jewels, foreign car, and a nigga talking about dough and his rims, trying to impress, but what she found was a laid-back, black ass nigga with Rocawear jeans, wife-beater, white T and white DC's.

"Anything. Show me your town."

"We'll go to Ruby Tuesday—and this isn't my town. I've been down here three months. Love the city, but it's not as easy to make it as people say." Angela gave him directions.

"No matter where you go, you have to work— nobody givin' away shit." Strong took in a full glance of Angela's outfit and body. "So where you from?"

"Seven-City, VA. You don't know?"

Strong smirked. "Seven-City, VA?" He opened the door to the restaurant.

"Yeah, the Hampton Roads consist of seven cities— VA Beach, Norfolk, Chesapeake, Portsmouth, Suffolk, Hampton, and Newport News, home of VA's, Allen I." Angela had been in this guy's presence for thirty minutes and she was totally relaxed. She was already feeling him. Nobody pulls her in like that.

"I heard that. So where you from in the seven cities?" Strong was enjoying every moment of this fine-ass, young shorty "reppin" VA. *A bitch from the crib. If she's a real bitch from out the way, she supposed to know how to read, figure out, and adjust to a nigga like me and pull me in.*

"You from LE?"

"Right down the street. L and J."

"I got peoples in Richmond. I've been through there going cross the Bay Bridge."

"Then you go right past where I grew up." Strong wanted to pull her in too, see what she knew. "I've been out your way to Norfolk—Norfolk and LE niggas ain't shit."

Angela looked at him. "You crazy. You won't fuck around there. Real niggas done came out of the seven cities." She was in ghetto form and didn't give a fuck. *This is me*, she thought; *I ain't frontin' no more.*

"Who? Name ten niggas from Tidewater that I heard of?" Strong had her going.

"Stacy, Speed, Donnell, Lo Max—that's Norfolk. I can go to the Beach. Goddamn, I can go to Bayside—that's the school I graduated from—and name ten—Lee-Lee from

Bayside niggas, Big Lloyd from Southgate, Pimp . . . I forgot where Pimp was from. He got along with everybody; he floated LE, Bayside Arms, and Northridge. Everywhere."

Black's heart dropped. Pimp went to school with him. He had gotten gunned down, two tragedies that hit Bayside hard. And Boot. He kept his shit so on the low, nobody ever thought he was even hustling. She was naming everybody he knew. Her names brought him out of his daze. All the niggas from out the way who were true hustlers and got caught slipping opened his eyes and made him smarter.

"Bo, Lo. Poppa—"

"I don't know none of them niggas," he lied.

Out of nowhere she said, "I bet you heard of Black, from Lake Edward. And I know you heard of Kenny Speed. Both of them niggas ain't nobody to even fuck with," she said seriously, as if she knew.

Strong's attention was caught, but he knew she didn't know Black, and she ain't know Speed. Just heard shit just like everybody else.

An hour passed quickly. He threw the amount on the table, and they were out. He pulled in front of her job.

"I've enjoyed myself. Thanks for lunch, Strong. I didn't give you much of a chance to talk, huh! I guess I needed somebody to talk to."

"So what's your situation, Angela?"

"What you mean?"

He gave her a "be serious" look.

"Well, I'm like kind of involved. I cut it off and I'm just trying to pull it together. I don't know what I want from you, Strong. I don't know nobody here except for my friend I moved here with—I don't fuck with the girls at the club. Just get mine and I'm out."

Black began to figure he had her pegged wrong. Maybe she was trifling and about games, chilling with him and giving him that "I-got-a-friend" shit, and she didn't just live with him and she had moved from VA with him too. *What did he look like?* "Right." He looked into Angela's eye, catching her light brown eyes, then her slim neckline, straight to her cleavage, down her thick, brown legs. He had to find out what was up with her.

"You leavin' tomorrow?" she asked, not wanting to get out.

"Yeah. Why you ask?"

"I would like to see you later. You have to eat dinner, right?" Angela held her head down.

"Yes, I do." He reached out and touched her hand. "Give me a call and we'll catch up." Strong leaned with his back against the door and stared at Angela.

"Before I go, can I ask you three quick questions?"

He looked at her like it was okay.

"One—do you have a girl?"

"No."

"Two—where you from?"

"VA, Richmond."

"Three—what do you do?"

"Promote shows."

"That show the other night at 201 Courtland?"

"Yeah . . . when the artist performed. Triple Strong Entertainment, baby, we doin' it big."

"I look forward to seeing you later, Strong. Then I'm going to talk to you and really tell you about Angela, okay."

"Definitely." *She had to really be bad news for him not to fuck with her,* he thought to himself as he watched her walk into the building, dressed like a businesswoman, with the ghetto button turned off.

Strong grabbed his phone and dialed Lo.

"What the deal, cuzzo?"

"Fuck y'all niggas doin'?"

"Workin'. What else?"

"What's all that noise, nigga? Y'all bullshittin'. Where y'all at?"

"We up here by the restaurant," Lo said.

"When Dee say we openin'?"

"They say in a week," Lo told him. "Pass me that Belvee."

"Who up there with you?"

"Poppa, Mike-Mike. Poppa gettin' ready to burst to Virginia Beach General. He just had a baby. His girl had a few problems, so she gonna be in there a few extra days. So he been hangin' over there. I'm gonna dock his pay." Lo laughed. "Kev with Dundee?"

"Dundee gone to kill somebody," Mike-Mike yelled.

"That nigga stupid." Strong laughed. Tell Poppa congrats. I got to pick something up for him.

"Lo, I met this girl here, from L and J Gardens. Her name Angela. Graduated from Bayside in '96."

"Brown skin, nice titties, real cute?"

"Yeah."

"Poppa, you know that girl Angela?" Lo asked. "Went to Hampton from L and J. Always out LE with that red bitch with grey eyes."

"Walk around like she the shit, fuckin' niggas' lives up." Poppa let Lo know he knew who she was.

"Who? Angela?" Mike-Mike sipped the Belvee out the bottle, passing it to Lo. "Tell Strong don't fuck with that bitch. Give me the phone. Heah, Strong."

"What up, Mike-Mike?" Strong knew he was about to hear a story.

"Her and her peoples be trickin'. One of these big-money niggas had a party and niggas was tryin' to trick.

That one you hollerin' at all right. Only thing, she killed two niggas—I mean one nigga killed two niggas over her. Then he ended up dead."

"Who?"

"The one who shot them. She had a baby by one of the dead niggas. Her cousin was somewhere one night saying she hadn't fucked a nigga since the other one got done up and that a bitch turned her out. Say she ran to ATL chasin' that pussy-eatin'-ass ho, but you know she triflin', leavin' her baby behind some bitch eatin' her pussy—" Mike-Mike took a break from the story— "Somebody give me a black."

"Give me the phone, Buc." Lo took the phone. "Yo, I think some of that shit true, but Buc fucked up a story."

"Yeah, but that's a lot information. I just took her ass to lunch. She supposed to be hittin' a nigga later. I know she is."

"Damn right!"

"So she live with a bitch, Lo. Damn! Nigga can't be jealous over another ho." Black laughed.

"Yeah, bitch got to at least think she can get pregnant when you bust in them—that brings out that deep love." Lo stepped away from everybody. "Yo, I've been meanin' to talk with you. When you was gone, there was some cats who came in and handled shit. Say they were from Up Top. They were definitely gettin' it. They opened at a studio called Notorious Records & Notorious Tapes & CD's & Notorious Gear and they had some more shit but not 'round here.

"They came in for a minute, held it down, then they burst. They got the club on Bonny Road, Donzi's. Well, anyway, they back. They moved in Lake Edward on both sides—families—and it's about seven or eight wild-ass niggas, and they ain't scared. But you know I don't give a damn about that. Check this—niggas talkin' like Mont and them gonna start fuckin' with them."

"I ain't worried about that."

"So . . . do I need to call Black, or can Strong handle this?" Lo laughed. "'Cause I don't like that nigga brother anyway. Something in my pocket got his name on it." Lo felt the 9 mm bullet.

"If you go, you gotta go correct. That nigga rude, Lo, but we ain't there yet. Business first. Let's see how much dough here. I'll be back tomorrow." Strong hung up and headed to Ant's house to finish his business.

"Goddamn, this shit hot," he said as he pulled into his driveway that went completely around.

Ant greeted him at the door. "Come on in."

"This shit is nice, kid."

"Yeah, this my dream. No matter how much money I make, this is me—five-bedroom, playroom over the garage, office, pool, three full baths, exercise room, three-car garage, and plenty of land. Shit, you can't get that in VA. This shit ran three hundred and seventy-five thousand. In VA Beach you know it would've cost three-quarter of a million—easy."

"No doubt."

They finished making proper arrangements. Strong was going go meet Ant's peoples in VA. Ant was going to make sure a nigga was in VA every week with twenty kilos of cocaine and two kilos of heroin.

From there Strong would put it in the streets. A lot of work and a lot of risk. But for the dough and the chance to live an elegant lifestyle, it was all going to be worth it.

"I'm headed to the other side. Gotta check this shit on the corner. This shit gettin' ready to get poppin' and we need every fuckin' dollar," Lo said.

"Don't let shit pop off over there; that shit hot enough," Poppa said, "after Dundee set shit off. Then them New York niggas be settin' out there, shootin' and playin' like it's a game."

"They'll find out soon enough. They think hustlin' in buildings was something. Wait 'til they get a taste of those LE hallways and back alleys." Lo smiled.

"Let's go, Lo. We need to get to the liquor store and catch up with Kev. I'm ready to get rollin'."

"Man, they say that X fuck you up mentally," Poppa said.

"But it make me feel good physically. I get drunk, take me two X and I'm rollin'. I don't smoke weed. I'm all right. And my hoes love when I'm rollin'. I eat up some ass, pussy, and I fucks hard. Bitch I fucked last night love me."

"That girl was a trick, Buc." Lo finished off the Belvedere.

"Why you gotta say that?" Mike-Mike was serious.

"Get the fuck in the car before you be walkin'."

"You see more when you walk, but I appreciate the ride." Mike-Mike got in the car.

Poppa understood how niggas drank, smoked, tooted, and did whatever to keep going. But being fucked up all day was beyond him. He pulled up on the other side and saw niggas at the park, standing on the corner, standing on E. Hastings, and up and down the back alley. He parked on E. Hastings.

Lo and Mike-Mike was standing outside talking. Several other youngsters had gathered because the altercation was beginning to get out of hand. Three guys stood outside of a winter-green Mercedes truck M320 with New York tags.

Poppa strolled up, intercepting some harsh words by one of the New York cats, who was trying to tell Lo they had as much right to hustle out LE as the niggas who been out here all their life.

Lo didn't argue.

"No, you don't have that right," Poppa told him. "If you trying to carve a spot, Lake Edward is not the place."

One of the cats leaning on the truck said, "Right now, all we trying to do is work the front part of LE, from Newtown on; we'll take it over later." His crew began smiling.

"Well, I ain't one to fuss and argue," Lo said. "So I'm gonna tell you for the safety of your peoples you put out here—you better stand out here with them because next time I see any niggas on these corners that don't work for us—gotta go!"

"You threatenin' us?" The New York cat stepped on the curve.

"Take it how the fuck you want." Poppa didn't give Lo a chance to answer.

"You need to calm down, playboy, and step back," one of the other New York cats said. "Come on, partner—these niggas don't know." They climbed in the truck and rolled out.

Poppa stood there as the Benz truck disappeared. "I was waitin' on you Lo, so I could tell Strong you started it."

"And I was waitin' on you," Lo said. "Shit, he told me to chill out and not to heat up the spot."

Poppa turned to all the niggas standing on the corner. "If you not out here makin' money, you need to go home. These work areas are gettin' ready to be cleared of all extras. Don't be the example."

Youngsters and non-hustlers began to move. They knew when shit was in transformation. It got crazy.

"I'm out, son. Goin' to check on my family. I'll be back later." Poppa jumped in his Suburban. "Yo, y'all, hold this shit down, and remember, if anybody comes out here makin' money, it's takin' from you," he said to Scotty and Pee-Wee.

"Actually y'all suppose to handle this corner. Don't have Dundee around this bitch wildin' out."

"Yeah! Handle your muthafuckin' corner," Mike-Mike yelled, "before I come out here and run it my god-damn self." Then he climbed in the Lex.

Lo was laughing. Scotty and Pee-Wee flipped him off.

Lo pulled in front of Precision Cuts on Baker Road. He saw the Intrepid that Dundee had rented. They were standing out front when James, the owner, came out. "Y'all got to clear my walkway." James' brother, Pop, walked right behind him.

Mike-Mike said, "Go to hell, nigga. You don't run—"

Next thing you know, James had a nice-size pocket-knife to Mike-Mike's throat.

Pop put his hand around his back. "What? What?"

Everybody started laughing. Dangerous games were a part of life around the way. It was funny, but everybody knew it could get serious real fast.

Kev pulled up in his CLK430 with a shorty in the passenger side. He jumped out and joined his team. The girl walked inside the nail shop to get her nails done.

"What the deal, baby?" Kev gave everybody a pound. Then he signaled to Pop, and they climbed in the CLK and burst across the street into Lake Edward, only to return moments later.

James jumped in his 3.5 Acura, Pop followed, and they burst.

"What up, Kev?" Lo and Dundee asked.

"I thought y'all niggas were together?" Lo said.

"Naw, he wants to trick." Dundee pointed at Kev.

"Shit, I got to fuck too."

"Nigga, I'm tryin' to figure out how you pulled them niggas in," Lo said. "They movin' at least half a brick."

"Brick in half," Kev said. "Niggas know how to get it." He walked in the nail shop to check on his new, young shorty.

When he returned, Lo was telling Dundee about the disagreement with those New York cats. "They knew things were going to kick off sooner or later, but for now it was time to get this money. "I'm going across the street to the apt."

"Me too. I'll be over there in a second." Dundee wanted to hang, but he knew that wasn't his place. He was a soldier for Poppa, but if he ever got with Strong, he would become a lieutenant. Then he would gain new respect. His time was coming. He was the nigga out LE. He'd been hustlin' in Lake Edward forever, the place he was born and raised, and had to reign over niggas. He moved two kilos a week. Not Poppa, him, and it had to be recognized.

Angela walked into her apartment. She stood in the doorway, traumatized—Shannon had come in and took all of the TV's, the couch, and all of her clothes.

The thousand dollars she'd stashed in the drawer was gone. She pushed all her things off the dresser to the floor and screamed. She pressed her hands to her eyes until they hurt. *This will never happen again. Not in this lifetime, ever again.* Her hurt turned to anger.

She picked up the phone and called the front office. They were around her house in minutes, putting a new lock on the door.

She ran some bath water and called Strong.

"Hello."

"Heah, this is Angela. Are we on?"

"Of course. I'm stayin' at the Westin on Peachtree, Room 612. What time you comin'?"

"Seven thirty, eight."

"See ya."

She got out of the bath. Her body glistened from the baby oil she squirted in her bath water. She slipped into her robe and looked in the mirror.

"Angela, I'm disappointed with you. Your life is a shamble, but you from VA, bitch—you better bounce back."

She knocked on the door. He didn't answer. She knocked again. The door opened, and she walked in. She caught a glimpse of his back with BLACK across the top and REIGN at the bottom. His left tricep read ST8, and the right tricep read RAW.

He walked to the room and returned wearing Pelle Pelle powder-blue velour sweats and a wife-beater. "You early. Seven thirty or eight usually means eight thirty or nine."

"How were you going to be spending your time until I got here?" she watched his muscles flex with every movement of his arms.

"Sparkin' and getting' my head right." He picked up his Backwoods. "Want some Hennessy?"

"Sure. What you got to go with it?"

"This weed."

They both laughed.

"No. I meant soda or juice, or better yet some Alizé— the gold-colored Alizé."

"I don't need shit fuckin' up my Henny, but here is some Alizé." Strong handed her the bottle. Then he lit the Back and turned on the radio.

She sat there feeling like she wanted to tell him her life story. Being in his presence made her feel good.

He walked out of the room. When he returned he had put on his jewels—stainless Breitling and a platinum chain with a platinum cross, flooded with diamonds and hanging down to his stomach. Nothing big, but an eye-catcher.

"So what did you have to tell me? You gonna tell me about Angela from Seven-City, VA?" He smiled.

"Yes, I am going to tell you all about Angela from VA and about Angela who lives in the ATL." She let out a deep breath and began to tell Strong about Ray, Mac, Damien, and Li'l D, all the way to her best friend Rome dying so tragically. By the time she got to physically fighting Shannon, going home and her shit and money gone, her eyes watered, and the tears covered her face.

"I don't know how I got here, but I'm here. Could you begin to understand?"

Strong took in Angela's every word. He decided then that if this bitch was telling the truth, she was at a new point in her life. "Let's go out for a ride; I can put my final miles on the rented Cadillac."

"I got a rental too—they gave me a convertible Sebring."

"For real? Then you drive; you know the land, and the wind can blow in my hair." They both laughed and headed out the door.

They rode up Peachtree to Buckhead, checking out the many clubs on Pharr Road.

Inside a club called the Living Room, Angela found herself standing in front of Strong as he stood there holding his double Henny and a Heineken.

She moved like a skilled dancer.

He leaned back and enjoyed the beauty of this young girl as she seduced him. He looked around at everything and every woman going by, but they didn't matter. Strong looked at her and smiled.

"Don't you have a plane to catch in the morning?"

"Yeah, why?—Don't you have to work tomorrow?"

"Yeah, but I'm all right."

"I'm all right too," he said, his platinum glistening from the flashing lights in the club.

The deejays decided to slow it down and played a slow melody by Aaliyah.

She turned to Strong, moved closer, and stared into his eyes. She broke the stare as his arms went up to sip the Henny he held with his left hand and secure the Heineken he had in the right. (Its purpose was really for niggas who acted up.)

She placed her body against his.

He placed his arm on her back, making sure to spill no Henny, to let her know she was secure, and they fell into a moment.

When the rugged sounds of Pastor Troy that came blasting through the speakers broke the mood, she eased back.

Out of nowhere, two guys came up. " 'Cuse me, fool," the boy said with a mouthful of gold, almost stepping between Strong and Angela.

The other guy stepped closer to Angela. "You tryin' to make that money tonight, shorty?"

Angela felt like shit. This is the shit that came with dancing, everybody thinks you fuck for money.

A feeling shot into Strong's gut. They might be saying fuck me, or are these country niggas this stupid? "Are y'all niggas really tryin' to talk to her or you tryin' me?"

Angela prayed. *Please let this guy walk away, God. Please.*

"Take it how you want, f—" Before the big guy could finish, the Heineken bottle shattered his gold teeth, splitting his lips and nose.

Angela turned and quickly slammed her glass into the other guy's head, shocking Strong.

Black grabbed Angela's hand and eased out the club as the crowd grew larger. They got to the car and got out as quickly as possible, making their way down Peachtree back to the hotel. Strong came in and poured a drink.

She went to the table and began rolling.

He removed his T-shirt and DC's then walked in the bathroom to wash his face. He returned and sat down.

She passed him the Back already rolled and lit.

He hit the L hard and then exhaled. "Next time, you get the fuck out the way."

"Shit, next time I'll know it's coming. I thought it was, but you still caught me off guard."

Angela was glad he finally spoke. It was a long ride back to the hotel in silence, and she thought it better if she just kept her mouth shut and followed his lead. "I'm sorry that happened." She held her head down.

"Heah . . . Never say sorry . . . makes you sound weak." Strong rubbed her back.

"I know you can take care of yourself, but you don't need to get caught at the club dancin'. Your rent will still get paid."

"When you comin' back to Atlanta?" she asked, resting her head on his chest.

"Now that I have a reason, real soon, cutie; real soon."

"Every reason in the world."

She put her arms around him and kissed him. She laid her head on his chest and he hugged her, and they fell into a deep sleep.

Strong arrived at Norfolk International at noon. He went and got a drink as he waited on Dee, flyin' in from Charlotte at 12:45.

Dee walked in and ordered a Henny straight.

"What the deal, son? How Chantel?"

"She good to go. Workin', studyin', doin' everything but taking care of her man. I got to damn near kill myself before she'll stop and pay some attention. She'll get me smiling, then go right back to her business."

"She just tryin' to get hers, man. She's a good girl; you know you can count on her."

"Yeah. Sometimes it takes more. So what's up with you?"

"Twenty joints and two things of diesel."

Dee reminded him, "We don't fuck with that."

"We do, and you need to connect, make some calls. You know how you do. I don't have no choice; I already got it, so it got to be moved."

"True." Dee finished his drink. "Let's get outta here. Ant's peoples suppose to be here with those thangs by three; they left Atlanta at six."

"So what you get into beside handlin' that shit with Ant?"

"Stopped at Strokers. Had to straighten a nigga and met the baddest bitch—body like Tricia with bigger titties."

"Heard that. Better watch those ATL hoes. When you goin' back?"

"In about two weeks. And she from the crib," Strong said as they made their way through the airport.

Kev approached them with his new partner. "What the deal, baby? Y'all know Pop?"

"Yeah!" Pop said.

Dee remembered James from back in the day out Norview. He was always known for getting it and keeping a top-of-the-line bitch, but his little brother was young. Now the talk was he's runnin' shit, while James ran the barbershop and other business. James was playing it smart, but Dee knew he still had a hand in the game, because there was one addiction he had to satisfy and that was getting on his knees with those dice. And Dee knew why Kev and Pop saw eye to eye— the same reason their eyes were low and red, and the smell of weed drenched their clothes.

They got to the parking lot and jumped into Pop's '97 S320 Benz sitting on 20's with TV's in the headrest. They rolled out LE to the apartment on Baker Road.

Kev took Strong to meet Ant's peoples. They picked up the whip and brought it back to the townhouse in LE with the garage.

Strong got on the phone and began making calls. He had product and was determined to move it. He met Mont, Speed, Poppa, and Lo. No sooner than it hit the garage, it hit the streets. Strong even got Speed to buy a quarter kilo of diesel to try. (Strong knew he'd be back in the next couple of days.)

Dee jumped out of the 2000 bronze-colored Yukon Denali sitting on 22's as he jumped out in front of the restaurant. "What's the deal, baby?"

***

The restaurant was open, and business was off the hook. At first they thought it might become a neighborhood hangout, but then Dee had the idea to advertise Moms' and Aunty's work. He went to Buda Brothers, the area's hottest radio personalities, and they pumped the restaurant across the airwaves. With commercials and neighborhood fliers, business increased. Once the Web site was built, and packaging and distribution began, it was unbelievable.

Dee stepped up, giving dap to his brother's team. He was cool with everybody, but Strong kept him away from all that bullshit for a reason. The only niggas that came to his spot was Kev and Lo, and that wasn't that often.

"We see who makin' all the money." Mike-Mike jumped inside the Denali. "Give me fifty dollars, Dee."

"You know I'm scramblin', nigga." Dee stepped up on the curve, letting the new navy blue Wallabees scrape the concrete.

The khaki shorts and navy-colored Sean John shirt let niggas know he wa'n' hardly scrambling. In the last month Strong had made close to a million dollars. He'd moved eighty kilos of coke and over ten kilos of heroin and wa'n' nothin' stoppin' the flow.

Dee walked inside the restaurant, leaving the truck in front running, and walked in the back getting hugs from Moms. She still hadn't seen Strong because he didn't go to her house at all.

Dee told her that the dough came from the promotional shows that were being done in ATL and Charlotte.

He seasoned four wings, floured them, dropped them in the grease. Got some fries and dropped them.

He talked to his moms while his food cooked. She had aged tremendously in the last decade. Through her struggles, she continued to put God first. Dee knew that it was through her prayers and by the grace of God they were here. Their family was destroyed once before, but he knew there was no way it was going to stop. Strong was feeling secure in his system and was seeing money he hadn't seen in a long time.

"You givin' the Lord His share of this money?" Mom asked.

"Yes, I paid some tithes," Dee said seriously.

"Stop lyin'. You ain't been to church. You need to give the Lord at least one Sunday. It would make me feel so good to look and see my son in church."

Then a look of sadness came over her face.

Dee knew her thoughts went to Black and Junie.

She started mixing her potato salad to clear her head.

Dee kissed her on her sweaty forehead, threw his wings, fries, and scooped up some greens and walked back out front. He was standing out front with Kev, Lo, Mike-Mike, Poppa, Pop, and Dundee, when Strong pulled up in his new Cadillac Escalade. This was going to be Moms first time seeing him in four years.

He pulled in front of the Denali. They were grill to grill. Dee watched as the navy blue Timbs hit the sidewalk. Maurice Malone jeans and white T-shirt, Strong joined his team that was out front hollering at the many females going in and out of the restaurant, the nail shop, NY Hair Salon, or Stellar, the beauty supply store.

The restaurant was in a prime location. Always a view.

Strong walked over to Dee and grabbed a piece of chicken. "Everything a'ight?"

"No doubt. Waitin' on you, kid."

"What's goin' on, Strong?" Mike-Mike said. "You goin' to put me with Monica, shorty's cousin?"

"Gotta see. They don't know who I am; they don't know I'm connected to LE, son. Know what I'm sayin'?"

"Yeah! I see what you sayin'." Mike-Mike sipped his Heineken.

"You know we don't need no shit up here—need to do something with that," Strong said.

Mike-Mike went and sat in Strong's truck. Dee and Strong looked at each other and walked inside. Lo followed.

Black peeped over the shutters. He looked at Moms. He always knew he would see her again, but he always prayed it would be while she was standing. He walked in the back.

"Heah, Ma," Black said as she stepped out.

She stopped in her tracks. A look came over her face, her eyes turned glassy, and the tears fell. She threw her arms around his neck, squeezing with all her strength.

Black held his mother. He knew she was praying and he wanted and needed her prayers.

She placed her hands on his chest and stared into his eyes for about two minutes. "So you okay?" She wiped her eyes.

"I'm all right, Ma. I'm all right."

"The police still lookin' for you."

"Naw," Black lied. But he wasn't worried about the police. His only worry was trying to duck these ruthless cats trying to take his, and the Feds.

"Stop lyin'—I wa'n' askin' you, I was tellin' you. They still come by from time to time."

"Don't worry, Momma." Black gave her another hug.

Auntie walked into the kitchen and set bags down. "What the hell—" She hugged Black. She understood her sister's happiness. They had shared the same heartaches and tragedies.

"So what you doin' in here? Ain't the police still lookin' for you? Yo' mamma said they knocked on the door the other week. Get your ass outta here and be careful."

Black walked back into the dining area, giving Dee a pound and a hug, then a pound to Lo.

"So what's up, cuzzo?" Lo asked. "You know the fifth annual Lake Edward basketball tournament is comin' up?"

"You still gettin' a squad?"

"Hell yeah! Kev playin'; him, Dre, Li'l and them niggas."

"Just makin' sure. Niggas gonna be out that bitch. New whips and all, just like a car show. Mad teams comin' from Norfolk, and them niggas across the water that fuck with Allen I. You know them niggas comin' with phat-ass shit."

"No doubt."

"What y'all niggas know?" Lo said going back outside.

They were standing in the front, checking bitches, hollerin' at hoes passing by, never being disrespectful because it was a place of business.

"So when do we close on those other two houses?" Strong asked.

"Next week. I know you enjoyin' your condo," Dee added.

"Who would ever think I could buy that back— three-story with an elevator, loft and Jacuzzi, with a clear view of the Chesapeake Bay." He went deep in thought. "I go in there, Dee, and sit on the couch, roll some of that 'dro in a 'Sweet Backwoods' and I sit there and through that glass on the water, I find peace." Strong stared into nowhere.

"Better enjoy it. Paid dude thirty thousand above askin' price, that he got in cash as soon as he signed the contract. Shit, he broke his hand signin' that shit."

They all laughed.

"Know what, Dee? I been to ATL once and chilled with Angela since we met. I want to fuck with her. I want her in the ATL. But I want to bring her here, so I can really enjoy that condo."

"Do your thing, son. Nigga can feel a bitch. I know I can. So if you see her bringin' you happiness, bein' up under you, fly her ass in for the tournament. Parties, cookouts, you know the deal.

"So what you gonna do with the new shit? I can't believe you went all out. That shit is off the hook— five bedrooms, four full baths, three-car garage in Indian River Plantation. You way out there in Virginia Beach."

"That's where I can sleep. I'm gonna enjoy my shit like Scarface—by myself . . . until I find a wife."

"Don't compare yourself to that muthafucka," Dee told him.

"Naw, kid. I would of did the whole family—nobody's family matters but my own."

Dee had called Freddie Mac, a well-known realtor, once he had spoken with William L. Tyler, CPA, his accountant for E Corp, the restaurant, and Triple Strong Entertainment. Money was being pushed through all the businesses and getting a loan was never a question. The condo Strong was in on the Chesapeake Bay, as well as the condo Dee owned, were both bought under no doc loans. Dee put down thirty percent on each property, and the bank financed the rest. No documentation whatsoever. Freddie Mac was the fucking man. Now with this new accountant, it was five percent down for any property in the US.

***

"We have to get a base," Strong said. "We have to get safes put where they never have to be moved. We sittin' around here with three hundred thousand in the refrigerator and another three hundred thousand in the trunk of the parked car. I'm riding around with two hundred thousand in the trunk. We need these houses. Next time we go to ATL, we buyin' cribs. I want some fly-ass shit. Spend about seven hundred thousand."

"Gotcha. You only got to tell me once." Dee smiled. He had already peeped some fly shit in the ATL.

"Vianna suppose to be closin' on a house in Alpharetta, up GA400 in North Atlanta. She found a four-bedroom, two-and-a-half bath for two hundred eighty thousand. I gave her the eighty-four hundred down. Money safe there. Tricia been lookin' at houses too. The realtor sent me some pictures through the Internet. House over in Stone Mountain—four-bedroom, three full baths, and a two-car garage for one eighty, fifty-four hundred down. Let me show you." Dee reached in the truck, pulled out his laptop, and showed Strong pictures of the house.

"Find me one like that—I think Angela will like that. Then I can have a comfortable spot, and I can use her apartment for heads comin' down visitin'."

"No problem. I'll put dude on it."

"Oh, I still want some nice shit for us. Show them ATL muthafuckas how we really get down. Let me holla at Poppa. So what's up, Poppa? How's the family?"

"Not good. Girl had the baby couple days ago and something not right. They won't let her come home, so I got my other little one. Shit ain't no joke."

"Check this—front Dundee those five bricks. Get Lo, make them niggas come here and get that money. Tell him to set it up and holla back. Make sure it's in our favor . . . we talkin' about five of them thangs."

Poppa and Dundee walked over to Poppa's rental, and everybody started dispersing.

Then Dee's phone rang.

"Hello, love," Vianna said. "You busy?"

"Talkin' to my brother. What's goin'?"

"Tell him I said hello. I got the loan officer everything. They just verifyin' funds. We should be closin' at the end of July," she said with her high-pitched voice. Vianna kept going on and on about how she was going to decorate. "I'm gonna let you run. Call me later. I love you."

Soon after, Poppa called Strong to tell him Dundee's peoples were coming in the morning.

"Got some shit goin'. Gettin' ready to make moves into Carolina. It's on," Strong told Dee.

"Get it, son. I'm talkin' to this cat I know from Norfolk State. He was tellin' me how the white folks put their money into insurance companies, savings and loans, and it's secure. He was also sayin' something about trust funds, basically lettin' attorneys control your money. You makin' enough to let people handle your money making sure it's secure. Yours, the restaurant, that's over a mill a month—gotta do something to secure that."

Strong knew Dee would make sure they never ended up broke like they did before. He knew his brother was on top of every cent of this money.

Strong's phone rang, and so did Dee's. It was Tricia calling. She told him that she was a week late and was never late.

D had stopped using condoms with Tricia two months after they met, and for two years she never got pregnant. He thought she couldn't, even after she had a child already. *How stupid was I,* D thought.

Strong was still on the phone. "So what's your plans when you get off?"

"The same as everyday—go home, kick back, sip on some thug passion since the thug I got a passion for isn't here. So I'll put on one of your T-shirts, spark an L, light some candles, and relax. I'm missin' you, Strong."

"So . . . I'm gonna be in VA Beach for the weekend at my beach house. You wanna fly in?"

"Yeah! When? I'm off tomorrow."

"No. You have an appointment tomorrow at ten. A real estate agent from Re/Maxx gonna pick you up, take you and show you five cribs. Choose what you like, and we'll see if we can make this happen."

She was speechless.

"Okay. So afterwards . . ."

"Yeah, soon as you finish. Take pictures, so I can see your choices." Strong smiled.

"Fuck you smilin' about?" Dee said. "Actin' all soft and shit."

"I'll call you when I get home," she said passionately and hung up.

"She comin' in?"

"Yeah. Tomorrow. You seen my niece, kid?" Strong asked Dee.

"Yeah, she doin' good, growin' the hell up. Her moms cussed me out. Told me don't come around or she was goin' to call the police."

Strong grinned at the thought of Tara wilding out. Tara was mad cool, but when it came to Dee, it was definitely a thin line between love and hate.

"She got reason to hate you, man."

"Look who talkin'."

"We talkin' about you," Strong reminded him.

"Nigga, I was young, she was young. I never had that much money. Shit, I felt the money was enough for her and my daughter. Money came, and the bitches came and never stopped. I was wrong a lot of times, but things happen in life. Fuck it—love me. Just love me," Dee said.

"She ever call you back?"

"Yeah. I just gave her a stack of fifties, two grand to be exact, and my phone number. She called like twenty minutes later. She say maybe I can get her later if she ain't got to watch her little brothers."

"What?"

"Yeah. Bitch done had two more young 'uns and still no man. I went and saw her. She look good and doin' good." Dee asked, "What about you?"

"Shereena in Florida. Married, doin' well. So I called her moms. We gonna meet later when she get her for the holiday. And Tia, I've always stayed in touch with her. Me and Tia was close. She knew my moves before I knew them. And she knew my moves when I broke out. Somewhere along the way, she became my best friend and I'll always have love for my baby momma. Even if I'm not with her, she will never want for anything—I'm on some real shit. And believe me, her and my daughter are fine." Strong gave his brother a pound. "I'm gettin' ready to burst; I got business."

Chapter Ten

"It's F-r-i-d-a-y and I just got paid Ready for to-morrow to-show-my-niggas-ass . . ."

Dundee came out of 7-Eleven singing, thinking about the twenty grand he'd just made off his peoples from Carolina.

He got in the rental, which Scotty was driving and said, "I got to go to the mall. Need some new DC's and Timbs."

Pee-Wee sat in the back smoking, not giving a fuck. "You buyin' me something?"

"Hell, naw—y'all muthafuckas makin' more money than me."

"Talk yo' as off, nigga," Pee-Wee said; "we don't hear that shit."

"Y'all make mad dough off those packages," Dundee said. "I might see two grand."

"Kill that shit, Dundee—you got us," Scotty said.

Dundee knew Scotty knew about the twenty thousand. Scotty was to Dundee like Dee was to Strong, older, with Dundee looking up to him like a big brother.

"There's Lo and Mike-Mike in front of Precision Kuts." Scotty said. "Ain't that Kev . . . comin' from Brandywine?"

"Yeah! Pull over there. See what them niggas doin' today."

"I still can't believe what them niggas did to Bo and Rome," Pee-Wee said.

"That was that nigga Strong work. Nigga rude," Dundee said. "I couldn't even look at that shit; I turned my head."

"And you want to work right with that nigga—see what happens when you cross him," Scotty said.

"I ain't gonna cross him if I get in. I just got to get Poppa out the muthafuckin' way. He gettin' my money;" Dundee pointed out. "He ain't never put in no real work."

They parked and jumped out the car.

"Where the cookout at, niggas?" Mike-Mike asked.

Dundee pulled his pants up that were almost to the ground. "That's why we came over here."

Lo laughed. "You a funny nigga."

Mike-Mike told Lo, "Tell Kev Strong said get a cookout poppin' at Bayview Park. Tell everybody out LE."

As Kev approached, Lo said, "You, Strong said get a cookout goin'."

"I ain't got no money." Kev stood in front of them in a new Phat Farm sweats and T-shirt, white DC's, and jewelry dangling.

Pop and James walked out of the barbershop.

"What y'all got on this LE cookout?" Kev asked.

"Got my lips on whatever y'all cook," James joked.

Niggas laughed.

Pop wanted to know. "When y'all doin' something?"

James threw a fifty to Kev and went back in the shop. "Let me call some hoes."

Lo called Poppa.

"Yo! Poppa said whatever in the pot he'll match it. Buy some T-Bones," Lo yelled.

In a matter of minutes, Kev was holding four hundred and fifty dollars. "Match four fifty, Poppa."

"A'ight. Carry that shit to Murray's—a thousand dollars. Tell everybody out the way. I'll check y'all when I leave the hospital. I got to pick up my other child."

Lo could tell something wasn't good. "You all right, Poppa?"

"Yeah, man, I'll be all right."

Kev picked up the phone and called Strong. "Poppa matched. We got a gee, headed to Murray's Steakhouse, discount meat market."

"Fuck you talkin' 'bout?"

"Lo said *you* said get together a cookout."

"I ain't said shit."

"You a lyin'-ass nigga, Lo." Everybody started laughing. "It's on now, nigga. Get it poppin'."

"Where y'all at?"

"Precision Kuts. Brandywine."

"Oh, where they doin' this?"

"Bayview—right, Lo?" Kev said loud so Lo could hear, but in the phone for Strong to catch.

"Tell Lo, since he lied, to spend five hundred at the liquor store." Strong's phone beeped. "Call Dee, tell him what's up, and to holla at a nigga." He clicked over to the other line. "What?"

" 'What?' Is that any way to answer the phone?"

"Naw, cutie. How are you?"

"Fine. I looked at the houses and it came down to two. Beautiful. I can't wait to show you."

"Okay, baby, I can't wait to see it."

"I got something to ask?" she said quietly.

"What?"

"Do you have anything really planned for us?"

"Just ask, don't play."

"Dream don't have anything to do over the weekend. She quit the club too after I ain't show up. She said that was her signal, but she ain't got no plans. I know she'll love VA . . . especially this weekend."

"Bring her. And I did have plans, but we'll work around that."

"You sure?"

"Yeah. Buy one-way tickets. You may need her help driving back, so I guess it worked out. Call me and let me know what time you comin' in."

"I will. I went shopping. Got a surprise for you."

"Holla soon." Strong hung up and looked at his phone to check the time. *Fuck—one o'clock; the day gettin' away.* He called Poppa. "Everything all right?"

"No doubt. Went smooth. Lo got yours; he said he'd see you. I'll check y'all niggas at the park."

Poppa checked his phone to make sure it was on vibrate. He knew he wasn't supposed to have it on in the hospital. The streets were the only thing that was going well.

His girl had his daughter a week ago and was still in Norfolk General and they couldn't tell him nothing. And his three-year-old son was asking for Mommy every day and he didn't know what to say.

He sat down with his girl's aunt and held her hand.

Her moms walked in and gave him the dissatisfied look she'd always given him. She made no secret of her dislike for Poppa; always telling him and her daughter that she could do better.

Poppa spoke to her aunt, telling her there was no change and that he was leaving for a while.

"Go on—you look better goin'."

Poppa couldn't take it. "Your daughter up here fucked up and you still actin' the fool. Damn!" He threw his hands up.

She looked at Poppa and yelled, "You disgust me. Get out of my face—nothin'," and sat back down by her daughter's bedside.

Poppa jumped in his white Excursion. It was the Fourth of July weekend. Ballin' time—parties, cookouts, and here she was laid up. He turned up his sounds and turned on the DVD and dropped the screen. He paid the attendant and rolled out, headed to Newtown Road.

He rolled through Lake Edward. Wa'n' nobody out there, but niggas on the corner gettin' money, workers, and fiends. It was almost deserted. He turned on East Hastings.

"Yo, Poppa . . . goin' out the park?" Pee-Wee asked. He was out hustling his last few bags.

"Now that's where everybody at."

Pee-Wee jumped in the truck.

"You dirty?" Poppa asked seriously.

"Naw, nothin' but money," he said, pulling out a bundle of twenties.

They rode down East Hastings and headed out.

"That lady still got that wreath on her door."

"Hell yeah, and Dundee talkin' about killin' her because she suppose to testify against him," PeeWee said.

"Young nigga better slow down," Poppa warned.

"One on one, Poppa—he wants your spot."

"I know. Like they say, keep your enemy's close; he'll fuck up his own self. But he's a money-gettin'ass nigga."

"You got that shit right. That's because he know niggas from everywhere. And he don't give a fuck—he'll sell to anybody, rob anybody, and kill anybody. True live wire."

"Believe me, he knows that nigga talks and acts wild, but he know who Poppa is. I was doin' bids when y'all niggas was at the park eatin' dirt."

Pee-Wee laughed.

They pulled up at the park. People were playing ball, but most were standing around listening to the radio/ CD boxes being played. It was about a hundred people out, and cars were still coming.

"Not bad for short notice, huh." Lo gave Poppa pound.

"What the deal, big Poppa?" Dundee gave Poppa a pound too.

Girls started hugging Poppa, kids were running around, it was going good.

Lo saw Dee pulling up into the parking lot. He met Dee so that he would park beside him. Dee parked and got out.

"Pop your trunk, fam," Lo said to Dee, opening the back to his new wintergreen, dark-tinted Benz wagon sitting on chrome.

Dee opened the hatch as Lo tossed the trash bag in the back.

"A hundred grand. Today's deal."

"Bet. I'll take care of it. Let's see what's goin' on over here." Dee checked out the crowd. He showed love to everybody and made a drink. "Where Kev?" he asked Lo.

"He comin'. Had some shit to take care of with Pop."

Dee pulled out his phone and hit Strong. "Fuck you at?"

"I got to meet Angela. Her moms picked her up from the airport, so she spendin' some time with her child. Then she gonna get dropped off at the park. She brought a friend too."

"What she look like?"

"I don't know, but she use to dance too. I know that."

"Word, word."

"Somebody got to get her—you or Kev—I don't give a fuck!"

"I'm keepin' my options open, nigga. How long you be?"

"I'm here."

Dee turned just in time to see the Escalade rolling by, headed to the parking lot.

Strong came strolling up—black Rocawear jeans, black Timbs, and white T-shirt. When you looked around, that was all you saw—white T-shirts. LE cats had a new style, crisp white new T-shirts everyday. Even the street vendors that set up shop near hair salons, and convenience stores had white T-shirts for five dollars. It was like private school, you made your fashion statement by your jeans and shoes.

"What the deal, Strong?" niggas yelled as they gave him dap. He walked up to Dee gave him a pound and a hug. Really to say, another day together is another great day.

"What the deal, Poppa?" somebody yelled. "Fuck up with those steaks?"

"Better eat those muthafuckin' hot dogs and hamburgers and be grateful," Dundee hollered.

People started laughing.

The nigga wanted to say, "Fuck you, Dundee," but didn't know how Dundee would take it.

"Yo, yah hoes get these kids somethin' to eat. Matter a fact, I want a picture with all these kids holding a hot dog in one hand and a hamburger in the other—I don't give a fuck how old they are." Lo started going around gathering kids.

Kev, Pop, and James had pulled up in the 3.5RL AC. When Kev saw Lo running around grabbing everybody's kids, he asked, "What the hell that fool doin'?"

"He want a picture of all these bad-ass kids from Lake Edward holdin' hot dogs," Dundee explained. I'm gonna go get some Bayside Arms kids and North Ridge kids, bring out here and get them started early.

Everybody fell out laughing. They thought about all the Lake Edward against Bayside Arms fights.

"Know what, we all used to fight LE against North Ridge, LE against Carriage Houses. Why nobody likes us?" Scotty asked.

"That shit was just to stay in practice," Strong said. "Because what happened when we went out Green Run, First Colonial, Chesapeake or Norfolk, even if you didn't like each other, we all became Bayside niggas. And is there a stronger force?"

"Hell naw. Let niggas step out on this muthafuckin' block." Pee-Wee did the LE holler.

Kev, Pop, and James were standing around listening, catching up on history. Pop and James were from Norview, and Kev was from Memphis, so they could relate to the pride niggas had and were holding down their hood.

"Fuck all that fightin' shit; show some love," Mike-Mike started giving all the kids hot dogs and hamburgers for the picture as Lo lined them up.

"Shut up, Mike-Mike," Pee-Wee said, "If you put the cup down you could get something done."

"Last muthafucka who talk shit to me, they found them burnt to fuck—blacker than a muthafucka—with his hand on his seatbelt." Mike-Mike laughed.

No one else laughed. They just looked at him and shook their heads.

"He doesn't know what to say out his mouth," Poppa said.

"Fuck them niggas and fuck all y'all. If somebody wanna fight, come on."

Niggas looked at each other and ran a dove on him, mushing him into the ground, punching him. He jumped up mad, but what could he do.

"Who them hoes over there at the table being anti-social," Lo asked.

"They with us. They from out Norview," James said.

"Well, introduce me to something." Lo walked toward them, followed by James and Mike-Mike.

Another four girls had just got out of a Ford Explorer and two more out of an old Volvo.

"Check these bitches," Kev said. "Those four tight, but these two hoes walkin' by themselves is off the hook."

"For real. Let me get my dibs in." Pop walked over and introduced himself to Dream and Angela. Dream's body grabbed him; Angela's beauty drew him right to her.

Kev automatically eased to Dream, her shoulder-length hair gleaming. He stepped close enough to catch the scent from her hair. He could tell the shit was just done. Her short wrap-around dress left her breast partially exposed and swung with the flow of her ass. "I'm Kev." He smiled his bright, white smile that bitches loved.

"I'm Dream," she said laying her perfectly manicured hand on her breast, right where her nails met her cleavage.

"And I'm Angela." She looked at Pop with her light eyes, half-open, barely moving her glistening lips. The only bitch he knew that had that type of natural beauty was on TV.

"I saw y'all get dropped off. So if you need a ride that's my AC over there sitting on them twenties." Pop smiled, and they began smiling at his comment.

"Well, you better catch his ride 'cause my shit in the shop," Kev said as if it was a joke.

"Oh, it's in the shop, huh!" Dream said it like a line they'd heard many times before.

They all laughed.

"Actually, we're tryin' to find Strong." Angela squinted in apology.

"No problem, baby. Let me show you to him."

They headed in the direction of Strong and Dee, and Kev and Dream followed, tuned in to their own conversation.

"Thought I had found my wife," Pop said as he approached Strong to give him a pound to say no disrespect. "Your bitch is bad."

Angela hugged him and kissed him on the cheek.

"Nice to have met you," Pop said before turning to walk away.

Kev and Dream was slowly strolling up, laughing and smiling.

"Well, that's Dream over there talking to dude. And this my big brother, Dee," Strong said with a feeling of pride. "And this is my little brother, Kev." Strong gave him a pound to let him know he was on his job—somebody had to get that extra.

Kev said, "Dream, this Strong; this is their other brother, Dee."

"Nice to meet you," Dream said.

Dee stared at her pretty white teeth, beautiful lips, the side view of her dress pulling from the wide hips, allowing her ass to set out and fuck niggas up. *Too beautiful to be real. This bitch is bad.* "Goddamn!" Dee shook his head. "Whew."

The girls looked at each other.

Strong and Kev gave half smiles. They knew exactly what he meant.

"Don't act funny. Y'all better get somethin' to eat. All this shit out here—steaks over there, some still on the grill; chicken, dogs, sausages, baked beans, that shit on the table."

They heard some arguing going on at the other table.

James came walking over by Dee and Kev. "Need to get Mike-Mike, man. He over there callin' girls hoes and bitches and they ain't with it."

"Lo got him. If not, tell Pee-Wee," Kev said.

All of a sudden Dundee's baby momma jumped on one of Dundee's girlfriends. Niggas was on the court arguing. It was time to go.

"Y'all ridin' with me." Strong headed to the truck, and the girls followed.

"Where you want me to drop you, Kev?" Dee asked loud.

"I'm all right. I'm rollin' with Strong."

"You don't want to crowd his truck; I got plenty of room."

Everybody caught on and laughed.

Kev hugged Dream. "I ain't leavin' my baby. I ain't got no car, and I guess you stuck with me." He gave her a big smile.

She got in the truck and sat down next to Kev, closer than she had to be. "I guess I'm stuck with you."

"What the deal, cuzzo?" Lo ran to the BMW wagon with Mike-Mike by his side. "Hit niggas later," he said, and he was out with Mike-Mike hanging out the window yelling.

Dee climbed in his Yukon and picked up his phone to dial Dog, his childhood friend still stationed in New Jersey. The military was treating him good—he'd bought him a home and an Escalade. They had talked earlier and he was supposed to be coming in town. Dog had been to Charlotte twice and ATL numerous times.

Dee dialed Big gees number. Him and Big G hadn't swung out in a while.

"Hello." Big G sounded mad as always.

"What the deal, partner? What you doin'?"

"Fuckin'! I'm fuckin' and you don't disturb me because you can't find no pussy."

"Ain't nobody tryin' to fuck yo' big ass." Dee laughed. Big G was the only big pimp he knew. Other big muthafuckas got pussy, but Big G always got his share and everybody else's.

"Why you ain't come to the park, stupid?"

"Told you—I was fuckin' some ass."

"Like you couldn't come out, then go back. You on some bullshit. Holla."

Dee dialed Chantel. There was no answer. He dialed her cell, she didn't answer. He got his laptop and searched her grandmother's number in Plymouth, NC.

"Hello," the older lady's voice answered.

"Hey, grandma. Chantel there?"

"Yeah, hold on. That boy gonna hunt you down, ain't he?" She gave Chantel the phone.

"Hello. You didn't answer earlier. Did you get my message?"

"Naw, I ain't even check them shit."

"So what the deal? When you be home?"

"Next week for sure!"

"A'ight. Call me later. We headed to dinner. Bye." She hung up.

Damn, Dee thought to himself, *she was always straight and direct. No softness whatsoever.* Chantel was never soft or very affectionate, but she was dependable, smart, and true. And what he liked most of all—she gave him a sense of security to know he had a hell of a woman behind him.

Dee then dialed Vianna. There was no answer. He called her cell.

"Hello."

"What da deal?"

"Why? You here?"

"No. What difference do it make? Where the fuck you at?" Dee hated that smart-ass shit.

"I'm on my way out College Park. I'll be out that way until tomorrow; my family doin' somethin'."

"A'ight. Was that hard?"

"Yeah. You always out of town. I want my time. I'm lonely. I get tired of goin' to my family shit by myself."

"So what you sayin'? Speak up now. I told you, if you want to go your way, say something. Don't fuck around and get caught up, get fucked up."

"I didn't say all that, Dee; you just don't understand."

He could hear the trembling in her voice.

"My job is sending me to Oakland for four days for training. They are putting me up in the Wynndam out there, October twentieth to the twenty-fourth. Do I have to go by myself, or will I have some company? Don't answer now because I don't wanna hear no excuses. Please try. I'm giving you enough notice. I don't ask that much of you and—"

Dee held the phone to his side, thinking, *Yeah, yeah, yeah.* He held the phone back up to his ear, and she was still flowing.

"Yo! I'm comin'. I ridin' with you," Dee said, not talking to anybody. "I'm gonna holla back."

"Yeah," she said with attitude.

Dee hung up. He started the truck and headed out to the exclusive neighborhood of Church Point across the street from Bayview Park. Several stars lived in the same neighborhood—Teddy Riley, Bruce Smith, and many other corporate millionaires. Dee rode through and stopped in front of his newly built home. *Life had taken a turn for the better.* He looked around at all the beautiful homes and wondered how many of them were purchased through illegal funds.

His phone rang. It was Strong seeing what he was up to. Him and Kev were at the condo chillin'.

"Let me holla at Kev."

Dee asked Kev, "You 'right, nigga?"

"Damn right. Go to the spot with the garage and look in my room."

"Bet. I'll holla." Dee lit his Garca Vega. He turned the truck around.

As he was pulling off, he heard someone yell, "Dee."

He slowed down and looked around. Then he heard it again. He looked to his left and saw the young lady standing in the driveway of one of the finer homes. He knew the face but not the name. He pulled over to the girl's driveway as she made her way to the truck.

"Heah, Dee," she said. "It's been a longtime."

"Yeah, it has," he said with a confused look to let her know he wasn't quite sure of their connection.

"Stacy—I used to be with Maria and them when you had those parties in your sports bar."

Dee remembered Maria, but he didn't really remember her or anything about her, just her face.

"Okay. How are you? I remember the face but not your name."

"Yeah. I was smaller then; I was the quiet one."

"I heard that." Dee looked her up and down. "How old are you, cutie?"

"Twenty-two."

Damn! This cutie was only sixteen or seventeen hangin' in my shit. I was twenty-four then. "So what you been up to all this time?" Dee looked into her eyes.

Her slanted, bright eyes were dazzling. With perfectly arched eyebrows, flawless skin, and small lips, her small, white, tight-fitting shirt came down to her waist and covered the largest prettiest breasts. She moved around as if she was restless, showing off that small waist and phat ass.

"I've been doing hair for the last four years. It's been goin' well. I live over here with my grandparents. I take care of my grandmother when my granddad's on the road.

"He started Mt. Zion Baptist Church downtown on Granby Street. Now he got five churches in Richmond, Roanoke, and North Carolina. What about you?"

"I sold my sports bar, broke out to ATL, and been down there for a couple years. Gettin' ready to do a club down there, so I'm back and forth."

"That's good. Whose house—you and your girl?"

"Naw, I'm rollin' solo. And you?"

"Not attached."

Dee twisted his mouth to let her know he thought she was lying.

"I'm for real. I was with this guy for four years. Two of those years he was locked up, I was true for real. He came home and wilded out. That was a year ago and here I am."

"So you don't have friends?"

"No. Because most guys lookin' for something. And if I'm with a guy, I'm with him forever—him and him only—I don't go for anything else."

"I heard that. Stacy, it was good seein' you again. I got to get ready and run."

"When are we going to talk, Dee?" She stared into his eyes. "I enjoyed talking with you."

"Me too, cutie."

"I work every day except Sunday and Monday. I'm home after six usually, so stop by sometimes or just call." She gave him the number, and he left.

He was headed to Lake Edward when his phone rang. He looked at the phone's caller ID: 770. "Hello, baby," he said. "How are you?"

"I'm fine. Sittin' here with Kay. We goin' to put some shit on the grill tomorrow. Tonight we goin' to the KAI YAH. We smokin' a blunt now, sippin' on some apple martinis we made."

"Be careful out there tonight. You know it's the Fourth weekend—drunken muthafuckas actin' a fool."

"I know. I'll call you when I get in, okay."

Dee couldn't wait to get back to Tricia. He pictured her getting out the shower and strolling around the house in her thong before getting dressed. She never knew that drove him crazy.

Dee never meant to ever compare any of the girls he was engaged with, but the things Tricia did, no one could match. Nobody cooked, waited on him, pampered him like her. Nobody rubbed his body all the time, gave massages like her. Nobody knew how to tone down his anger when shit was in an uproar. And nobody took care of his body like Tricia. Before sex, she would ensure the dick was hard.

When making love she knew how to move, gave it to him however he wanted. She gave him sex at the drop of a dime, anytime he had the desire.

When he wasn't in the mood, she would be the aggressor until he was in the mood. And whenever that time of the month came, he was still well satisfied. Her man was always taken care of, as she would say.

"If you go anywhere else, you just a fucked-up-ass nigga . . . because I never tell you no."

He thought of Vianna and Chantel. They were financially stable, educated, and they loved him with their heart, but the only one who even had a chance of keeping him was Tricia. He couldn't help being who he was, but when it was time to fuck, he had to fuck. *The hell with being with a woman who fucks when she wanna fuck and suck dick every blue moon.* Dee had a simple theory—what one bitch won't do, another one will. That don't have shit to do with love.

Kev and Dream decided to give Strong and Angela some privacy. Kev figured getting her away from her friend improved his chances anyway. He took the S500 that was in the garage—it now had VA tags with the state seal and a slight tint—so him and Dream could drive up the coast until they reached the Atlantic Ocean.

Kev realized that the beach was an aphrodisiac. Any girl who wasn't used to the beach, like Atlanta bitches and New York bitches, it always got them. Not to mention the beach house, Escalade, and Benz.

Dream was definitely looking at Kev and Strong as a perfect picture of urban elegance.

Strong walked out of his game room holding Angela's hand. He stepped on the elevator and rose to the second floor. The candlelit room allowed them to see their silhouettes on the wall as he hugged her, stepping off the elevator. He made them drinks, and she rolled an L. They sat in the Jacuzzi, looking through the glass that rose from the second floor to the third, exposing a perfect view of the Chesapeake Bay.

"I lived here all my life and never knew they had shit like this, not even fifteen minutes from the crib. It's amazing. The view is perfect, so are you." Strong kissed her neck and massaged her shoulders.

***

The sounds of the buzzer woke Strong and Angela. Kev forgot the code and was at the gate trying to get in. Strong buzzed him in.

Angela grabbed her silk robe to cover her silk spaghetti-strap nightgown. She walked out of the room and looked out at the water. *This shit is off the hook.* She went to the loft and glanced over into the family room. "What the deal, peoples?" She leaned on the rail, looking down at Kev, Dream, and Strong. "What today's plans?"

"Tournament start at eleven; it's nine now. We play at two. It will be hot as hell by then. The tournament is two days. It should be off the hook."

"Should be," Angela said. "They have it every year, and that shit be off the rocker. Niggas come from all seven cities. It be like a car show. Real car show."

Strong and Kev looked at each other and smiled. Kev said, "I need you to drop me at Kenny Bug Shop on Monticello, so I can pick up my whip. That nigga said he'd be done by eleven."

"Well, let me shower, because once I go out the Lakes, I ain't comin' back this way until tonight," Strong said. He went upstairs to the bedroom.

Afterwards Strong, Kev, and the girls jumped in the Benz and left. Kev was driving with Dream by his side, headed downtown. Her brown legs sticking out of her beige skirt damn near had him off the road. *What the fuck was happening?* He had enjoyed her every way possible the night before and couldn't get the black thong out of his head.

She laid her hand on his. She was definitely feeling him.

Strong leaned back, enjoying being chauffeured around.

They pulled up to The Music Shop, where they had just finished putting the TV's in the headrest. They pulled the new platinum CLK55 out of the garage. (Kev had traded his other car in and got this; the CLK320 just didn't have the power, nor was the one he looked at a drop.)

Kev looked at his whip and smiled—the new convertible CLK was going to shit on niggas— eighty thousand rolling on wheels.

Strong and the girls headed to Imperial Motors, the exclusive car lot. You could go in and request what you like and in days they would have it. Strong wanted another truck for the ATL. He knew if he got Angela a truck, then he would have transportation when he hit Atlanta. They pulled up on the lot, and Angela and Dream looked at each other and smiled.

The owner greeted Strong by name. Through Strong's team alone, the car lot had made a fortune.

Thirty minutes later, Angela was leaving the lot in her new G5 Benz truck, allowing Imperial Motors to get another eighty thousand. She was overjoyed. Most niggas allowed you to drive their shit, if they cared for you or to let other cats know you belong to them, but to just show love and buy you a whip and a crib . . . Angela was like, *Whoa!*

Strong told Angela to follow him back to the crib so she could in return drop him off. She followed him, and he returned his car and jumped in the truck. This shit was nicer than the Escalade, but he wanted the Cadillac for VA.

She pulled on Witchduck Road to a storage, and Strong got out.

Angela asked him, "You gonna be a'ight?"

"For sure. What time is it?"

"Eleven. That Triple Strong Entertainment is you?" Dream asked.

"Yeah, I sponsor them. My cousin Lo got a team too for the restaurant. I'll meet y'all out at the courts in a couple hours. Kev and them definitely goin' to win the first round. Probably play again about four."

"That's good. We goin' to run to McArthur Mall and pick up a few things," Angela told him. "Need anything?"

"No, I'm all right."

"What's your size anyway?"

"Thirty-eight waist, thirty length and triple X shirts. Size eight-and-a-half Timbs and DC's."

"Gotcha."

Strong began to walk away.

"Heah, give me a kiss, nigga. You buy me houses, cars, clothes, but I catch hell gettin' a kiss."

Angela and Dream laughed.

Strong leaned down and gave her a kiss, and she pulled off smiling.

Angela picked up her phone. "I don't know why my girl ain't called me. Let me try this bitch again."

"If she truly your girl," Dream said, "she'll call you."

After picking up a few things at McArthur Mall they went by Angela's moms to change before going to the courts. On her way down Baker Road she saw some of her old Bayside team hanging out at 7-Eleven and pulled over. She hadn't had a chance to talk to Fat Joe or Quan since she'd seen them at Rome's and Ski's funeral.

They didn't know who she was when she first pulled up.

She got out the truck.

"Goddamn, girl. What the hell!" Fat Joe said. "I guess the ATL treating you good or that bitch treatin' you good."

"I ain't fuckin' with her no more—I got a man, son." Angela gave him a pound like a nigga.

"Heah, Quan." Angela hugged him as he approached. She smelled a certain stench. She looked at Quan up and down. His Timbs were dirty as if they'd been through three winters, three summers, and were on their way into winter number four. His jeans looked as if they could stand on their own and his once-white-turned-beige T-shirt was hanging like he had it on for days.

"What's up, Angela?" Quan barely lifted his head.

She touched his cheek and looked in his eyes. She could tell he was looking for more than weed. She looked over at Fat Joe with disgust in her eyes.

Fat Joe signaled for her to walk with him. He wasn't with Quan, but had seen him up there just like her.

Dream got out the truck and walked in the store. She came out with two cranberry juices. She was so fine, Joe stopped and Quan lifted his head. Some other cats were trying to holler, but she paid them no attention.

"So what's goin' on, Joe?"

"Not a whole lot." Joe stepped over to his Durango and grabbed a small package out the door compartment. He took two toots and shook his head, then handed it to Angela.

She took two toots and handed it to Dream in the truck. Dream finished it off.

"How Quan get fucked all up, Joe?"

"Fuckin' with them niggas on the other side. You know all I do and ever done is smoke and toot this here." He showed her another bag. "But niggas out here is losin' they minds—tootin' coke, heroin, takin' X, and puttin' crack in weed. That's what got him."

"I hate to see my nigga like that," Angela said.

"They say your girl doin' the same thing, but she ain't gone yet. Monica still lookin' good, but she tootin' probably over seven, eight grams a day."

"For real! I been callin' her since I came in yesterday and she ain't answer or call me back. How she supportin' that habit?"

"This was the part of the conversation I didn't want to have—she fuckin' with your boy Ray."

Angela's head snapped back to attention. "What?"

"Yeah, Ray started hustlin' and blew. You know he soft, so he had to fuck with those Carriage House niggas. Somehow he got dough, found a connect, and got those niggas scorin' from him. He movin' weight and Monica right there."

Angela laughed. "Not Ray."

"Oh yeah, your cousin—the bitch you was stayin' with before you left—was around here talkin' shit on you, talkin' 'bout she help shorty turn you out and how she was carryin' you to Atlanta to work."

"My cousin's a stupid bitch. I left here on a good note, but that ain't my first time hearin' that shit. I'm gonna see her soon."

"You goin' to the courts?" he asked getting in his truck.

"Yeah, I'm behind you."

"Sorry, girl, my nigga was just catchin' me up. Seem like my girl fuckin' with my high-school love and she probably ashamed—I don't want that gay-ass muthafucka."

Quan walked up to the truck. "Can I hold somethin', Monica? I mean, Angela."

She handed him thirty dollars. "Quan, please get your shit together. We all make mistakes and choose the wrong paths, but we can bounce back."

"I'm tryin', An. I'm tryin'."

They pulled up by the courts. It was so packed, you had to park several blocks away. Angela couldn't see it and drove closer to the crowd.

"Damn, niggas gettin' it around this bitch," Dream said.

"Niggas goin' to jail around this bitch—that's what they doin'," Angela told her. "Let me break this shit down for you. See over there"—Angela pointed to a group of niggas sitting and parked by the apartments behind the picnic tables by the courts, the Bentley's, 600 Benz—"that's Allen Iverson peoples. They come from across the water, Hampton and Newport News; they are truly rich and got backin'. They ain't about no trouble, just hollerin'.

"See those guys over there with the Escalade, Yukon Denali, and those little BMW's and the Lexus—those cats from Portsmouth and the Beach—they run with Timberland and Pharrell. They got money, some of them, but they in the industry so you know."

They both said soft at the same time, "Fuck 'em!"

"Now over there, the clique with the 4Runner, Yukon, Q45, Tahoe—them niggas hustle out Carriage House. They got money and they chill-ass niggas. Love to have a good time, but they get rowdy and rude at times. Now over there in the parking lot where the black Lexus is sitting, black Avalon, white Mountaineer, Porsche— those cats from Bayside Arms and Northridge right down the street. We go to school with them."

"And those LE niggas over there where my baby CLK sittin'?" Dream asked. "Look at his fine ass. Don't even know it's us. Pull over there. They got four cones over there; maybe you can get a space."

Angela pulled up by a cone. Kev noticed her and moved the cone behind Poppa's Suburban. All eyes were on the G5 truck as the girls stepped out.

As soon as Angela's Dolce and Gabbana sandals hit the pavement, she noticed Monica. The black Dolce and Gabbana shorts hugged her hips and flowed with her movement as if they were painted on.

"Shinin', ain't you, girl?" Kev said to Angela.

She looked at him through her D&G glasses. "Like the muthafuckin' sun, nigga," Angela told him. She knew eyes were on her.

Some were her peers. They knew Angela, but they didn't know her like this.

Angela saw Monica across the court sitting on the CL600 "drop" being driven by Ray, staring his ass off from the time the G5 truck pulled up.

Monica saw her talking to Kev. She thought her truck was nice but didn't consider Kev to be any competition. He wasn't large as Ray and Ray had money now. Kev wasn't from VA and she didn't know him, but she knew he drove that platinum CLK.

"Give me a hug," Kev said to Dream, sitting in the truck; "need some good luck. We barely won that last game."

Out of nowhere you heard the roar of motorcycles, and all eyes went to the ZX9R Kawasaki hanging in the air down Newtown Road with an airbrushed picture of Junie on both sides with RIP. The rider was draped in royal blue and black, with a silver half helmet. Behind him was Lo and Pop on the Suzuki 1200 and Ducati 900ss, chromed from front to back like the other two, with loud Muzzy pipes.

Dee pulled up and jumped off the bike. Niggas gathered around checking out the paint job, some asking who Junie was.

"That was y'all's older brother?" Angela asked.

"Yeah," Dee told her. The pain of Junie's loss hit him again. He looked around and went over and hit the blunt that Pee-Wee had.

Angela looked over at Ray. By this time, Monica had made her way closer to the end, near Angela.

Angela knew that bitch wanted to talk.

"Here come Poppa. Move the other cone."

Poppa pulled up, shining in the convertible Cadillac, El Dog. He jumped out wearing a wife-beater, showing off his tats, jeans sagging, and Timbs.

"Fuck goin' on, my niggas?" Mike-Mike yelled, jumping out the Suburban with the Grey Goose.

"Put that shit up, Mike-Mike," Lo said. "Ain't no police out here. They at the restaurant eating; all of them."

Everybody laughed as he continued to take the Goose to the gut.

"Pass it here then, son."

"Who gonna win the car show?" Scotty asked.

"I already see who won that shit," Poppa said. "That hot-ass Bentley drop—rich-ass niggas. Nobody can fuck with that athlete money. Then strong second is between Kev and Ray, big ballers."

"Shit, Ray ain't no baller—his dad died and left him that business. He ain't want it, so his dad partner bought him out—three hundred fifty thousand," Mike-Mike said.

"Well, the nigga got weight and be gettin' it. If he had a quarter mill then, he might have a million now," Kev said.

"Cats say he soft, but nobody really fucks with him."

"Shit, his ass done got robbed a couple times. I know." Lo said it like he was the one that did it.

"Yeah, but two cats dead and one dismembered," Mike-Mike added. "They lookin' for the other one."

"They ain't lookin' for the other one," Lo said. "I ain't use no mask—fuck him and his muthafuckin' team."

Poppa looked at Lo.

"Ray is a punk-ass nigga, but he gettin' it and nobody fucks with him because of his cousin, Speed. Speed that nigga first cousin."

Those who knew who Speed was stared at each other and then at Lo. Everybody knew Lo was a wild nigga, but he wa'n' ready to fuck with Speed.

Out of nowhere, a black Dodge Viper and royal blue Corvette ZR1 came flying down Newtown, past the courts, doing about a hundred.

Everybody stopped and looked except for the cats playing ball.

The tinted-out Viper and ZR1 pulled up in front of Poppa, and the tinted window came down. It was Javonne, that neighborhood cat that hustled alone, light-skinned nigga with three golds in the top row of his mouth. Rocked dreads, twists, whatever you called them, with a headband around his head, pulling them back. He skidded off, racing down Lake Edward Drive.

"Fool gettin' that money, hustlin'-ass LE nigga," Poppa said.

"That's my peoples, but he ain't never put me on. He a'ight though," Dundee said.

"We good, nigga." Poppa gave him a pound.

Angela noticed Monica talking to Fat Joe. He went to school with most of these niggas and had no beef. Angela walked across the street. "Watch my girl, Kev." She looked at Dream.

"Nobody wanna fuck with this Memphis bitch," Dream said.

"I thought you from Atlanta," Kev said.

"I live there now, but originally from Millington."

Just then, the coordinator got on the loud speaker and announced the next game.

"I gotta run. Don't let nothin' happen to my girl, Poppa—that's my future." Out of all the girls he'd been through, this shorty was on. He fucked around and took the condom off just the night before and that shit was incredible.

"Don't play, Kev. Goin' home the right way is a dream for Dream." They smiled.

Kev noticed Dundee and Javonne trying to park where the cones were. He yelled, "Move the cones, Pee-Wee."

Angela walked up to Monica and Fat Joe. They looked each other up and down. Angela noticed Monica was dressed head to toe in Burberry shorts, bikini top, showing her pierced belly button and banging-ass body. Her Burberry hat complimented her lightly tinted three-hundred dollar Burberry shades that covered her grey eyes. They both knew they were tight.

"So you can't answer my shit because you fuckin' with that bum-ass nigga"—Angela pointed at Ray—"and scared to be a woman and say that."

"I knew you'd act like this and I ain't got time . . . nor do I want to hear any bullshit about how I handle mine."

"Monica, I know Ray fake and you coachin' him. He playin' what he thinks is a game and if he knew shit about it, he would know it's far from a game. And I know you—if he go broke tomorrow, you out."

"I learned from the best. My old roommate taught me to get it all at any cost," Monica said, hiding behind the three-hundred dollar shades.

"That was low. You ain't shit. You always held me responsible, but I'm livin' with that shit, Monica."

"I know you are, An. I know. Look, I know you don't want him, and if I don't drain him, some other bitch will." Monica held her hands up. "I thought you forgot the game—fuckin' with dirty-ass bitches."

"That's my past, girl. My past."

"So who you fuckin' with, girl? Kev?"

Kev had been in town a short time but had made his mark as a pretty boy with braids. Him and Pop were getting it, and they were running through some hoes.

SCURRRRRRRRRRRRRRRRRRRRRRRR!!!!! was all you heard. Then the streak of bright yellow flew by, getting the attention of every living soul. The bright-yellow Lamborghini came to a sudden stop. The driver made a doughnut, and smoke clouded everybody's sight. Then he took off, beaming toward Poppa.

The car had everyone's attention, until a streak of silver flew by doing one hundred twenty miles per hour, and stopped on a dime. The driver threw the Ferrari GT in reverse. He was going backwards at about sixty and came to a dead stop.

Then the driver punched it, and the car did doughnuts in a perfect circle until it looked like a compact platinum bullet. He burst toward Dee and Poppa and stopped, then burned rubber, sitting still for about fifteen seconds.

When the smoke cleared, Ant jumped out the Lamborghini as the doors went up, and Strong got out the Ferrari.

Strong approached Dee and Poppa while Kev, Lo, Dundee, Pop, and JaVonne all crowded around the Ferrari. Ant walked over to the cats with the Bentleys and 600's.

"That shit nice," Poppa said. "Doors open like a spaceship—off the fuckin' hook."

"The nigga shit is hot," Dee said. "I like silver and the way that shit look; but the bright yellow screamin'.'"

"What them shits cost?" Poppa asked.

"Ferrari, two-hundred and thirty thousand, and the Lambo was fifty more."

"For a goddamn toy." Poppa shook his head.

"You can get out the truck, girl. You a'ight out here," Strong said to Dream.

She was getting ready to get out anyway because Angela had called her. She stepped out the truck. Strong couldn't help looking as she stepped to the sidewalk.

He saw the most blessed ass and hips, low-cut jeans with a bikini string going into her ass. Her tight half-shirt covering those firm thirty-six-D's that were trying to come out of the bra and free themselves.

Many girls were hating, not because of the outfit, but the body was a dream. She walked across the street, catching every eye, including even Monica's.

"So you and Kev kickin' it?" Monica asked Angela after all the commotion died down.

"Naw, girl. I fuck with his brother Strong, the guy with the white Iverson jersey and the two long platinum chains."

Monica stared and couldn't believe what she was seeing. The braids he had when she knew of him were gone. "Who Black?"

"Who? Hell naw. I said Strong, the one driving the silver sports car."

"Angela, what you say? You fuck with him?"

"Yeah, he bought that truck, girl, and we got a house."

"Girl, that is Black. The guy beside him is Dee, and the one with the dreads is Lo. Remember I told you about them a while back."

"Yeah, but I thought—" Angela got quiet as Dream approached.

"Dream, this is Monica, Monica, Dream," Angela said, not really giving a fuck.

She looked over at Black, known as Strong to her. She now understood why she was drawn to this guy—they were from the same place. She knew he had his reasons for hiding his identity, but her feelings hadn't changed. Her eyes caught his. He stared at her, and she blew a kiss.

Black gave a half smile as Monica and Dream looked on.

Dream looked over at Strong. "She got a nigga there."

"You ain't lyin'. You ain't lyin'." Monica looked over at Black.

Black stepped back on the curve as the bright yellow Hummer pulled on the grass up by where Black Russian Entertainment was setting up.

Mont and Grip jumped out with some wild-looking nigga hopping out the back—half his head was braided, and the other half was all over his head. Tall, thick, dirty-looking cat, looking like he just got off work. They walked over to Black, showing love as many did.

The directors called for the next game. It was a squad from the Lakes that Lo was sponsoring and the other squad was sponsored by Mont and those Carriage House cats, which consisted of young ballers that came to play.

"What the deal, Lo?" Mont asked. "How much faith you got in your team?"

"Holla, nigga—don't play." Lo watched as Ray whispered in Grip's ear.

"Thousand a man," Grip yelled.

Lo thought about five grand. He knew Kev, Little, and them cats were unbeatable and he had five thou, but not to lose. But he couldn't be made to look small; he'd rather go broke first. "Sound good."

Everybody moved closer as the guys stepped to the court.

"Wanna up it, Lo—ten a man?" Mont asked.

Lo looked over at Kev, who'd overheard the bet. "Hell yeah," Kev said, "I got twenty-five."

Angela and Dream came and stood by Strong, Dee, Lo, and Poppa as they watched Kev ball.

"We got another fifty over here," a nigga yelled across the court from the Carriage House side.

The score was about even and it was the third quarter. "Stop fuckin' with that nigga, Lo—bet it up; I got you," Strong said.

Angela and Dream looked at each other, eyes wide. Angela looked across at Monica leaning on Ray. She knew at that moment her and her girl had the two biggest ghetto celebrities there were, and it felt good.

"Twenty-five a nigga. Let's keep it simple. What?" Lo yelled.

All eyes fell on Mont and Ray. Mont looked at Ray and, after a couple-seconds stare, turned and said, "Bet."

It was on. These cats ran until they bled from the concrete scrapes and 'bows thrown throughout this game—if that's what you want to call it.

"Get them niggas, Kev," Dundee yelled when Kev hit three.

"Show a muthafucka something," Mont yelled.

"Here it go, here it go . . . aaahhhhhh!!!!!!" Mike-Mike yelled as Li'l slammed that shit and damn near broke the goal."

"Play that ball. Fuck 'em," Rell yelled.

"LE niggas ain't shit." Ray laughed—alone.

Those who overheard got quiet and stared.

Mont and Ray ended up winning by a jump-shot. The tournament was over for the day.

"Can I get that?" Ray hugged Monica.

"You won, but you lost in character. You disrespected LE, so you forfeited your rights to *your* money," Mike-Mike told him. "That's the rule—never disrespect the Lakes, muthafucka. You must of lost your goddamn mind."

"Fuck all that," Ray said. "Y'all muthafuckas playin' and I'm more serious than a muthafucka."

"Comin' out your mouth like that—how serious are you?" Lo picked up the basketball and slammed it into Ray's face. "Carry yo' bitch ass—I ain't givin' you shit."

"Your card has been pulled my nigga," Mike-Mike said.

Kev was still upset about losing and was acting a little hostile. "Let's burst, Lo. Fuck these niggas."

"Fuck you, pretty muthafucka—don't make me tongue-kiss your ass out here," Mont said.

Kev looked at this big muthafucka. His split-second hesitation allowed that wild-lookin' cat to come from nowhere with a broken bottle and slam it into the left side of Kev's face. Blood splattered as he rushed Kev, tackling him to the ground, and raising his hand to stab him again.

Shit happened so fast.

Lo kicked the nigga in his chest and knocked him off Kev, reaching in his waist for the nine. His hand was stopped by the hold that Grip had on his hand, and his other around his throat, forcing him backwards, trying to push Lo to the ground. But the right blow that Poppa delivered to his ear took all the strength out his ass as he dropped to his knees.

In one smooth swoop Mont made his move on Poppa, who grabbed his neck with both hands and, with his own momentum, took Mont off his feet and slammed him on top of the CL600, leaving his bodyprint.

Ray grabbed Poppa around his arms and locked his, as the wild-ass nigga jumped back up, and all Poppa saw was this crazy-looking guy with half his head braided and the other out coming at him with the same broken glass. Ray had Poppa's arms stuck.

Poppa twisted his body and turned his head, anticipating what was about to happen. In the split second, he heard the words, "Hail Mary, look at me now—"

Pow!!! *Pow*!!!!!

Ray's grip quickly came loose just in time to see the wild-ass nigga's body drop beside Kev, leaning on the table under the shelter. The cut was wide open from the jagged bottle, and he had lost a lot of blood.

Dundee pointed the gun at Ray as he dove toward his car.

Pow!!! *Pow*!!! *Pow*!!!

One bullet grazed Ray's left arm.

Black had made his way back across the street from talking to JaVonne once the commotion started. "Get him to Bayside."

The girls were frantic. Dream was upset as if Kev was really her man.

Angela sped off toward Bayside with Dream, Kev, and Mike-Mike. The police sirens got closer real fast.

Mont grabbed Grip. "Nigga, you got two strikes, and I'm on paper—we got to go. Sorry!" Mont and Grip jumped in the Hummer.

All cars were skidding out as the police hit the Lakes.

Black knew he had to go and quick. He couldn't get caught out there. He looked at Dee. Dee knew the deal and threw him the bike keys as he caught the keys to the Ferrari, parked with the Lamborghini away from the ruckus over by all those rich niggas and entertainment cats.

Dee glanced around as he walked to the Ferrari. Black's whole team was gone. He was talking to Stacy and she had disappeared right when the conversation was heating up before the gunshots. He'd told her she was going to leave with him, if she wanted his company. He climbed in the car and pulled off. He had to get to Bayside and check on Kev.

Suddenly Stacy stepped up. "You made a promise."

"I got to go to Bayside; it's on you."

She jumped in.

He smirked as he eased away from the scene of the crime.

By the time they arrived at Bayside, the whole clique was there, except Black and Dundee. Kev had to have thirty-two stitches and was granted a lifelong scar. They decided to keep him because he had lost a lot of blood. Kev was out of it—they were pumping blood into his body and had tubes up his nose. That wild nigga had got him good.

Poppa, Lo, Mike-Mike, Angela, Dream and Stacy had all walked back out to the emergency room parking lot.

Moments later, Dee came out with a sad look. "What the fuck happen? I was standing there talking to shorty and all of a sudden, all hell broke loose."

"Shit happened so damn fast," Mike-Mike said. "But it was Lo fault—he started it."

"Shut the fuck up, Buc—ain't nobody with that shit tonight." Lo looked at Pee-Wee and Scotty, who had just pulled up in Scotty's girl's car.

"Fuck . . . you can't beat my ass," Mike-Mike said. "You should of fucked up them niggas instead of letting that nigga snatch your ass up."

Lo grabbed Mike-Mike. Mike-Mike grabbed him back, and they started tussling in the parking lot.

"Chill out, man," Scotty said. "Y'all niggas still actin' the fuck up and Kev in that bitch fucked up. That shit wa'n' suppose to happen."

"Heah—" Pee-Wee looked at Stacy—"I know you."

"Dog." Stacy remembered him from one of the young hustlers out the Lakes that Pee-Wee used to fuck with.

"Yeah, a'ight. How you been?" Pee-Wee looked at her as she stood by the Ferrari. He looked at Dee with a wicked smile and shook his knotty head up and down as if to say, "You got one, son."

Dee's phone rang.

"What's poppin'?" Black asked. "How Kev?"

"He a'ight. He got mad stitches in his head and they keepin' him overnight for observation. He lost mad blood."

"Okay. Where Poppa and them? They ain't answerin' their phone."

"You know you got to turn shit off in the hospital. Everybody out here."

"Tell them to get to the house on West Hastings. Come through the back way through Norfolk—it's hot as hell out there. Tell Lo his bike out here. Pop went back up there and got it; both of them in the back. Where the CLK?"

"Lo got it here. Him and Mike-Mike fightin'."

"Tell them niggas I said get around here."

"Yo, Strong said he at the spot on the Hastings and y'all need to get round there," Dee said to Poppa and Lo.

"Angela and her girl still there?" Black asked.

"Yeah. Got to clean the back up; some blood got on her seats."

"Tell her to clean that shit up. She'll be a'ight. Fuck that truck—long as Kev a'ight. Fuck, I got to call his peoples; he ain't suppose to be here." Black said he knew his conversation with Polite wasn't going to be pleasant. "So what you goin' to do?"

"Ride for a second. I'll holla later," Dee told him.

"I need you to go with shorty and make sure they clean her shit out good. Pay somebody or take it up by Military Circle to the car wash."

"Man! Shit, I don't feel like doin' all that shit."

"Then tell her to hit me," Black said and hung up.

Dee showed her where the car wash was and hit them off lovely to just clean it up and not to ask a thousand questions.

After a thorough cleaning inside and out, the Benz truck was like new, and the girls were on their way. They were leaving Sunday, and Angela was ready to finish enjoying her weekend. But Dream wasn't feeling VA no more.

Before they left the parking lot, Dream pulled up beside Dee in the whip.

"Dee, Dream wants to stay at the hospital and sit with Kev."

"Go ahead. Leave her here; he'll love that. Make him feel better."

Dee smiled. *Go take care of my little brother,* he thought, saying thanks to God again as he remembered the doctor's words, "A few more minutes and he'd been gone."

Dee punched it, headed for Interstate 64. He wanted to chill with Stacy for a few before heading to the club.

They raced up and down the highway, kicking and enjoying the exotic sports car. After a long and intense conversation, he dropped her off and headed home to get right for the club. Her conversation was nice, and she made it clear that she wanted a relationship, she wasn't just giving her body up for fun. So he decided to catch her another time.

He hit Strong. They were still out LE.

"What the deal, son?"

"Gettin' my head right, sitting here. Just popped two of those 'jumpoffs,' sippin' Henny with the Backwoods burnin'. Nigga is ready for the club. Goin' to Donzi's?"

"I don't know. Tryin' to figure out all this bullshit. Niggas beefin' gonna fuck up money. Hold on, my phone beepin'." Black looked at the caller ID. "That's Mont—let me call you back."

"What's the deal, Strong?" Mont asked. "Callin' to make sure we still in business." He knew the importance of a connect. He could score from Ray, but his prices were nowhere near Strong's. And his cousin was scared of him just like many other niggas in Tidewater. Felt he'd never get his paper. But Speed still held him down.

"That young nigga was one my brother soldiers. He hot as hell about everything, but you always dealt with me."

"Yeah, we still good. Couple changes, but I'll put you on to them next week."

"A'ight, one other thing—that one fifty."

"Who you make your bet with?" Strong asked.

"You know that's your peoples, so I thought it was—"

"Again, Mont, who'd you make your bet with?"

"Lo."

"A'ight, that's who you see."

"Tell him to call me; I don't got his number."

"One," Strong said and hung up. Then he told Lo to call him, so he didn't feel like Lo was ducking him.

"What you need, kid?" Lo asked Mont when he answered the phone.

"You know what I'm lookin' for, son—don't play."

"First of all, I made the bet with Ray, and I ain't payin' him shit. And I really ain't payin' you shit."

"Who you think you fuckin' with? The last nigga to fuck with me I—"

"Naw, nigga. *I* was the last nigga, and you ain't shit in my book. Now this shit is done." Lo hung up the phone.

Black was standing there. "That was one of Grip soldiers that Dundee killed," Strong said to Poppa with a stern look. "He's lookin' for payback and Mont lookin' for his dough."

"Nobody gives a fuck," Lo said. "He was gonna take Poppa's life—it was his or Poppa's. Fuck him."

"I'm with Lo," Poppa added. "They set it off, and that nigga paid for what he started. Fuck that dead muthafucka," he said, answering his phone. He stared at the number for a second till he remembered it was the hospital. He took a deep breath and answered. "Yeah!"

"Hello, Poppa, this is Auntie. You need to get down here. Princess has taken a turn for the worse. It looks real bad, Poppa."

She heard the silence in the phone, then a low, "I'm on the way." Poppa wasn't going to accept that. *Princess ain't goin' anywhere.* They had two kids together and she'd been his rock before he did his bid. She was there when he came home, waiting with open arms.

Princess always fussed about him being in the streets; she always felt he could do better. But this was all he really knew, and this shit was making them mortgage payments, day care payments, feeding her and those kids, and was going to open his studio he had in the works that him and Dee had discussed. Princess was going to be so proud that he had a business.

"Yo, I got to run—it's Princess; she's not good." Poppa headed for the door.

"Give me a call, Poppa," Strong said.

"Let us know what's up, fam. One!" Lo added.

Dundee sat for a second talking to Lo and Strong. He was tired of paying dues, but moving up constantly. "I'm out. I'm gonna ride by Virginia Beach General and check on Poppa," Dundee said. "I got to make sure he a'ight. He quiet, but he will snap—like his ass did earlier; dude got dropped with a one-piece."

Lo hyped the story. "Naw, check this, Strong—I'm five foot ten, so I know Poppa about five foot eleven, Grip six foot two, Mont about six foot one. Poppa had Mont off the ground and slammed his ass through the god-damn hood."

"Strong as a bitch. Mont big boy," Strong said. "Go check on my nigga, let us know. I was goin' to Donzi's, but I'm goin' to chill."

Strong hit Angela. "Heah, baby," she answered.

"Where you?"

"Gettin' ready to catch up with some friends and go to Donzi's. Why? What's up?"

"I'm headed to the condo, sit back look at DVD's."

The phone was silent. Neither was saying a word. She knew by the silence he was waiting for her response. "I'll meet you there in twenty minutes."

"Twenty minutes," he said and hung up.

"The club better not be that important. Give up those keys, Lo dog," Strong said.

"Damn! Thought I had the Benz tonight," Lo said.

"Get your bike, go home, and get your own shit. I ain't drove no CLK 55 before," Strong said as if it was a big thing. He headed to the condo and dialed Dee.

Dee was headed to Donzi's already. "What's up, son? You on your way?"

"Naw, I'm goin' in. Look, tomorrow or Monday I need you to get me three hoopties that run real good—old Honda, Lumina, Delta or some shit. I got a new set up that gonna make me sleep better. I need this done Monday."

"Bet. I'll holla," Dee said hanging up. The Ecstasy had kicked in, and he was smoking his second Backwoods to the head of this new shit called "Sour Diesel," which had him in rare form. His body was feeling great, and all he wanted was to get around some of the finest bitches in VA. It was great to be home; he was rolling, and he was ready.

Dee pulled to the front door of the club and stepped out the Ferrari as the doors went up. The line was down the sidewalk, so eyes were on the exotic piece of machinery, waiting to see who was driving.

They watched as the four-hundred-and-ten-dollar crocodile-embossed sandals hit the concrete, neatly covered by a khaki-colored linen set. Dee scanned his surroundings through the gold-andwood, tinted Ralph Lauren glasses. His four-thousand-dollar hexagon link bracelet filled with four-carat set in platinum and ten-thousand-dollar platinum watch with the diamond bezel let lookers know he was for real.

Security stepped up. "Can't park here, player."

"Valet park that shit."

"No, you can't park here—I don't care about your money."

Dee already knew he had a hater trying to show out for the crowd like he showed nobody favoritism. "Call Youngblood." Youngblood was head of the security force and also was married to Dee's and Black's first cousin, Janielle.

"Tell 'im Dee out here. Sorry he missed the restaurant, but I hope my sister got his plate to him. Tell 'im that."

Moments later, several security was showing him love: parking the whip, and escorting him in with no pat-down, no charge, as if he was the star performing that night.

Youngblood stood talking with Dee for about five minutes with two other security cats around Dee. Youngblood introduced Dee as his brother-in-law. Each time Dee shook the hand of security, he palmed a fifty. They assured him he would never have that problem again.

Dee headed upstairs to the bar, greeting many guys and girls from years back, new ballers, same hoes and definitely new young hoes that were not playing. Dee walked to the crowded bar. He saw three young ladies ordering their drinks. He checked their style. They looked nice, but ordinary. He continued to listen to deejay Devastator rip shit like he always done.

Suddenly a gleam of light caught the corner of Dee's eye. He glanced down at the ring. She was wearing that big-ass diamond on the left hand, letting every nigga know she was spoken for. The diamond tennis bracelet and diamond earrings, the short Chanel skirt, Chanel top, and Chanel open-toed sandals with her toes beautifully pedicured with a mixture of colors, let every nigga know she was being well taken care of. She stood eye to eye with him (he'd always preferred a shorter woman). She stood talking with her friend who was dressed nice, but not with the same class and taste.

Dee walked to the bar and walked close to her, almost on her hip, crowding her personal space.

"Please order me a double Hennessy straight and a Corona." Dee threw his left hand on the bar, getting closer, where people looking on might think she was with him, making sure she got a glance of the Christian Dior watch with the diamond bezel.

She turned, moving away with attitude across her face. She glanced at the watch, the bracelet, the linen, the crocodile sandals, and then her eyes went straight to the slightly tinted Polo's, and in one quick motion returned to her original position, slightly closer with a slight smile on her face. In her nose sat the tantalizing smell of the Burberry cologne.

"I need a Hennessy straight, double and a Corona with lime," she said to the bartender. "That's all you want?" she turned and asked Dee.

"Naw, that's not all, but we'll have to find time and talk about that." Dee looked into her eyes. He pulled a small stack of fifties, peeled off one, and handed it to her, got his drinks, and took a step back.

"Here's your change," she said, tapping Dee.

Dee waved his hand. "Did you get yours and tip her?"

"Yes, and thank you." She had gleaming white teeth, beautiful brown skin. Her long, black, healthy-looking wrap made him want to run his hands through it. Her eyebrows arched, and she had deep, dark pupils like Tiffany from *In the House*.

"Thank you. I couldn't fuck with that line."

"Patience. Have to learn patience," she said.

"I want what I want now. So I work hard so I can have it like that. So what up? I don't need no drama in my life though, shorty." Dee reached down and rubbed her hand, then her ring finger.

"That's my husband's. He asked me to wear it. He's married. And drama don't come with this. Always a lady."

"What's your name, cutie?" Dee tried to stay in pimp mode, which was hard while rolling. The social, smooth, and sensual part of him began to come out. He was feeling the bitch and could tell she was feeling him.

"Lady—that's my name." She smiled.

"Yo' momma ain't name you Lady," Dee said with attitude.

"Wilma Lady Hill—don't tell me. What's your name?"

"Dee," he said as the fine-ass, light-skinned girl caught his eye. He seen her before. Where?

The girl looked at Dee and headed toward him. Lady looked up at the girl coming. She stared as she walked up and hugged Dee as if she knew him.

"How you?"

"Fine and you?" He squinted his eyes to let her know he wasn't sure where he knew her.

"Monica—Angela's friend. I saw you earlier at the game. Didn't get a chance to meet you." Monica's team of girls looked on.

"Dee, a'ight."

"A'ight. Let me holla in a sec," he said putting her off, but she was fine. Then he remembered seeing her with dude sitting on the Benz. His mind started racing. Bedroom talk was a muthafucka.

He turned to Lady and assured her he would catch her before leaving.

Lady stepped off, but the look she gave Monica let her know she wasn't happy.

He quickly turned back to catch Monica's hand. "So what the deal? Your man let you out tonight?"

"Shit, he headed out of town."

"Niggas got to handle they business. You know how it is—money first."

"Yeah, when you the man, don't let niggas use you just to be down."

Dee could read Monica. She ran her mouth too much, trying to impress, like she knew something. So he pressed the issue as he moved to VIP. He ordered a bottle of Moët. He didn't like it, but the young hoes who weren't used to money thought it was something.

"So you just left your man home by himself and you bounced?"

"Naw. He home with his boys puttin' their little change together to go score."

Dee kept pouring. The champagne had her ass going. "What he buyin'? A ounce?" Dee laughed as if it was a joke.

"He talkin' about fifteen bricks," she said. "Fifteen bricks probably this big."

Dee knew them niggas had some paper. "I don't know why guys mess up money; they need to buy real estate. Buy a house; put that money there. Stop fuckin' it up, simple niggas."

"He got a big house."

"How big?"

"You seen them houses off Independence and Holland, that new complex. The ones in the back, the biggest. He got money."

"Guess so. So what's up with you? Goin' home from here? Or you hangin' out?"

"Tell me what's up?—I don't play for free."

"Whoa . . . I ain't got it like that."

"Then you playin'. Let me stroll a minute." Monica got up, and two girls from her crew followed.

Dee picked up the phone. He couldn't hear, so he walked out front. He called Black, but he wasn't answering. He dialed the condo.

Black knew nobody had that number, so it had to be important. "Yeah!"

"Shorty up here say her man home gettin' ready to score fifteen bricks.

"Who?"

"Yo' girl buddy, Monica. Her man, nigga with the CL drop."

"Ray?"

"I guess. He home with his mans and them with dough." Dee finished telling Black where the nigga lived and everything.

Black wasn't going out on a humbug, but he called Lo, told him to holla at Dundee and take a ride.

Lo called Dundee. When Dundee scooped Lo, he had Scotty with him. They drove out Holland Farms and rode around until they saw the drop-top Benz, a Q45, and Expedition.

They parked across the street, two houses down. They sat in the car with a 9 mm, .45, and the shotgun Scotty had.

Two guys pulled up in a Land Cruiser. One of the guys jumped out and ran inside.

"He waitin' on dude. As soon as he come out, we going in," Lo said.

"Let's do this, baby—my kind of shit," Scotty said.

Dundee sat not saying a word. This wasn't his type of shit. He sold drugs, not rob niggas, but he wanted to show niggas he was with anything.

They were so into going in the house, they thought nothing of the black, tinted Range Rover that rode by.

"How many niggas you think in there, Lo?" Scotty asked.

"Maybe three. Four at the most."

The other guy came out and got in the truck.

Within seconds of the truck pulling off, Scotty took the lead and knocked on the door. Lo was glad he came. This woulda got done without him, but Scotty and Lo had came up together, and when Lo got under Black, Scotty was robbing niggas like Black.

The door just opened—they thought the other guy had forgot something. Scotty put the shotgun in his chest and pushed him to the stairs.

Lo went to the left, Dundee to the right.

Dundee made two niggas get flat on the floor. Lo went through the living room to the kitchen and went upstairs the back way. He met Scotty at the room door.

They burst in the room over the garage. There stood Ray and some other cat.

"Bag it up, son," Lo said to Ray.

Ray began to bag slowly, praying the two nines didn't go off.

"He think it's a game, Lo," Scotty said, shotgun still in dude's chest.

Lo pointed the nine at the cat standing on the wall. *Pow!* He shot him in the chest. "You next," he said, busting Ray in the side of his head.

Ray gathered the money in the bag and walked downstairs with the cold steel sitting on the back of his neck.

As they hit the stairs, Lo yelled out to Scotty, who'd laid the guy down and slowly pulled the trigger to the shotgun. The sound scared Dundee, Lo, and the nigga coming in the door with the two .45's locked and loaded.

Lo kicked Ray in the back as he tumbled down the stairs, while the bullets from Lo's nines and Speed's .45's scattered.

Scotty ran down the back stairs, blasting a shot at the front. Speed jumped to the den, as him and Dundee exchanged gunshots. Dundee scattered to get away, catching a bullet in the foot.

Scotty bust another shot at Speed, takin' out the big screen. But two shots to Scotty's shoulder and neck left him in a puddle of blood.

Lo was shot in the thigh and stomach.

Dundee scrambled to the steps and grabbed the bag as the bullets came raining down.

Lo began shooting, and Speed pulled Ray away from Lo's shots.

Dundee saw this as the perfect time to make a run and dashed out the door, hopping and letting off shots at Speed and Ray. Ray fell from the stray that caught him in the spine.

The sirens got closer as Dundee sped away with Speed right behind him as they bypassed the police racing to the scene. Both cats were on paper and they had to leave. Neither could do anything for anybody locked up.

Speed musta turned off. Dundee raced down Independence and hit the interstate. He pulled in his driveway to the back of his house, went inside, and called Poppa.

Poppa never answered, so he counted the money. Three hundred thousand. *Damn! Jackpot!!!*

He tried Poppa again.

Dundee's phone rang. It was Poppa. He was at the Virginia Beach General when they brought Lo, Ray, Scotty, and the other two cats' bodies in.

"What happened?"

"Lo called me in to rob Ray. We bust in and scooped the dough. We gettin' ready to burst and Speed came through the door."

"Goddamn." Poppa closed his eyes and rubbed his forehead.

"He killed Scotty and Lo. I think I killed Ray."

"Lo got shot five times and he ain't dead," Poppa said. "Ray fucked up. Say bullet's in his spine. Scotty, Jake, and two more cats dead. For a couple hundred grand. Goddamn! Let me make a call and tell his peoples."

Poppa called Black and told him what had just happened.

Black said, "Call Dundee and tell him meet me at the apartment on Baker and to bring that money."

Dundee was sitting in the house, almost in tears when Poppa called. The fact that Scotty was gone had sunk in.

Dundee, Poppa, and Black stood on the balcony of the apartment. Black couldn't go to the hospital, and Dee wasn't answering his phone.

Black made the call he dreaded to make.

Tony T answered the phone.

Black let Lo's brother know what had happened so Moms and Auntie could go to Virginia Beach General. Then from every direction the red, white, and blue lights came flashing down Baker Road.

Dundee stood there and watched ten police cars surround his townhouse and kick in his door.

"Ray must of told. Thought I killed the son of a bitch."

"Well, you didn't. Now he puttin' the police on you. And they got Lo," Black said, digging for his phone that was ringing. "Yeah!"

"Fuck goin' on, stickman?" Speed said angrily.

"Fuck you mean, my nigga?" Black answered, his voice slightly raised.

"What y'all niggas fuck with my cousin for?" Speed lowered his voice. He had gotten real calm.

"I just heard about this shit—some beef carried over from the courts."

"Naw, baby. Yo' peoples robbed my cousin for three hundred thousand and left him in a wheelchair. Payback's a bitch, nigga."

"You better recognize who the fuck you talkin' to."

"Talkin' to you, son. Better soak it in, because when I see you we goin' to hell, baby. Straight to hell," Speed said and hung up.

"Where the other hundred thousand?" Black looked at Dundee.

"That's it—two hundred thousand. Word to my mother."

Black looked at Poppa and walked back inside. His phone rang. It was Tony calling from Virginia Beach General. Lo was going to be okay. Even though he got hit five times, there was no major damage.

Moms and Auntie had the staff in an uproar. They let them see Lo for a second. He did open his eyes. Tony told Black that all Lo said was three hundred thousand.

"There's police outside his door and they have him cuffed to the bed."

"Take care of Moms and Auntie," Black said hanging up. He looked at Dundee. "Lo said three hundred thousand. Speed said Ray said three hundred thousand. Speak now or live with your decisions."

"That's Lo's; I got my hundred." Dundee looked at Black as to say, "I'm not scared."

"Everybody think like that young nigga, but we are a clique. The only way we gonna have longevity and prosperity is to hold each other down. You ever lived like you livin' now?"

"Naw, man." Dundee looked at Poppa.

"Without me and Lo, this shit stops; with us, everything stays good in life—don't ever do that again. LE niggas . . . 'til we die."

"No doubt. Sorry," Dundee said. "You need to go get that foot checked," Poppa said.

"We all right, partner. Now we move forward." Black handed Poppa twenty-five thousand and kept the same for himself, putting the rest up.

Dundee hopped over to the couch. He told Black everything and how it went down. Now Black saw why he got up outta there. Now he knew Lo was going down for all that shit, because Ray was going to tell—it was his house and they had robbed him.

Chapter Eleven

Dee walked back in the club and ordered another double Henny straight and Corona. The bitches in the club was off the hook. The Ecstasy had him ready to freak, but the weed kept him from bouncing off the wall. He walked back to the second floor and found his VIP spot, sat down and ordered a bottle of Dom Perignon. He popped the champagne and poured a glass. He felt good.

He sat there watching as people came by, showing love that he hadn't seen in awhile, guys and girls. He realized then that the clubs in Atlanta was off the blinker, but it felt good to be home, to see niggas he'd been clubbin' with since Circle Bingo and Big Apple days.

Then two loud-ass niggas came up. Dee jumped up, hugging the niggas. It was Shawn and Smiley, two Norfolk hustlers who had a good piece of Norfolk and Portsmouth locked. Smiley was always a grimy money-getting nigga. Whatever was whatever. "Let's do it," was his attitude, as long as he got paid, and he always had a hustle.

Shawn was more laid-back, quiet type nigga. Got his money quietly, played fair, but if you ever got him wrong, sooner or later you got got. He usually ran with rich niggas, stars, and fucked a lot of hoes. "Fuck you been, nigga?"

"ATL, son." Dee shook his head.

"Heard the strip joints like no other," Shawn said.

"I'll come down there and have all those hoes callin' this dingy-ass Norfolk nigga Daddy. I heard them hoes got some paper," Smiley added.

"No doubt, kid. Houses, cars, jobs. It's poppin'," Dee said. "And all those gay niggas don't want no pussy."

"That's some bullshit." Shawn got a champagne glass and poured some Dom. "When you gonna open another sports bar?"

"As soon as you get some of your peoples to invest," Dee told him. "We'll do one for about one point two million. Have that shit bangin'."

"Well, we got four together. What you got?" Smiley asked. "I got four; all we need is four more. Shawn the man. All he got to do is go to Sweet Pea, Bruce Smith, Joe Smith, Allen I, Alonzo, Missy, Timberland."

"Goddamn, nigga, you fuck with everybody from Norfolk who done made it." Dee poured some more champagne in all three glasses.

"Dee, how many hoes you got in ATL, pimp?"

"I got two. I told myself I wa'n' goin' down there with all that, but you know, them hoes pulled me in," he said, giving niggas a pound.

Shawn pulled out a Dutch and split it, dumping the tobacco on the floor to roll the "labo" he had in his pocket. These niggas was gleaming—they had to have a hundred gees on in jewels between the two.

"I got four hoes. Real relationships with four hoes," Smiley said. "Keys to they houses, they cars—kids love me—and it's been goin' on for over seven years right here in Norfolk. So I know ATL callin' me."

Dee and Shawn laughed, but Smiley had a serious look.

"This the crazy part—I love all these hoes. People say it can't be done. But I'll kill a nigga over all four hoes."

"Tell him, Shawn."

Shawn shook his head in agreement and lit the Dutch.

"How many hoes you done fucked in Norfolk, Smiley?" Dee asked.

Shawn looked at Dee as if to tell him, "Don't get me started."

"About sixty in the last decade. What about you? I've seen you run hoes, Dee."

They both started laughing, remembering a time they'd bumped heads.

"Shit, I'll say about seventy or eighty," Dee said seriously.

"You ain't lyin', son. I know you. And I can say Shawn probably done fucked over a hundred hoes."

We laughed, but we both knew the hoes loved Shawn. They called him quiet and fine, and he was killing them all.

"So how you fuck four hoes like that. I fuck, but a nigga dick die out every now and then. Been fuckin' with that X—that shit make sex off the hook."

"I used to have that problem. Them old heads up at the Long Shoreman Hall turned me on to these." Smiley handed Dee two light-blue, diamond-shaped pills. "Viagra, nigga—for old heads who can't get hard and for young niggas who just want to fuck nonstop."

Dee looked at the pills and put them in his pocket.

"You got that X?" Shawn asked.

"All day long. AOL's, Mitsubishi, tweety birds. What?" Dee felt a deal coming on.

"Mad niggas doin' that shit, but it's hard to come by," Smiley said.

"Not no more. Twenty a pop all day," Dee said.

"I want a thousand," Shawn said.

"Twelve then. Tomorrow." Dee handed him one to try.

Shawn took it. "Tomorrow."

Just then Monica and her crew came by. Dee signaled for her to come over. They all came and began talking.

Dee was thinking he would like to fuck with this bitch. She was fine as hell. "So what?" he asked her in her ear as she leaned into him, "You want to get down?"

"One thousand and you got me all night."

Dee knew this bitch wa'n' getting a gee a night from niggas in Norfolk. "I don't want all night."

"Then five hundred from—" She looked at her watch. "It's one now . . . from now to six."

"Give me your number," Dee said as he put it in his phone. "I'll call you at three thirty. I want from four to five. You might make two hundred. I'm gonna hit you as soon as I get settled." Dee knew Ray wa'n' giving that bitch no real dough, still out here tricking.

He grabbed his dick, raising up from the table. He gave Smiley and Shawn a pound, telling Shawn, "Hit me up tomorrow."

"How y'all niggas know Dee? Y'all from uptown?" Monica asked.

Smiley smirked. "Who the fuck don't know Dee?"

"Niggas want to know his brother," Monica said.

"Whose his brother?" Shawn asked.

"Black."

"Black who? That Norview cat with the clothing store," Shawn said, "or Black from Grandy Park, or Black that run with Shampoo."

"Oh yeah," Smiley said, "Black from out Lake Edward. Back in the day they say he killed about ten New

York niggas. Say he had mad bodies and never did a day."

"Okay, did he run with that nigga Lo with the dreads and the patch on his eye?" Shawn asked.

"Now remember when they found them two niggas at the mall dead, one in the back seat and one in the trunk."

"The nigga you talkin' about is Lo Max. Tall, black, skinny nigga with dreads. Wilder than a bitch."

Shawn looked at Smiley. "That's Dee peoples? That's why he always look like he flippin' keys with a asshole full of money."

"Because of his brother. I didn't know that shit."

"Come on," one of the girls said to Monica. "Broke-ass niggas not spendin' shit."

"Niggas ain't gonna spend shit with your nasty ass, bitch," Smiley said.

"Bitch, fuck you with your stinkin'-ass breath—that's why I moved."

"Bitch, you better recognize a pimp when you see one." Smiley jumped up and kicked her in the mouth with his Timbs.

Her head snapped back, just to catch a slap when it came back up. The slap took her off her feet.

Monica grabbed Smiley, and the other girl began hitting him.

Shawn grabbed the other girl by the hair, slinging her to the ground, and still holding her ponytail in his hand.

"Please, Smiley, don't beat her like that," Monica yelled as Smiley slapped the girl.

Monica was glad to see security grab Smiley. He turned on security and began head butting him until he let go. The other tried restraining him, and again Smiley grabbed him and began butting him across his nose until blood spread across his face.

Out of nowhere, Youngblood scooped Smiley up and slammed him to the ground. He tensed his body, but he went up again and the next slam took everything he had in him. He was cuffed and carried out.

Shawn was right behind them as they carried his man out. He was walking to the car mad as hell. "Security didn't have to do that."

He walked past a Quest van. Three niggas sat inside. "You need to tell Smiley to calm the fuck down."

"He'll be all right."

"That's why he got his ass whipped and your bitch ass let it happen."

"Fuck all you niggas."

They began laughing. They were drinking and smoking and joking so much, they never saw Shawn come back across the street from his car.

Pow! Pow! Pow!

Dee dropped to the ground in the parking lot. He was talking to Lady, trying to get her to roll with him, and saw when Smiley came out cuffed up.

Then he saw Shawn dash back across the street and his black, chromed-out Supra hit Independence Boulevard and disappeared.

Shawn left two kids dead in the Quest, and taught one kid a lesson—never fuck with niggas you don't know.

Dee knew it was time to go. He looked at Lady. All the sweet shit was over. "What you gonna do?"

She got in and they were out.

Dee took off toward his condo. Lady sat beside him, her right leg thrown across her left, leaving an exposed upper thigh that he couldn't help touching while she rambled on about how she'd been married four years, and her husband was a producer or some shit. He had a studio and was pushing mad artists. He offered her and their two kids the world but was never home, so she shopped and fucked up a great deal of his money.

They walked inside.

Dee decided he wanted to fuck hard if this bitch gave him some pussy, so he walked in the kitchen and took one of the pills Smiley gave him to see how it worked. Then he poured himself a drink and sparked his Backwoods.

She sat there smoking her Newport cigarette.

He put on his Dave Hollister CD. By track four he had Lady laid back, kissing her neck and rubbing her breasts. He lifted her shirt and felt the lace bra that fastened in the front. The Ecstasy had him ready to freak.

As he kissed her neck, she began to moan and slide down in the sofa. He removed her blouse to see her beautiful breasts fill the gold bra. Lady stood in front of him in a gold bra, gold thong, and Chanel sandals, her diamonds gleaming.

Dee's dick was rock hard. He took her hand and guided her to his room.

She strolled to the bed with her ass jiggling.

Goddamn! His body felt so good, and his dick was throbbing. He removed his clothes down to his boxers. "Let's shower," he said, walking into his bathroom.

She undressed fully and stepped into the shower. He washed her down and she did the same.

When they came out and dried off, she pushed him back on the bed and began kissing his neck. It felt good, but she was sucking hard.

"Don't leave no marks on me," Dee said seriously.

"Don't worry, I won't," she said softly and kept kissing and nibbling until she reached his chest. She took his nipples into her mouth and sucked, then nibbled on the ends until she felt his heartbeat speed up. She reached down and stroked his dick. She knew he was ready the way his dick was jumping. She leaned down and placed her lips on his dick.

A sensation shot through his body.

She began sucking his dick like it was the best tasting piece of meat she ever had. The saliva ran down his balls into his ass cheeks. Lady kept sucking intensely as she massaged his balls. Then she turned him over with his ass in the air.

He flowed with it because she was making his body feel so incredible.

She got on her knees and pulled his dick back between his leg and sucked from behind.

"Whoa! Whoa!" was all he could mutter.

She kept going as she reached up and placed her finger on his asshole.

He jumped up and spun around. "Fuck is you doin'?"

"Oh! You never had a woman touch you there?"

"Hell naw. Don't fuck around."

"Look, Dee, relax. Aren't you secure with your sexuality? You know you ain't gay. I'm just playin', tryin' to make you feel good." Lady placed her head back on his head. Again she rubbed his balls until his knob was really wet. She laid him back, lifted his legs, and began to lick his balls, then his ass.

He jumped, but she kept going until sensations floated up and down his body. She eased her slim finger into his ass, and he shifted uncomfortably. Then she pressed her finger forward. Dee felt as if he was going to pee, but nothing happened.

Of all the bitches he'd fucked in his life, none ever made him feel this good. The feeling was rising from his feet through his body. He thought he was coming, then all of a sudden his entire body went numb. This feeling had his entire body shaking for about two minutes.

Lady sucked down every drop until he pushed her off his dick.

Dee laid there with a limp dick until he caught his breath. He felt like a bitch that had been turned out.

Lady lay on his chest and rubbed his stomach.

He wasn't pressed on no ass.

Then she grabbed his dick again. It rose instantly.

Damn! Dee took her in his arms and laid her back, climbed on top of her, and slid in.

Her pussy was burning up. It grabbed his dick and was pulling with every stroke. She brought her legs back real wide so he could get in tight and rub against her clit with every stroke. She began to buck wildly as he slammed his dick with authority until that feeling came again, and he let off a load to fill her up. Lady came at the same time too, and he collapsed in her arms.

"Damn, it's almost four o'clock. Let me go." Lady jumped and ran to the bathroom. She returned wearing her bra and thong. She walked back to the living room and slipped into her clothes. Then she kissed Dee and exited out the door.

Dee climbed in the shower and cleaned up. He went and laid in the bed and flipped on the TV. He grabbed his dick and squeezed it. He picked up the phone and hit Monica. "Hello."

"What's up, Dee?"

"You—let's do this; meet me at the Clarion."

"See you in about twenty minutes," she said and hung up.

Dee threw on his Pelle Pelle baby-blue velour sweatsuit and white DC's with the baby-blue stripe. He got to the Clarion and got a room. He took another Ecstasy pill.

She arrived and after smoking a Back, she tooted four times.

His X had just kicked in, and it was trick time. His dick throbbed at the thought of getting into this young girl.

She undressed, stood in front of him wearing a black bra and black thong on her red body.

He stood in the bed, holding his dick. "Crawl over here and suck this dick."

She crawled and sucked his dick, licked his balls. He even pulled his leg back and made her lick his ass.

He turned her over and slid in from the back. Every time he got excited and started pounding, she would slide up and keep him from getting deep.

He pulled her hair and her neck came back, as he slammed dick into her.

She wriggled until she broke his grip.

He picked her up and turned her on her back, grabbed his dick, and slid it into her, pushing his legs against hers so they would stay wide. Dee started bucking like a horse, cupping her under her shoulders and going crazy. He couldn't come, his dick hurt and throbbed, but it was rock hard. He kept going.

She yelled, "Stop! Stop!", and tried to push him off, but he heard nothing, felt nothing.

He fucked hard until his sweat dripped in her face. The tears ran as her pussy became dry and raw. The harder he fucked, the more she fought . . . until he finally bust. Out of breath, he collapsed thinking he might die.

She grabbed her clothes and headed out the door.

He lay there holding his rock-hard dick, feeling good. He was ready again.

Monica searched her caller ID on her cell, nervously looking for the number Angela had called from. *There it is.*

Her mind was in shambles. She rode past Ray's house and saw yellow tape around it. She ran home to catch Channel 5 news and heard about what happened at Ray's home. The announcer said, "The owner of the home was in Virginia Beach General in critical, but stable, condition."

Angela finally answered her phone. She was laying beside Black at the condo. She sat up. "What up, girl?"

"That muthafucka you fuck with, girl, is a beast. He's a fuckin' beast. He killed Fat Joe, and Ray laid up in the hospital now."

"Slow down," Angela said, her head racing.

"You said Fat Joe—Oh my God—and what?" Angela wasn't about to say Ray's name while Black was lying next to her.

"Yeah, Ray's fucked up too. Scotty died. It was on Channel 5. Yo' nigga did this because of that shit."

"Kill it, girl—you reachin'."

"Ask him. That was Fat Joe; we grew up together, Angela," Monica cried. "All of us, from Bayside Elementary to Bayside Middle to Bayside High." She cried even harder.

Angela felt her pain. She was hurt, but she never fucked Fat Joe like Monica did. *And what the fuck was he doing around Ray house anyway?*

"Ask him. You know I'm right. I'm going to the hospital to check on Ray; you owe him that much."

I ain't owe Ray shit. "Bye," Angela said.

"Are you goin'?" Monica asked.

"Yeah, I'll see ya." Angela hung up the phone and looked at Black. "Something happened."

"Yeah, I saw it on Channel 5."

"Saw what?" Angela tried to see what he knew.

"Tone down, girl." Black held his left hand out, showing a down motion.

"My best friend from childhood is dead. My girl is fucked up. I got to go check on some things."

He got out the bed and slipped on his boxers and wife-beater. He picked up his Back and pulled on it. "I don't care where you go or what you do, but don't interfere in that street shit and don't go visiting at the hospital." Black knew the police was watching who was coming and going.

Angela stopped at the bathroom door. "Why not, Strong? Tell me why?"

"Just don't—now leave it alone." He was tired of the conversation.

"Fuck that. You—"

Next thing you know, her naked body was pinned against the wall between the dresser and the bathroom door. She was on her tiptoes, the dresser pushing into her side, and his hand around her neck and pushing against her windpipe.

She blacked out for about five seconds. When her vision became clear, her eyes were wide, her mouth open, and her skin was darkening.

"Don't ever challenge me. You haven't been around long enough." Black threw her body across the bed, making her body slam against the oak headboard.

She jumped up and stood on the bed. "I'm tired of muthafuckas puttin' they hands on me." She charged across the king-size bed.

He grabbed her neck and tossed her as he moved to the side, but her momentum made her fall through the closet door. "Bitch, you don't know who you fuckin' with," he said, picking up his Backwoods. "Now clean this shit up." He walked downstairs and stood in his family room and looked through the clear glass at the waves rushing the shore.

"Black, I can't be goin' through this. I love you, but I can't. I'm gonna leave the keys to the truck and catch a cab." She stood at the banister overlooking the family room.

"I said you weren't goin' because the police is probably watchin' everybody goin' in and out. You get hot, Black gets hot. Strong ain't wanted, but Black been locked up twice and is wanted in three states. Black got two felony charges. If they catch Black right now he'll be gone a long time. Strong loves you. But Black will put two in your muthafuckin' head and be gone in sixty sec," he said, still looking over the water, and pulling on his Back, never turning around. "Before he get locked up behind your ass."

She walked back in the room and began cleaning up. She couldn't believe what she had just gone through. But she did know two things—she wasn't going to the hospital; and she wa'n' leaving her muthafuckin' truck.

Chapter Twelve

Kev was supposed to be in Memphis, but he spent more time in VA with Black, waiting for his move farther South and had become accustomed to VA. Him and Dee were on their way by the hospital to check on Poppa's situation. They were getting off the elevator and ran into Monica.

"What's up, Monica?"

"I can't fuck with you—you are dangerous."

"What the hell you talkin' about?"

"You know what you did," she said. "I know."

Kev leaned closer to her. "Be concerned if you want, but don't let your mouth make your whole body end up in a canister floatin' in the Dismal Swamp. Be careful, Monica."

"I know that nigga ain't givin' you shit, or you would not be trickin'. Let me tell ya how you can put fifty grand in your pocket," Dee added.

Her eyes popped open. It seemed as if the anger was gone. She shut her mouth and stepped on the elevator, shook.

Dee decided to carry his ass home. He had thought about staying home, letting her come over, but she just fucked Ray. She wa'n' gettin' him, triflin' bitch.

He was tired, so he punched the Ferrari. As he flew past Witchduck Road, two state troopers sat on the right. He looked at his speedometer—100. He knew he was going to jail.

They shot out after him.

He got off on Newtown, but by the time he reached the Boulevard, they had him. He got a reckless driving, eluding the police, no seat belt, and they towed the Ferrari.

They carried him to Princess Anne.

It was six o'clock then; he didn't get a call 'til ten.

Dee finally got in touch with Black. He sent Tony to bail him out. His bail was set at ten thousand. Tony gave the bondsman one thousand and Dee walked. He had to pay one fifty for towing.

Black took the car and keys, but he gave Dee forty-five thousand for schooling them on Ray. At least that made him smile.

Dee rode over to Bayside Hospital. Moms and Auntie was there. It was Sunday and the restaurant was closed. Auntie assured us that he was out of danger and he was going to be okay.

Kev was ready, so he picked him up with Dream. She was looking rough, but she was there for Kev, with the badges on the side of his face. They went to his crib to clean up and shower.

He left Dream there, while him and Dee ran to check on Lo. After he heard what happened, he was even more outraged. He had never witnessed so much drama in a day.

They pulled in front of the hospital. Poppa was standing in the front looking like a zombie. They'd forgot his girl was still here.

"You a'ight, Poppa?" Kev asked.

"Girl slipped in a coma. What I do to deserve this?" Poppa said.

Big, strong-ass nigga wiped his eyes. Kev couldn't understand, but Dee could. Dee had lost a girl before, and he knew Poppa was scared. He felt for him, but words meant nothing at this time. His life mate was in trouble, and it was nothing nobody could do or say at this time.

Dee and Kev walked upstairs to check on Lo. The police was outside the door and they wouldn't let them visit. Dee didn't have ID and Kev was too stressed to argue.

They walked back downstairs. Poppa was gone, so they got in the whip and headed back to Black's condo.

They must of rode for fifteen minutes in the Dodge Intrepid listening to the sounds of some underground shit by Fifty.

"Stop lookin' so sad, son. You still pretty," Dee said.

"I know. I just feel fucked up inside," Kev said.

"Why? The nigga that did that paid for it—with his life. That's done."

"You right. Just feel funny."

"Need to chill, kid. Everybody ain't built for this shit—day-in-day-out hustlin' . . . not knowin' what the next day gonna bring. If you find a nigga that's been in this shit for ten years or better, he's cold and he built for shit most niggas can't stand. This shit ain't easy. You got to be smart, stay ahead of the game, get money, and— most of all—stay alive.

Niggas who fuck with this shit crazy and you better know it."

"Dee, you smart as hell. You ever killed anybody?"

"I've caught three in my lifetime," Dee said slowly. "Two over bitches and one over my brother. The one over Black, I dropped him point-blank range, to the back of the dome in the club. I will never forget how his body fell. I see it over and over, but it doesn't bother

me, because I did that to protect Black. I'll do that anytime. My brother's all I got.

"The two over them hoes keep me fucked up. Young
niggas like you let that pussy get them open and they
lost their mind. Now one was ready to take my life. The
other I think was trying to be hard and show out. Never
pull a burner to play— this lifestyle is not a game; it's a
way of life."

"So why keep playin' in it? You don't even sell drugs."

"The richest niggas sell drugs. There's many other
hustles that get you close to that money. Do what you
know. And I stay close in the game because of the
money, bitches, cars, the respect that comes with the
car you drive, the money you got, and the bitch on your
arm. I been here too long. I love the 'not knowing what
tomorrow brings.'"

They pulled up to Black's condo, where they saw the
Black Yukon Denali XL, parked with handicap plates,
from New Jersey.

Kev knew who it was. He knew what he was facing.
They walked inside. Kev walked over and hugged his
cousin.

"Look what happens when you out of my care," Polite said.

"We goin' home, son. I'm gonna go back and forth
for a second, but you can handle Memphis. Me and
Strong gonna work somethin' out. Bring 'em in to Tennessee from Atlanta. We'll be a'ight." Kev felt good. He
knew he'd still be with Black. *Only a phone call away.*
He loved Polite, but he learned from Black.

"You not leavin' for a couple weeks, let's get Lo back
and rollin'. Check this out."

They all walked to the table.

"We'll show Lo and Poppa before you leave. You gonna bring your peoples, Pop and them, in under Poppa. Grip just got picked up on that kid's murder. Somebody said he thought the kid was snitchin', so he was going to do him. When they stopped him, he had a half brick of 'hard' (crack). I don't know if he talkin' or what. And Speed fuckin' up. I don't know what he doin'. So this is the change. We changing the cribs out LE that they been to. We got three cars—each gonna have a stash. We meet at the malls, Wal-Mart's, big parking lots. Park on opposite sides, go in the store, and swap keys. No more hand to hand—key to key, car to car."

Dee looked on. *Real smooth.*

Kev thought it was good also.

Polite just realized how he was going to run Memphis. "I'm goin' to Memphis tomorrow. I'll see you in two weeks. Now let's find a restaurant."

They all left out, jumping in the Denali XL.

Black called Angela, and her and Dream met them at Piccadilly. Dee called Stacy. She was there in a flash.

They finished eating and walked outside. Dee walked the girls to the truck. They were getting ready to head back to the ATL. They both had work Monday morning.

"Y'all should be gettin' back about one," Black said. He walked over to Angela.

She hugged him. "When will you be home?" She held him tight.

"About three weeks—in time to close the house. Go ahead and put down the deposit and sign the papers for the one we picked."

"Be careful, Black." She smiled. "I can't lose you."

"You won't. Don't you worry, you won't."

Kev stood on the other side of the truck in deep thought with Dream.

"I don't believe in that corny shit—love at first sight and all. But I've never enjoyed myself with anybody Kev like I did this weekend—minus the craziness. I never thought VA was like this."

"Know what, they say VA is for lovers. I guess you found that out."

"They need to say VA is for hustlers. Because y'all niggas is gettin' it." She pulled him closer and kissed him, throwing her tongue around in his mouth.

He kissed her back, not giving a fuck about all the church folks coming and going.

"Look, Dream, I'm gonna be straight. I want you to go to Atlanta and straighten out all your personal shit . . . because I'm comin' in a couple weeks."

"All right, Kev. There's nothin' to clear up. My plate is clean—school, work—and I want you to know my door is open to you."

"I'll be goin' to Tennessee in a couple months. Once I plant my roots, I want you there. Think about it; we'll talk later." He kissed her again, and they hugged.

Black and Dee watched as their girls rolled away in the G5 truck, looking pretty, headed for the ATL.

It was Sunday night—reggae night at Club Ritz on Military Highway. Bitches were off the hook.

Polite, Kev, Black, Dee, and Poppa were sitting at a table drinking and talking business.

Poppa was looking sad because his girl hadn't gotten any better.

Black was staring into space. He wanted to go home and climb next to Angela. The two days she was home had spoiled him.

Kev was sipping on his Hennessy and deep in thought.

"What y'all think of this club?" Poppa asked.

"It's all right. Nice crowd," Dee said.

"I know the niggas. They ask me to come in and get down for a third," Poppa responded.

"How much?" Black asked.

"A hundred gees."

"Shit ain't bringin' in that much," Kev said.

"It's okay. I see makin' it back. I need an investment," Poppa said.

"Talk to this attorney and this accountant before you do anything. Let them say it's a good deal, and draw up paperwork to make sure you get yours back and everything is legit." Dee handed Poppa two cards.

Polite asked, "So VA still wild as hell?"

"Yeah, this shit off the hook," Mike-Mike said. "Poppa gettin' ready to buy the club—free liquor and free beer all night."

Everybody started laughing because they knew he was serious.

Black had his eyes glued to the door, with all the beef going on. He wasn't comfortable at all.

"Heard you got locked up, Dee," Mike-Mike said. "Fastest car in the world and you stop. Muthafuckas wouldn't have got me." He acted out a getaway.

Stacy walked up with three of her friends. Dee had called her. He wanted the company of this young, beautiful, innocent-ass girl. She spoke, and Dee walked them to the bar, with Polite rolling beside one. We later found out that he could still fuck; his dick wa'n' paralyzed.

"How Lo doin'?" Poppa asked.

"He gonna be okay after we see what the police gonna hit him with," Black said.

"That Ray nigga gotta go—he's the one who gonna fuck around and put Lo away," Kev said, feeling like if he killed someone he'd feel better about his life, his face, and his fucked up heart.

"Where Dundee?" Black asked. "Did you take care of that?"

Black had told Poppa to give Dundee his apartment he had for tricking. Poppa didn't really use it since his girl had been down; he was always with her since her complication earlier in her pregnancy.

Dundee needed a low spot. The police was on a manhunt for him. A two-time felon, he had three murders and wasn't about to give up his whole life to get locked up.

"Yeah, he straight. He over there with Pee-Wee. You know without Scotty they fucked up," Poppa said.

"Feel you," Kev said.

Then they heard a phone ring.

It was like a chain reaction, as everyone grabbed their phone.

Dee answered.

"Hey, baby. What you doin'?"

"Sittin' in the club, sippin' on some syrup, listenin' to the sounds."

"You need to call me back," Tricia said. "I got some news for you."

"Holla. What's up?"

"I haven't seen a period in two months."

"So we need to handle this shit soon." Dee loved her but didn't want any more kids right now.

"Handle what?"

Dee walked to the room with pool tables and couches so he could hear better. He wasn't expecting this conversation tonight.

"You ain't havin' another baby right now. Barely take care of the one you got. This ain't the time. You better set up an apartment. Shit, I care for you, but I don't love you like that."

Actually he did love her, but he had to convince her not to have this baby. He didn't want that now, and plus, how the fuck could he tell Chantel this? Shit, fuck all those other hoes—Chantel was going to go off. There was no way this could happen.

"You can fuck around and have it. I'll take care of it if it's mine, but I'm not gonna be there. You on some bullshit."

"Fuck you mean 'if it's yours'?" she said loudly. "You know goddamn well I haven't fucked anybody else. You are a sorry-ass nigga. I would of never thought you'd act like this."

Dee felt bad. He knew she hadn't fucked anybody.

"I ain't gettin' no fuckin' abortion. I ain't killin' my baby." Tricia screamed. "My momma raised four of us by herself; I can do two."

"Fuck all that shit you talkin'. I'm out." Dee hung up.

She called back several times, but he never answered.

His mind stayed on Tricia. She was beautiful, and a wonderful homemaker. He knew she would be a great mother to his child. It suddenly hit him that he actually wanted a child. His only daughter was almost ten and a brand new baby would be something great. Here he was telling Tricia to get an abortion, not because of timing, but because he didn't want to hurt Chantel, who'd been trying unsuccessfully to have his baby for the last year. Then here comes this young girl who shows love like no other woman, takes care of him like no other, and he wants to put her through hell because of his love for another woman.

Damn! His mind was racing. He looked at his phone and a feeling ran through his body. He was scared to answer. He felt like shit as he watched the phone ring until it read "1 CALL MISSED." He noticed his team rushing out the door and ran outside.

Poppa was on the ground beside his Suburban, balled up, his hands over his face, and crying like a baby.

Black and Kev tried to help him to his feet, but he had no strength. He jumped up and put his fist through his driver side glass, before he leaned against the truck and continued to cry.

"What's goin' on?" Dee asked running up.

"His girl just died. Her aunt just called," Black told him.

Stacy and her crew walked outside to see what was going on. "What's wrong, Dee?" she asked. "Is everything okay?"

"No. My people's girl just died—his baby moms."

"This been a hell of a weekend. Y'all won't never forget *this* Fourth."

"Never," Dee said. "Somebody need to drive him down to Virginia Beach General."

Kev took his keys and helped him in the passenger side, and he and Mike-Mike carried him to the hospital. He had stopped crying and fell into a deep stare. His eyes were swollen.

For the thirty-minute ride all Poppa did was stare straight through the windshield, never blinking an eye.

They reached the hospital and ran upstairs. As he headed to the room Princess was in, he met her mother.

"Where were you?"she scolded. "My daughter died lovin' your no-good ass—you ain't shit."

Poppa walked past her and fell into the arms of Princess' aunt. They hugged as more tears fell.

Her mother was going on and on, crying and fussing about Poppa not being any good.

Finally Kev stepped up. "How you think Poppa feel? You lost a daughter, but he lost the mother to his two kids, and his wifey. He left here to raise two little kids. You need to chill out and be considerate."

"Fuck that! He ain't raisin' shit. I'm takin' those kids—he won't even fuckin' see them."

Poppa lifted his head.

"You's a ignorant bitch," Mike-Mike said.

"No you—" was all that came out of her mouth before she felt the back of Mike-Mike's hand.

"Shut up. Poppa doin' everything in the world to show you respect. I don't know you and don't give two fucks about you. Now carry that shit outta here."

She ran down the hall, screaming her peoples or somebody was going to kill everybody and Poppa.

Dee was headed to his condo with Stacy. Her crew had gone to the hotel with Polite and Black.

Stacy entered the condo and was very much impressed. "So who house is that in Church Point by my grandparents?"

"Mine. All mine."

She made herself comfortable. "I heard that."

They sat down. He poured some Hennessy and lit his already rolled Backwoods. He was in deep thought as he took long pulls. He stared at Stacy. He could only push her away for so long.

Stacy wanted Dee and she wanted all of him. She didn't want to play as she told him, but he took it to heart and wasn't pursuing her.

She had on her tight black jean shorts, white top that tied in the front and exposed her belly, and black and white Nikes.

He passed her the Back.

She took her pulls, sat it in the ashtray, and leaned over to kiss him. She was scared, and it showed; she had never been so forward.

But Dee met her, took her in his arms, and began kissing her from her lips to her neck. He undid her shirt and unsnapped the bra. Her beautiful breast fell out and he began sucking them, easing her out of the tight Liz Claiborne shorts.

He wasn't pressed for this, but he wanted it since it was here to get.

He had on his velour sweatsuit with an elastic waist, so his dick was out in seconds. After pulling her panties to the side, he pushed his dick to her entrance, looking in her eyes as he pushed.

She opened her legs and slid back on the couch. "It's been a while."

He looked into her dazzling brown eyes and cute face that looked so young and innocent. The deeper he stared, the more he realized that she wasn't a freak. She was a young woman in search of love: a pleasant young man doing something with himself, who would be there for her mentally, spiritually, and sexually. She wanted the same thing Chantel, Vianna, and Tricia wanted.

He had too much on his plate. So why pull her into all that? Just show her how the nigga she do decide to fuck with should treat her.

He stood up and pulled her into the bedroom and removed her shoes and panties. He ran some hot bath water in the Jacuzzi tub. He bathed her as the jets massaged her body. He dried her down and applied lotion to her, massaging her body from neck to toe. She was lying on her stomach, so he pulled her to her knees and pushed her chest and face to the bed. So her ass would be high up, exposing every bit of the fresh, inviting pussy.

Her clit was larger than most, so as he flicked his tongue across it she jumped. Then finally the slow licks from her clit to her ass relaxed her until she fell into a world of pleasure. No nigga had ever licked her like this.

Dee's tongue slid in and out of her wet pussy. He positioned his mouth so he could use his top lip to push up the skin that covered the clit and he sucked lightly so the clit came out as he ran his tongue in a slow circular motion. He felt her breathing getting harder and speeded up the motion until she lost control. Her legs went further back and got wider and she grabbed the top of his head and the moaning began. He felt her about to come, could taste her pleasant juices flowing, so he sucked again on the skin covering the clit as his tongue roamed.

He placed a finger inside of her as he continued to eat her. Her pussy kept squeezing his finger. She was ready. He stood and removed his Polo boxers and slowly slid into her tight vagina—even with the wetness.

She caressed him as if she had never felt anything so good.

He took several strokes, cupped her head into his arms, as he stared into her face. He slowed down, gaining control.

She opened her eyes; he stared deep into hers and the feeling began to run. From his feet, up his leg, through his penis, and kept going until his eyes shut and his body went numb.

He collapsed, rolled over, and she slid up under him. He hugged her and realized she felt real good.

***

The next couple months were hectic. Poppa's girl dying left him fucked up and fucking up. He wasn't on time for shit. He was like a zombie. His girl mom's was putting him through hell. She had him in and out of court trying to keep his kids. She was going off at the funeral—she even tried to spit on him.

Lo was moving again. He was moving slow, but he kept his nines close by. He was out on a five-hundred-thousand-dollar bond. Black took fifty thousand from him and Dundee's robbery, gave it to Brandy, who was there to bail him out. Brandy had been with Lo before his last bid on his last good run. He treated her good—and a lot of other hoes—but whenever he seemed to get into some shit, she was there to pull his ass out.

Lo was charged with breaking and entry, two counts of murder. His biggest problem was the firearm he had. He was a felon—automatic five years.

Then he had Ray to worry about. He was going to testify and that would put him away for sure, especially if he rolled up in a wheelchair. He had a court date for late November, but the attorney assured us he wouldn't see the courtroom until sometime in 2000.

Kev had gone to Memphis. Him and Polite were running things there. They met Black every other week in ATL. That made up for the money Mont and Grip was bringing. Shawn and Smiley called. Black had them scoring from Lo. JaVonne had got down. He was from around the way and didn't respect Poppa as a hustler, but he would buy from Lo. No money had ever stopped.

***

Black and Dee stood in the middle of Black's living room with the high ceilings, wide foyer, with the three-hundred-thousand-dollar chandelier. He had an elevator in his house that went up to the second floor. Six bedrooms, five full baths, three-car garage, family room, formal dining room, game room, pool, workout room, office, closed-in deck with Jacuzzi. $1.7 million dollars well spent.

At first Black said he was gonna get some hoes and decorate, but he didn't want them knowing where he lived. The idea was quickly dismissed when Dee introduced him to Yvonne Jasline Taylor. She was thirty-three, graduate of Temple University in Philadelphia, PA and was becoming known as one of the top interior designers in the state.

Dee had met her at Homeorama. She had won the contract to design all the homes up at Homeorama. He began talking. She was used to dealing with more white folks, so to work for some young black brothers was going to be a challenge. They didn't know the name of all the fancy shit, but Dee and Black knew what they liked.

When she first met Dee at his $750,000 home in Church Point, she was all business. Pants suit, heels, hair in a bun with Liz Claiborne eyewear. She carried big books to show her work and give ideas. Dee sat for six hours picking out shit for every room. She charged one hundred and fifteen dollars an hour for consultation, and started him a running tab, meaning pay for everything later.

She finished the living room and dining area and we were at eight thousand for window treatments, matching dining chairs, and vases and shit. By the time the house was finished another hundred thousand was spent. And the house was laid like a model. She took pictures for her book to show future clients.

When she met Black it was like straight chemistry. They began talking and exploring his home at 10:00 A.M. They finished after ten that evening. They talked business. A lot of business.

Lunchtime, since it was a beautiful day, he asked Yvonne to move her ML 500 Benz truck, so he could pull out the Ferrari. They rode up the to the coast to Virginia Beach Resort, went inside to the Trade-winds, four-star restaurant that overlooked the Chesapeake Bay.

She was impressed. He was like no other client she'd dealt with. Cats in the music industry always talked about themselves, bragging about what they're getting ready to do. Those ball players think everybody want them, but Black, he listened.

If he agreed he let her know, if he didn't feel it, he let her know before she wasted all her breath. He was direct, but he also wanted her feel.

The beauty of the home was picture-perfect, her best work. She didn't only take pictures, but it sparked an idea to walk through the home and put it on video. Black's home was plastered in *Home* magazine, *Robb Report*, *Millionaire*. With all her education, success, and her jump in lifestyle, that nigga Black had her open.

"So where's Yvonne?" Dee asked, sparking a Back.

"She should be through in a little bit. Let's go in the game room with the trees."

"Can't smoke in your own shit, nigga."

"You know the deal—shorty treat it like it's hers. She also made that ninety-one hundred mortgage payment last month."

"Yeah, let's go in the game room," Dee said smiling. "So what's goin' on? When you goin' back to the ATL?"

"Shit, I don't know. Poppa still fucked up. He can't run like he want to because social service makin' sure he on point with those kids."

"I would of probably had somebody kill that bitch," Dee said. "Send Lo and Dundee."

"Shit, they a fuck it up—don't even know how to rob a nigga."

They laughed.

"How things workin' out with Shawn and your boy?"

"They comin', DaVonne comin', and those young New York niggas peoples got tore off. Them niggas scorin' from Dundee now. Them little niggas workers. When you goin' to ATL?"

"Couple days I'm goin' to Cali with Vianna. So I'm going to Charlotte, then to the ATL, burstin' Friday morning. Cali . . . going back to Cali." Dee gave Black a pound.

Dee shook his head. "Man, shorty pregnant,"

"Who? Tricia?"

"How you know?"

"She called me, cryin', talkin' twenty miles per hour for about twenty minutes."

"Damn! She loves you, son. Bitches know a real man. She see it all in you."

"Yeah, but one thing—Chantel. Man, fuck! I live and breathe that girl. If everything a'ight there, I'm okay; if shit fuck up there, I can't even get a peace of mind."

"Yeah, but you only got one child. You gettin' too old to be killin' babies."

"She said she ain't, anyway. She said her moms did four by herself, she can damn sure do two."

They both smirked at her boldness.

"Guess you ain't got no choice."

"I guess not. Where the girls?"

Black had picked his daughter and Dee's daughter up. They had grown so fast. "Nine years old, looking like little ladies," Black said when he picked them up Friday night.

They were in the back whispering, like they were having their own private conversation going. They decided they were going to live with Black. Dee's daughter said he had more than enough room. Black's daughter said everybody could live there—her, her sister in Florida, her cousin, and even her mom.

They had spent Saturday up at the restaurant with grandma, and since the restaurant had opened, they were getting their hair done at NY Hair Designs, two doors down. So all day they ran from the restaurant, to the beauty salon, looking beautiful as ever with their long hair hanging down their backs, dressed cute as hell in jean sets, new white Reebok Classics.

They ran back to the beauty salon, bursting inside.

"Y'all not goin' to be runnin' in and out. Come here!" Leah, the shop owner, said. She sat them down, talking to them.

Dee always loved when she took the time and showed them special attention. She was someone for them to look up to and model themselves after. She was young, beautiful, owned two businesses, and had a Lexus that let every nigga know she DO4SELF.

They listened then jumped up.

Thirty minutes later they were back at the shop, until grandma threatened to find a switch.

The little ladies hauled ass in the room with their dads. No warning of any sort. Just burst in the room, interrupting the conversation.

"Heah, Daddy."

"Heah, Uncle Dee."

"What up, little ladies?" Dee hugged them.

"What y'all doin'?"

"Playing my PlayStation."

"I heard y'all runnin' up and down the stairs. Better be careful. I don't got time to sit at no hospital. If you fall and bust your head, I'm going to give you a towel and leave you here."

"Daddy, you crazy."

"We ain't gonna get hurt; we know what we doin'."

"Y'all get outta here—we smokin'," Black said.

They ran out excited and happy, just like kids should be.

"They somethin'," Black said.

"Yeah, I know. Just pray their life goes well."

"We ain't worried; they straight—we gonna make sure of that."

"Yeah, but a parent never know what they child have in store or how they will turn out."

"You right, but we'll leave that in the hands of God. Just pray for them."

"Like Momma do?"

"Just like Momma. Shit, I know it's her prayers that keeps me here. Damn sure ain't mine. No more time than I give the Lord."

"Need to start goin' to church with Tony, Momma, and Auntie."

"Yeah, Tony the godson. He ain't fuckin' with this shit here," Black said. "He's gonna make something of himself. For sure."

"Hell yeah, goin' to Regency University. Military payin' for it. Studyin' theology. He got God on his side. How can he lose?"

"Strong, Strong," they heard the voice hollering.

"We in here," Black yelled. He opened the door.

Yvonne walked into the smoke-filled room. "Y'all know the girls here."

"They know what we do. Wait 'til y'all have me a nephew. He gonna know too." Dee knew that kind of talk would aggravate her.

"I'll be goddamn!"

They laughed, but not at her.

"You wanna go to Cali for three days? Leavin' Friday."

"Hell yeah. I ain't never been to California," she said.

"You scared of those Cali hoes—they'll eat your ass up." Dee said joking.

"Can't no bitch fuck with it. Don't let the Chanel and long hair fool you. Better recognize how this Philly bitch get down," she said turning up her nose.

"Dee and Vianna goin' to Cali," Strong said. "Her job."

"What about Chantel?" she asked.

"We ain't ask you all that. You goin'?"

"Yes, I am. I ain't lettin' Strong go out there with you. You are corrupt. Don't fuck up my man." She hugged Black.

"I got to get ready to go before traffic get bad." She was taking the girls shopping. She enjoyed them. She didn't have any kids of her own yet, and spoiling them was something she loved; and telling them things about being little ladies. She even let them hang when she went to the spa. The ladies gave them little robes, and put clear polish on their feet and nails. They never wanted to go home when it was time.

"Yo, I talked to Lo and them earlier. Niggas gonna pull the bikes out—nice-ass day. What's up? Pull out the triple X," Dee said, referring to Black's Honda 1000.

"Got shit to do. Some of us gotta work. This good life don't come easy." Black waved his hand around, bringing attention to his extravagant home.

"I say that's for sure. But straight up, son, you got enough dough to chill. You can go wherever, put down new roots, and live comfortable forever. I got some new shit for us anyway. Gonna make us millions." Dee finally got the nerve to tell his little brother it was time to change their way of living.

"Where that shit come from? We livin' better than we ever have. Things rollin' good—fuck you talkin'."

"You got a heavy-duty high security safe with half-inch solid steel reinforced doors holdin' over three million upstairs. You got a safe at my house holding one and a half million. You got a safe in your condo with a couple hundred thousand.

Then Triple Strong is worth—what—another four or five. You done came off. Look, this is the plan— go to Atlanta and start Triple Strong Building Corp. Buy land, build houses, and sell. Spend six hundred thousand and sell for one point two mil-lion—real flip."

"Shit sounds good. Do your thing. I'll send Angela to real estate school. She ain't doin' shit anyway, sniffin' her ass off, spendin' up my god-damn money. She brings home like nine hundred every two weeks, but she spends two thousand a week. Know what, Dee, this shit is me. It's not just the money, it's the game—I love it. I love the players, I love the streets, I enjoy the fear I put in niggas, not knowin' what the fuck I'm gonna do. I love goin' to the parties with all the rap artists and entertainers, and I shine."

"You ain't got shit to prove. Most of them niggas rappin' about the life you live or life I live ballin' with these bitches drivin' hundred-thousand-dollar cars." Dee smiled.

"You know the greatest nigga was B.I.G., and the realest nigga is Fifty."

"Where 'Pac fit in?"

"I ain't no 'Pac fan, so I put couple niggas before him, startin' with Jiggah. Black, I love this shit too—having the homes, cars, bikes, jet-ski and enough money to do whatever I want with these hoes. But I want to know that we gonna grow old and be hangin'. Come pick each other up, play golf. I don't know. Just get old."

Black knew what he meant but he was a hustler. He loved the thrill of game, never to be separated from Dee, or the streets.

"Don't worry, we gonna be a'ight," Black assured him.

"A'ight. Love ya, man." Dee hugged his brother and made his exit.

He was on his way to his condo when Monica called. She was still upset about things, but she wanted to know more about the fifty thousand.

They pulled out the bikes and met Monica at the restaurant. She was back in with Ray and he had moved. She was helping him adjust to being in a wheelchair. One of the bullets had ruptured his spinal cord and disabled him from the waist down.

She told Dee where Ray lived and who was there with him. He might even get lucky and catch Speed there. Dee called Black.

Ray had to go because his testimony was going to put Lo away for a long time.

By the time Dee finished his conversation, many other bikes had joined him. Some of the guys were even riding girls. Dee looked at Monica, looking sexy in her tight jeans and black boots. She could definitely ride.

"So you ride?" he asked.

"Yeah, I'm ridin' with you." she answered while going to lock her car. She put on Dee's extra helmet.

They never noticed the black Range Rover parked in
front of Food Lion.

Black called Lo. He knew this had to be done right.
Lo decided he wanted to call Dundee, who let Black
know that he was ready, not only to be brought in on
this, but also to be offered better prices and a promo-
tion to it.

Dundee was on the run and still moving six kilos
a week, three from his cousins in Carolina and three
he worked. He stayed in the street two to three days
straight; not washing, rocking the same clothes, grind-
ing.

Black met them at Lo's spot, and they rode over to
Ray's new ranch-style duplex with ramps and shit, off
Witchduck Road, called Witchduck Lakes. He'd bought
a beige Mercury Mountaineer with special attachments
to drive.

They watched as they rode past the house. It was two
others in the home. Lo was turning around at the end
of the street when he saw the black Range Rover coming down toward Ray's house.

"Bingo, niggas," Black said. "This me. I'm gonna
catch him goin'." He jumped out the truck and ran
through the houses.

When Speed put his keys in Ray's door and saw
Black coming up, he panicked—he had left his gun in
the truck. He was only gonna be there a second. His
eyes widened as he took off, his body hitting the corner
of the house as he ran like a cheetah.

Black was hot on his tail. He'd caught him slipping
and he had to go.

As Speed dodged between the cars and buildings,
Black had the nine out, one in the chamber. Speed ran
back by the dumpster, not knowing his surroundings.

Black was the only nigga name he had heard ring in the streets like his. When you heard Speed or Black, real niggas put up their guards, and bitch niggas broke out.

Two bullets ripped through his black leather Nautica, and he fell on the cold concrete, leaning against the dumpster. *How could I slip like this?* The cold steel that now rested on his temple let him know it didn't make a difference.

Black pulled the trigger and watched his body go totally limp, then he ran back to the house.

Dundee and Lo were already inside. They had a nigga and a girl flat on the floor in the kitchen. Ray was sitting in his chair with Lo's .357 to his head.

Black shut the door. "We got like two minutes. Where the money, nigga?" Black knew that you always asked for dough, even if it's not any—you never know.

"Ain't no money, kid. Took it all the last time," Ray said.

Black pulled the guy up from the kitchen floor. As Ray looked on, he took a hollow, sharp rod and jammed it into the guy's sternum and pushed it straight up to his aorta then slammed him down to the floor, his body now held up only by the kitchen cabinets.

They watched him sit there. Every time his heart beat, blood gushed out on the floor.

"In the closet . . . in the beige leather coat." Ray watched his cousin sit in a puddle of blood, life slowly draining from his body.

Dundee grabbed the coat and threw the money on the table.

Black grabbed the stacks. "Eighty thou. Come on, son, gots to be more—I got to eat." Black pulled out a syringe and needle and laid it on the table. He walked over to the kitchen. Dude was slumped over not moving.

Black grabbed the girl by her long, beautiful hair, snatching her up from the floor in one quick motion. Tears ran down her face, and her body trembled. He took her head and slammed it into one of the sharp edges of the wall. Blood poured down her face. He turned the stove on up high, still controlling her every movement by the grip he had on her hair, and pulled her face near the bright orange flame.

"It's the bag in the closet. That's it, man, my last. I'm done." Ray hung his head low.

"We know that, nigga." Lo bust him in the head with the butt of the gun.

Dundee opened the bag. "Bingo."

Black pushed the girl on the floor and grabbed the needle. "Hold him."

Lo hit his ass about four times with the gun and grabbed his arm. Black pushed the needle into his arm and squeezed.

Ray thought they were giving him heroin to kill him by overdose, but Black had pumped embalming fluid into his vein. "We out—don't leave no witnesses, Lo," Black said, headed for the front door.

Lo pulled a large Ginsu from the rack. And before the girl could move, he slammed the knife into her head and left it. She fell beside Ray, who was going crazy in a rage on the floor, bouncing around hollering.

They left out.

Black knew Ray was dead. The embalming fluid was going to flow through his bloodstream and burn every organ it hit. Black smiled. He knew they were done too.

Monica had her arms wrapped around Dee as he did one hundred miles per hour down 264 with a pack of bikes behind him. Dee hit the top of his helmet and began patting, and everybody slowed down to sixty while riding past the state troopers.

He patted Monica's hands to tell her to hold on, as he dropped the bike down into fourth gear. He gunned the gas, the RPM shot up, and he popped the clutch. Quickly, he got a tight hold of the grips as the front tire rose in the air and he did a wheelie down the interstate. When the front tire hit the ground he was running ninety. By this time the state troopers pulled out with their lights on.

He quickly punched it.

In a split second he was running one hundred and thirty with Monica's grip taking his breath. He saw the exit, broke it down, and exited on Interstate 44.

Once out the curve he punched it again. He knew once he hit Newtown Road he'd be home free. He saw exit 15B Newtown Road. *Yeah, got they muthafuckin' ass.* He patted Monica's hands to hold on.

Newtown exit was a sharp curve. He had to lean hard, but it meant nothing. He'd done this a thousand times.

He fell into the exit and leaned. The curve was sharp, and he leaned harder, adrenaline running. Dee felt Monica's body resisting; she was trying to lean the other way. The bike began to shake and at that moment Dee saw the gravel. Leaning hard, he tried to break it down, but it was no use. He was headed for the guard-rail doing fifty. A split-second decision had to be made: Hold it and get wrapped up in the guardrail and bike or get the bike away from him.

He laid it down. As his body hit the hard, rugged road, he saw the bike crash and Monica's body hurl into the guardrail, breaking her neck and killing her instantly.

His body slammed into the rail, cutting his pelvis wide open and breaking his back. He lay in the street gasping for air, blood draining from his pelvis onto the road.

The other bikes stopped. Kev ran up and looked at Dee, his insides hanging out. Kev had to grab his stomach. Then he looked into Dee's eyes. "Come on, big bro, please hold on. You gonna be a'ight. Come on, Dee, Black need you. You can't leave Black. Come on."

Dee stared at Kev, and tears fell from both eyes. Then Dee forced a crooked smile and closed his eyes.

Kev picked up the phone and dialed Black.

"What's up, son?"

Kev didn't say anything. Nothing would come out.

"Kev, fuck you at? Me, Lo, and Dundee stuck in all this traffic on Newtown.

Kev wiped his eyes. "Dee just wrecked."

"What?" Black looked up and saw the ambulance and rescue squads trying to get to the exit. "Not in the exit?"

"Yeah. You see us?" Kev said.

"That's Dee, Lo. It's Dee." Black jumped out the car and ran across traffic, up the exit. He was outta breath, but he couldn't stop. "God, I know you wouldn't. I know you wouldn't. I know you wouldn't. I know you wouldn't." He saw Dee and collapsed beside his body. He tried to move, but his body was numb and he could not breathe.

Black's heart had dropped into his stomach. He wanted to die. He took Dee's head into his arm, hugged him, and cried.

Kev hugged Black and cried as the ambulance and police came and moved them, placing the bodies in bags.

Black looked at the bike now torn to pieces. The picture of Junie was staring and didn't have a scratch. He looked into Junie's eyes and felt empty and alone. He walked over to Lo, who sat on the guardrail, his fist tight to his eyes.

They walked back down to the car in silence. Dundee drove to the restaurant. Black and Lo walked inside to the back.

The restaurant became silent when Moms let out a stabbing scream that only came with death. She held Black and squeezed him until he broke down again.

Tony walked to the front, his eyes bloodshot red from crying. Customers knew something was wrong. Tony turned off the sign and closed the store.

Mom, Auntie, Tony, Lo, and Black sat at the table in silence.

"It's time to start new—Virginia's been hard on us," Tony said.

"All of us," Black said. "All of us." He stood up and walked in the back. He stood at the back door looking into Lake Edward. What the fuck was he going to do. "Damn! Dee," he said out loud. "You wa'n' supposed to leave me like this." He couldn't stop his eyes from watering. This was the first time in his life that he was scared.